UNRAVELED

THE UNTANGLED SERIES

BOOK 1

IVY LAYNE

GINGER QUILL PRESS, LLC

Unraveled

Find out more about the author and upcoming books online at www.ivylayne.com

Contents

Also by Ivy Layne

THE UNTANGLED SERIES

Unraveled (October 2018)

Undone (Early 2019)

Uncovered (Spring 2019)

SCANDALS OF THE BAD BOY BILLIONAIRES

The Billionaire's Secret Heart (Novella)

The Billionaire's Secret Love (Novella)

The Billionaire's Pet

The Billionaire's Promise

The Rebel Billionaire

The Billionaire's Secret Kiss (Novella)

The Billionaire's Angel

Engaging the Billionaire

Compromising the Billionaire

The Counterfeit Billionaire

Series Extras: ivylayne.com/extras

THE ALPHA BILLIONAIRE CLUB

About

UNRAVELED

Summer

Evers Sinclair is dangerous.

One flash of that teasing smile, and I know he's going to ruin me.

He makes my body shiver and my brain melt.

He's also a huge mistake.

Girls like me don't land guys like Evers.

But every time he knocks on my door, I let him in.

I thought we understood each other.

I thought we were playing the same game.

I was wrong.

Evers

I've never had a problem mixing business with pleasure.

Until Summer.

I was supposed to keep an eye on her, not take her to bed.

Once I had her where I wanted her, I couldn't let her go.

I'm going to have to move heaven and Earth to win her back.

And that's the easy part.

With the Russian mob after us and her father dragging us to hell...

I don't just have to win her back, I have to keep her alive.

Chapter One

SUMMER

The knock at the door startled me so badly I almost dropped my curling iron. I wasn't that late, was I? I wasn't supposed to be downstairs for another...

Oh, crap. I *was* that late.

Unplugging the curling iron and giving my lashes a quick swipe of mascara, I rushed to the door, swung it open, and froze.

It wasn't Julie, here to pick me up for a girls' night out.

No, standing in the door was my very own, personal Achilles' heel.

The devil come to tempt me.

Eve with the Apple.

Okay, bad analogy. Evers Sinclair could be a devil, but he was no Eve.

Evers Sinclair was male temptation incarnate, and I'd never been able to resist him.

He smiled at me, lips curved into a grin seasoned with mischief and filled with promise.

That grin always got me, even when I'd resolved to resist him.

Especially when I'd resolved to resist him.

He leaned in my doorway, one arm braced against the frame, his ice-blue eyes doing a slow perusal from my head to my toes, heating as they took in my deliberately-tumbled blonde curls, little black cocktail dress, and mile-high spike heels.

"Going somewhere?"

His voice was all flirtation, but his eyes said something else. Something I couldn't quite read.

Annoyance?

Irritation?

That couldn't be worry, could it?

Giving an internal shrug, I stepped back to let him in. I'd given up on understanding Evers Sinclair. Evers walked in as if he belonged in my apartment, dropping his overstuffed briefcase on the chair by the front door before heading into the kitchen to help himself to a beer.

Popping the cap off the bottle, he turned and leaned against the counter, taking a long swig.

"I like the dress," he said, lids heavy over those cool blue eyes, gaze smoldering.

Ignoring the flash of heat at the look in his eyes, I rolled my own. "It's new," I said.

"You didn't answer my question," he said smoothly, his gaze tracing the V-shaped neckline of my dress and the generous display of cleavage framed by black silk.

His eyes peeled the dress off my shoulders, stripped me naked. It had been three weeks since I'd seen him, and I'd felt his absence every day.

The heat growing in my belly kicked up a notch. I gritted my teeth and pushed it back. I did not have time for this. My body didn't care. It never did where Evers Sinclair was concerned.

He showed up, smoldered at me, and my body was ready to go.

"Which question?" I shot back, always ready to play the game with Evers, even against my better judgment.

Since the moment we'd met, he'd been getting under my skin. As hard as I tried, I couldn't quite work him back out.

"Are you going somewhere? If it's a bad time I can leave."

I stopped, the quick retort frozen on my tongue. I took another look at Evers, seeing past his distinctive eyes, his broad shoulders and sharp cheekbones, past the beauty to the man beneath.

He was tired, I realized with surprise. More than tired, he looked exhausted. His face was drawn, lines bracketing his mouth, purple-gray smudges beneath his eyes.

I had no idea what he'd been doing since the last time he'd shown up at my door, but whatever it was, he looked like he needed nothing more than a good meal and a solid night's sleep.

I bit back the sarcastic retort on the tip of my tongue and told him the truth. "I am. I'm sorry, I didn't know you'd be coming by and—"

"Hot date?"

I wasn't imagining the edge in his voice. I debated how to answer.

It wasn't any of his business if I did have a hot date. We had a thing, yeah. A thing neither of us had ever bothered to define. A thing that was definitely not exclusive.

I didn't know who he was with when he wasn't with me. I could never bring myself to ask. That way lay heartbreak.

Evers Sinclair was a player.

He was not a one-woman man, and he never would be.

I'd known from the start I had a choice. Take what he was willing to give or walk away.

It had never occurred to me that he would care if I saw other people, but the way he'd asked *hot date?* didn't sound nonchalant.

Again, I went with the truth.

"Not tonight. You know my friend Julie?" Evers nodded. I'd mentioned Julie before. She and I had known each other since college. "She and Frank broke up."

"That was a long time coming," Evers commented.

He'd never met Julie, but he'd heard me bitch about her boyfriend more than once. Frank was an asshole who didn't deserve my sweet, funny friend, and she'd finally figured it out. Hallelujah.

"I know. She caught him flirting with the waitress when they were out to dinner, which would have been bad enough, but when he disappeared to the bathroom for a little too long and she went looking for him—"

"Let me guess, she walked in on him in the back hall with his hand up the waitress' skirt," Evers said dryly.

I shrugged a shoulder. "Close enough. The waitress smacked him—apparently, she had better asshole radar then Julie—and then Julie kicked him in the nuts and walked out."

"Good for her," Evers said.

That was the thing about Evers. He was a player and a flirt, but he was honest about it. He'd never once made me a promise he couldn't keep. Never once implied that he could give me more and let me down.

He was a player, but he wasn't a liar.

That was the only reason I could make this crazy arrangement work. Well, that and the sex.

The sex was amazing.

Fucking fantastic.

Fantastic fucking.

Hell, however you wanted to put it, getting in bed with Evers Sinclair was worth the dangerous game we were playing.

I was going to end up getting hurt.

I knew it, but I couldn't seem to stop myself. He was dangerous, but he was Evers.

Just like the second piece of chocolate cake. I kept telling myself *only one more bite* and found myself going back for more.

Over and over.

Eventually, I was going to work up the willpower to give him up completely.

Eventually. But not tonight.

I picked up my purse from the kitchen counter, removing lip gloss, wallet, and emergency cash, transferring them to the small black purse that matched my dress.

"Julie's finally past the sappy movie and ice cream stage and she wants to go out. Get dressed up, you know, have a little fun and discover a new, post-Frank world."

"And you're playing wing-woman?" Evers asked, taking another pull on the beer, his eyes lingering on the short hem of my dress.

"Something like that," I said, the trail of his gaze heating my skin. I found myself wondering if I could bail. I wasn't the only one going out with Julie and—no.

No.

I was not bailing on a girlfriend for Evers.

No way.

This was Julie's night. Ditching her for hot sex, even

stupendously hot sex, was not cool. I pressed my thighs together, willing my body to stand down.

I swear, one look at Evers and my hormones leapt into overdrive.

He took another pull on the beer and didn't say anything. Something in the line of his neck, the tilt of his jaw made me think he didn't like the idea of me being Julie's wing-woman.

I fought back the urge to make an excuse, to explain that I wasn't going to pick anybody up, I was just there to support a friend.

It wasn't any of his business what I did.

That wasn't what we were.

I didn't know what the hell we were, but I knew it wasn't that. It wasn't explanations and promises.

It was moments of time.

It was the present, not the future.

I knew that. So why did I find myself saying, "I won't be late. If you want to hang out, I have leftover Chinese in the fridge from last night. Orange beef, your favorite, and some egg rolls. You can eat dinner, watch the game until I get home."

My stomach lurched.

Why did I say that?

Evers had never been in my apartment without me. He'd never spent the night. We'd fallen asleep together, too exhausted to move after a marathon of sex, muscles wrung out, nerves fried with pleasure. In the morning, he was always gone.

Why had I offered him my leftover take-out, my couch, and my TV? And why did he look relieved?

My phone chimed with a text. Julie, downstairs waiting. I didn't have time to figure out the mystery of Evers Sinclair.

"That's Julie. I've got to run. Do you want to stay?"

Evers set his beer on the counter and prowled toward me, cool blue eyes intent on mine. "Come here," he growled, reaching out to pull me into his arms. His mouth landed on my neck just below my ear, sending sparks through every nerve in my body.

Evers could play my body like an instrument, and he did. Moving his lips down the cord of my neck, his strong arms absorbed my shivers, his leg nudging between mine, hand dropping to cup my ass, urging me closer until I ground against him, shuddering under his mouth, the caress of his lips, the heat of his tongue on my skin.

Lifting his mouth, he nipped my earlobe before whispering, his breath hot in my ear, "Have fun. Stay out of trouble. When you get back I'll fuck you until you can't walk."

I thought *promises, promises,* but the words remained unspoken, short-circuiting between my brain and my mouth. All I could do was gasp as his teeth nipped my jaw and his mouth fell on mine.

Evers Sinclair knew how to kiss. Like, he really knew how to kiss. I wrapped my arms around his neck and held on for dear life, his lips opening mine, tongue stroking, his hands everywhere.

A heartbeat later I was flushed with heat, hips rolling into his, every inch of me wound tight.

Desperate. For him.

My phone chimed again, the high-pitched sound cutting through the haze. Reluctantly, I eased away, sliding my hips out of his grip, dropping my hands from his neck, breaking the contact between our mouths.

I had to go.

I had to go, but I didn't want to end that kiss.

7

I already knew I was a mess, hair all over the place, cheeks flushed, lip gloss smeared across my cheek.

I didn't expect the flags of red on Evers' cheekbones, the tight set of his jaw, the glitter in his eyes. His hands flexed at his sides as if he wanted to reach out. To drag me back.

On shaky legs, I stepped away, hiding the roil of my emotions, lust, and want. Longing.

"I have to go," I said inanely. He already knew I had to go. Why wasn't I leaving?

"Go then. I'll be here when you get back."

His words sounded suspiciously like a promise. *They aren't*, I told myself as I considered one more kiss, then thought better of it.

If I kissed him again, I'd never leave my apartment, and Julie was waiting.

Grabbing my purse, I headed for the door without another word. Standing at the elevator, I lectured myself.

Be sensible.

This is Evers Sinclair.

He might get bored and wander off before you even get home.

Don't count on him being there.

Don't count on him for anything.

I warned myself, but I didn't listen. I never had where Evers was concerned.

I had no idea what I was doing with him. We were a total mismatch.

From the moment we'd met we hadn't gotten along.

He was bossy, autocratic, arrogant, and an incorrigible flirt. Evers wasn't my type in so many ways. I favored serious guys, usually cute, but not hot. Guys with normal jobs and normal lives.

I sound exciting, don't I? But that's the thing, I'm not

exciting. I'm a perfectly normal girl with a perfectly normal life. A least I was, until the day Evers swept in and turned everything upside down.

I was at a conference in Houston, kind of bored, kind of having fun, looking forward to the weekend when I was expecting a visit from my best friend, Emma.

Evers had appeared out of nowhere, claiming that Emma was in danger and she needed my help. If I'd heard that line from anyone else I would have laughed him out of town. Especially since he refused to tell me what the trouble was or how she needed my help.

I'd known, the way best friends always know, that Emma was involved in something, but that didn't mean I trusted Evers. Still, I'd gone with him, all the way to Atlanta, bickering the whole time.

I couldn't help myself. He was so high-handed. He strolled in and expected me to do his bidding just because he said so.

It hadn't helped that every time I looked at him, my knees went weak.

Back then he'd worn his hair almost military short, and it left every inch of that chiseled face on display, from his dark brows to his ice-blue eyes, his sharp cheekbones and full lower lip.

His face is enough to make a girl swoon. His body kicks the whole package up a notch. I didn't have to see beneath the suits to know that Evers Sinclair was sex on a stick.

So out of my league. So very much out of my league.

We'd bickered and flirted, and that had been it.

Until Emma's wedding.

A little too much champagne, an argument over the wedding cake, and before I knew it, I was backed into a wall behind an arrangement of potted plants, Evers' hand on my ass under my bridesmaid's dress.

I could blame the champagne for falling into bed with Evers, but that would be a flat-out lie. It had nothing to do with the champagne and everything to do with Evers Sinclair.

Damn, that man knew how to use his hands. And his mouth. And everything else.

We'd spent Emma's wedding night locked up in my hotel room. And the night after. And the night after that.

Then I'd flown home, he'd left town on a job, and I wrote off Evers Sinclair as a wedding insanity mistake.

Maybe not a mistake.

It's hard to call sex that good a mistake.

And what's wrong with having a fling every once in a while? Every girl should have a fling. Except I was a serial dater. I didn't fling. One-night stands seemed like too much work for not enough payoff.

With Evers, it was all payoff and no work. When I bumped into him again a year later at a client's party, my body went on full alert the second my eyes met his.

I'd convinced myself I'd forgotten Evers, but my body hadn't. Not for one red-hot second.

Evers had his own gravity, a magnetic pull that drew me across the room, demanding my attention even when I was in the middle of a client's party. At the end of the night, he'd been there, lounging against my car, waiting.

I'd invited him home, we fell into bed, and our non-relationship was born.

He showed up every once in a while, knocking on my door with no notice, and I always let him in. Every now and then, I'd text, and he'd come. I'd never been to his place and wasn't exactly sure where he lived. Somewhere in Atlanta.

I was in Marietta, northwest of the city. Close enough that we could have seen each other more often, but neither of us offered or asked for more.

I didn't ask because I knew I wouldn't get it, and Evers because he didn't do more. More wasn't his thing.

Julie was waiting in front of my building, the car running, music blaring through the open windows. She was ready to party, but she didn't miss a thing. A grin bloomed on her face when she saw me.

I snapped my seatbelt into place as she said, "Your lip gloss is smudged."

"I still have lip gloss?" I lifted a hand to wipe my lips. I'd have been shocked if Evers hadn't kissed every speck off my lips. I pressed my knees together at the thought.

Down girl, tonight's not about you. Not until you get home. If he's still there.

Julie stared at me for a minute before her eyes flared wide and she glanced at my building. "Is he up there? Did he come by tonight?"

She thought my weird thing with Evers Sinclair was the stuff of fairytales. Evers Sinclair of the Atlanta Sinclairs. She imagined he'd fall in love with me, and we'd live happily ever after in a little mansion in Buckhead.

I gave a mental snort. Not likely.

I couldn't see Evers settling down, and if he did, it wouldn't be with someone like me. Someone normal. Average.

He'd find some society princess or a former model. An actress. Somebody with flash. With flair. Someone exciting enough to fit into his life.

Evers Sinclair came from a long line of Atlanta Sinclairs who, a few generations back, had founded the premier security agency in the country.

They protected royalty. Celebrities.

Designed security systems that put Fort Knox to shame.

He was James Bond come to life, from the perfectly-tailored suit to the Aston Martin. I wasn't the first to get caught in his orbit, and I wouldn't be the last. I was just enjoying the ride.

I shook my head at Julie. "He's up there, but don't worry about it. Tonight is about you."

Julie hesitated before putting the car in gear. "Are you sure? I mean, we can go out any night. He hasn't come by in a few weeks, and—"

"I'm sure," I insisted, irritated that even Julie thought the world should stop for Evers Sinclair. "If he wanted to know if I was free, he could have called. He shows up, he takes what he gets. Tonight is for you. He can wait."

Julie leaned over and threw her arms around me in an awkward hug, considering our seatbelts. "You're the best friend, Summer. Most girls would have ditched me for a hottie like Evers Sinclair."

My libido bitched at me when I said, "I'm not most girls, and he'll be there when I get home."

I hoped.

I really, really hoped he'd be there when I got home.

Chapter Two

SUMMER

I tried to throw myself into girls' night out. I did. I hadn't lied, tonight was important. Julie needed her friends and some fun.

I did my best. I had a drink. I flirted with a guy down the bar who Julie thought was cute and lured him in so she could give him her shy, sweet smile.

Julie was a catch. Pretty, smart, easy-going, fun. Good job.

She'd settled for Frank, but she hadn't had to. She was going to find a good guy. I knew it. Maybe not tonight, but eventually.

It was closing in on ten, Julie and the other girls diving into a round of shots, when Julie leaned over, nudged me, and said, "Go home."

"No, I'm having fun, I swear, I—"

Julie rolled her eyes. "You're not having fun. You're a sweetheart, and I love you for being here, but go home. Somebody should have amazing sex tonight, and it's not going to be me."

"You don't know that," I protested, though I did know that. We both did. Julie may have been four drinks and two shots into the night, but she'd never picked up a guy in a bar, and I didn't think she was going to start now.

"I'm not," she affirmed, "and we both know it. I'm getting drunk, Steph can drive me home, or we'll get a rideshare and I'll pick up my car tomorrow. Go home. He might not be back for a few weeks or a month, and I'm not going to be responsible for you not getting any. You get cranky when you go without."

She wasn't wrong. "Are you sure? I don't want to bail on you."

"You're not bailing, you idiot. I would have dropped you in a heartbeat if he'd been waiting in my apartment."

"Liar." Julie never would have dropped me for a guy. Friends first. "If you're sure," I mumbled, already pulling up the rideshare app on my phone.

I rode home in an aging sedan, staring blindly out the window, trying not to squirm in my seat as I imagined all the things I wanted to do to Evers when I got there.

He would have stripped off the suit coat. Loosened his tie. I wanted to slip the buttons of his shirt free, one by one.

Push it off his shoulders and down his arms, baring all his smooth skin.

Trace every line of muscle on his chest down to his abs.

Slide his belt from the buckle...

I pressed my knees together, the heat between my legs already out of control.

He always did this to me. So fucking hot.

Half a lifetime passed before I slid my key in the lock and opened my door, so ready to jump him that if he'd been in the foyer, I would have had him on the floor.

Instead, my apartment was quiet but for the murmur of

an announcer's voice coming from my living room. The end of the game was on, the volume low, the only light the flicker of the television.

Evers lay stretched out on the couch, feet propped on the arm, fast asleep. He looked almost boyish with his eyes closed, his hair mussed, his smirk of a smile wiped away.

I reached out to brush his hair from his forehead, a rush of tenderness taking me by surprise. Snatching my hand back, I stared down at him in horror.

I could not feel tenderness towards Evers Sinclair.

Tenderness wasn't lust.

Tenderness was feelings. I could not have feelings for Evers.

I had feelings about sex with Evers, sure.

Great feelings.

Amazing feelings.

That was it. I did not feel tenderness for him.

I did not want to lay down on the couch next to him and trace my finger along his lower lip, stroke my hand down his back and cuddle into his warmth.

No, I wanted to wake him up, strip him naked and have sex with him.

That was it. Sex.

Having feelings for Evers was a recipe for a broken heart, and I was keeping mine in one piece.

I turned my back on him, needing to get my bearings. Seeing him so defenseless in sleep had caught me off-guard. I couldn't afford to be off-guard with Evers.

This thing between us only worked because I followed the rules I'd set up with myself from the beginning.

No making more of it than it was.

No expectations.

No demands.

No feelings.

Quietly making my way to the kitchen, I set my purse on the counter, looking around for my key ring. I'd removed my door key earlier, but if I didn't put it back on the ring, I'd lose it. I finally spotted my jacket on the chair by the front door and remembered I'd tossed it there when I'd come home in a rush to get ready.

Evers' briefcase sat on top, the zipper half-open. He must have done some work while he was waiting. I picked it up to grab my jacket, and the handle slipped through my fingers, the jacket and bag spilling to the floor.

Maybe that last round of drinks had hit me harder than I thought. I felt giddy, not tipsy. Definitely not drunk, but the mess at my feet said different.

I dropped to my knees to put everything back. It wasn't too bad, only a few files, a pen, and a half-eaten bag of sunflower seeds.

I slid the first two folders in the briefcase, barely glancing at them except to note the Sinclair Security logo, a slightly pretentious combination of a royal crest, a lion, and the company name. The third folder caught my eye.

Neatly typed on the label were the words 'Smokey W.'

Smokey W.

My heart skipped a beat.

Smokey W. was my father's name.

Why would Evers have a file with my father's name on it?

I sat back on my heels and stared down at the bland manila folder, mind racing. My father's given name was Clive Winters, but everybody called him Smokey.

He and my mom were hard-core hippies, had been forever, and you can probably guess why my dad was called Smokey.

He was a big believer in the spiritual and medicinal benefits of marijuana and partook regularly. He hadn't been the most reliable of parents. Smokey Winters was a man-child—irresponsible, immature, but fun.

If I'm being honest, I don't know if I could say he was a good dad, but he'd always loved me.

I hadn't seen him as much as usual lately. He and my mom split a few years ago—she wasn't a stoner hippy, she was an energetic activist hippy, and she'd grown tired of being the only adult in her marriage.

I loved them both to pieces, but I hadn't given my mom a hard time about leaving my dad. I got it. Boy, did I get it. I loved him, but I wouldn't want to be his wife either.

Since the divorce, he hadn't been around much, and lately, he'd been... off. Weird.

Tense.

Smokey Winters was never tense. He was chemically incapable of being tense. He made sure of it.

I'd been meaning to call him, sit down and see what was up, but work had been crazy, and I hadn't gotten around to it.

Why did Evers have a folder with my father's name on it?

What the hell was going on?

Feeling absolutely no shame at invading his privacy, I opened the folder and flipped through the pages. My heart turned to ice at what I saw.

Reports on me.

Reports going back all the way to Emma's wedding.

Reports on my father starting six months after the wedding and continuing regularly. Reports on his movements and activities. Comments on me. What I was doing. Where I'd been. Reports on my clients.

I didn't understand most of it. It was written in code, almost all of the relevant language abbreviated so that it meant nothing to me, but based on the dates I could decipher a few.

1.26.18 Su.W. ctc Sm.W. Cl mt Atl. Su.W. Il 2d. Sm.W. mt B

January 26, 2018. I'd called my Dad on the way to a client meeting in Atlanta before I flew to Illinois for two days to assist another client. I only remembered because I'd had a flat tire on the way to the airport and come close to missing my flight.

Since my client was meeting me there, and she was deathly afraid of flying, the flat tire had caused an avalanche of problems. I'd handled it. I always did. Handling things was what I did best, but the day was etched in my memory as one for the record books. The day from hell.

And Evers had been watching, documenting the whole thing. While I'd been standing on the side of the road, freezing my ass off, splattered by ice as cars flew by, he'd been there. Somewhere. Watching me.

I had no idea what Sm.W. mt B meant. Sm.W. was my father. Based on Su.W. mt Atl, I thought mt stood for meeting. B? No idea. Not that it mattered. My dad's life wasn't my problem.

I flipped through more of the file. Page after page of cryptic notes. Me, my father. A few on my mother, spanning over two years.

The ice in my heart turned to nausea. I thought of Emma and how she'd met her husband, Evers' brother, Axel. Emma had been a job. Axel was investigating her on behalf of a client for suspected embezzlement. She'd been innocent, but that wasn't the point.

She'd been a job.

Just like me.

I was a job. My mouth watered, and, abruptly, I realized that I was going to vomit. I set the folder on the floor and rose, walking deliberately to the bathroom, then racing as my mouth flooded and my stomach hitched.

I hit my knees in front of the toilet and threw up a night's worth of frothy drinks and shots, everything inside me turned upside down, inside out, body heaving as my head spun.

I sat there for what felt like a year, my clammy forehead braced on my arm, leaning over the toilet, my mouth sour, breath shallow, heart racing.

I couldn't get my bearings.

I should have known. I should have known it was a lie.

I'd had the good sense to keep my distance from him. I'd thought it was because he was a player. A flirt. I didn't want to fall for him and get my heart broken.

The stab in my chest told me I'd fucked it all up.

I hadn't kept myself safe at all, and my heart was breaking anyway.

I hadn't even known it could. Not over Evers.

I'd tried so hard to keep him at a distance. I'd thought I could keep my heart safe if it was only sex. I'd thought I was protecting myself. He couldn't break me if I didn't let him.

Wrong.

I was an idiot and he was a liar.

I'd thought I knew him.

I'd thought I was in control.

Seeing the last two years in black and white, I'd been so blind. He'd been watching me, chronicling my every move and reporting it to... Who? Why?

Why was he investigating me and my father? None of this made any sense.

I hadn't done anything. I couldn't imagine my father had, either. He didn't have enough motivation to do anything. There was nothing in my life that justified this kind of invasion.

I worked, had fun with my friends, and for a while I had an affair with Evers.

He was the most exciting thing to happen to me in years. And he was a lie. He was a fucking lie. He wasn't here for me. He was here for a job.

Not anymore.

Not for another second.

Mechanically, I stood, leaned over the sink and turned on the water to brush my teeth. When I was done, I set my toothbrush back in its holder. Flushed the toilet. Washed my hands. Replaced my father's file back in the briefcase beside the others. Zipped it closed.

I left it on the floor and went to wake Evers.

Every step to the living room fell like lead. I stood over Evers, fists clenched at my side, staring down at him. His eyes flashed open and warmed, a sleepy grin spreading across his face.

It halted abruptly as he took in my expression.

"Hey, what's wrong?"

"Get. Out." I couldn't bring myself to say any more than that. Couldn't trust myself not to choke on the words, was desperately afraid the tears prickling the back of my eyes would spill down my cheeks.

I would not cry in front of Evers. No fucking way.

He'd lied to me. He'd used me. Fine, that was done.

I'd been a fool, but I didn't have to let him see me cry. He already knew he'd lied to me. He didn't need to know he'd hurt me.

Evers rolled to his feet, instantly in command of his body, of the room, of everything.

I stepped back and repeated myself.

"Get. Out."

"Summer, did something happen?"

I wasn't playing this game anymore. Flirty, mischievous Evers wasn't going to cajole me out of my mood to get what he wanted. Forget that.

"I saw my father's file in your bag. I know you've been watching me this whole time. I don't know what you want. I don't know why you're here. But get out. Do your job somewhere else."

His face went blank. Most people would jump straight to defensiveness, making excuses or accusing me of snooping.

Not Evers. A wall went down behind his eyes, his jaw set, and he straightened his shoulders.

"Summer, if you give me a minute, I can explain."

The flirtation was gone, the glint in his eyes extinguished.

This wasn't charming Evers, this was Evers on the job. Hard. Cool. Detached. This was what he hid beneath the smooth veneer. What he hid from me.

"Can you?" I demanded. "Can you explain lying to me for a year? Watching me? Taking notes on everything I do? Is there anything you can say that makes that okay?"

We locked eyes, Evers' ice-blue assessing, analyzing. He was flirty and sexy, but behind that façade, he was a cold-blooded machine. I knew it. I'd always known it.

I'd fooled myself into thinking he left the machine at the door. I'd been wrong.

"Summer," he started, "it's complicated."

"Just tell me one thing, Evers. At Emma's wedding, was that premeditated?"

"No. Absolutely not."

That was something. I would have bet anything our first hook up had been an accident. A collision of lust and champagne resulting in two spectacular days in my hotel room.

I already knew the answer to my next question. "And last year? At my client's party?"

A muscle flickered in the side of Evers' jaw before he admitted, "I knew you'd be there."

"So it was a setup. This whole thing is a setup."

The muscle flickered again. He nodded.

My heart squeezed, and I blinked hard. Tears pressed the back of my eyes. My nose tickled. I had about a minute before I lost it.

I felt it coming, the wave of anger and pain rising too fast for me to hold it back.

I couldn't talk to him anymore. I wouldn't. There was nothing he could say to justify this.

He wasn't my boyfriend. This wasn't real.

It was convenient sex, and it was over. Turning my back on him, I walked a few steps down the hall to his briefcase, still on the floor where I'd left it. Scooping it up with one hand, I turned for the door.

Evers' hand closed over my elbow, stopping me in my tracks. With a jerk, I pulled free, reaching the door with him a pace behind. I swung it open and tossed his briefcase into the hall.

"Get. Out. I don't care what you have to say. Leave. This is over. Get your information some other way."

"Summer, at least let me explain."

"What is there to say? Are you going to tell me why

you're investigating me? Are you going to tell me whose job this is? Why you're really here?"

Evers stared me down, his silence my answer.

"That's what I thought. Don't come back."

I watched him leave, briefcase in hand, his long, smooth stride carrying him to the elevator without a hitch.

If I'd known how soon he'd be back, I wouldn't have thrown him out the door.

I would have shoved him out the window.

Chapter Three

EVERS

"Clive Winters is missing,"

My head jerked up, and the droning boredom of the meeting came into sharp focus.

"What did you say?" I asked, watching my older brother Cooper carefully.

He picked up a pencil and pretended to scribble a note in the file in front of him.

He wasn't taking notes. Asshole was fucking with me.

Clive Winters, a.k.a. Smokey Winters, was *my* case. Or, it had been until I'd fucked everything up, and my brother Knox had taken Clive off my hands.

Cooper opted not to answer, only raised an eyebrow at me. I turned in my chair to face Knox, slouched in the big armchair beside me, an absurdly-big gas station travel mug in his hand.

He gave me a bland look and said, "What?"

"You fucking lost Smokey Winters? How the fuck did you lose him?"

"Why are you so riled up?" Knox asked in that same bland tone he knew drove me nuts.

Brothers. I'd die for any one of them, but they were a bunch of assholes.

"I care," I said, gritting my teeth, "because he was your case."

Knox shrugged his shoulder and took a long sip of coffee. "If it meant that much, you wouldn't have blown the deal in the first place."

He was wrong. I'd blown the case *because* I cared. For the first time in my career, I'd tangled together business and pleasure and ended up tied in knots.

Knox was right. I'd fucked the whole thing up.

"Maybe if you'd joined the twenty-first century and stopped using paper files, none of this would have happened," my older brother Axel commented with a sly smile.

Axel ran the Western division of Sinclair Security and lived in Las Vegas. He wasn't in Atlanta often, but he'd shown up the night before, saying only that he was in town on business.

I hadn't had a chance to pry the details from him, but his presence at our meeting told me something was up. Something more than Clive Winters going missing.

Used to the ribbing but unable to ignore the urge to fire back, I said, "I like paper files. Fuck off."

Fuck off. The generic response to brotherly teasing. It worked about as well as it usually did. Not at all.

Axel had a point. Using paper files had been stupid. An old hang-up I'd refused to let go until it had been too late. These days there wasn't a scrap of paper to be found in my office. Every piece of case information was safely stored behind multiple layers of encryption.

I wasn't going to get caught again. Not that it mattered. The worst damage had already been done.

Axel wasn't ready to let it go. "How everything got fucked up doesn't matter. What matters is that Summer's father is off the grid. He's a ghost. We need to find him. Yesterday."

"Is that why you're here?" I asked him.

"In a way." Axel shared a long look with Cooper. "Show him."

Cooper pulled a page from the pile on his desk and handed it to me. Numbers in a list, arranged in columns, notes in Cooper's precise handwriting along the side.

Account numbers, dates, amounts. Payments. Or transfers.

I took in the names, the timeline. Money moving from a hidden account under a shell corporation we suspected our father had set up before he disappeared. Money moving from our father to William Davis, now deceased, and from Davis to fucking Clive 'Smokey' Winters.

Fuck me. This was not good.

Our father, Maxwell Sinclair, had disappeared five years before. We'd thought he died when his car shot through the railing of a bridge into a river swollen from rain.

No body had ever been recovered. A few months ago, information had come to light that suggested Maxwell Sinclair was no more dead than I was.

Dead or alive, he'd left us a mess.

I grew up thinking my father was the king of the universe. He protected celebrities. Royalty. Everyone loved him. Respected him.

That hadn't been enough for Maxwell Sinclair. Since well before I was born, my father had been dabbling on the dark side.

I could only assume he did it for the adrenaline rush. We didn't need the money. He'd inherited tens of millions from my grandfather, and Maxwell had always been good at making money grow.

A few years before he disappeared my brothers and I had taken over leadership of the company. Since then Sinclair Security had almost doubled in size.

Whatever my father was up to, it wasn't about money. From what we'd been able to uncover, he'd roped in an old friend, William Davis, and together the two of them had been into all sorts of ugly shit. Running guns, illegal adoptions, and worse.

The question was what the hell did Clive Winters have to do with any of this? My father and William Davis I could see. They'd been tight since high school, gone to college together, and William, who'd died recently, had been a nutcase.

I didn't have any trouble imagining William operating without a moral compass. And my father? I was learning I knew a lot less about Maxwell Sinclair than I'd thought.

But Smokey Winters... Smokey Winters was a hippie stoner who coasted on alimony from his wife and a family trust he'd managed not to bleed dry. Occasionally, he supplemented his income by slinging weed.

He wasn't very good at it, considering he smoked half of what he was supposed to sell, but Smokey Winters was one of those guys who always managed to get by, one way or another.

I couldn't see him fitting into any puzzle that included my father and William Davis. Yet, here he was, in black and white, in numbers and dates and hefty transfusions of cash.

I stared at those numbers, at Cooper's neat handwriting, and my stomach drew into a knot. Cold, greasy fear settled deep inside me, tendrils spreading to my heart and up my spine.

Summer.

My father was into some bad shit, and if Smokey Winters was involved, that put Summer a hell of a lot closer to any of this than I wanted her to be. If her father was involved, she wasn't safe.

Fuck.

Summer.

Just thinking her name made me want to shut down, to get up and walk out of the room. I didn't want to think about Summer here. She shouldn't have anything to do with my father's mess.

From the beginning, from the first time I laid eyes on her, on those long blonde curls and her bright blue eyes, she'd made me crazy. Crazy and stupid. Never in my life had I screwed up so badly with a woman.

"Emma doesn't know about your fuck up," Axel said, not pulling his punch. "I'm going to be around more until we figure out what's going on with Dad, and eventually she's going to want to come to Atlanta to see Summer. I suggest you fix whatever you did before she finds out, or she's going to kick your ass."

"I'm not afraid of your wife," I said with a sneer.

Axel only raised an eyebrow. "Liar."

"If you're not afraid of Emma, you're an idiot," Knox cut in.

I wasn't afraid of Emma Sinclair.

Okay, I was a little afraid of Emma Sinclair.

Emma was an excellent sister-in-law. A redhead with a sharp mind and a bombshell body, she'd hooked Axel the first time he laid eyes on her. She wasn't a ball buster, but she was tough, and she didn't take any crap.

If she found out I'd screwed over her best friend in the entire world? My ass was grass.

"I still don't get why you lied to Summer," Knox said.

"It was easier," I muttered.

"Easy, maybe. That's not why you lied."

Knox wasn't a talker. He saved his words, only using them when they'd do the most good. Or the most damage.

I didn't want to hear what he had to say, but there was no chance he'd let it go.

I should have kept my mouth shut. I didn't.

"Really? Then tell me, oh, wise one, why did I lie?"

"Because Summer Winters scares you shitless. You do know you're not Dad, right?"

Heat flooded my brain and I saw red. Only force of will kept me in my seat.

I ground out, "Shut the hell up. You don't know what you're fucking talking about."

Knox knew exactly how close I was to taking a swing at him. He only sipped from that ugly oversized mug and said, "Go ahead, be pissed. Doesn't make me wrong."

I was. And it didn't.

"Knock it off," Cooper said, eyeing both Knox and me. "Why he lied doesn't matter. It's done. He fucked up and now he's going to fix it."

"Why am I fixing it? If I fucked up so badly why don't you put somebody else on the case?"

Just the thought of one of my brothers 'fixing things' with Summer made the knot in my stomach wind tighter. She wasn't mine anymore, if she ever had been. That didn't mean one of them could have her.

I handed the paper with the banking information back to Cooper. He took it, shaking his head at me in exaggerated patience and a little pity.

"It has to be you. Believe me, I like Summer. I'd love to spare her dealing with you. You'll be lucky if she doesn't try to kill you in your sleep. But it has to be you. Summer is our best chance right now at finding her father. Knox and I are going to keep on his trail, but he's vapor. Summer, we can track. And the perfect opportunity just fell into our laps."

Under his breath, Axel muttered, "You're gonna love this one."

"What? Is she all right? Did something happen to her?"

Cooper shook his head. "Summer's fine. You remember she does work for Cynthia Stevens?"

I nodded. Summer's job was odd, but she was good at it. She was a kind of virtual assistant for a handful of high-profile people. For some she was hands-on, traveling to work with them a few days a month. Some she interacted with only over the Internet, managing their email or social media. Booking flights and arranging appointments. Whatever they needed, Summer handled. I'd known she worked for Cynthia Stevens here and there.

Cooper nodded again. "Cynthia decided she wants to come home while she preps for her next role. Her ex has been a problem. Rehab didn't take, and he won't leave her alone. He claims he wants her back. Cynthia wants to be near family, and she doesn't want the friction of handling daily life. She had Summer rent the Rycroft estate. Cynthia, her entourage, and Summer are moving in."

"Guess who's doing the security?" Axel asked with another sly grin. Fuck me. He went on, "Cynthia requested you, personally."

"I don't do protection details anymore."

"You're making an exception for this one," Cooper said flatly, his tone brooking no argument.

This morning had started badly and was only getting worse.

Fucking hell.

Cynthia Stevens was the granddaughter of Rupert Stevens, a close friend of my grandfather when he'd still been alive. She was old Atlanta, raised for cotillions and charity luncheons. When she'd run off to Hollywood at eighteen, everyone figured she'd be home within six months.

Instead, she'd busted her ass, waiting tables and taking bit parts until she got her first break. She was beautiful, high maintenance, and talented as hell.

Cynthia Stevens was a diva. She was also my ex.

Slowly, desperately hoping this was a bad dream, I said, "You want me to put together a detail, headed by me, to live in the Rycroft place with Cynthia Stevens and Summer? You realize this is going to be a disaster, right?"

Cooper shrugged a shoulder, his dark eyes, so like our father's, locked on mine. "It doesn't have to be a disaster. You've been moping around here ever since Summer kicked you out. This is your chance to fix it. While you're at it, figure out where her father is and what he has to do with Dad."

"Cooper—"

"No, Evers. I don't want to hear it. Knox is right, you fucked up with her because you were scared. You want to bury your head in the sand and pretend that's not what happened, go ahead. Lie to yourself. If she didn't matter, you wouldn't have cared when she kicked you out. You would have moved on to the next woman and not given Summer a second thought. That's not what happened, is it?"

"When's the last time you got laid, Evers?" Axel asked with a smirk.

Fucking brothers. "None of your business, asshole."

"There's your answer," Knox filled in.

I'd let them set me on fire before I'd admit that I hadn't so much as kissed another woman since I'd walked out of Summer's apartment.

I'd thought about it, wanted to in a vague *I should get laid* kind of way. Since Summer, no other woman had grabbed my interest. I didn't want anyone else.

"And what about while you were with her?" Axel pushed.

"I wasn't *with her*. We had a thing," I protested.

"Jesus, you're like the stereotypical commitment-phobe. How many other women did you sleep with while you had your *thing*?" Axel asked, his words dripping with sarcasm.

"Not everyone is looking for domestic bliss, Axel. Ever since you got married you've been a know-it-all pain in the ass."

"He was a pain in the ass long before he got married," Cooper said. "If anything, Emma's made him more tolerable."

True, but I wasn't going to admit it.

"Answer the question," Knox said evenly.

I didn't want to answer the question. Answering the question would tell them everything they wanted to know about exactly how wrecked I was over Summer.

"None, okay?" Maybe now that I'd admitted it, they'd stop needling me and move on.

No such luck.

"So, she was just a hookup," Axel said, "but in the year you were keeping an eye on her—and sleeping with the target—you didn't so much as touch another woman. Do I have that right?"

I didn't dignify his question with an answer.

"But she didn't mean anything. You're over her."

I made a sound in the back of my throat that was supposed to be a yes. I couldn't make my mouth form the word. I wasn't even remotely over her. I'd been working my way around to figuring out how to win her back. How to explain.

It had started innocently enough.

My brothers and I had grown up side-by-side with the Winters family. While the Sinclairs were well-known and had a nice chunk of change in the bank, our lives didn't come close to that of the Winters.

Notorious for scandal and billionaires a few times over, to us, the Winters were family. So, when Emma's best friend turned out to be an estranged cousin, we decided to keep an eye on her. She'd seemed legit, but when long-lost relatives come out of the woodwork, nine times out of ten they're aiming straight for the bank account.

No one was taking advantage of the Winters family on our watch. Defying expectations, Summer hadn't made any attempt to reach out to the rest of the Winters family.

She'd established her business in Atlanta, made friends, went out for drinks or to the movies. Dated here and there. Though the Winters' high profile would have helped her attract clients, Summer stayed far away.

I could have watched her from a distance. I didn't need to make contact. But I hadn't been able to stop myself. In every area of my life, my self-control was absolute. Until it came to Summer.

Cooper flipped open his laptop and started tapping keys. Without looking at me, he said, "I'm sending you the Stevens file. They move in on Friday. You need to take a team out to the house, make sure it's secured, and be there when she arrives. Details are in the file." He tapped the final key and looked up. "This is your chance, Evers. Don't fuck it up again."

I stood, eager to get out of the office. Out of the building. I needed to clear my head and think. I'd been looking for a way back in, but babysitting an ex-lover while trying to win back another was a disaster waiting to happen.

A disaster, and my only shot.

One way or another, I'd figure out how to make it work. I wasn't going to fail.

Not with Summer.

Not this time.

Chapter Four

SUMMER

Rycroft Castle looked like it belonged in a different century. In another country. Maybe in another dimension. In the center of an oversized lot in Buckhead, surrounded by trees that buffered the sounds from the road, it was easy to imagine I'd walked straight into a fairytale.

The massive house looked like it had been built centuries before. In fact, it was the dream of a tech billionaire who'd fallen in love with the idea of building his very own castle in the heart of Atlanta.

He'd had money to burn, and he'd poured it into Rycroft Castle, importing the marble from Italy, the bar from a pub in Ireland. Fashioned after a French château, with three-inch thick creamy limestone walls and a slate roof, it loomed over me, both imposing and fanciful.

Sporting an indoor pool modeled after a Roman spa, four separate kitchens, a theater, card room, three formal parlors, a music room, and a wine tasting room bigger than my condo, it was hard to imagine the owner had given it up.

After a few years of living in Rycroft Castle, he'd grown bored and moved out, focusing his attention on a modern monstrosity in Silicon Valley, closer to his corporate headquarters. He still owned the place, renting it out under special circumstances to high profile guests. When Cynthia Stevens told me she wanted to come home for a few months but had no intention of staying with family, I knew exactly who to call.

She was going to go crazy when she saw this place. Cynthia was larger-than-life, with a talent as overwhelming as her beauty. A princess to the core, she'd fit right in at Rycroft Castle.

Of all my clients, Cynthia was my favorite. She could be a diva, and like most wealthy and successful people, she wanted what she wanted when she wanted it. Cynthia was high on standards and low on patience. She was also funny and kind.

I wouldn't say we were friends, exactly. I'm a glorified PA and she's an Oscar-winning movie star.

But Cynthia never treated me like the hired help. She'd told me once that she saw her team as partners all playing a role in creating the persona that was Cynthia Stevens.

If any of my other clients had asked me to move in and manage their lives full time, I might have balked. Not that my other clients were bad, but there's a big difference between working remotely and living in the same house with someone. Especially when they were your employer.

I wasn't quite sure how this is going to go, but for Cynthia, I was willing to give it a shot. She'd had a rough year, and her upcoming role would be demanding, physically and emotionally. She needed this break, this time at home. I was going to help her make it happen. I'd lightened my load with my other clients, clearing my schedule as much as possible so I could focus on Cynthia.

I was in charge of almost every aspect of the move to Rycroft Castle, except for the security. Cynthia wanted to handle that personally. I was hoping that meant she was bringing a team with her to Atlanta.

Celebrity security in Atlanta usually meant... Nope. Not thinking about him. Cynthia was bringing her team from L.A. I was sure of it. Problem solved.

Looking up from the list on my tablet, I watched two men in matching polo shirts carry Cynthia's Louis Vuitton trunks up the wide limestone stairs to the front entry. I knew better than to ask why she needed ten full trunks for a mere two months.

I'd be unpacking them soon enough, and I was sure I'd find umpteen pairs of shoes, piles of dresses, and anything else Cynthia thought she might need for two months of rest and seclusion.

I'd planned to have the movers out of the way and Cynthia's things unpacked before she arrived. The rumble of an engine up the drive told me that wasn't going to happen. If she was anything, it was unpredictable.

An oversized white SUV came to a stop in the circular drive, directly in front of where I stood at the base of the stairway. The passenger door swung open, and Cynthia emerged, tumbled platinum locks shining in the summer sun. Her apple-green eyes landed on me and a wide, genuine smile stretched across her face.

"Summer, darling, you're here!" Her spike heels tapped across the cobblestone driveway, Cynthia gliding toward me as if the surface were smooth as glass.

She wrapped me in her arms, wreathing me in a cloud of sweet perfume as she pressed her cheek to mine on one side, then the other, making a kissing sound with each gesture.

"I knew you'd have everything in hand. We're here a little early. I just couldn't wait to get started. This place is magnificent!"

"Wait until you see the inside," I said, returning her hug. "I haven't unpacked your trunks yet, but I've already gone shopping, supervised the cleaning service, and double-checked the sleeping arrangements. I'll give you a tour soon as we get settled. I haven't had confirmation from the security team. We need a walkthrough on the system."

Cynthia waved a hand in the air dismissing my concern. "The security team will be here later this afternoon. We can talk to them then. Plenty of time to get settled first. These two will do for now." She gestured behind her at two hulks in suits who had emerged from the SUV.

Ignoring them, she looked up at her new home. "This place is a dream. I didn't even know it was here. Show me around. I think this is going to be a wonderful few months."

She looped her arm through mine, and we climbed the stairs to the house together. Room by room, we strolled through Rycroft Castle, and Cynthia's smile of delight made all my work worthwhile.

The sumptuous luxury of Rycroft fit her to perfection. When I showed her the expansive master suite, she cooed with delight. Only in a house like this could I unpack every one of those ten trunks and still have room in the closet.

"Now, where will you be?" she asked. "I didn't bring everyone. Just Viggo and Angie. But there will be some people popping in and out while we're here. I have to do combat training for the movie, and my acting coach will be coming out a few times to work with me on the script. Other than that, I want things to be quiet. Peaceful. I need peaceful."

I reached out and squeezed Cynthia's hand in mine, understanding immediately. For the past year, Cynthia had been embroiled in an ugly divorce. Her husband, also an actor, had a series of bombs at the box office and had consoled himself with liquor and other women.

Cynthia didn't talk much about Clint Perry, but I'd seen with my own eyes how deeply in love they'd once been. In an effort to stop the divorce, he'd gone to rehab, quit drinking, and sworn off other women.

Cynthia had been hopeful until a month before when he'd shown up all over the tabloids with an ingénue young enough to be his daughter half-naked on his lap.

A few days later, Cynthia came up with a new plan for the summer. Get out of California and go home. Away from Hollywood. Away from the paparazzi. Away from Clint.

Clint hadn't taken her departure well. He'd insisted everywhere—the tabloids, on social media, in endless voice-mail messages—that the pictures weren't what they looked like.

He hadn't been drinking. He hadn't been fucking around.

But Cynthia was done. Clint swore he wasn't going to let her go. Cynthia had blocked his number and arranged for extra security.

Rycroft Castle had been designed with no expense spared, including the security system. That wasn't good enough for Cynthia Stevens. We would have security on-site, twenty-four seven, as long as we were there. She needed peace, and she had the money to pay for it.

I led Cynthia down the hall from the master suite. We descended a set of stairs, went down another hallway, and climbed a second set of stairs to arrive in another wing of the house, this one tucked away from the owner's wing and the main section of Rycroft Castle.

Originally designed for key members of the staff or guests who didn't rate top-notch rooms, this wing was little more than a long hallway with bedrooms on either side, six of them total. One for me, one for the head of security, two more for Viggo and Angie, the last two for any additional staff that might come and go.

Typical of Rycroft Castle, even the second-rate rooms were far from plain. Plush wool carpet, silk drapes, and marble in the bathroom. I was going to get spoiled.

Our small wing was almost self-sufficient, with a beautifully-appointed sitting room at the end of the hall, complete with a large-screen television, two couches, and a kitchen with stainless appliances, a double oven, and wet bar.

In Rycroft Castle, even the staff lived better than I did, and my condo wasn't shabby.

"Darling, tell me you've arranged for lunch," Cynthia said. She followed a very strict diet, as you'd guess, but she never missed a meal. Cynthia loved her food. It was one of the things I liked best about her.

It took a lot of time, effort, and self-discipline to pull off the façade of a renowned actress. Cynthia did what she needed to do. She had a healthy dose of vanity to give her motivation, but I'd seen her tuck into a cheeseburger with relish, even if she ate less than half of it.

I led her from the staff hallway back around to the main staircase and from there to the kitchens. The cook and two housekeepers had arrived the day before. They were staying in a suite of rooms over the five-car garage.

As we entered the kitchen, the cook, a portly woman in her sixties with steel gray hair, took one look at Cynthia and blushed a fiery red. Used to her celebrity making people nervous, Cynthia flashed a wide, welcoming smile and held out a hand, covering the cook's nerves by saying, "It's a pleasure to meet you, you come highly recommended. I appreciate you taking on the challenge of my menu. I know it's frustrating to have so many requirements, and I appreciate your patience."

I knew for a fact the cook had scowled when she'd seen the list of Cynthia's do's and don'ts. Now, faced with Cynthia's smile, she babbled her delight at the chance to cook for Cynthia Stevens. She assured us that it would be an honor to make sure that every meal surpassed Cynthia's expectations.

I thanked her before she passed out from excitement and asked, "When should we expect lunch?"

"In about a half-hour, if that's all right, ma'am," she answered with barely a stutter.

I looked at Cynthia who said, "'That will be just fine. We'll take it in the main dining room. Thank you so much."

With another dazzling smile, she turned and strode down the hall leaving a cloud of perfume in her wake. I followed behind, tapping items off my to-do list and making notes.

Give Cynthia a tour. *Done.*

Introduce her to staff. *Done.*

Unpack trunks. *TBD*

Lunch. 3om.

Meeting with security. *Undetermined.*

"When are we meeting with security?"

Cynthia waved her hand in the air. "Sometime after lunch," she answered, "I need to check my phone. They texted. They said the property is secure. I'm just going to have a wander until lunch."

I knew when I was being dismissed. That worked for me, I had trunks to deal with. "I'll start with the unpacking and meet you in the dining room for lunch."

"Fine," Cynthia said, scrolling through the screen on her phone, already distracted. I headed for the stairs, hoping to make a dent in organizing Cynthia's closet before it was time to eat.

I only made it through three trunks, mostly shoes and day wear, before the cook called us to lunch. We were just finishing our meal when Cynthia's phone beeped with an alert. Looking down at the screen, a secretive smile spread across her face.

"The security team is here," she murmured. "This should be fun."

Finally, the long-awaited meeting with security. Cynthia had uncharacteristically insisted on handling the arrangements herself. She'd resisted any attempt of mine to help coordinate the logistics. She hadn't explained why, and I hadn't pressed. What Cynthia wanted, Cynthia got. I was paid well to make sure it happened.

I should have pushed for an explanation. I should have demanded answers.

I should have done anything but let Cynthia take the driver's seat.

If I had, I wouldn't have felt like I was going to lose my lunch so soon after finishing it.

"Summer, be a doll and get the door, would you?"

I opened my mouth to tell her no one was there when, as if cued by a director, the sound of church bells echoed through the main level. Trust Rycroft Castle to have a door-bell that belonged in a cathedral.

Dutifully, I pushed back my chair and rose. "Of course. Would you like me to order coffee in the parlor?"

"That would be fine, thank you, Summer. I'll meet you there."

I texted a quick message to the cook on my way to the front door. Turning the heavy iron handle, I swung the door open and turned to stone.

Evers Sinclair stood in front of me, a knowing grin on his face.

Chapter Five

SUMMER

My heart sank. I should have seen it coming. Why had I convinced myself there was any chance Cynthia had brought her team from L.A.?

She'd grown up in Atlanta. She'd probably grown up with the Sinclairs. And even if she hadn't, Sinclair Security was the best. Evers' brother Axel managed her security on the West Coast, though he didn't handle her personally. It looked like Evers would be different.

His ice-blue eyes were impenetrable and fixed on mine. A wave of dark hair fell over his forehead. My hand itched to push it back, to run my thumb over the grooves beside his mouth.

He'd looked tired the day I'd thrown him out. Now, the bright July sun highlighting every detail of his face, I wondered when he'd last slept. Beneath his tan he was pale. Drawn.

I quashed the worry blooming in my heart. So what if

he was worn out? Not my problem. It had never been my problem.

My eyes landed briefly on his full lower lip, then flicked away. Evers Sinclair had been a thorn in my side since the day we'd met.

I fought the urge to grit my teeth and mustered every ounce of professionalism I had. In an even, calm voice I said, "I assume you're representing our security team?"

Evers' lips curved in that charming smile that dropped panties from coast-to-coast. Not mine. Not anymore.

"Winters. I forgot you worked for Cynthia."

"Liar," I said flatly.

I hated when he called me Winters. I'd worked for Cynthia when he'd been investigating me. I didn't believe for a second he'd forgotten.

From behind him, I heard, "Ev, the girl's got your number. Are you going to get out of the way or should we do this meeting on the steps?"

I stepped back to let them in the house. Evers moved past me, and the man behind took his place, holding out his hand with a grin. I took it and shook, meeting a pair of amused sea-green eyes. A little shorter than Evers but still way taller than me, Evers' partner was broad shouldered, with sandy, close-cropped hair, and a stubbled jaw.

Based on the bump on the bridge of his nose and the scar running over it, his nose had been badly broken at some point. The old injury only added to his roguish appeal. All in all, he was more than handsome. Compelling. Downright hot.

Too bad he didn't do anything for me. Since the disaster with the jerk standing beside me, I hadn't had any interest in men, even one as good-looking as this one.

"I've heard all about you, Summer Winters," he said with a wink.

I realized immediately that he knew what had happened with Evers, probably knew my file inside and out. Before I could be annoyed, he held out his arm, placed my hand on it and started to lead me into the house.

Ignoring Evers, he smiled down at me and said with a hint of a drawl, "I'm Griffen Sawyer. I'm working with Evers on this assignment. This place is amazing, isn't it? We put in the original system, and I saw it while it was under construction, but I haven't been back since. Seems like a shame it stands empty most of the time. We meeting in the front parlor?"

He didn't wait for me to answer, leading me down the hall to the formal living room. Evers stalked behind us, scowling at Griffen.

"You don't have to lead her to the parlor," he grumbled under his breath. "She knows where it is."

Griffen glanced over his shoulder. "I'm a gentleman. Unlike some people."

Evers responded with a low growl.

I ignored him. The side of Griffen's mouth quirked up, and he looked down at me, his eyes meeting mine before one closed in a slow wink. Startled, I barely caught myself before I grinned back.

It looked like Griffen was ready to mess with his friend. I didn't know why Evers would care if Griffen flirted with me, but I was happy to poke at him any way I could.

Throwing him out of my condo hadn't been nearly enough punishment for his betrayal. I wasn't above aggravating him if I had the chance.

Cynthia swanned into the room, her arms held wide in welcome, pink lips curved in a dazzling smile.

"Evers. Evers Sinclair. Darling. It's been so long." She threw herself into his arms, linking her hands behind his neck and pulling him down for a smacking kiss right on the mouth.

I looked away, my chest burning as their lips met. Evers' hand rested on her back, her fingers stroked his neck. My lunch rolled in my stomach.

He wasn't mine. He'd never been mine. And Cynthia was my boss.

Griffen cleared his throat. Cynthia stepped back, noticing him for the first time. "Well, aren't you straight out of central casting. Rugged and handsome. I don't believe we've met," Cynthia said, giving Griffen a long, slow, appreciative smile.

She held out her hand. Griffen took it in both of his, bending low over hers in a courtly gesture that should have looked silly and didn't.

"Griffen Sawyer, ma'am. It's a pleasure to meet you."

"Oh, no, don't call me ma'am. Cynthia's fine. We're all going to get to know each other very well. We don't need to stand on ceremony."

With horror, I thought about the room I'd reserved upstairs for the head of security. *Please let that be Griffen*, I thought, silently cursing Cynthia for keeping me out of the security arrangements.

There was clearly something between her and Evers. She was friendly and touchy, but she didn't kiss men she'd just met. She'd kept the security to herself so she could arrange for some company along with safety.

At the thought, bile rose in the back of my throat. I hoped they were going to meet in her room. I couldn't take hearing them across the hall.

Ugh, it was very possible I was going to vomit. I swallowed hard. Of course, they'd meet in her room. She was the princess. She wouldn't go to him.

Gesturing to the two white sofas flanking the cold fireplace, Cynthia said, "Business before pleasure. Let's sit and go over the arrangements."

We sat, Cynthia beside Evers and me beside Griffen. Evers eyed the space between Griffen and myself even as Cynthia slid closer to him, leaning in and setting her hand on his knee, her long pink nails curving around his thigh. She said something under her breath, and Evers turned to answer in a murmur.

To me, Griffen said, "How long have you worked for Cynthia?"

"For a few years," I said, sure Griffen already knew every detail of my employment history with Cynthia Stevens.

I wasn't sure why he'd asked until he eased closer to me and stretched his arm behind my back along the top of the sofa, his fingers landing on my shoulder. Evers' ice-blue eyes flicked up, catching Griffen's movement, and narrowed, a muscle clenching in the side of his jaw. I felt more than saw the smirk on Griffen's face.

"She going to give us trouble?"

"Hmm?" I asked, losing track of the conversation.

"Cynthia," Griffen said in a low voice as we watched Evers talk to the client in an intimate tone we couldn't quite decipher from a few feet away.

"Oh, no. No, I don't think she will. She's usually very sensible, and the situation with Clint has her on edge."

"Good. That's good. Nothing worse than a client who gets in the way."

His fingers brushed my shoulder again. Evers had his eyes on Cynthia, but that muscle in his jaw flickered. In any other situation, I would have discretely moved away from Griffen's touch. He seemed nice enough, but that was too much contact for a guy I'd just met. I stayed where I was. I knew he was only touching me to needle Evers, though I didn't get why.

"Is she good to work for? Cynthia?" Griffen asked, his voice low enough that the pair on the other couch couldn't hear.

"Usually," I said just as quietly.

I thought about my answer. She was great to work for. Generous and kind and no more demanding than anyone else in her position would be. So why was I ready to stand up and walk out of the room? Why did it matter?

I was the one who'd ended things with Evers.

I didn't want him back.

I didn't.

I'd never really had him in the first place. He'd been using me. Lying to me. Whatever he had going on with Cynthia, it was none of my business.

I thought about my mortgage payments. The new car I was saving for. Cynthia was generous. She expected a lot, and she paid for excellence. Walking out would be unprofessional. If I was anything, I was damn good at my job. I wasn't going to abandon her because my jerk-of-a-not-really ex-boyfriend had shown up.

Taking a breath to steady myself, I said, still in that low, barely-audible tone, "She's great. Really great. She's a little flamboyant, and stubborn, but she's a good person. My favorite client," I said, almost completely meaning it.

I did mean it. I wasn't going to let Evers Sinclair screw up a great working relationship.

Across from us, Evers straightened, leaning a little away from Cynthia and turning his attention to Griffen and myself. "'There's not much to review," he began. "We'll have security teams on the property twenty-four seven. A team of two in the house. A second team of two patrolling the grounds and the perimeter. The property is walled, which makes our job easier.

"We upgraded the motion sensor cameras last week. We have a control room set up on the lower level. Someone will be manning the monitors around-the-clock. No one will get on this property without us knowing about it." Looking directly at Cynthia, he said, "I'd prefer you keep the alarm on while you're in the house."

Cynthia shook her head. "I'm not doing that. The gardens are beautiful, and I love to be outside."

"At least the pool is indoors," Evers said under his breath. "You don't leave the house without a guard. Understood?"

"Understood," Cynthia said with a wry smile. "I don't want to feel like I'm in prison, Evers, but I'm not a fool."

Throwing that statement into question, she reached into her pocket and withdrew a folded piece of paper.

"I do have a challenge for all of you," she said, smiling sweetly up at Evers and then sympathetically at me. "Now, don't kill me, but I decided we have to have a party. A kind of welcome home get-together. Nothing elaborate."

She met my eyes and gave an apologetic shrug of one shoulder. "Summer, honey, I know this is throwing a lot at you, but if anyone can make it happen, it's Summer Winters."

"No parties," Evers said with finality. I choked back a laugh.

He glared at me. "Problem, Winters?"

"No, no problem," I said.

There *was* a problem, but it wasn't me.

Chapter Six

SUMMER

"I'm having a party, Evers," Cynthia stated in a tone I knew well. "You're in charge of security. You figure it out. This is the guest list," she said, handing it to Evers. He skimmed it carefully as she went on, "Next Friday. You should be able to work that out. The guest list is small. No more than seventy-five."

I gave Cynthia my most professional *I can handle anything you throw at me* smile. A party for seventy-five in a week? No problem.

Who was I kidding? Major problem. I knew Cynthia. This would not be pizza and beer. My mind raced, searching through myriad mental lists. Caterers. Equipment rentals. Flowers.

Cynthia was impossible. How could she do this to me?

I didn't need to ask. Cynthia wanted it, and it happened. That was the way it worked. *How* it happened was on me.

Evers silently reached across the table, handing me the guest list. He said nothing, but something in the set of his shoulders, the way he wouldn't meet my eyes, put me on alert.

Before I could move, Griffen leaned forward and plucked the list from his hand. He skimmed it before silently handing it to me.

I started at the top, reading quickly, familiar with many of the names. Cynthia was Rupert Stevens' granddaughter, so I expected to see Rupert, his wife Sloane, Cynthia's parents, her sister and brother, all of whom still lived in Atlanta. I read further, recognizing many of the highest echelon of Atlanta society, as well as a few artists and local performers.

I was halfway through the list when my eyes snagged on a name and my heart stopped in my chest. Vance and Magnolia Winters. Below them Aiden Winters, and below him his brother Jacob Winters. I didn't have to keep reading. The entire Winters clan was on the guest list.

This was a problem. A huge problem. A problem so big it turned throwing together a party in a week into child's play. My hand shook as I set the list on the coffee table and said, with only a slight tremble in my voice, "This doesn't seem like a good idea, Cynthia. I know you want a party, but with everything that's going on, with Clint—"

"I want the party, Summer. I did not come here to hide. I haven't been back in ages, and I want to see everyone. Would you rather I go to the country club?"

"Of course not," Evers cut in. He glanced at the guest list, then to me, and finally back to Cynthia. "And we don't want you to feel trapped here. But a party is irresponsible. At least give us more time to plan—"

"No. I don't have more time. I'm only going to be here for two months, and if I wait a few more weeks for the party

I'll barely have time to see everyone after we're re-introduced. No. It has to be next Friday."

She stood, brushing the wrinkles from her skirt, and tossed her platinum locks over her shoulder, sending us another dazzling smile. "You're all the best at what you do. Go out there and do it."

To Evers, she said, "Figure out how to keep the house secure during the party." And to me, "You've worked miracles before, Summer. I know you can do it again. I have complete faith in all of you."

I shook my head as she turned and glided from the room, the sweet scent of her perfume lingering after she was gone. I shook my head in disbelief.

"How does she do that?" I asked myself aloud. "Just when I'm about to strangle her, she says she has absolute faith in me, and I'm ready to hit the phone and make this ridiculous plan happen. If I didn't like her so much I'd strangle her."

Beside me, Griffen chuckled. "Can you do it? Throw together a party in a week?"

"I can," I admitted. "It's going to be a long few days, but I can." I looked down at the list of names on the table between us and then to Evers, waiting for him to say something. He remained silent, his eyes on the door Cynthia had walked through moments before.

I'd figure out what to do about the guest list later. I had more important things to deal with. I would have preferred to have this conversation in private, but asking Griffen to leave would give Evers too much importance.

He didn't know how badly he'd hurt me. If I had my way, he never would.

Leaning forward, I met Evers' blue eyes with a hard look. "Why are you here?" I demanded. "And don't tell me it's all about Cynthia's security. Obviously, you're old friends, but I know you don't handle protection details personally anymore. So why are you here?"

Evers sat back and crossed his arms over his chest casually, propping one ankle on his knee. He stared at me for a long moment, his eyes unreadable, before he said, "When was the last time you talked to your father?"

I sucked in a short breath. I hadn't expected him to say that. I'd expected him to dodge the question. To lie. Again. I tried to shift gears, to remember the last time I'd talked to my dad. "A few weeks ago?"

"Did you see him or talk to him by phone a few weeks ago?" he asked, one eyebrow raised.

"I talked to him on the telephone. I called to check in, say hi. We didn't talk long. He said he was in the middle of something. Why? What's going on?"

"Your father—"

Griffen pulled his arm from behind me on the couch and leaned forward, bracing his elbows on his knees. "Ev, she doesn't need—"

"Shut. Up." Evers flashed a quelling look at Griffen, who ignored him.

"There's some stuff going on with your dad," Griffen said, giving me a sympathetic look. "You don't have to worry about it. We have it under control."

Evers glared at Griffen. "I told you to let me handle this."

"You're doing a piss-poor job so far," Griffen shot back.

"If something's wrong with my dad, I want to know," I said, "What the hell is going on, Evers? Why are you here? Why now?"

Evers dropped his foot off his knee, his arms falling to his sides, dropping the illusion that this was casual. He leaned forward and propped his elbows on his knees, mimicking Griffen's posture.

Eyes level on mine, he said, "Do you want the truth? I can tell you right now you're not going to like it. Griffen is trying to spare you. I was trying to spare you. I know now that was a mistake. You're pissed about that, and I get it. But be sure you want to know."

"I want to know," I said immediately.

Evers shook his head. "You have to be sure. And if I tell you, you have to keep your mouth shut. Your father is part of a bigger situation, and if I trust you with this information, you have to promise me you'll keep it to yourself."

"Evers," Griffen warned, shaking his head. "This is too much. She doesn't need to know." He turned to look at me, sympathy in his eyes. "Summer, I know he's your dad, and I know Evers here fucked everything up with you before. But this deal, it's an ugly mess. If you're smart, you'll let us do our jobs and keep everyone safe, and if you hear from your dad, you'll tell us right away. You don't need to get involved."

I looked from Griffen to Evers. I saw it in Evers' eyes. He didn't want to tell me whatever it was he knew about my father. But he would. Maybe this was his way of apologizing for what had happened. His way of trying to make it right.

Not that it mattered. We couldn't change the past.

This was my dad we were talking about. He wouldn't win father of the year, but he was mine, and I loved him. After I'd kicked Evers out, I'd probed gently, but Smokey stonewalled every time. I knew there was something wrong. He'd been different. Tense. Sometimes he went days without returning my calls. If Evers knew why, I needed him to fill me in.

"Tell me," I said simply.

Evers let out a long breath.

"We don't know the whole story yet, but my father was involved in some... shady dealings. He was working with an old family friend who recently died."

"I thought your father was dead."

With a wry, almost bitter laugh, Evers said, "So did we. It looks like that might not be the case. We've been tracing every piece of information we have, trying to find out what he was up to and where he is. We got a hold of bank records that show significant amounts of money moving from my father to his partner, and from there to Clive Winters."

I laughed. Smokey Winters involved in shady dealings? Unless those shady dealings had to do with packing a bowl or buying a bag of weed, Smokey wouldn't be interested.

I shook my head. "You must have made a mistake. I know my dad's kind of a wing-nut, but he doesn't have it in him to—"

"It's not a mistake."

"But some numbers, some bank transfers, they don't prove anything," I protested, still shaking my head.

Evers took another deep breath, looking at the coffered ceiling above for a moment before he said, "Summer, I've been watching you and your father for a while. You know that."

I gritted my teeth but said nothing. There was nothing to say.

"Your father gets around. A lot more than you think he does. We knew something was going on, even a few months ago. We didn't know what, and we had no clue it was related to my father. Now, it looks like everything's connected."

"If you didn't think it was connected, if you didn't know what he was up to, why were you watching him?" I snapped my mouth shut the second the words spilled out. I already knew the answer. I'd figured it out not long after I broke things off with Evers.

Evers said gently, "You know why."

"So, what, you needed to keep an eye on me and you figured you'd do it from my bed? What did you think I was going to do? Knock on their gates with my hand out?"

"We had to be sure. They're like family."

I didn't say anything. There was nothing to say.

It all started with the Winters family. Our last names weren't coincidence. We were related, though I wasn't exactly sure how. It didn't matter. We'd never met, and if I had anything to say about it, we never would.

The guest list lying on the coffee table would be a problem. I was usually visible at the parties I managed, but for this one, I'd stay as incognito as I could.

I'd made a promise, and I planned to keep it.

"What do you want?" I asked.

"I want you to help me find your father. And I want you to think carefully. Has anything happened lately that's unusual? Strange phone calls, things out of place in your condo? Anything."

Gears turning in my brain, I stared at Evers and asked in a whisper, "You think I'm involved?"

"No, but—"

"Evers, what's going on?"

"That's what we're trying to find out."

Chapter Seven

EVERS

I walked down the wide hall of Rycroft Castle re-familiarizing myself with the layout now that it was occupied. The cook was busy in the main kitchen preparing the evening meal.

That afternoon, while we were arguing about the party, the rest of Cynthia's staff had arrived. She was traveling light, only bringing her stylist and trainer. Angie, the stylist, had disappeared into the master suite to deal with Cynthia's wardrobe.

Cynthia herself was in the gym on the lower level with Viggo, her trainer and masseuse. I had a feeling he was more than her trainer and masseuse. None of my business.

Cynthia was going to be a handful. The second she'd curled her fingers around my leg, I knew she hoped to pick up where we'd left off all those years ago. I didn't want to bruise her ego. Cynthia was bossy and demanding, but she'd been a friend.

I had to set her straight. Before Summer, I might have

been tempted. Who am I kidding? Before Summer I might have taken her straight to bed.

Since Summer threw me out? Not even the spectacularly-beautiful Cynthia Stevens could hold my eye. There was only one woman I wanted, and she despised me.

I didn't need to walk the house. I knew the layout of Rycroft Castle better than I knew my own place. I'd been through the blueprints multiple times, had inspected every inch of the more than 16,000 square feet.

No, I was pacing the halls so I could end up in this narrow hall behind the kitchen, outside the closed door of the housekeeper's office, now Summer's domain. Her voice bled through the door, drawing me like a magnet.

If Griffen touched her, smiled at her, fucking winked at her one more time...

I ran out of steam at the thought. What was I going to do about it? Beat him up? He was only doing it to get under my skin, and we both knew it. It shouldn't have worked.

I knew he was messing with me, knew he had far too much loyalty to ever make a move on a woman I had feelings for.

I knew I could trust him. And still, if he so much as laid a finger on her again... The brush of his fingertip across her bare shoulder played on a loop in my brain.

Griffen wasn't allowed to touch her. Not when I couldn't.

I was alone in the hallway, no one to see my weakness. Slouching against the door frame, I rested my forehead against the cool, thick wood of the office door, absorbing the clear, light tones of Summer's voice.

"May, you're an angel. I owe you one. I owe you a million. I'll be by tomorrow morning if that's not too soon."

64

A pause, punctuated by light tapping as if she were bouncing a pen against her desk.

She laughed, sounding delighted and a little relieved. "That would be absolutely perfect. I can't thank you enough." Another pause, then, "Well, their bad luck is my good fortune. This is a huge weight off my shoulders. I'll see you tomorrow, no earlier than ten. Thanks again. Yep, you too."

Summer fell silent. I was reaching for the handle before I realized what I was doing. Snatching my fingers back, I moved away from the door, away from Summer, down the hall until I reached the stairs to the lower level.

I had to get my head on the job. Cynthia had a crazy husband out there, and she was famous enough that we had to worry about garden-variety fans and stalkers. Axel had given me the rundown from her L.A. detail, some of whom would be rotating in here in Atlanta, so I knew this wasn't a vanity job.

Cynthia needed tight security, and I needed to stay sharp. She'd hired Sinclair Security because we're the best. She'd asked for me because she assumed I'd take a special interest in the job.

She couldn't have known how right she was. The one person I wanted more than any other was living inside the walls of Rycroft Castle. I would do whatever I had to keep Summer safe.

No one was getting in this house. No one was getting on the property. Not while I was around to stop them.

The lower level of Rycroft Castle was as expansive as those above. I took a quick look through the wide double doors to the Roman spa, a decadent indoor pool and hot tub. Crowned by a painted domed ceiling held up by white pillars, the entire space was built entirely of white limestone, including the custom gourmet kitchen and bar. You could throw a hell of a pool party in Rycroft Castle.

I passed the workout room and yoga studio, strains of music and the clang of weights interrupting the silence of the empty hallway.

Then the wine tasting room, six hundred square feet of custom woodwork, high-tech temperature-controlled storage, and every accoutrement a wine lover could ask for.

A little further down the hall was the small interior storage room we'd repurposed into our command center. I gave a single rap on the door to alert Griffen and swung it open.

He sat in front of the L-shaped desk, lounging in his chair, feet up. From the back, he looked half-asleep, entirely relaxed. His eyes gave him away. Sharp, alert, they moved from screen to screen, resting just long enough to absorb every detail before checking the next.

Without looking up, he said, "Everything good?"

"Fine. Cook's making dinner, the two maids are straightening, Cynthia's with Viggo working out, the stylist is unpacking in Cynthia's suite, and Summer is in her office trying to make miracles happen."

At that, Griffen tore his eyes from the screens and looked up, his expression of disappointed scorn almost driving me a step back.

"What?" I asked, already knowing the answer.

Griffen shook his head in disgust. "You are one of the smoothest bastards I've ever met. I've seen you charm a woman into your bed in five minutes flat. So how did you fuck up that meeting so badly?" He laughed, shaking his head at the disaster that was my life. "Seriously, I wish I had that shit on video, otherwise no one would believe me. Fucking idiot."

"Yeah? Like you could have done better," I said, trying for scornful and hitting pathetic instead.

He was right. I had fucked up the meeting. When it came to Summer, that was par for the course. I opened my mouth, and I fucked up.

"I wouldn't have called her *Winters* for one thing. Jesus, what is she, one of the guys on your softball team?"

"I don't play softball, asshole."

Griffen just shook his head again. "And acting like you didn't know she worked here? What the fuck was that?"

I slumped against the closed door and let out a gust of air, admitting, "I don't know. I don't fucking know. She just—"

I ran out of words. How to describe what was wrong when I didn't even know myself?

I'm charming. I'm good with women. I'm really fucking good with women. I open my mouth, and the perfect words come out. I always know exactly what they need to hear, when to reassure, when to challenge. When to flirt and when to be blunt.

Then I met Summer, and all of it went out the window. First, I bossed her around, then I started calling her *Winters* when I saw how much it annoyed her.

Like an elementary school boy pulling a girl's pigtails, I did anything for a reaction. For her attention. At first, it was fun, the way her eyes sparked blue fire when she was pissed off. I hadn't planned to take it further. Not really.

She was my sister-in-law's best friend, and that had complicated written all over it. My thing was fun. I'd never been interested in complicated.

But I couldn't get her out of my head. The silky blonde curls, her round ass, her full, pink lips. That laugh. The way she glared at me when I pissed her off. Fucking hot.

And then the wedding. Her hotel room... I'd never had sex like that in my life. It wasn't fucking. It wasn't just getting off, having some fun and scratching a mutual itch. It was more.

I hadn't believed in more, hadn't particularly cared about it. That weekend with Summer woke something inside me.

A need I'd never acknowledged.

A need that hadn't existed until Summer. It was feral and hungry, and she was the only thing that could satisfy it. I saw her, and I wanted. Straight from my gut, from the marrow of my bones, I had to have her.

It was fucking terrifying. My brother Knox was right. She scared the hell out of me. I didn't need anybody. I'd had my shit on lock until she came barreling into my life.

Suddenly, there was a black hole right in the middle of my world, and only Summer could fill it.

I'd run from that hotel room determined to live without her. My head was clouded with lust. It would fade if I just stayed away. Except it didn't fade. It got worse.

I'll never forget the sheer, brutal relief when Cooper tossed me her file and said someone had to keep a closer eye on her.

I wasn't giving in to the need, I was only doing my job. I thought I'd figured it out. Keep an eye on her, talk my way into her bed, and get the girl without risking anything.

"Yeah, well, you fucked that up," Griffen said, his voice cutting through my thoughts.

For a moment, I wondered if he'd been reading my mind before I remembered he was talking about the meeting. I scrubbed my palms over my face and shook my head.

"I know, man, I know."

"You have got to talk to Cynthia. If you're not going there—"

"Of course, I'm not going there. Jesus. You think I'm going to sleep with Cynthia?"

"Hey, no one would blame you—"

"Don't be an asshole," I said. "I want Summer. I'm not sleeping with Cynthia. I'm not sleeping with anybody."

"No shit. That's why you're so cranky." He chuckled at his joke.

"You're fucking hysterical," I grumbled.

"I know, it's a curse."

I opened my mouth to insult him again when a soft knock sounded on the door. Turning, I opened it to see Summer standing there in her navy shift dress, blonde curls still caught in their professional bun, silky strands falling around her face. She shifted her weight nervously, drawing my eyes to her hips, my hand starting to reach for her before I thought better of it.

Slow. I had to take this slow.

"Do you have a minute?" Summer asked.

I wanted to say, *For you, I have eternity*. I opened my mouth and out came, "Sure, Winters, what's up?"

She was a fucking mojo vampire. She came near me and she sucked up all my game, leaving me nothing more than a stuttering adolescent.

Scrambling, I said, "Let's go down the hall to the wine room so we don't distract Griffen."

I reached out to take her arm, dying a little as she smoothly sidestepped out of reach. Fuck.

I followed her the short distance back to the wine room. She leaned against the rustic wooden table in the middle, half sitting on one of the stools made from an old wine cask, looking down at her fingers, fiddling with a ring.

So many things I wanted to say.

I'm sorry.

There's nothing going on with Cynthia.

Tell me what to do to fix this and I'll do it. Anything.

I asked, "How are the party arrangements coming along?"

"Pretty well, actually. I got lucky, and one of my favorite caterers had a last-minute cancellation. I'm stopping by tomorrow to review the menu, but I think we can transition everything to Cynthia's party."

"Lucky for both of you," I said.

The side of her mouth quirked up in a grin. "Lucky for me, lucky for May. Not so lucky for the groom who walked in on his bride servicing his best man a week before the wedding."

"Ouch."

"I know. I feel bad that I'm so relieved, but it solves a huge problem. I can finesse almost everything but the food. I'm headed out in a few minutes to pick up a special order from my favorite stationery shop. I'll be up all night addressing the invitations to have them ready for the courier to deliver first thing tomorrow. Then I just need to find musicians and arrange for flowers and decorations. Those are the easy parts. Well, easy compared to swinging catering for seventy-five in less than a week."

"Good news," I said. I wasn't lying. For Cynthia to demand a party for seventy-five with barely a week's notice and expect Summer to pull it off... I had a vague idea how much work went into something like that. A week didn't come close to being enough.

With no idea what I planned to say, I took a step closer and opened my mouth, "Summer, I—"

"I thought of some things that you might need to know,"

Summer said, her head down, eyes on the ring she twisted around her finger.

It couldn't have been clearer that she didn't want to hear my apology. I wasn't sure I blamed her. I should never have lied to her in the first place.

When she caught me, I should have done anything but stare at her in silence. She'd been so angry. The guilt, the fear of losing her, had choked me until all I could do was walk away.

That was the past. I had my second chance, and this time I wasn't walking away. I pulled up one of the wine barrel stools and sat.

"Tell me."

Chapter Eight

EVERS

S he twisted the ring in one direction, then another, before she looked up with a sheepish expression on her face. "I don't even know if this is important. I could be making something out of nothing, but you asked if anything weird had happened."

"I did. Has something weird happened?" I'd asked, but I hadn't expected an answer.

Summer shouldn't be a target. She had nothing to do with whatever her father and mine were wrapped up in. She barely saw Smokey Winters. He wasn't exactly an attentive parent.

"It's probably nothing, but a few weeks ago somebody tried to break into my building. They broke the lock on the back entrance that the super uses. Tried to get up the elevator, but the security is pretty good—"

She broke off, probably remembering all the times I'd bypassed it without any trouble. "Or maybe it's not."

"Did they get into your place?" I asked adrenaline spiking up my spine, sharp and cold.

"No, but I've been getting weird calls. Hang-ups from unknown numbers. I figured it was telemarketers or a wrong number. And there's this client—"

"You have a new client?" She couldn't have a new client. I would know. Knox would have put it in the report.

"No. I turned him down. He, uh, he creeped me out."

I abandoned the stool and moved closer. Summer shrank back. *Slow*, I reminded myself. *Take it slow.*

Holding my ground, I said, "He creeped you out? How? Did he touch you? Did he—"

"No. We only spoke over the phone. I didn't meet him in person. He claimed he wasn't local, said he traveled a lot, and one of my other clients recommended me, but when I asked more questions, his answers didn't fit."

"Do you have any information on him? Age, where he's from?"

"Some. I can send you the file. I asked some general questions. He said he was early fifties. He had an accent. He claimed he was Greek, but I had a friend in high school whose father was born in Greece, and this guy didn't sound like him at all."

"You turned him down?" She nodded. "Have you heard from him since?"

"No. I told him I was too busy, that I wasn't taking on new clients, and he said that was fine and hung up. I wouldn't even mention it, but there was something about the conversation that felt off. He asked personal questions. He mentioned my family—"

"Get me the file. I'll check into it." She had good instincts. I'd bet she was right, and that call had not been from a prospective client. Fuck.

"And you're absolutely sure you don't know where your father is. If you're protecting him, I understand, but—"

"I don't know, Evers. I don't know where he is. If I did..." Her voice faded away.

"I know he's your dad," I said softly, "I know you want to protect him. But this is over your head. He's not safe out there. And if you get involved, neither are you. If you hear from him—"

"I'll tell you. I already said I would. I have to get back to work." She straightened and moved to walk past me.

I blocked her, and she stopped abruptly, taking a step back to keep distance between us.

Every step she took from me drove the need to touch her higher. It clawed at me, demanding I close the few feet separating us. Demanding I take her back. Make her mine again. I saw myself reach out, pull her into my arms. That would be too far, and I knew it.

"We need to talk," I started.

The fire in her blue eyes flickered out, leaving them cold and hard. "No, we don't. We had a thing. It's over. Now we both have jobs to do. Let's just stay focused and we'll get through this. Our main concern is Cynthia."

"Forget Cynthia," I shot out, "I don't care—"

"I do. She's my client, and this is my job. It means something to me and I'm not going to mess it up because of you. Get out of my way. I have to get to the stationery shop before they close, or I won't get the invitations out in time."

"I'll go with you."

"No, you won't." Summer's eyes were sparking fire again. I'd take her furious over cold any day. She propped a hand on the jut of her hip. Her round breasts strained against her dress. Keeping my distance was killing me.

"It's bad enough that you're here," she said, temper spilling over. "I don't want to see you any more than I have to."

Her voice choked a little on the last words and I felt sick. That was me. I'd done that, fucked things up so badly she just wanted to get away from me.

All I wanted was to get closer.

"Look," I said, trying to sound reasonable when I felt anything but, "until we figure out what's going on with your dad, I don't want you out there by yourself. You're safe on the property, but outside the gates—"

Summer scowled up at me, gritting her teeth. "Then find someone else. Anyone but you."

"Griffen will go with you," I said grudgingly.

"Fine."

Hating the idea, but knowing Griffen would keep her safe, I stalked back to the control room so I could send my partner out to watch over my girl.

I could feel the frustration coming off me in waves. I couldn't watch over her. She wouldn't let me explain. I was backed into a corner, and the only thing on my side was time.

I'd wasted enough of it with Summer already. Too much time. Screwing around. Not being honest. Treating what we had like it was a game. Like it didn't matter.

Just as I reached the door to the control room, my phone went off in a series of high-pitched alerts.

"What's that?" Summer asked from behind me.

I swung open the door, and a cacophony of shrill beeps flooded out. Before Summer could ask again, I ushered her into the room. "Stay here. I'll be right back."

Griffen told her, "Perimeter alarm. Someone tampering with the gates."

I don't know what else he said. I was headed for the gym at a brisk jog. I walked in to find Cynthia flat on her back on a yoga mat, one leg extended into the air, her half-naked trainer leaning into it, stretching her hamstring and glutes, looking like he was about to do a lot more than that.

"We have an issue with the gate. I need Cynthia in the control room now."

Cynthia could be headstrong and a diva, but she was smart. Viggo moved and she rolled to her feet with grace, snagging a towel off the stack by the door as she hustled down the hall.

The control room doubled as a safe room. It wasn't as robust as the safe room attached to the master suite, but it would do the job. Cynthia preceded me into the room and came to an abrupt halt when she caught a glimpse of the scene on the center monitor.

Clint Perry stood at the wrought iron gates barring entry to Rycroft Castle. A bouquet of roses in one hand, he pressed the intercom button with the other, repeatedly, breaking only to shake the gates until they rattled.

I'd learned from experience that most actors, particularly leading men, looked a lot smaller in person than they did on the screen. Clint was the exception.

He was known for playing oversized, broody action stars. In person, he was even more oversized than on screen, with wide shoulders, hulking biceps, and thighs that looked like tree trunks. If he'd been drinking or using, it hadn't affected his workouts.

He was missing the brooding frown his fans knew so well. His eyes were desperate. Broken. A part of me, a part I ignored, wanted to hit the button to open the gates, to let the poor guy see the woman he loved.

Project much?

Unlike Clint, I hadn't cheated on Summer. I hadn't so much as looked at another woman since the day I picked her up at her client's party over a year before.

Some of the accusations against Clint Perry—his relapse, drug use, attempted harassment—were unproven. His infidelity was a matter of public record. Literally, considering he'd been caught screwing a starlet on a public beach. His mug shot had been a meme for a while.

"I'll go out and talk to him," I said to Griffen. "I'd rather not call the police and alert the press if I don't have to."

"Isn't he violating the restraining order?" Cynthia asked, her voice shaking. Summer stepped closer and put her arm around her employer, giving her one of Summer's trademark tight hugs.

I wasn't going to think about how much I missed those hugs. Such a simple thing until they were gone.

"He is," I affirmed. "He's not allowed to come within 300 yards of you, your vehicle, or your place of residence. I'll go talk to him, see if he can be reasoned with before we have to take this a step further."

"Be careful, Evers. If he's been drinking, he's not stable. He's not usually violent but..."

Cynthia squeezed her eyes shut and trailed off. I'd assumed she and Clint were just another Hollywood marriage. That she would divorce him and move on. I wondered if I'd underestimated her. If beneath that perfect façade, she hid a broken heart.

"You three stay here. Don't open the door until I come back."

"Got it, boss," Griffen answered, rising to follow me to the door. "Be careful out there," he said in a low voice.

"Always." He shut the door behind me, the flick of deadbolts loud in the quiet hallway.

Locking them in the control room was probably an over-reaction, but I wasn't taking any chances. Not with my client, and absolutely not with Summer.

I left my weapon in my holster as I jogged down the long driveway to the gates. I hoped I wouldn't need it, but it was good to know it was there. When he caught sight of me, Clint stepped away from the button on the intercom, coming to the center of the gates, the bouquet in his hand.

"Clint Perry," I said coldly, "are you aware that you're breaking the terms of Cynthia's restraining order?"

"I know," he said, sounding defeated and desperate, a dog who'd been kicked too many times and couldn't stop crawling back. "I just need to see her. I need to explain. She doesn't know. It was all lies, and she doesn't know. I never would have—"

"Except you did. Over and over. She doesn't want to hear it, man. She's trying to move on. She came all the way across the country for some peace and quiet, and if you really cared about her, you'd give her that."

"I just need to see her," he said again. The repetition, his desperation, made me think he was using or drunk, but his eyes were clear, his pupils normal. His voice was sad but steady.

He was a wreck. A mess. It was like looking in a mirror.

"Look, I feel for you," I said. "But that doesn't change what I have to do. Do you understand? Either you get off this property in the next two minutes or I call the police."

Clint Perry's eyes went wide, and he shook his head, backing away from the gate. "Don't do that. Look, man, we don't have to go there. Don't call the police."

"You're not leaving me much choice. The lady has a restraining order, which you are violating. She doesn't want you here. She's afraid, and every second you stay, you're making it worse. I'm counting. Two minutes, starting now."

I lifted my watch and made a show of tracking the

secondhand. Clint swore under his breath and turned on his heel, heading to the rental car parked by the street.

I didn't think he'd be much trouble. He was an ass. Desperate enough to fly across the country. Desperate enough to risk arrest. But there was something about him that told me he was an annoyance. An irritation. Not a danger.

I stood inside the gates and waited until he'd started his car and driven away. My gut might tell me he wasn't a danger, but that didn't mean I'd relax our vigilance.

Cynthia needed a break from this man, and he didn't have to hurt her physically to do damage. Just being here eroded her peace of mind. Wore her down.

Down the street, almost out of sight, brake lights flashed on. A car starting. A car that had been parked where no one ever stopped.

The narrow, winding road through Buckhead that led to the gates of Rycroft Castle did not have sidewalks. There were no homes nearby where a visitor might park on the shoulder. This wasn't that kind of neighborhood.

Clint Perry didn't ping my radar, but those brake lights made me uneasy. Clint could have brought his own security. Would he want a witness when he broke the restraining order? Why would he start using security now when he never had before?

Clint wasn't the reason for those brake lights. I jogged back up the drive, making a mental note to add cameras along the street.

Back in Rycroft, I knocked on the door to the control room, a quick pattern of three knocks, followed by two slow ones. The locks clicked open in rapid succession. Summer stood there, blue eyes searching my face, scanning down to my feet, only relaxing when she saw I was in one piece.

Saying nothing, she stepped back to let me in. Cynthia, who'd been sitting in a chair beside Griffen, stood and threw herself against me, burrowing against my chest. I wrapped my arms around her, stroking a hand down her back.

Cynthia had been flirting with me since I'd arrived, but that was her default. She was a lot like me; she flirted as easily as she breathed. It didn't mean anything.

This hug wasn't flirtation. This was fear and pain, nerves strung to the breaking point. Summer looked anywhere but at me holding Cynthia, crossing her arms over her chest and conspicuously studying the monitors, now showing nothing more than the empty grounds and gardens.

Cynthia shuddered in my arms, not crying, but so tense she was having trouble breathing. I didn't have the heart to push her away.

"Everything's okay," I reassured her. "He left. You saw on the monitors. He can't get through the gates, and he didn't seem to mean any harm. Not this time."

"Will he be back?" Cynthia asked, tremulously.

"I don't know," I said honestly. "I think it's likely, but if he does come back I doubt it'll be today. I want you to stay in the house for the rest of the day. Can you do that?" Cynthia nodded.

Looking to Summer, thinking of the brake lights, I said, "I'm taking you on your errand."

With adrenaline buzzing in my veins, I couldn't bring myself to leave Summer in anyone's hands but mine. Before Summer could object, Cynthia pressed herself harder against me, looking up with limpid eyes.

"No, absolutely not. You're staying here with me. If Summer needs security, Griffen can take her."

Griffen shot me a look and raised an eyebrow. Never mind that I'd been about to let Griffen take her twenty minutes before. Never mind that she'd be safe with him, especially considering I wasn't absolutely sure she was under threat.

Logically, I knew all that was true. Still, I said, "Cynthia, you'll be fine."

The diva made her appearance. Cynthia straightened and propped her hands on her narrow hips. "I know I will. Because you're staying here with me. You're the head of security and I'm the client. That's your job. Summer will be perfectly fine with Griffen." Looking over her shoulder at Griffen she said, "Won't she, Mr. Sawyer?"

The apologetic glance Griffen shot in my direction surprised me. I expected him to smirk at seeing me thwarted once again. He must have known how close I was to the edge.

Grudgingly, I gave in. "All right. Griffen, it's closing in on five o'clock. Take Summer to the stationery shop before it closes. There and back, no detours. Got it?"

"Got it, boss." Griffen slid his arm around Summer's shoulders as he led her from the room, sending me a sly wink. Asshole.

I shook my head as Cynthia said, "I need to shower after that workout. Come with me to my suite."

Great. The stiff set of Summer's shoulders told me she'd heard every word.

Fuck me. Cynthia didn't know, hadn't done it on purpose, but the last thing I needed was for Summer to think I was banging her boss.

Chapter Nine

EVERS

Rycroft Castle was quiet. Finally. Cynthia had too much wine at dinner, overcompensating for the stress of the afternoon, and insisted we all gather in the theater to watch a movie.

Summer was the only one who escaped, pointing out that if she didn't finish the invitations no one would show up to Cynthia's party. The rest of us piled into the theater room, popped some popcorn, and watched an absurd, repetitive chick flick Cynthia just had to see.

I understood that she didn't want to be alone. I knew she was under a lot of pressure. And if she forced me to watch another movie like that, she was going to have to find a new head of security.

Griffen stayed in the control room watching the monitors. I was supposed to be in bed, catching some sleep before my shift in the control room.

I couldn't do it. I couldn't lay down in that bed across the hall from Summer and find sleep. I tried. I stared at the ceiling. Counted sheep. Closed my eyes and remembered

Summer. Her soft skin, the smell of her hair. The way she'd fall asleep against me, her arm draped across my chest.

The way she'd trusted me and the way I'd ruined it all.

I'd never spent the whole night with her. I'd wanted to. Thought about it so many times. But when I got close, when I convinced myself just once wouldn't make a difference, I'd hear my father in my ear.

Never let them get their claws in you, kid. Just fuck and go. They all say they love you. Say they want a ring. A family. What they really want is your freedom.

My dad was an asshole when it came to women. He cheated on my mom constantly. I never understood why she put up with him. She'd once told me, after a few too many gin and tonics, there'd never been a divorce on either side of the family, and she had no intention of being the first. Lacey Sinclair was not a quitter.

Upholding tradition didn't seem worth a lifetime of misery. When we got word my father was dead, I'd swear the look in her eyes was relief.

My father liked the idea of molding the next generation of Sinclairs. He'd pat me on the back and say, *You're just like me, kid. A ladies' man, too smart to get tied down.*

I knew he was wrong. The cheating. The way he treated my mom. I didn't want to be him, no matter how much he saw himself in me.

In the hidden chambers of my heart, I was terrified he was right.

That dead look in my mother's eyes when he came home smelling of perfume. The way she went straight to the bottle to drown it out.

I couldn't do that to a woman. I wouldn't.

I focused on my job, on building Sinclair Security into more than just the premier security agency in the country.

We had ambitions, my brothers and I, and a woman, a family, didn't fit.

That's what I told myself. Despite seeing Axel fall in love, I'd been so sure it wasn't for me. I'd had no idea what I was missing, moving from one empty fuck to another. No clue how miserable I'd be once I had a taste of something real and lost it.

Was she sleeping across the hall now? Tucked under the covers, the crease of the pillow on her cheek, gold lashes fanned across her skin?

Was she wearing one of her cute tank top and boxer-short pajamas that made her look like a college student? Or one of her silky bits of lace she said she wore because she liked the feel of the fabric on her skin?

Without even thinking of it, I reached beneath the covers and palmed my half-hard cock. I'd been on the edge of an erection since I'd seen Summer earlier that afternoon. My cock and my hand hadn't spent this much time together since I hit puberty.

I won't lie. After Summer threw me out, I thought about going to another woman. Hell, I'd tried. Once. Every other female left me cold.

I squeezed my fingers hard on the length of my cock and stroked, remembering the smell of her, lemon and flowers and woman. The tight, clasping heat of her pussy. The bounce of her breasts when I fucked her. The way she kissed me when I was inside her, hungry and demanding and so fucking sweet.

With a grunt of sheer frustration, I rolled from the bed and threw myself into a cold shower, gritting my teeth as my soap-slick hand pumped my cock. Summer, her teeth biting her lip, pupils dilated with orgasm. My mouth sucking her breasts.

When I came, the pleasure was hollow, a momentary relief that did nothing to assuage the craving deep inside me. My hand was a poor substitute for Summer, barely better than nothing at all.

I stepped out of the shower and dried my hair, deciding to walk the house. Clearly, I wasn't going to sleep. I'd make sure everything was quiet—though I already knew it was, considering that my phone was jacked into the monitoring system. I could make myself a cup of herbal tea or some shit in the kitchen. Maybe see if I could hunt up a shot of whiskey.

Lit by moonlight and silent as a tomb, Rycroft Castle left me feeling as if I'd stepped back in time. The place was unbelievable. Over the top. And this is coming from a guy who's been in and out of some of the best homes in Atlanta. In the country. I practically grew up rattling around Winters House.

Rycroft Castle was something else. As I'd expected, the place was sealed up tight. Quiet outside. Quite inside. I didn't stop in the control room, knowing Griffen would give me crap for being awake.

Done with my rounds, I made my way to the kitchen, hoping I'd find a box of herbal tea. I thought wistfully of a few fingers of whiskey. The bar was stocked with the best, but I had a shift in the control room in less than six hours, and I didn't want alcohol in my system. Bad enough that I was short on sleep.

I pushed through the swinging door to the kitchen and stopped at the unexpected gasp of surprise. Summer, wrapped in a white terrycloth robe, her blonde curls in a messy knot on the top of her head, a tea kettle in one hand and a box of tea in the other.

"Exactly what I was thinking," I said. At her look of

confusion, I tilted my head at the teapot. "I couldn't sleep. I thought I'd make a cup of tea."

"You drink tea?" Summer asked, looking from the box of herbal blend to me and back again.

"Not usually," I admitted. "I figured it couldn't hurt."

"Do you want me to make you a mug?" Summer asked, her voice quiet. Hesitant.

"If you don't mind, I'd appreciate it." So polite. I fucking hated the distance, but it was better than me being a jackass and her hating me even more.

"How are the invitations going?" I asked, floundering for something to say.

Summer set the kettle on the gas burner, dropped a teabag in each of the mugs she'd pulled from the cabinet, and turned around to face me. Leaning against the counter, she looked down at her fingers, the tips stained dark with splotches of ink.

She stretched her hands, using the heel of her palm to press her fingers back on one hand then switching and doing the same to the other.

"They're done. It took forever, but they're done."

"All of them? Seventy-five invitations?"

"Yep. At least we kept it short. Just Cynthia Stevens cordially invites you, etc., with the date and time, RSVP to my phone number."

"Your hands are sore?"

I watched her rubbing her fingers. She'd been in her office for hours working on those invitations.

She shrugged a shoulder. "Calligraphy always makes my fingers sore. That much of it..."

I crossed the room, holding up a hand when she started to back away.

"Don't. I know you're angry. I know you hate me. But let me help."

Summer didn't move. Her weight balanced on the balls of her feet, she reminded me of a doe startled in the woods. The slightest wrong move and she'd bound away.

I reached out and took her fingers in mine, keeping my distance but pulling her hand closer. I pressed my thumbs into the meat of her palm, massaging the tight muscles. Her knuckles were red and swollen.

"Your fingers must be killing you," I said.

"Yeah," she breathed.

Sidling closer, I changed my grip on her hand, working my thumbs into her palm, massaging her strained muscles, chasing away the pain one sore finger at a time.

I glanced up once to see her slumped against the counter, head dropped, eyes closed, teeth sunk into her lower lip. It took everything I had not to pull her into my arms.

My kneading fingers moved from her hand to her wrist, then her forearm where her muscles had tightened into hard knots. Seventy-five invitations, all in calligraphy. Normally I liked Cynthia, but this party was bullshit. She worked Summer too hard. Expected too much.

"Feel better?" I asked.

"Mmm-hmm," Summer answered, her voice fuzzy with exhaustion. I recognized that tone. She was only minutes away from passing out.

"Turn around," I said softly.

She didn't answer but pulled her hand from mine and turned, giving me her back. Brushing stray tendrils of hair off her shoulders, I closed a hand around the base of her neck and squeezed. She let out a low groan.

"Your muscles are like rocks. Your shoulders are so tight."

"Bending over my desk for hours," she murmured. I worked my thumbs into her traps, loosening the tension, relaxing her, doing everything I could to drag out the moment. To keep touching her.

She sighed, sagging with fatigue as her strained muscles eased. I wanted to tell her to go to bed, to get some sleep, but I didn't want to leave. I worked my thumbs around her shoulder blades, and she let out a moan of pleasure that had my cock rock hard in an instant.

Leaning into her, I dropped my head, my lips grazing her hair, breathing in the lemon and flowers scent of her.

"Summer," I whispered, "Summer. I—"

Chapter Ten

EVERS

She turned her head—maybe to move away, maybe to say something—and my mouth grazed the warm skin at her temple. She went stiff for a heartbeat before she shifted to face me, lifting her face to mine, her eyes shadowed and impossible to read.

Following instinct, I dropped my mouth to hers in a soft, gentle kiss, giving her all the time in the world to move away.

"Summer," I breathed against her mouth, my lips brushing hers with a tenderness I'd never known until her. "I missed you so much."

Cupping her cheek in my hand, I deepened the kiss. She tasted the same. Better. Everything I remembered and more. I dropped my arm around her back, pulling her flush against me, the need inside me breaking through, pushing me to kiss her harder, to take more. To take everything.

The shrill of an alarm sliced through the heavy quiet in the kitchen. Summer stiffened, jumping back, her arms swinging wide in surprise and panic, knocking over the mugs and almost hitting the boiling kettle behind her.

I tugged her clear of the stove, letting go when she jerked from my grip and wrapped her arms across her chest. I pulled my phone from my pocket and checked the screen.

The perimeter alarm again. This time in the back of the property. A gate in the wall adjoining the neighboring lot. I pulled up Griffen's contact and called. Faster than running down the stairs.

"Where are you?" he demanded.

"Kitchen. I've got it."

"You sure?" he asked.

"I'm right by the door."

"Be careful. The camera can't get a solid view, but it's not Perry."

"Got it." I slid the phone in my pocket and looked up to see Summer watching me, her eyes wide with nerves and a hint of fear.

"Is it Clint again?"

"Someone's trying to get in the back gate. Tampering with the lock. We don't have a good angle on the camera, which means they know it's there. Griffen said it doesn't look like Clint."

"If it isn't Clint, who is it?"

"That's what I'm going to find out," I said, reaching behind me out of habit to check that my gun was in my holster. I pulled a small earpiece from my pocket and slipped it in my ear. Griffen popped online with, "Got me, boss?"

"Got you," I murmured back.

"Shouldn't you call the police? If someone's trying to break in?"

I resisted the urge to laugh. She was tense. Brittle. Break-ins and angry spouses weren't Summer's life.

"This is my job, Summer. I can handle it. Go to your room. There's nothing to worry about."

"I'll wait here. Go. I know you need to go. I'll be right here. Come tell me what happened so I know you're okay."

"I'll be right back. I promise."

I left Summer in the kitchen and raced to the side door of the house, headed straight for the wall surrounding the property. I was through the access door by the garage in less than a minute, sprinting down the length of the tall limestone wall as silently as possible.

In my ear, Griffen said, "Must have spooked him. He's taking off. Headed north along the wall."

A shadow moved ahead of me. A tree swaying in the breeze, a cloud passing in front of the moon, or my intruder. I put on an extra burst of speed.

"He's off the cameras. Last I saw he was still moving north along the wall but about twenty feet west, just out of range. He did recon."

Fuck. This was not looking like Clint Perry. Clint did not do recon. Clint Perry showed up at the gates with a sad bouquet of flowers looking like a kicked puppy. This was something else. Fucking fuck.

To my left, I caught movement in the dark. Definitely not Clint Perry. Shorter and leaner. And fast. Fucking fast. The figure took off, weaving through the trees, slipping in and out of the dappled moonlight, feet crunching branches.

I got close enough to see a flash of dark jeans. A black hoodie, a face white as a ghost. A mask. I was closing in, hand outstretched, thinking *almost, almost* when I was jerked off my feet, the rasp of rough fiber against my throat.

Experience and training served me well. I had my hand beneath the rope just before it drew tight, my feet leaving the ground as I was hauled up, too busy trying not to suffocate to track my assailants.

I managed to get my weapon back in its holster and my other hand beneath the rope, stretching the noose until I could breathe. Amazing what a little oxygen can do for your outlook on life. Sucking in deep breaths, I pulled at the noose, shoulders straining, body swinging wildly. I tried to ignore the bite of the noose into the back of my neck, wincing as the rough fibers dragged at my skin, scraping my chin, my nose, until my head popped free, and I was dangling six feet above the ground.

Compared to almost dying by hanging, the drop wasn't a big deal. I'd lost my earpiece. A quick look told me that I was out of range of the cameras and my target was gone. I was alone, the woods around me silent but for the chirp of crickets and the faint rustle of leaves on the night breeze. Reaching up, I rubbed the raw skin on my neck where the noose had pulled tight. My fingers came away sticky with blood.

I stood there for a second, getting my bearings, making absolutely sure I was alone. There'd been two of them. One smart enough to stay off-camera. They must have planned to use the rope to go over the wall if they couldn't get through the door. When that plan hadn't worked, they'd been prepared to kill me.

I moved back in range of the cameras, giving a wave to let Griffen know I was all right. My trip back to the house was slower than my departure. I covered the distance in silence, using the shadows of the trees to hide, searching for any sign of the intruders. Nothing.

At the door to the garage, I called Griffen. "Lost my earpiece. Meet me in the kitchen."

"What happened?" Griffen asked, tension pulling the words tight.

"There were two of them. I was almost on the one at the gate when the second one got me. Tried to string me up. By the time I got free they were gone."

All Griffen said was, "Fuck."

My thoughts exactly. Summer was in the kitchen, exactly as I'd left her except for the steaming mugs of tea on the counter. When she spotted the smear of red on my fingers she sucked in a breath.

"What happened? You're hurt! Who the hell was out there?" Her voice rose in panic. The last thing I needed was for Cynthia to find out we'd had an intruder. I wanted to keep the client calm, not scare the hell out of her.

In a low voice, I said, "I'm fine. Don't wake Cynthia. She sees this, she'll panic."

"Did Clint hit you?"

Griffen pushed open the swinging door, took one look at me and said to Summer, "Would you get a wet towel?" To me, he said, "The back of your neck is a mess. Lean over so I can take a look."

I did, bracing my elbows on the kitchen island, dropping my head so Griffen could assess the damage. His fingers probing the raw, torn skin weren't gentle. I swore under my breath.

"It's a nasty scrape. Bloody, but you'll survive." I started to stand, and he said, "Stay there. I'll be right back with the first-aid kit."

"I don't need first aid," I grumbled.

I'd dump my head under some water to clean up the

mess and I'd be fine. Summer wet a handful of paper towels in the sink and approached.

"Shut up and lean your head down so I can see."

I didn't know if I should be happy or terrified. Summer was going to put her hands on me. That put a checkmark in the happy column. On the other hand, I was bleeding, and she probably wanted revenge. I'd take whatever she dished out.

"Lean down more," she ordered, "you're too tall."

I did, and she dabbed at the raw skin on the back of my neck, cleaning away the sticky blood that had already started drying in my hair. Griffen came back and rummaged through the first-aid kit.

He handed a bottle to Summer. "Here, pour some of this on it."

Summer uncapped the brown plastic bottle and poured what I soon learned was peroxide over the back of my neck. Leaning over, her full breasts pressing against my arm, she blew gently on the torn skin. I'd get strung up on a tree limb any day for this kind of treatment.

"I don't understand why Clint would hit Evers," she said. "He hasn't been himself lately, but he's never hurt anyone. I know he plays a tough guy in the movies, but before he started drinking so much, he was a really sweet guy."

Before I could think better of it I said, "It wasn't Clint Perry."

Summer pulled back. At the loss of her heat, I almost let out a moan.

"I don't understand. If it wasn't Clint, then who was it?"

Griffen cleared his throat. Summer didn't take long to catch on. "You think this is about my dad. Or your dad."

"It's one explanation," I said, starting to stand.

She shot out a hand and pushed me back down. "Let me put some antibiotic on that."

If Summer was going to touch me again, I wouldn't argue. I stayed where I was as she smoothed antibiotic goop across the back of my neck with gentle fingers.

"It's not bleeding anymore." She unwrapped an oversize bandage from the first aid kit and pressed it over the worst of the scrape, asking, almost idly, "What did this?"

"Rope," I answered shortly.

Her hands fell away. "Rope? What do you mean? How could a rope have done this?"

"It was a noose," I clarified. I didn't want to tell her, didn't want to see horror spread across her face. "I'm fine."

"But you—" Her eyes fixed on my neck, her face pale. "They could have—"

"I'm fine," I said again. I wanted to wrap her in my arms, to show her how fine I was. Not the time. I settled for taking her hand and giving it a strong squeeze. "It takes a lot more than two guys and a rope to take me out."

"Not if they get lucky," she muttered darkly.

"They didn't."

Summer's eyes, heavy with concern, studied my face before she looked to Griffen then back at me. "You really think this has something to do with whatever our fathers are involved in, don't you?"

"We're still untangling the mess," I said. "We don't have the full picture yet, but what we do know..." I shook my head, thinking of the swamp of shit we'd uncovered. "We don't know who they were working with yet. I'm not sure I'm ready to find out."

Summer let out a long sigh, her shoulders slumping in exhaustion.

"My dad, he's just not that kind of guy, you know? He's

unreliable and lazy. I can't see him being competent enough to get involved with anyone who's actually dangerous."

"I know," I said. "I know that's what you think. But the people we think our parents are? That's an illusion. It's what they want to show us. What we want to see. Sometimes there's a lot more beneath the surface. And sometimes it's all bad."

Chapter Eleven

SUMMER

I t may sound weird, but my office is one of my favorite things about Rycroft Castle. Weird because in all of the over the top glamour of Rycroft, my office was fairly spartan.

Tucked behind the kitchen and laundry room, it was barely bigger than one of the generous walk-in closets upstairs, but it was bright, cheerful, and all mine.

I suppose it had been designed as the housekeeper's office. Much like the rest of Rycroft, the owner had spared no expense outfitting it. White beadboard stretched floor-to-ceiling framing a built-in desk, bookshelves, and drawers. An enormous bulletin board, also painted white, covered most of the wall behind the desk.

At the far end was a narrow window that looked out into the gardens behind Rycroft Castle. I'd only been at Rycroft a few days, but already the office felt like home. Probably because I'd spent hours there the night before writing up invitation after invitation. I can't describe my sense of relief at seeing the courier depart with his box of crisp white envelopes to deliver. One great big item checked off my to-do list.

I'd spent an hour with May going over the menu for the party. It wasn't hard to transform the sit-down dinner May had originally planned into a light buffet and heavy appetizers. The waiters hired to handle the wedding were more than happy to take over our job as was the equipment rental company.

I scanned my list, ticking off items, deciding what I would deal with later and came to a halt at one I'd been avoiding.

—*Call Mom*

I love my mom. She's amazing. Fantastic. When I grow up, I want to be just like her. Minus the protests and arrest record. I'm not chaining myself to any redwoods.

She's strong. Self-assured. As far as I can see, the only mistake she ever made was sticking with my dad as long as she did, but no one's perfect. Normally, I'd love to grab the phone and spend a half an hour catching up.

The problem is, Paisley Winters knows me inside and out. She can read me like a book, one she'd written herself. It was eerie.

I'd long ago given up trying to pull anything over on her. On top of that, I'm a terrible liar. Not that I had anything to lie about, exactly. This job had me turned upside down and inside out.

Being in the same house as Evers was wearing on my nerves, even if the house was the size of a castle. My mom would hear it in my voice. I didn't want to talk about Evers. There wasn't anything to say. We had a thing that wasn't a thing, and I'd ended it. Simple. Almost nothing.

That *nothing* was a raw wound. Every time I saw him it opened a little more. I tried not to think of the night before.

His hands working the stiffness from my fingers. His lips on mine.

I've missed you so much

He was playing me again. Why?

I couldn't think about it. Evers was one more problem than I had time for.

I stared at my phone. Mom always said do the hardest job first. Then it's over with, and everything else is downhill. It was good advice. Advice I tried to follow, usually. With a sigh, I unlocked the screen and hit her contact in my speed dial.

"Baby, I was wondering when you were going to call. How's the new job? How's Cynthia? I can't believe you're staying in a castle. You have to send me pictures," my mom said in a rush of enthusiastic affection.

Just the sound of her voice soothed. She was a fountain of energy, always excited, always full throttle. An endless source of love. My heart squeezed. For just a second, I wished desperately that she were here.

Taking a breath, I tried to force my mind into a happy place, to block out all my uncertainty, all my nerves, so she wouldn't hear them in my voice.

"Mom, you know I can't send you pictures. But Cynthia is great, and Rycroft is unbelievable. You should see the downstairs. It's an actual Roman spa, all white stone with a big blue pool and a mural of the night sky on the ceiling. It's crazy. There are five kitchens."

"Five kitchens? What does anyone need with five kitchens? Who wants to cook that much?"

"Mom, if you live in a castle I'm pretty sure you don't do your own cooking."

"Good point," she said with a giggle. "But it's good?"

"Other than Cynthia deciding at the last minute to

throw a party for seventy-five next week, everything's great," I lied.

My mom let out a gasp. She knew just enough about my job to understand the insanity of a last-minute party for seventy-five.

"You're kidding. Is she nuts? What are you going to do? I don't suppose Cynthia Stevens wants a backyard barbecue."

I laughed. I couldn't help it. The thought of Cynthia at a barbecue just didn't gel. "No, no. She invited the most upper of the upper crust of Atlanta. I don't think they do barbecues. I got lucky, and a wedding canceled for the day after Cynthia's party, so I was able to scoop up the caterer and some of the vendors. Stayed up half the night addressing invitations, but the worst of it's over now."

"Is that why you sound so tired?" she asked, shrewdly.

"Probably," I said, hoping she would buy that explanation.

"How's your dad?"

"Dad?" My parents had divorced amicably, my father too relaxed—meaning perpetually stoned—to get too excited about anything. My mother wasn't angry with him, just fed up. They'd been friendly in the years since the split, but I couldn't remember the last time my mom had asked after him.

"When I talked to him he said he was headed to see you."

A chill crept over my skin. I hadn't seen my father in months. "When was that, Mom?"

"Oh, I'm not sure. A month ago? Maybe a little more? He called to—" she cut off, but she didn't have to. I knew what she was going to say. I had to give my mom credit. She had plenty to complain about with my dad, but she always tried to show me his best side.

"He called to borrow money," I finished for her.

"No, that was the weird part. He didn't ask for money, just wanted to know how I was doing, how you were doing, and said he was going to head your way and spend some time with you. I didn't say anything because I wasn't sure he'd follow through, and I didn't want to get your hopes up."

"I haven't seen him, Mom. We talked a few weeks ago, but he didn't say anything about coming to see me."

"Well, you know your father," my mom sighed. A familiar sound when she was discussing her ex-husband. "That's partly why I didn't tell you. It seemed a little unlikely he was headed your way, considering he was all the way up in Maine."

"Maine? What was Dad doing in Maine?"

"I don't know, he didn't tell me. I wouldn't have known he was there, but I recognized the area code when he called. Bobbi Jenkins, you know my friend in the Audubon Society? She lives in Bangor. Same area code, so I saw the 207 on the call and thought it was her."

"Well, he's probably off on some adventure somewhere. I'm sure he'll turn up eventually," I said.

I wasn't going to tell my mom what Evers claimed was going on with my dad. For one, I wasn't sure I believed him. Not that I thought Evers was lying, exactly. It just seemed so unlikely.

He didn't know my dad. I did. Smokey had barely stirred himself enough to come to my college graduation. The thought of him being neck deep in some complex criminal enterprise? No. No way. I didn't want to worry my mom, but I did want her to be careful. At least until we knew what was going on.

"Mom, if you hear from him, if he shows up, would you

let me know? I need to talk to him about something. It's no big deal, but he's not answering his phone so—"

"Of course, sweetheart. I doubt he'll call. I don't hear from him that often. But if he gets in touch, I'll tell him you're looking for him."

"No. No, don't tell him I'm looking for him. He'll think I'm going to lecture or something. See if you can find out where he is and what he's up to, then let me know."

"Gotcha," Mom said. I knew I could trust her to do exactly as I asked. Mom was dependable. Always. I kept her on the phone a few more minutes, soaking in the sound of her voice.

When she was done telling me about her latest trip somewhere out west to protest something to do with national monuments, I realized how long we'd been on the phone.

A wave of homesickness swamped me as I ended the call. I wanted my mom. I wanted her chewy quinoa cookies that tasted like dirt and her patchouli incense. Funny the things you miss after you leave home.

All the stuff that drove me nuts when I was a teenager took on a nostalgic cast. I would have eaten a plate of those cookies just to spend the day with my mom. Maybe, when this job was over, I could carve out a week and go visit her.

Pushing my seat back, I prepared to hunt down Evers and pass on the info that Smokey had been in Maine about a month ago. I'd been avoiding him all day. I should at least have asked him how he was.

I couldn't forget the jolt of fear when I'd seen the blood on his fingers and realized he was hurt. The twist in my stomach at the bruises on his neck, the skin torn from the noose. Someone had tried to kill him. If they'd been lucky, they might have succeeded.

Maybe I should have let him explain yesterday in the wine room. Maybe I shouldn't have cut him off and walked away. But why? What would be the point? Every time I thought of the night I'd thrown him out, anger filled my heart, bitter and hot.

The anger was a smokescreen, and I knew it.

He'd lied. That wasn't okay. But he'd never made me any promises. He never said I was his girlfriend. Never said he cared about me. Never said that what we had was more than convenient, casual sex.

I was the one who read more into it. I was the one who made it complicated. As much as I wanted to blame Evers for my heartbreak, I was responsible.

I was angry at him, but more than that, I was furious with myself. I knew he was out of my league the first time he called me *Winters* with that irresistibly sexy smirk.

A man like Evers would never fall for a girl like me. He was wealthy. Gorgeous. He'd grown up in high society and had a job like an action hero. I'm a normal suburban girl who's just pretty enough, just smart enough, to get by. I like my job and I make good money, but when you get down to it, I'm a glorified assistant.

Not a good match for James Bond. I knew the clock was ticking the whole time we were together. Eventually, he'd get bored and wander away. Finding out that he stuck around to keep an eye on me for his friends was too humiliating to bear.

He'd been a jerk, and I'd wanted more than I could have. Simple as that. I needed to get over it.

I finally tracked him down by the pool. If we were over, if he didn't matter, then why did the sight of Cynthia in his arms make me want to vomit?

They didn't hear me when I came in. One of the doors

was already open, and whatever they were talking about, they were engrossed in each other. Cynthia must have been swimming because her tanned skin gleamed, rivulets of water still streaming down her legs, in between her breasts, across her flat stomach.

I knew how hard she worked for that body and didn't want to do any of it myself, but I couldn't help my envy. Cynthia was older than me, even a few years older than Evers, but it didn't show. Every inch of her was sleek and toned except for the full breasts straining the minuscule fabric of her white bikini.

Only a woman with a spectacular body could pull off a bathing suit like that. Cynthia didn't just pull it off. Through the envy in my heart, I had to admit she looked spectacular. Her platinum hair was piled on top of her head to keep it out of the water, and her makeup was perfect.

She was photo shoot ready, leaning into Evers, one hand on his shoulder, the other on his chest. As she murmured in his ear the bitter flavor of jealousy coated my tongue.

I cleared my throat and said as neutrally as I could, "Excuse me."

Cynthia turned to look at me with a smile, but Evers started and stepped back. He would have extricated himself from Cynthia's embrace if she hadn't tightened her fingers on his shirt, keeping him in place.

My brain blanked out. Her red nails against his white shirt, the perfection of Cynthia and all the gorgeous that was Evers—they were a supernova of beauty, incinerating everything in their path, including me.

I stood there, staring, and all I could think was that they looked like some glamorous, perfect version of Barbie and Ken. Cynthia was the kind of woman who could claim a man like Evers. Not me. Never me.

Cynthia raised an eyebrow. "Summer? Did you want something?"

I cleared my throat, realizing that I was standing there with my mouth open, staring at both of them like an idiot.

What did I want? Why was I here?

I'd walked in, seen them together, and every cell in my brain had shorted out. Clearing my throat again, I said with a stutter, "I, uh, um, wanted to give you an update on the party."

I'd rather hide in my office until I forgot the burn of seeing Evers with Cynthia, but I did have to update her on the party, and I might as well do it while I was standing there like a fool.

Evers stepped back, gently removing Cynthia's hands from his shirt. He looked at me for a long moment before he said, "I'd better get back to work," and strode from the room.

I watched him go, noting that the abrasions on his neck were perfectly camouflaged by the collar of his shirt. I wanted to follow him, ask how he felt, if it hurt, if he was okay.

Cynthia also watched him go, her eyes on his ass. When he cleared the door, she let out a low whistle of appreciation, then shrugged one perfect shoulder and lay down on the padded lounge chair beside her.

I cleared my throat again. "Bad timing. I'm sorry."

Cynthia waved a hand in the air "It's fine. I'll get to him later. Now, update?"

Back on familiar ground, I ran down the list of things I'd done to get the party organized. Cynthia smiled in appreciation when I finished.

"Summer, you are a miracle worker. I knew you could make it happen. And music? What are we doing about music? I don't think I want a full band, but I don't want a stuffy string quartet or something like that."

"I figured that, and I found a small group, no vocalist, that does popular covers. Mostly oldies. Some new stuff. All of it upbeat and lively."

"That sounds perfect."

She lay her head back against the lounge chair and closed her eyes, for a moment looking like she was about to take a nap. Faint shadows lurked beneath her eyes, showing through her almost flawless makeup.

"I'll get back to work—"

"You and Evers know each other, don't you?" Cynthia interrupted, her eyes popping open, her clear, green gaze focused on me. Before I could answer, she said, "Oh, that's right, your friend is married to his brother."

Glad for the simple explanation, I agreed. "Yes. We met a few years ago."

"And that's it? You're just friends because his brother married your BFF? You never..."

"We're just friends," I said, hoping Cynthia would buy it. I wasn't a very good liar, and I couldn't think of any way to explain my relationship with Evers that wouldn't open a door into a conversation I didn't want to have. Not with my employer. Not with anyone.

Cynthia tapped one red nail against her raised knee and turned her eyes to the door through which Evers had so recently disappeared. "You don't mind if I make a run at him?"

Her eyes flashed back to me, reading every nuance of my expression as I struggled to hide my feelings. Pasting a bland smile on my face, I shrugged a shoulder and said, "Sure. He's a big boy."

"That he is," Cynthia agreed. "We had a thing, a long

time ago. Nothing serious, but I wouldn't mind doing it again. For old times' sake. He might be just what I need."

The thread of sadness in her last words pulled at me. I found myself asking, "Are you okay about Clint? That he's here?"

Shutters came down over Cynthia's bright eyes and she studied her nails, buffing a nonexistent smudge. "I wish he'd just give up already. He keeps emailing me. Leaving messages. He says the relapse was a lie. That the press made it up."

"And the girl?" I asked, softly.

"He swears that was a lie, too. She was looking for publicity and set the whole thing up."

"Do you believe him?"

"I don't know," Cynthia said, her voice small and sad.

Suddenly angry at Clint, I reminded her, "Calling you is breaking the terms of the restraining order. If you turn your phone records over to the police and report him—"

Cynthia's eyes flashed up to me and the sadness in them made me want to give her a hug. I held back, sensing she didn't want that kind of sympathy right now.

"I don't want to call the police on him, Summer. I want my husband back, but the man I married is gone. The man I married didn't have a drinking problem. He didn't do drugs. He didn't sleep with half of L.A. to hurt me. Now I just want it to be over."

"Hopefully, soon it will be. Then you can move on," I said, torn between wanting Cynthia to be happy and feeling sick at the idea of her finding that happiness with Evers.

As if conjured by my thoughts, Evers strode through the open door, his eyes on alert, face blank. I recognized that look. Something had happened.

"Cynthia, I need to borrow Summer. Griffen is in

charge of the staff. He's got everything under control, and you'll be fine until we get back."

"What happened?" I asked. It couldn't have anything to do with Cynthia or he wouldn't need me. Which could only mean it was...

"There's been a break-in at your father's place."

My stomach sank. A break-in at my father's place could be a coincidence. Or it could be further evidence that Evers was right, and my dad really was in trouble.

"Evers, can't someone else handle it? If it's a break-in, can't you just call the police?" Cynthia asked, her eyes studying both of us.

"No, we can't," Evers said without further explanation. "Cynthia, I mentioned this might happen. We'll be back later. Until then, Griffen has everything under control." Looking at me, he raised an eyebrow. "Summer? Let's go."

Chapter Twelve

SUMMER

Questions flooded my mind. I wanted to badger Evers with them, to find out everything he knew about my father. At the same time, I didn't want to talk to him, which made questioning difficult.

I followed him to his car in silence, clutching my phone in my hand, and decided to take the easy way out. We'd have a long drive to my dad's place.

Mumbling under my breath, "I have to make a few calls," I pulled out my phone and hit the number of the florist. We were reviewing the list of flower arrangements when Evers left I-85 for the road to Augusta.

Where was he going? We'd need to stay on I-85 to get to North Carolina and the small mountain town where my Dad had been living for the past few years. I ended the call with the florist, made a few quick notes on my phone, and set it in my lap.

"Where are we going? This isn't the way to my dad's."

"Not your dad's place in Asheville. Your dad's place in Atlanta."

"My dad doesn't have a place in Atlanta," I said, confused.

My dad didn't have enough money to have a second home. The look Evers gave me was gentle, with just a touch of pity.

"He bought it a few years ago."

"But why—" I cut myself off and fell silent. So many why's.

Why would my father get involved in criminal activities with Evers' dad?

Why would my father have a second home and not tell me about it?

Why would my father do half of the shit he did?

I'd never had an answer for the last question, and I don't know why I thought I'd find one for the first two. My father had always lived in his own orbit, his own needs his main concern.

"So, where is this place of my dad's? And how did you know it's been broken into if no one's called the police?"

"It's a little bit outside Stone Mountain, and we had it wired. Just in case. Your dad hasn't been back in a while."

Evers' comment tugged my memory. Something about my dad I couldn't remember. Something about him being out of town. I shook my head. It would come to me eventually. Between juggling the details for this party and dealing with Evers, my nerves were fried. My brain wasn't much better.

If we could just get through the party on Friday, I could relax. A little. There was still my missing dad, Evers, and Clint Perry to worry about. Relaxation seemed very far away.

Evers must have known where he was going. He navigated through the suburban streets and country roads easily, finally pulling to a stop in front of a brick ranch house that looked like it hadn't been touched since the fifties.

Weeds grew high in the yard. The bushes beside the front door were overgrown. A crack in one of the front windows spread like a spider web. The curtains were pulled, blocking the view inside.

I followed Evers to the front door. I barely had time to wonder how we were getting in when he pulled out a key and unlocked the door.

"How do you have a key to my dad's house?"

Evers didn't answer, just slanted me a look. "The place is empty. We already checked for evidence, lifted a few prints, but we don't have much. The two who broke in wore masks and gloves. Almost nothing to go on."

"Then why am I here?" I asked, looking around the disaster of my dad's small house with dismay and more than a little embarrassment.

"Take a look around, and see if anything is out of place or doesn't belong. If there's something missing that should be here."

A hysterical giggle erupted from my chest.

See if anything was out of place? *Everything* was out of place.

Couch cushions tumbled on the floor. Drawers upended, their contents scattered all over. Beneath the mess of the break-in, it was clear that my father hadn't cleaned his house... ever.

A glass bong sat on the coffee table, lighter beside it, the bowl still half-packed with pot. A half-empty baggie was carelessly covered with a magazine. Whoever had broken into the place, they weren't interested in drugs.

"Evers, I wouldn't know where to start. I've never been here before."

"It looks like he left in a hurry." Evers poked his head in the bedroom, took a quick pass at the bathroom and commented, "All his stuff is still here."

I followed him into the bedroom and saw what Evers meant. A stick of deodorant, toothbrush, and toothpaste sat on the bathroom counter. A used towel hung on the rack. His shoes sat by the side of the bed as if he'd toed them off before laying down.

It looked as if he'd gotten up and walked out the door fully intending to come back. Instead, he'd disappeared. Had something spooked him? Had he left alone?

I couldn't begin to guess. I opened a drawer in his dresser to find a pile of unmatched, yellowed socks mixed with worn boxers. He hadn't bothered to hide the small baggie of pills or the folded wad of cash. I didn't touch either, just let out a long sigh and said, "Evers?"

Evers came up behind me, studying the contents of the drawer. My cheeks flushed with shame. This was my dad. Drugs, cash, and secrets, barely hidden in a careless mess.

"He wouldn't have left that behind," Evers commented.

"Probably not," I agreed. Not the cash or the drugs. Definitely not both.

I stood in front of his dresser, staring at the pile of loose change on top, thinking. Something wasn't right. I picked up a key ring I didn't recognize. A sinking feeling hit my stomach when I saw what was beneath.

"Dad's ring," I whispered. Evers picked up the gold ring and turned it in his fingers.

"I've seen this ring before."

"What do you mean you've seen this ring before? It's my

dad's ring. He's worn it for as long as I can remember. He never goes anywhere without it."

"It's not your father's ring," Evers said quietly. "It's your grandfather's."

"My grandfather's? How do you know that?"

Evers held out the ring, turning the monogram in the light so I could see it clearly.

MWC

"Marshall Carlisle Winters. Clive's father. Your grandfather. Marshall Winters was Daniel and Amelia's Winters' brother. The black sheep of the family. He left home when he was young and never went back."

I stared at Evers in disbelief. I didn't know who Daniel and Amelia Winters were. I knew I was related to the Winters family of Atlanta in some way, even knew the names of the current generation. More than that? I was in the dark. My blank stare must have told Evers that I was lost.

"You really don't know? You don't know any of this?"

"No. I never knew my grandfather. My dad never talked about him. He never talked about any family. Always said we were on our own."

Evers turned the ring over, studying it. "Your grandfather, Marshall Winters, was the oldest child in his generation. The story is he went to Korea in nineteen fifty with the Army, came home with a Korean bride, and his father went nuts. Kicked him out. From what I get, Marshall, Daniel, and Amelia's parents were old-school. Intolerant and inflexible. Marsh took off with the wife and disappeared.

"Amelia and Daniel looked but couldn't find them. He showed back up in nineteen sixty-three with no wife. Stayed less than a month—he was drinking, there were drugs, a big family fight, and Marsh disappeared again. We traced him to San Francisco. He became kind of a counter-culture hippie hero for a while. Married another hippie, and they had your dad in sixty-five as far as we can tell."

"I knew he lived in San Francisco when he was young. He said his father died when he was a teenager. I don't know what happened to his mother," I said absently, my mind reeling.

"Your dad never made any attempt to contact Hugh and James. Or Amelia. You moved all the way to Marietta, right in their backyard, but you didn't contact them either. We waited. Assumed you would, but you stayed away. Why?"

"My father made me promise not to," I said quietly, trying to make sense of what Evers was telling me. Did that make the youngest generation of Winters my second cousins? I'd have to look it up. Either way, we were related far more closely than I'd guessed.

"What do you mean your father made you promise not to?" Evers asked, sliding the ring into his pocket. I thought to object. If anything, the ring was mine, not his. But more than ever, I wanted to find my dad, and Evers was my best bet.

"I don't know. When he found out I moved here he was furious, told me not to get any ideas, that they weren't our family, that if I tried to talk to them, they'd just throw me out. He made me promise, made me swear I'd stay away. He got so worked up over it I agreed. Honestly, I didn't realize quite who they were until I got here. I mean, I'd heard of them—everyone's heard of them—but in Atlanta, the Winters are like royalty.

"My idea about touching base, giving them a call, seemed stupid. They must have family coming out of the woodwork looking for a handout. I didn't want them to think I was looking for something. I figured my father was probably right, and I'd made a promise, so I stayed away."

"They could have helped your career," Evers commented.

My spine went poker-straight. "I've done fine without them."

"You have. More than fine," Evers said, and a swell of pride filled me. "But I don't get why your father made you swear not to see them. It doesn't make sense."

"I always figured he held a grudge. Or something happened he didn't want to tell me about. Maybe he tried to see them, and they threw him out?"

"Not as far as I know. James and Hugh are gone, but my Dad didn't have any notes in the file about Clive making contact."

"How long have you been watching us?" I asked, thrown by the idea that Evers' father had a file that went back to a time when James and Hugh still lived.

"My father is paranoid," Evers said in answer. I took that to mean that I didn't want to know. A startled laugh escaped me. "What?" he asked, looking at me with a raised brow, a shade of worry in his eyes.

"Just thinking how thick my dad's file must be. All the trouble he gets into. His friends."

"He's not the average dad."

"No," I said, thinking of my childhood wish for a normal dad. One who would take care of me instead of needing me to watch out for him. "No, he's not."

"The Winters know you're behind Cynthia's party. They know who you are."

"I assumed they knew who I was since they had you spy on me to make sure I didn't cause any trouble," I said bitterly. Evers didn't contradict my harsh words. Instead, he surprised me.

"They want to meet you. I tried to talk them into waiting until we know what your father is mixed up in, but they don't care. Aiden said it's time."

"Why? Why now? If they've known all this time who I am, that I was around, why wait?"

Evers rubbed a hand against the back of his neck and looked away. "It's partly our fault. You seemed innocent enough, but your dad has always been sketchy. They've had enough scandal in their lives. When you turned up, practically on their doorstep, I talked them into waiting. Then, by the time I was sure you weren't a threat, your dad—"

Evers shook his head. "Maybe we're all a little overprotective. I was a kid when James and Anna were murdered and in college when Hugh and Olivia died. The media were relentless. Vicious. Your father is a loose cannon, and when we saw what he was capable of, we wanted to keep him far away from the family."

"And that meant keeping me away," I said, putting the pieces together.

"We could have handled it differently," he admitted. "Maybe we should have. Jacob liked you when he met you during Axel's thing. He voted to bring you into the family."

"And you talked him out of it," I said flatly.

"Not at first. Not until I looked into your dad."

I sighed. I wanted to be angry. Looking around the shabby, sordid disaster of my father's life, I couldn't argue with the Sinclairs wanting to keep us away from their friends.

I didn't want their money, but my dad would have hit them up for cash while they were still shaking hands.

"It doesn't matter now," Evers said. "I talked to Aiden yesterday. They want to meet you before the party."

"I... I wasn't going to... I saw the guest list and..."

Evers laughed and shook his head. "What were you going to do? Hide? I've seen you run parties before, you're out on the floor the entire time. How are you going to manage the party from your office?"

My shoulders slumped, and I gave a little shrug, laughing at myself. "I hadn't worked that out yet. Honestly, I've had enough to worry about getting the party put together. And, just so you know, I could absolutely run the party from my office if I had to."

"Well, now you don't have to. They want to meet you. It won't be all of them. Vance and Maggie, Aiden and Violet, Charlie and Lucas, and Lise and Riley. The rest of them can't make it. Lucas and Riley work for us. They'll be at the party doubling as security, working undercover."

"Can we put it off? Do it another time?" I asked, nerves creeping in. The Winters family was larger than life. I wasn't ready to meet them. Not yet. Not with everything else that was going on.

"You might be able to put off the rest of them, but if you try to hide from Charlie, she'll hunt you down. Nobody told her about you, and she is pissed. You don't want to see Charlie when she's pissed. It was all Lucas could do to convince her to wait until Friday."

"But why? Why would they care? I'm a nobody."

Evers' eyes narrowed on my face, confusion and annoyance flashing through them. "You're not a nobody, Summer."

"I'm a nobody compared to the Winters family."

"No, you're somebody no matter who you're compared with. And you're a part of the Winters family. You think they have relatives coming out of the woodwork to hassle them, but they don't. You and your father. That's it. Daniel had two sons who are both dead, and Amelia never had children. They've lost enough family."

"This is weird, " I blurted out. "You don't understand, Evers, my dad made me promise. He doesn't get worked up about much, but he made me swear I'd stay away from them."

"Your dad's not here."

An idea occurred to me, and I looked down at my phone, wondering. "My dad's not answering my calls," I said slowly, gears turning in my mind, "but I wonder what would happen if I told him I was going to a party with the Winters. I wonder if that would get him to call."

Evers gave me a speculative look. "Do it. Call him. If you call now, he'll have plenty of time to try to stop you."

I pulled up my dad's number and hit the call button. As I'd expected, it went straight to voicemail. When I finished listening to my dad's vague half-asleep voice invite me to leave a message, I did.

"Dad, it's Summer. I've been trying to call you. Listen, remember how you told me not to get in touch with the Winters? Well, I'm doing a party next week, and they're all invited. They said they want to meet me. So if that's a problem, if you still want me to stay away, call me back, okay? I don't want to break my promise, but I'm not sure I can get out of it without a good reason."

I paused, the whole crazy situation swirling in my head, wondering what else to say. *Where are you? What have you done? What are you mixed up in?*

All I said was, "I love you, Dad."

There was nothing more we could do in the abandoned ranch house. I got back in the car while Evers locked up, clutching my phone in my hand. I willed it to ring. Willed my father to reach out. To call. To give me answers.

The party grew closer, and still, he didn't call. Every day that passed without hearing his voice, my worry grew.

Finally, the day of the party arrived.

Smokey Winters was out of time.

So was I.

Chapter Thirteen

SUMMER

I paced the hall outside my small office, every click of my heels on the hardwood floor winding my nerves tighter. Everything was ready for the party.

I was dressed, Angie was taking care of Cynthia, the caterers were set up, the band was here, and all of the guests had yet to arrive.

Almost all of the guests. The Winters family was assembled in the parlor. Waiting for me.

I glanced at the phone sitting beside my laptop on my desk. My father had never called. After making me promise, making me swear I'd never contact the Winters family, I told him we were meeting, and he said nothing.

I didn't have time to think about how much that scared me.

Part of me hadn't really believed that my dad was in trouble. Smokey Winters never got in trouble. He always managed to squirm his way out, leaving someone else holding the bag.

Not this time. This time, something was really wrong. I

did not have time to worry about it. Not tonight. I stopped pacing and smoothed my hands down my skirt.

I was being ridiculous. I'm an adult. A professional. I'm successful and smart, and there was no reason to be nervous about meeting the Winters.

The flutters in my stomach intensified. All of that might have been true, but I was still terrified. I ran a hand over my hair, tucking a stray wisp into my chignon.

For the party, I'd chosen a cobalt silk wrap dress accented with a silver scarf and matching silver heels. Elegant and striking enough to fit in, understated enough that I wouldn't draw attention from the real star of the party.

A quick glance at my watch told me that I'd better get this thing with the Winters over with before the rest of the guests arrived and Cynthia made her grand entrance.

I still couldn't believe we'd managed to pull this off. A last-minute party for seventy-five, and so far, everything was ticking along right on schedule.

I allowed myself just a moment to revel in the depth of my awesomeness. There was a reason my clients are loyal. I'm damn good at my job.

I clenched my hands into fists, letting my nerves run rampant through my body before I forced my hands to relax, rolled my shoulders back, and took a deep breath.

I could handle this. They were just people. If they didn't like me, well, that was their loss.

Just as I reached the end of the hallway, Evers appeared, taking my elbow in hand and walking beside me. Under his breath, he said, "Don't be nervous."

"I'm not nervous," I lied.

He was nice enough not to call me on it. We entered the room, and everyone turned. A man broke free from the group and strode forward, hand outstretched. This had to be Aiden Winters, the eldest and current head of the family.

He clasped my fingers in his, giving me a warm, friendly shake. Looking down at me in curiosity, he said, "You have the Winters' blue eyes. It's hard to tell from pictures, but I'd know those eyes anywhere. Just like Charlie's."

"I told you," a man said. He stood next to a woman about my age with chin-length auburn curls the same shade as Aiden's and ocean-blue eyes that were an exact match to mine. The man who'd spoken was a little scary despite his perfectly tailored dark suit.

He was tall, and that was saying something in a room full of men who all had to be over six feet. This guy could have been 6' 6", with broad shoulders and long legs. He would have made me nervous except for his friendly smile and the way he held his date in his arms.

"I'm Aiden," the first man said, confirming my suspicions.

"Summer. Summer Winters." I flushed. "But you already know that." My nervous laugh made me flush deeper. I hate being nervous. Almost as much as I hate blushing.

"Well, *I* didn't know. These guys are all in big trouble for not telling me," said the woman with my eyes and Aiden's hair. She strode forward and pulled me into a short hug, squeezing tight.

"I'm Charlie Jackson, but I used to be Charlie Winters. I'm this one's little sister," she said, nodding at Aiden. "And this is my husband, Lucas. He works at Sinclair with Evers and Riley and Griffen and the rest of the guys wandering around here. Sorry we're all ambushing you at once when you're supposed to be working, but we figured it would be less weird than running into you at the party."

Charlie's open friendliness disarmed me, scattering my nerves and leaving me grinning.

"It's a little weird, either way," I said, "but this is much better than bumping into all of you at the party. I, uh, I should have gotten in touch before, but—"

"I was about to say the same thing," Aiden said. "We shouldn't have let it go for this long."

"Life has been a little crazy," a tall, blonde woman cut in. She stepped forward, tugging her date along with her and held out her hand. "I'm Annalise. Lise. Aiden and Charlie's cousin. This is my husband, Riley. He works with Lucas and Evers and the rest of them. Over there is my twin brother Vance and his wife Maggie. Everyone else can't wait to meet you. They would have rearranged things if we'd had a little more notice, but—"

I shook my head, smiling. "Cynthia said it had to be today. She wouldn't hear of waiting another week or two."

"Summer sent out the invitations less than twenty-four hours after Cynthia sprang the party on her," Evers said, smiling down at me with something that looked like pride.

A gasp came from beside Aiden. With silvery blonde hair and lavender eyes, his date was so composed, so beautiful, she was a little intimidating. "A week?" she asked with disarming admiration, "How did you manage to throw this together in a week?"

"She's going to say it's no big deal," Evers said, "but she's been working around the clock to make it happen."

"Cynthia keeps me on my toes," I said diplomatically.

She might drive me nuts half the time, but she was a client and a good one. I'd never admit to anyone else how hard the last week had been. How exhausted I was, and how much I was looking forward to sleeping for twelve hours straight once this whole thing was done.

I soon learned that the woman beside Aiden was Violet, his girlfriend, named perfectly for the color of her eyes. Vance and Maggie came over, Vance giving me a firm handshake and Maggie a hug.

They were all so... normal. I mean, aside from being gorgeous and draped in designer clothes. Underneath all that polish, they were normal. They were friendly, and kind, and seemed genuinely interested in getting to know me better.

We chatted about this and that, mostly the Winters telling me about the various siblings and cousins who hadn't been able to make the party and planning an impromptu get together at their house. It was all so easy and comfortable, I lost track of time until Angie popped her head in the parlor and lifted a hand to draw my attention.

"Excuse me for just a second," I said and met Angie at the door.

"Cynthia's almost ready, but she has a plan for her big entrance, and she wants to go over it with you. She needs you upstairs, now."

"One minute. Thanks, Angie."

Evers stood, signaling Lucas and Riley. Lucas said, "Time to go to work." Leaning down, he kissed his wife's temple and murmured something in her ear that made her laugh.

"I'll try," she said with a sparkle in her eyes. Lucas winked and followed Evers and Riley from the room.

Vance shook his head at his younger cousin and said, "Like you could stay out of trouble."

His wife, Maggie, elbowed him in the side. She

reminded me a little of my best friend, Emma, with her red hair, bombshell figure, and kind eyes.

Proving that I hadn't read her wrong she said, "Don't let us keep you. I know you've been working hard to make this happen, and the next few hours are going to be busy. We'll make sure we catch up, set up something with the whole family so you can meet everyone."

"That would be great. I'd love to do this again when I don't have so much on my plate. I'm sure you've got my number," I said with a wink. "I'll see you around the party. Have fun," I said over my shoulder as I hustled out into the hall and up the stairs to Cynthia's side.

If only the rest of the evening could go as well as meeting my long-lost family, I'd be in good shape. Funny, I'd been so nervous, and in the end, they were just... really nice. Nice was good. I liked nice.

I was a little dizzy at the thought of suddenly having so much family. All these people who were connected to me going back generations.

A spike of resentment snuck in. My father had kept me from this, from those people. People who'd been happy to welcome me. Who wanted to be a family.

Why did he keep us apart?

Because everything is always about him, that resentful voice murmured in the back of my mind. *Because the only person he really cares about is himself.*

I pushed my father from my thoughts. Personal time was over. I'd met my family, they were great, and I'd think more about them later.

From now on, the night was all about Cynthia. This was her party, and she was the Queen Bee.

I pushed open the door to Cynthia's suite to find her sitting in front of the vanity, smoothing another coat of lipstick over her deep red lips. Angie had pulled her hair away from her face to highlight her dramatic cheekbones and almond-shaped eyes, gathering it at the crown of her head with a jeweled clasp and letting the rest fall in a wave of tousled platinum curls.

Narrow straps held up her dark red dress, the deep V in the front and back showing plenty of cleavage and highlighting Cynthia's perfectly-toned arms. The chiffon skirt floated around Cynthia in panels that shifted and swayed when she moved.

Standing still, the length was perfectly demure. When she danced it would show her legs almost to her hips. Tiny, perfectly-placed crystals gave the dress a shimmer that went perfectly with her hair. Cynthia sparkled with jewels and excitement.

I said with complete honesty, "You look fantastic. Just amazing."

Cynthia smiled at me, scanning me from head to toe. "You don't look so bad yourself. I love that scarf. It's perfect with that shade of blue."

"It is, isn't it? I bought it the last time I was out in California with you. It's just the thing to liven up the dress."

"I am so excited for this, Summer. You've done a wonderful job. I know I'm demanding. You're the only one who can put up with me. You're a miracle worker."

"I love putting up with you," I said, and despite how crazy the party had made me, I meant it. Cynthia could be a pain in the ass, but I loved the challenge. I'd get bored if I didn't have to scramble every once in a while.

Nothing is quite like the sense of triumph I get from knowing I'd faced the impossible and pulled it off with flair.

"Guests should be arriving any moment," Cynthia said,

her words punctuated by the sound of voices coming from below.

"It sounds like the first are already here."

"Not exactly the first," Cynthia said, eyeing me curiously. "Why didn't you tell me you're related to the Winters?"

I shook my head. "Because. It's complicated. I'll fill you in after the party. Seriously, we do not have time right now."

"As long as you promise. I don't like missing out on gossip. Give me the TLDR."

The TLDR. Too Long Didn't Read. I smiled at the term coming from Cynthia, who looked so much like an old-school silver screen goddess it was hard to imagine she'd ever seen an Internet forum, much less knew what TLDR meant.

"Okay, and then we have to focus. Short story, my father is their father's cousin. Which makes them my second cousins. I think. My grandfather was estranged from the family and my dad made me promise never to talk to them. But he's not around right now, and it was time. That's it."

Cynthia's eyes narrowed. "I don't think *that's it*. I think there's a lot more to the story, but you're right, now is not the time. So," she said, shifting gears, "obviously, I want to make an entrance. I was thinking, if you can let me know when most of the guests have arrived, we'll signal the band to play something fun. Lively. Then I'll come down the stairs and the party can really get started."

"What about *Shut Up and Dance*? When the band auditioned they played it—instrumental and a little slower than the radio version. It was fantastic. High energy and fun."

"That sounds perfect. Exactly what I want."

"I'll go let the band know. They should start playing any minute now. I don't think we should wait too long to—"

There was a brief knock on the door before it swung open to reveal Evers, his brow knitted, lips pressed in a firm line.

"What is it?" I asked. "What's wrong?"

"Clint is at the gate," he said, biting off the words in irritation. "My guys aren't letting him in, but they can't exactly conceal his presence, considering they're checking in other guests. I don't think he knew about the party in advance, but it's bad timing. With so many people coming through the gates, we're limited in how we deal with him. He's insisting he wants to talk to you," he said to Cynthia.

All her joy drained away, leaving her eyes strained, her smile flat. I wanted to march down the driveway and smack Clint Perry in the face. Or worse. Maybe Evers would let me borrow his gun.

It had been a hard year for Cynthia. She was excited about the party, and now he was trying to ruin this, too.

Cynthia stared at the ceiling, apparently lost in thought. Evers and I waited. After what seemed like a year, she sucked in a sharp breath, blinked hard and said, "Get him on the phone. He is not ruining my night."

"Cynthia," Evers said, "I don't think that's a good idea. He—"

"Get. Him. On. The. Phone."

"Okay," Evers said, pulling his phone from his pocket. He called the guard at the gate who was keeping Clint off the property. "Put him on the phone. She wants to talk to him."

He brought the phone down from his ear, covering it with his hand as he said, "You talk to him on speaker, understood? I need to hear what he says."

Cynthia nodded. "Is he there?"

Evers took his hand off the phone and said, "Perry, you're on speaker. Cynthia's here. She wants to talk to you."

"Baby?" Clint's familiar low husky voice sounded through the speaker. "Baby? I'm sorry, but I need to see you. I didn't know what else to do."

"Clint, I could call the police," Cynthia said, and I would have thought she was simply exasperated except for the pain hiding beneath her words.

"You're not going to call the police, baby. I know you hate me. I know you have a right to feel that way. I promise, if you just agree to talk to me one time, I'll go away and leave you alone. I'll give you the divorce. I'll give you anything you want. If you just see me one last time. I promise."

"Why?" Cynthia asked blinking rapidly to fight back tears. "What's the point? All we do is hurt each other. We can't go back, Clint. We can't save what was never there."

"Don't say that. Don't say that. I messed up. I messed up so badly. I ruined everything, and I know it. But I love you, and I know you loved me. Maybe you don't anymore, but you did, once."

"'That was a long time ago," Cynthia said, her voice thin and sad. I wished he would just get to the point so we could hang up and she could go back to being excited and happy.

Cynthia had spent a lot of this past year lonely and miserable. I hated seeing her slide back. Once upon a time, I'd liked Clint Perry, thought they were great together. Now? I wished she would call the police so we could have the satisfaction of seeing his ass thrown in jail.

"Just meet with me," he said. "One time. Let me explain and then I'll leave you alone, I promise."

"Fine," Cynthia snapped out, her sharp tone drowning out Evers' groan and my sharp intake of breath.

What was she doing?

She'd gone to all the trouble of getting a restraining order, and now not only wouldn't she use it, she was breaking the terms herself. I couldn't see how meeting with Clint was a good idea, but I was just the assistant. Cynthia was in the driver's seat.

Evers tried to talk sense into her. "Cynthia, this is not a good idea. I can't recommend—"

"Evers, set it up. I have a party to get to. You know my schedule. Find a time, and make the arrangements. Not here. Your offices. And Clint, after the arrangements are made, you leave. Immediately."

"Understood, baby. Thank you."

Evers took the phone off speaker and put it to his ear, sending Cynthia a dark look as he stalked from the room, barking at Clint over the phone. I gave Cynthia's face a quick look, relieved to see that she'd managed to hold back her brimming tears. Her makeup was still perfect.

I wanted to hug her, but Cynthia needed to shore up her defenses. A hug wouldn't help. Later, after the party when there was no one else to see, she might let me offer comfort. Not now.

Right now she had to get into character, and there was no character she liked playing more than the fabulous, glamorous, and unbelievably talented Cynthia Stevens.

Unable to help myself, I reached out and gave her arm a brief squeeze. In a low voice, I asked, "You good?"

"Fan-fucking-tastic," she answered, determination filling her voice. That determination had propelled her from waiting tables and doing toothpaste commercials to the Oscars. It would get her through tonight.

"I knew you would be," I murmured. "I'm off to check in with the band. I'll send a text when we're ready for you. I don't think it'll be too long. Based on the sound of voices downstairs, I think everyone was eager to be here on time."

Another quick squeeze of her arm and I left to confer with the band. Less than twenty minutes later, Cynthia swept in, serenaded by a lively beat as assembled guests clapped in appreciation.

Normally, I might give a discrete internal eye roll at her need for drama and attention. Tonight, after what Clint had pulled, I just hoped all that adoration filled the hole he'd left in her heart.

Chapter Fourteen

SUMMER

The next two hours disappeared in a blur of hors d'oeuvres, spilled wine, music, and laughter. So far, everything was going to plan. The food was delicious, not that I was surprised, knowing May. She was my favorite caterer for a reason.

Rycroft Castle was at its best in a party, and the guests got a kick out of the atmosphere. They were wealthy, some of them famous, and probably lived in mansions of their own, but Rycroft Castle was a step above.

I bumped into Charlie just as the party was hitting its stride. I stood to the side of the room, a glass of wine in hand, scanning for anything that might need my attention. She sidled up beside me, nudged my shoulder with hers and said, "This party is fantastic. Rycroft is amazing. I grew up in Winters House, which is pretty impressive, but it's not a freaking castle."

"I know. This place is just beyond. Every time I walk down the hall I feel like I'm in a different century," I said.

"Lucas and I flip houses. Well, I do it full time, he works

with me when he's not doing his thing at Sinclair. I just got my contractor's license, and I have a pretty good idea what this must have cost." She rolled her eyes and grinned. "This is what they mean when they say price is no object."

"It's one of the perks of my job. I usually work from my condo, but every once in a while, I get to stay in a place like this." I thought about it and corrected, "Okay, never quite in a place like *this*."

I'd noticed Charlie's husband Lucas and Lise's husband Riley mingling with the guests, their eyes sharp, alert. I didn't know exactly what they did for Sinclair Security, but both of them shared that cool, efficient veneer Evers had when he was on the job. Whatever came up, they would handle it. Nothing would get in their way.

When Lucas came up behind Charlie and me, I looked up to see his face and felt a trickle of concern.

"What is it? Is Clint back?"

Lucas shook his head. "Not a security problem, but I thought you'd want to know. I was outside when the band was taking a break. Heard them saying they're going to refuse to play past ten unless you kick in another grand."

I swore under my breath. "They can't do that. I have a contract. If you'll excuse me for a moment, I need to grab some paperwork and have a chat with the bandleader."

Lucas winked at me and said, "Good idea. We'll come with, just in case he gives you a hard time."

"I can handle it," I assured. I didn't want them to leave the party, but Charlie looped her arm through mine.

"Let us help. Lucas is excellent at looming and looking scary. He won't even need to say anything. He'll just stand there, and you can do your thing. More efficient that way."

I laughed and said, "Thanks, then. I'd appreciate it."

I worked my way through the crowd until we reached

the hall to my office. At the edge of the party, I said, "You guys can wait here. I'll be right back."

The din of music, voices, and laughter faded away as I moved down the hall, the sounds dissolving into the clatter of silverware and plates, the rush of the servers and May hustling in the kitchen.

I ducked past the kitchen, turned down the short hall to my office, and skidded to a halt. The door to my office was cracked, light spilling into the dark hall.

I'd left it shut. I'd checked. There was security all over the place, and it's possible one of the servers or May had been looking for something and checked my office, thinking it was another pantry or storage closet.

With a shrug, I strode down the hall and swung the door open, coming up short and staring in a moment of shocked confusion at the dark figure bending over my desk, clicking keys on my open laptop, my phone in one hand.

What the hell? Who would be interested in my computer? Too late, I realized the person at my desk was probably not a guest. I had to get the hell out and go for help.

I stood there for a second too long, jaw dropped, thoughts scrambled. The figure straightened, and I saw he was a man around my dad's age, dressed in a tuxedo like so many of the other partygoers.

The clothes aside, he didn't look like a guest. There was something in his dark eyes. Something hard. Cold. He shut the lid of my laptop and tucked it under his arm, sliding my phone in his pocket.

He took a step toward me, and I backed up, stumbling a little as my heel caught on the corner of the doorframe.

"What are you doing? You can't take that!"

Stupid. So stupid. He said nothing, answering with his

fist. His arm flashed out, the back of his hand hitting the side of my head hard enough to send me flying into the doorframe, the sharp corner smacking my shoulder, spinning me to the side. My heel twisted, breaking. Off balance, I stumbled, my ankle giving out beneath me.

Another hit, this one into my stomach, driving the breath from my lungs. I went down, falling on my ass and rolling, the back of my head smacking the floor. My broken shoe flew off, sliding across the floor as I gasped for air.

Looking down at me as if I were no more than a bug, the man calmly stepped over me and took off down the hall at a sedate, leisurely pace.

"Stop! Stop! You can't—someone stop him!" I tried to shout, but he'd knocked the wind out of me and my words were a harsh whisper. Scrambling to my feet, the floor tilting beneath me as my ankle wobbled, I wondered if I was going to throw up before I managed to get help.

I stumbled, my stomach hitched, and I fell to my knees, the drumming of my heartbeat in my ears turning into feet pounding on the floor.

Then Lucas was crouching in front of me, saying over his shoulder, "Get Evers."

Charlie's voice, high and strained, "I'll be right back."

"Summer, are you all right? What happened?"

He eased me to my side, helping me sit up. "Take a deep breath. You're okay."

"I came down the hall. Door was open a little. I left it shut. I know I left it shut. He was in there. He took my laptop and my phone."

"Who was in there, Summer? Did you recognize him?"

My vision slowly cleared, the chaos of thoughts in my head slowing. "No. I've never seen him before. He was maybe in his fifties? Dark hair. Dark eyes. Wearing a tux."

"Did he say anything?"

"No. Just hit me and took my laptop and my phone and walked out. I... I should have stopped him, but he hit me, and I fell, and then he was gone."

Evers strode down the hallway. "Where is she? What the hell happened?"

The second Lucas saw Evers, he stood, taking off at a jog. As he passed Evers he said, "Ask Summer. I'm going after him."

Evers dropped to his knees beside me, framing my face with his hands, turning my head in the light, looking for injuries.

"What happened? Where are you hurt?"

"I'm fine," I breathed, fighting to fill my lungs.

Evers looked to Charlie, who said, "He knocked the breath out of her, shoved her, but that's all."

He stroked a hand over my back, murmuring, "Just breathe. You're okay."

I made a noise in the back of my throat, my eyes squeezed shut against his tenderness.

"Take a breath and tell me what happened."

I told Evers what I'd told Lucas. He swore under his breath and sat, settling against the wall and pulling me into his lap, wrapping his arms around me and nestling my head in the crook of his neck.

"Lucas will find him," he whispered against my hair. "He hit you twice, in the shoulder and the stomach, and you fell and hit your head. Your ankle might be twisted, but nothing else? You're not hurt anywhere else?"

I shook my head, rolling my forehead against his warm skin.

"Summer?" he probed.

"No. Nowhere else. Still hard to breathe. Feel sick." I

couldn't seem to string together more than a few words at a time. A steel band was wrapped around my chest and my insides felt bruised. Sore.

From somewhere behind me, I heard Charlie say, "I'll go check the freezer for peas or something. A bag of ice for her ankle."

"I don't need ice," I said slowly, the tightness in my lungs finally easing, bit by bit. "I'm okay. I just need aspirin or something."

"You need to rest," Evers said, resettling me against him. "The team will find the guy who broke in."

As that thought filtered through, a bolt of alarm cleared my mind.

I couldn't rest.

I was the middle of throwing a party.

I had a job to do, and I wouldn't let Cynthia down. I struggled against Evers, trying to sit up, to get back on my feet.

His arms tightened, and he growled, "Where do you think you're going?"

"I have to get back to the party. Have to get back to work."

"No," Evers said baldly. "You're hurt. Once we get you settled I'll take a closer look and decide if we need to take you to the hospital or just call in the doctor."

"You didn't go to the hospital when you almost got killed," I said peevishly.

I wanted nothing more than to peel off my silk dress and crawl between the sheets of my bed so I could fall asleep and escape the growing ache in my shoulder, the throb in my ankle, and my pounding head.

It didn't matter. I'd get through it. A few hours and the party would be over. I could rest then.

From above me, I caught the rustle of silk and Charlie's voice. "When did you almost get killed, Ev?"

Evers shifted, and a second later the blessed relief of cold spread across my ankle.

"None of your business," he said in retort.

"Hmm," Charlie grumbled, and if I'd never met them before, from that short exchange I could have guessed they were the next thing to siblings.

We sat there in silence for a long minute, me soaking up the icy relief of the cold pack on my ankle, and Charlie clearly thinking hard.

Breaking the silence, she burst out with, "Oh, my God. Summer is her. Summer is your secret. Holy crap."

"Shut up, Charlie."

"I will not shut up. Did Lucas know?"

No answer from Evers.

I shifted my head an inch to see Charlie standing over us, arms crossed over her chest, glaring down at Evers, her eyes annoyed but her mouth stretched in a shit-eating grin.

Evers let out a huff of air. "I decline to answer the question on the grounds that it's going to get my buddy in trouble."

"He *did* know. That weasel. He's too good at keeping secrets." Charlie moved to the end of the hall by the kitchen and Evers' head popped up. "Don't. Stay here until Lucas gets back."

"Why? Do you think there's anyone else in the house?"

"No. I don't, but I'm not taking any chances. Lucas is doing his thing, Riley is leading the team securing the house. You're staying right here with us until one of them comes back to give us the all clear. There's enough to keep track of with all those guests out there, we don't need to make it harder."

"Cynthia—" I started to say.

Evers cut me off. "Cynthia is fine. I have two guys who won't let her out of their sight."

Griffen appeared at the end of the hallway "Lucas hasn't come back yet."

"Is he—?" Charlie asked, nerves in her voice for the first time.

"He took two guys with him," Griffen reassured. "I've got ears on him," he said, tapping a discreet earpiece. "He's fine, just trying to catch the guy who got in. Cynthia's covered. No one out there has any clue. We've got two teams sweeping the house, all exits secured. We can move Summer upstairs."

He'd no sooner finished speaking then Evers was rising, holding me in his arms as he stood and strode down the hall.

"I've got your shoes, Summer," Charlie said from behind us.

"I can walk," I said to Evers.

"You can, but you're not going to.

I tried not to be relieved. I needed to get back to the party. Back to work.

My body had other plans. Taken on their own, none of my injuries was that bad. A sore stomach, a bruised shoulder, a twisted ankle, a bump on the head. All together they left me feeling as if I'd been hit by a truck.

Evers set me down on my bed and put the ice pack back on my ankle. Over his shoulder, he said to Griffen, "Call Whitmore."

"She's a little banged up. She probably feels like hell, but she doesn't need a doctor," Griffen said.

"Call him anyway," Evers insisted. "She hit her head when she fell."

Griffen ignored him and strode to the side of the bed.

He leaned over, nudging Evers out of the way. Turning on the bedside lamp, he said, "Open your eyes and look up at me, Summer."

He studied my eyes for a moment. "Close them." I did. "Open." I did. "Pupils are reacting normally. Nausea?"

"Not really. Right after he hit me, but not now." I said.

"Take a deep breath." I did. My chest was sore, but my lungs were finally cooperating again. "Again."

After two more full breaths, Griffen nodded. He held up a hand, one finger extended. "Follow my finger." He moved his finger from side to side, then up and down. "Blurred vision? Dizziness?"

"A little dizziness," I admitted. "No blurred vision."

He flashed three fingers. "How many?"

"Three."

He tested me a few more times, threw some math at me and pronounced me in need of a painkiller and a good night's sleep.

"She's fine," he said to Evers, patting him on the shoulder.

"You're not a neurologist," Evers muttered.

"She doesn't need a neurologist. She's fine. You had it a hell of a lot worse than Summer, and you let *me* stitch you up. Relax."

I twisted to look at the scrapes on Evers' neck, mostly hidden by his collar. I reached out to touch them, and he caught my hand.

"You didn't tell me you needed stitches," I said, irrationally angry that he'd hidden how bad it was.

"I didn't. That was another time," he said absently, still holding my hand in his, his thumb rubbing my knuckles. "Don't you have something to do?" he asked Griffen.

Griffen sent me a wink and a grin. Then, more seriously, he said, "If you start to feel sick, your headache changes, you have any drainage from your nose or ears, confusion, or blurred vision, let Evers know. Basically, you should feel better from here, so if you feel worse, we'll take you to the hospital. Otherwise, I think you're fine."

"Thanks, Griffen."

He lifted his hand to his forehead in a jaunty salute before he disappeared through the door.

Charlie wandered to the window and peered through into the dark night. Mostly to herself, she murmured, "I like not knowing what he's up to when he's in the field. It's easier. I hate sitting here and waiting."

"He can handle himself," Evers reassured.

"I know," Charlie said with a sigh. "I know he can. I'll still feel better when he's back and I can see that he's fine."

She paced for what seemed like an hour, but was probably less than twenty minutes, stopping only when the door opened and Lucas walked through, Riley behind him.

Lucas met Evers' eyes and shook his head. "Lost him. I waited too long, but I didn't want to leave Summer alone when we didn't know what was going on."

"You did the right thing," Evers said immediately. "We'll have to check her office to see if he got anything else, or just the laptop and phone."

For the first time reality sank in. My laptop and phone were gone. Stolen. I had everything on them. What wasn't on my laptop was on my phone.

I reminded myself to relax. They were both backed up. Getting a new laptop and phone was an added expense, and inconvenient, but it wasn't the end of the world.

I didn't bother to ask. I already knew the break-in had nothing to do with Cynthia. Someone interested in Cynthia would have gone straight for her. Instead of my office, they would have headed to her bedroom to raid her lingerie drawer. A few years ago, she had a stalker who'd done exactly that.

Her housekeeper had walked into her bedroom, a stack of clean, white sheets in her arms, and screamed bloody murder when she saw a portly little man with a goatee pawing through Cynthia's underwear drawer, his pockets stuffed with wisps of silk and lace. Yuck.

After that, Cynthia had kicked up the security. This wasn't about her.

No, whoever it was had gone straight for my laptop and phone. I didn't have any digital information worth stealing. Somehow, I didn't think he was after the contents of my modest savings and investment accounts.

If he was looking for proof of contact with my father, he was out of luck. Smokey Winters wasn't the email type, and he hadn't called me in weeks.

"How did he get away?" Evers asked.

"The best we could tell," Riley said, "he went over the wall like some kind of goddamn spider monkey. It looked like he had the laptop strapped to his back and he just—" Riley mimed climbing. "By the time we got to the other side, he was gone."

"Fuck."

"Summer need a doctor?" Riley asked.

"No," I said, struggling to sit up. "Griffen said I was fine."

Evers turned, giving me a sharp look. "Don't even think about getting up. Keep that ice on your ankle and stay where you are."

"Bossy," Charlie said under her breath, earning a tiny giggle from me and scowls from all of the men in the room. She rolled her eyes at me and I smiled back.

"I have to get back to the party," I said. "Cynthia—"

"Cynthia is covered," Evers said shortly. "Nothing is going to happen to her. I'm staying here with you."

I opened my mouth to object, then took in the resolve in his ice-blue eyes, the mulish set of his chin, and kept my mouth closed. I didn't have the energy to argue with Evers, but more than that, I didn't want him to leave.

I was tired and beat up. Exhausted and scared.

Evers made me feel safe.

I didn't understand myself.

I didn't trust him. I was still angry with him.

And when I thought about who I wanted most, the answer was Evers. Only Evers.

I wished that this time it wasn't about a case. That this time it was about me and not his job.

Chapter Fifteen

EVERS

"Cynthia, I want you to reconsider this meeting with Perry. We both know it's a bad idea. He's unpredictable and—"

"I want him to go away, Evers. If this is what it takes, I'm doing it." She flounced across the wood-paneled bar, her heels silent on the thick Persian rug, and sat in a wide leather chair, scowling at me.

"Fine," I said shortly.

I was tired and not in the mood to argue with Cynthia about Clint Perry. I'd stayed up half the night sitting with Summer, watching her sleep.

I'd fucked up. Somewhere there'd been a hole in our security. The intruder must have had an invitation. The cameras hadn't caught him coming over the wall to get in, but they'd certainly caught him on his way out. Riley had been right, he'd scaled the tall limestone wall just like a fucking spider monkey.

Somehow, he got his hands on an invitation. He'd been close enough to Summer to hit her. Twice.

When I thought about what else he could have done, alone in her little office, Summer at his mercy—

I couldn't picture it without wanting to tear him apart. I was here to keep her safe. To get her help finding her father, yes, but mostly to keep her safe.

I'd fucked it up. After Riley, Lucas, and Charlie had left, she'd pushed me away and disappeared into her closet, emerging in a long T-shirt before she crawled into bed and murmured, "You can go. I'm fine."

I hadn't left. I made myself comfortable beside her on the bed, ignoring her protests that she was fine, waiting until she fell asleep. More than once, I'd stopped myself from reaching out to stroke her hair. She wouldn't allow that. Not yet. Maybe not ever at this rate.

When she was asleep, I left two guards on her door and went to meet with the rest of the team.

The guests had been filtering out, Cynthia tipsy, giggling, and having the time of her life flitting from one group to another, bestowing hugs and air kisses as she said goodbye.

It annoyed me to see her basking in the success of Summer's hard work while Summer herself lay asleep in bed, in pain and alone. Riley, Lucas, Griffen, and I met in the control room and had a quick debrief. After, I returned to Summer's room where I lay beside her, staring at the ceiling and listening to her deep, even breaths.

I left before the sun came up, knowing she wouldn't appreciate opening her eyes to see me beside her. Never before had I regretted my mistakes with her this much.

"You look tired." Cynthia watched me with curious eyes.

"I didn't sleep well," I admitted.

Cynthia stood from the deep leather armchair and sauntered across the room toward me, her eyes intent on mine.

Intent and predatory.

Oh, shit. I'd known this was coming. I still hadn't decided how to handle it. I didn't want to hurt her feelings, but there was no fucking way—

"You know," Cynthia said in a sultry voice, "if you're not sleeping well, I could help you with that."

She came to a stop in front of me and lifted her hands to rest on my chest, leaning in and tilting her head up, lifting her mouth to mine, perfectly positioned for a kiss.

Objectively, I looked at her and wondered how any man could tell her no. She was perfection from head to toe, every strand of hair, every curled eyelash, every toned muscle and rounded curve the feminine ideal.

There was nothing about her that wasn't gorgeously sexy, and still she left me cold.

I wanted Summer.

Cynthia was no substitute.

I wrapped my fingers around her wrists and drew them from my chest, backing up to put distance between us, searching for something to say that would explain without leaving her feeling rejected.

I liked Cynthia, and she'd been having a bad time of it where men were concerned.

I didn't want to hurt her. I just didn't want her.

I opened my mouth to say something, I wasn't sure what, when Cynthia pulled her wrists free and waved her hand in the air in dismissal.

"Don't bother. Whatever you're going to say is bullshit. You're not interested."

She didn't sound angry so much as intrigued. I was glad she wasn't angry, but intrigued made me nervous.

"I'm not. I'm sorry, it's not—"

Another wave of her hand, brushing away whatever I'd

been about to say. "I know, It's not me it's you, blah blah. Except it's not me *or* you, is it? It's Summer."

I went still. The last thing I needed was for Cynthia to butt her head in the middle of my problems with Summer. "I don't know what you're talking about."

"Good try. I've been watching you two. The way she won't look at you. The way your eyes follow her whenever you're in the same room. I'm not blind. I wasn't sure exactly what was going on, figured I'd make a run at you since you were here, and she said she didn't mind."

I started in surprise. "She said what?"

Cynthia shrugged and gave me a knowing grin. "I asked if there was anything going on, and she said absolutely not. Then I asked if she minded if I made a move, and she said you were all mine."

She strode behind the bar and opened the small refrigerator. Pulling a bottle of champagne from inside, she poured herself a flute and sipped, studying me like I was a bug under a microscope.

I've faced down people a hell of a lot more intimidating than Cynthia Stevens, yet under the weight of that gaze, I wanted to turn and run. This conversation was not going to go well.

"So, what happened? Did you fuck it up, or did she?"

Defeated, I went to the bar and poured myself a finger of whiskey. It was the good stuff, and I sipped slowly before admitting, "It was me."

"Not a surprise," she muttered.

"What's that supposed to mean?"

"Evers, come on. You're the original rolling stone. You go from one woman to another, flash that charming smile, remind them you don't make any promises, and then you're gone. You've been like that since you first discovered what your dick is for."

I grunted in half-hearted protest. Cynthia ignored me.

"Summer is not that kind of girl. Nothing wrong with taking your fun where you find it, but that's not her. I've known her for four years, and she doesn't sleep around. She doesn't do one-night stands. That's *all* you do. If somebody fucked this thing up, it's an easy bet it was you."

"Thanks a lot."

"I'm just being honest. You know I'm right."

I didn't say anything to that. She was right, and I was disgusted with myself.

"What are you going to do about it?" she asked, sipping her champagne. "Do you have feelings for her, or do you just want to nail her again?"

"It wasn't like that," I said, irritated at her words. I never *nailed* Summer. Even at the beginning, Summer was so much more than that.

"Then what is it? Don't tell me Evers Sinclair is in love."

"That's our business, not yours," I snapped back. If all she was going to do was make fun of me—

"You are," Cynthia said in quiet amazement. "You're in love with her. I never thought I'd see the day. You couldn't have picked a better girl. So, what's the problem? Did you finally find a woman you can't charm?"

I tossed back the rest of my whiskey to avoid scowling at Cynthia. It was generally a bad call to scowl at the client, but Cynthia didn't really count. We'd known each other too long, and this wasn't a business discussion.

"You might as well tell me," she said, sounding pleased with herself as she leaned against a table and drained the last of her champagne. "Unless you want me to ask her."

The threat was delivered in a sweet tone, but that didn't

make it any less of a threat. I sighed and poured myself another finger of whiskey, swirling the dark liquid in the cut crystal glass and taking a long sip before I answered.

"She was a job, okay? We discovered her when Axel met Emma. Found out she was related to the Winters. Her dad has issues, and we wanted to keep an eye on her. It seemed like too much of a coincidence, her turning up in Atlanta."

"You thought she'd knock on the door to Winters House with her hand out," Cynthia said quietly. "But she didn't, did she?"

"No, she didn't. It all went on longer than it was supposed to. Their lives got hectic and her father—" I cut off and shook my head. The Winters' problems, Summer's father, my father—none of it was Cynthia's business.

"Long story short, he's trouble, and until things calmed down for the Winters we thought it was best to keep them apart. I kept an eye on her."

"Oh, I get it. You kept an eye on her up close and personal."

I looked away. When she put it like that it sounded sordid. Ugly.

"It was like that, but it wasn't. The first time we—"

"Yeeees?" she asked, drawing out the word, prompting for more.

"The first time we were together it wasn't about work or the Winters. That was Summer and me at a wedding, a few too many drinks, and I just..." I floundered for words. "She's Summer. I lost my head."

Cynthia let out a wistful sigh. "I remember those days. Your head tells you to hold back and the rest of you dives right in. I bet she scared the hell out of you, didn't she?"

I was getting really fucking sick of people implying that

I was a coward. Just because I didn't do relationships didn't mean I was scared. I wasn't afraid. I was discerning.

Yeah, right. Whatever I had to tell myself.

"I saw her on and off for a year," I said, changing the subject from my cowardice, "and then she found out that she was a case, that we were keeping tabs on her and her father—"

"And she threw your lying ass out."

"Pretty much."

"So, what's your plan? You don't seem to be having any luck winning her back. She tenses up every time you walk in the room."

"I'm working on it," I said. "She doesn't trust me, and I don't know how to change her mind."

"You could start by telling her about us."

"There's nothing to tell," I protested. There wasn't. Cynthia and I never had more than a fling, and that fling was over a decade old.

"Trust me, Evers, it matters." Ready for my protest, she went on, "Not because there's something going on now, but because there was, and if she figures out you didn't tell her? You just look like a liar again."

"How am I supposed to tell her? Just blurt it out?"

I set the crystal glass on the wet bar, not interested in more whiskey. I didn't need a drink. I needed to figure out how to fix things with Summer.

"I don't know," Cynthia said, clearly amused at my dilemma. "That's for you to figure out. I'm just giving you some friendly advice."

The tap of heels sounded in the hallway, the gait slow with a slight hitch. Summer.

I was so occupied trying to figure out what I was going to say to Summer about Cynthia—what she might believe and what wouldn't dig me into a deeper hole—that I didn't notice Cynthia sidle up beside me.

I didn't catch the way she turned to face me, positioning herself so that whoever walked through the door would get a clear view of the two of us.

The door opened just as Cynthia rose up on her toes, threw her arms around my neck, and planted a hot, wet kiss right on my mouth.

Chapter Sixteen

EVERS

S ummer stepped into the room and came up short, letting out a breathy *Oh* of surprise. I clamped my hands around Cynthia's waist and pushed, trying to disentangle myself from her embrace.

She was like an octopus, her lean arms sticky tentacles that grabbed on and wouldn't be dislodged. I tore my head back from hers and caught a glimpse of Summer's red face, the flash of anguish in her eyes.

Her words barely more than a whisper, she said, "Excuse me," and dashed from the room.

"Cynthia," I growled, trying to pry her off of me, "what the fuck are you doing?"

Cynthia released me, tossing her hair over her shoulder with a grin and a wink.

What the fuck?

She gestured to the door of the library through which Summer had so recently fled.

"'There you go, champ. Now you have to explain. Maybe if you beg and tell her the truth about how you feel, you might have a chance in hell of winning her back. *Might.* But you'd better hurry."

"Thanks a lot," I grumbled, leaving the bar at a dead run, following the click of Summer's heels on the hardwood floor. I caught up with her outside the door to the library.

Grabbing her arm, I yanked her inside and shut the door behind us, turning the lock.

"It's not what you think," I said immediately, the cliché tumbling from my lips.

Summer straightened, wrapping her arms around her chest, refusing to look at me. "It's not my business. I didn't realize—but it's not my business."

"It is your business. And it isn't what it looked like."

Summer lifted her head, spearing me with a hot blue gaze, tears swimming in her eyes.

"It looks like you and Cynthia were kissing. You're both adults. It doesn't have anything to do with me—"

"It has everything to do with you," I burst out. "The whole thing was about you."

"I don't understand." Her voice cracked, tears spilling over her cheeks. She dropped her head to hide her face and pushed past me, intent on the door.

I was screwing up again. I was done making excuses. I needed to come clean. To tell her everything.

Everything.

Including the stuff I didn't want to admit, even to myself.

I stepped in her way, sliding to the side when she would have moved around me. "Just hear me out. Please."

Summer shook her head *no*, but she didn't move. I had to start talking, fast, before she took off on me again.

"Cynthia and I had a thing. A long time ago. Before she was famous. Back when she still lived in Atlanta. She wasn't my girlfriend. It wasn't serious. We hooked up once or twice when she came back, but not in years. It ended way before you went to work for her. There's nothing going on with Cynthia."

"Then why were you kissing her?" Summer studied the carpet between her feet, refusing to look at me.

"I wasn't kissing her. She was kissing me."

Summer let out a breath. "She said she was interested."

"She made it clear," I agreed. "And when I turned her down, she figured out that there's no way I would hook up with her when the only woman I want is you."

I waited for Summer to say something. Anything. She lifted her gaze from the carpet and stared me, eyes wide and watery, mouth closed. Waiting.

Shit. Of course, telling her I wanted her wouldn't be enough.

To me, wanting Summer meant everything.

I didn't just want to sleep with her. I wanted *her*. Wanted to talk to her and laugh with her. I wanted to fall asleep with her and wake up with her.

To me, *I want you* covered all of that.

From the hesitant look in her eyes, the confusion clouding her gaze, I knew it didn't mean the same thing to her. She needed more.

I tried again. "Summer, I screwed everything up with you. We started, and it was just about sex. I let you think it was always about sex. It was easier."

I stopped, scrambling, searching for the words. Everything going through my head sounded pathetic.

Summer shifted her weight from one foot to the other, dropping her hands to her sides as she realized I was at a loss.

I was failing her.

She was about to give up.

She lifted her hands and wiped away the moisture from beneath her eyes, sucking in a restorative breath. "It's okay, Evers. It's over. You don't have to explain. You don't owe me anything."

"That's bullshit. I have to explain because I've never told you the truth. I started out lying to you, and I kept lying. I don't want to lie anymore."

"Then tell me," she said quietly. "For once, tell me the truth."

I stared down at her, the words stuck in my throat.

I love you.

I want you.

I'm sorry.

Forgive me.

No sound came out. Finally done with my bumbling, Summer pushed past me and stalked toward the door, her wobbly ankle slowing her down.

"Wait," I shouted. "Wait."

"I'm done waiting, Evers."

"I love you," I burst out. "I'm in love with you and I'm scared to death. That's the truth. That's what I didn't want to tell you."

Summer turned to face me, her eyes wide with disbelief. "You do not love me," she said.

"I do. I do love you. I love you more than I ever thought I could love anyone. I knew that first night at the wedding. With you, everything was different, and I had no fucking clue what to do about it."

"At the wedding? Axel and Emma's wedding? After the wedding, you disappeared, and I didn't see you again for a year," she said.

"I know. And I spent that year trying to convince myself

that I was wrong. Deluded. That you weren't different. That I'd had too much to drink and was overcome by the wedding and all that shit. Then your file hit my desk and I was so fucking relieved, Summer. Relieved to have an excuse to see you again. I walked into that party and—"

I stared at her face, remembering that feeling in my chest the first time I saw Summer after a year apart.

Sheer, undiluted joy.

How could I have convinced myself it was only sex? Just being in the same room with her again had set my entire world to rights.

I was a fucking moron.

I tried to explain. "I walked in, and there you were. *A shot to the heart.* I never knew what that meant until I saw you again. The whole year apart I was bullshitting myself. Then you were there, and I knew."

Summer lifted her hands helplessly and dropped them to her sides. "Evers, I don't get it. If you knew you felt this way, why didn't you—I don't know—ask me out to dinner? Spend the night? Invite me to your place? Why didn't we date like normal people? Instead, you snuck in and out of my place like I was your dirty little secret, and I let you because—"

She fell silent abruptly. I wanted to chase down what she'd been about to say. Why? Why had she let me? Cynthia was spot on, Summer was not the kind of girl who let a man bounce in and out of her bed.

It wasn't time to pin her down. Not until I was done baring my soul.

"I don't know how to explain it," I said honestly. "It's just that I was always the one my dad said was like him. A ladies' man. A player. I loved my dad, but he could be a bastard. And he was a shitty husband. He cheated on my mom all the time. He'd say right in front of her that marriage was a trap. Love was a lie. That the only thing to do was fuck and run."

"He sounds like a real prize," Summer said.

I let out a wry laugh. "Yeah, that's my dad. I have no idea why my mom stayed. She deserved so much better. I think, in the beginning, she loved him, and she thought if she could stick with him, eventually, he'd settle down. I watched her fade away, start drinking earlier and earlier. She fell apart day by day. Year by year."

"Evers, none of that is your fault," Summer said, still looking a little confused.

"I know it's not my fault," I said, "but I wasn't going to do that to a woman I cared about. Promise her forever and then fuck her over. I wouldn't. My father meant to be faithful when he married my mom. He intended to be a good husband. He just... it wasn't in him. And I always thought, what if that were me? What if I made promises to a good woman and then I realized I couldn't keep them? I didn't want to be that man."

"So you didn't make promises to anyone," Summer said.

"No. I didn't. And for a long time, that worked. Until you. I met you and I wanted to make promises. I wanted something that would last. Something real. I was terrified I'd fuck it up. Turn you into my mom. I couldn't stand the thought of seeing the light in your eyes fade. I couldn't do it.

"I tried to keep things light. To put you in a box and keep you there, where there wasn't room for promises of love and forever. Where it was just moments of time together. I thought that could be enough."

I ran out of words.

Summer folded her arms across her chest again, but this

time she stood straighter, her chin lifted, her eyes level on mine.

"Okay, so if that's all true, tell me, honestly, how many other women did you sleep with the year that we were, you know—"

"None," I said immediately.

She raised an eyebrow. "Evers, we never made any promises to each other. Just tell me the truth. I know it's not any of my business, but I want you to tell me."

"None," I insisted. "I haven't so much as kissed another woman, touched another woman since I saw you at that party over a year ago." I thought about Cynthia in the bar. "Okay, correction, I guess I kissed Cynthia ten minutes ago. But that's it."

An unsettling thought occurred to me. I found myself asking, "Did you? If you did, it's not my business, but—"

"No. No one else. Not since a while before that party, if you want to know the truth."

She sounded a little embarrassed, but all I felt was relief.

"You went that whole year only seeing me every few weeks and you never went looking for another woman?" Summer asked, slowly.

"No, I'm telling you—"

"I believe you, Evers. But think about what you're saying. You're worried you're going to cheat. You're worried you'll be your father, but we weren't even together, and you were faithful. Don't tell me you didn't have the opportunity. Opportunity practically jumps in your lap."

I wasn't going to deny that. I'd had plenty of opportunities to be with other women.

Summer was right. I'd never thought of it that way. I

hadn't made her promises. She hadn't been my girlfriend, and still, I stayed true to her.

Because she was it for me. I didn't want anyone else. I never would.

Her eyes on my face, she waited, watching as I processed this revelation.

"So, Evers, the real question is, what do you want to do now?"

"I think that's really up to you," I hedged, my insides unsteady as if my entire world had shifted on its axis.

"I want to know what you want," she said, her chin set, eyes impossible to read.

She wasn't going to make this easy for me. I was very aware that she'd accepted my declaration of love but hadn't returned it.

Time to put my cards on the table and see how the hand played out. I closed my eyes for a second and let myself fall into fantasy.

What did I want? Really, truly, in the deepest part of my heart, what did I want?

Images unfolded in my mind, and suddenly, it was so very easy.

Opening my eyes, I looked down at Summer and stepped closer, reaching out to take her hand.

"I want you to be mine," I said. "Not here and there. Not for secret moments of time. For always. I want to wake up with you in the morning and go to bed with you at night. I want to argue with you and laugh with you. Cook dinner with you and dance with you. I want everything. And I want it with you."

If I expected her to soften, to fall in my arms, her tears turning into tears of joy as she swore her eternal love for me... If I'd expected that, I would have been sorely disap-pointed.

She studied me before she said, "What about marriage? Kids? Is that part of what you want?"

I'd always thought it wasn't. The example my parents set hadn't left me overwhelmed by the joys of married life. Still, I didn't have to think. I already knew my answer.

"Eventually, with you? Yes. Definitely marriage. I've always liked the idea of kids. Someday." Something occurred to me and I asked quickly, "Do you want kids?"

"I do. Someday. With the right man."

"And what about me? Is there any chance that could be me?" I couldn't remember the last time I'd been this nervous.

Summer wasn't mean-spirited. I didn't think she'd set me up to crush my heart under her heel. I'd hurt her, but Summer wasn't the kind of person who needed revenge. I hoped.

"I think you'd be a great dad," she said. Still not a decla-ration of love, but it was something.

"I know I'd give it everything I have," I said, tugging her closer. "But that's not really the question, is it? The real question is do you think I could be a great husband?"

"Are you proposing?" Summer asked, and for the first time since this conversation began her eyes were bright with a twinkle of mischief. From any other woman, at any other time, that question would have sent me racing for the door, a cloud of dust in my wake.

Not with this woman. Not now.

"No," I said, pulling her into my arms and lowering my head to rest my lips against her ear. "Not this time. Not right now. When I ask, you'll know it's a proposal."

Summer turned her head so my lips pressed her cheek,

her arms wrapping my neck, her body melting into mine. "So, you're going to ask?"

"Eventually. Are you going to say yes?" My lips brushed her chin, the lemon and flowers scent of her hair like coming home.

A laugh bubbling in her throat, she said, "Maybe. I have to think about it."

I dropped my lips to that spot just below her jaw that always made her shiver and sucked the tender skin there. "You're evil, you know that?"

"You deserve it," she breathed as I took another bite.

I did deserve it. And I didn't care. I could take whatever Summer dished out. I'd take it happily if it meant she was mine.

"I love you," I murmured into her neck. "I love you, and I'm not going to fuck this up again."

Summer leaned back and looked me straight in the eyes. "No, you're not. Neither of us will."

It was as close to a declaration as she was going to get. I'd take it. Glad I'd locked the door, I kissed her.

Chapter Seventeen

EVERS

I kissed Summer with everything pent up inside me. Love and lust and adoration. I kissed her for the months we'd spent apart, for everything I hadn't given her. Everything I'd denied myself.

My mouth claimed hers, and she claimed me back, kissing me with a hunger I'd missed more than anything. I couldn't get enough. It had been too long, too much time apart, exquisitely aware that she hated me. Afraid I'd never touch her again.

Now she was here, in my arms, and I was lightheaded with relief. If I'd had any idea how good it would feel to tell Summer I loved her, I would have done it a long fucking time ago.

Finally, I wasn't hiding what I felt. Wasn't trying to protect myself. Now it was just Summer and me, and she knew everything.

She knew everything, and she was kissing me like she'd never let me go.

I slid my hands down her back to close over her ass,

lifting her into my arms. Her skirt hiked up, and she wrapped her arms and legs around me, holding on as I carried her to the wide, deep sofa across the room.

The rest of the world fell away. There was no Cynthia. No staff. No fathers. No intruders. No attempted break-ins. No angry husbands. There was just Summer and me.

"I missed you," Summer said into my mouth, her fingers busy on the buttons of my shirt. I slid my hand beneath her back, searching for the zipper of her dress, finally finding it on the side and pulling it all the way down to the swell of her hip.

I sat up enough to yank off my shirt. Summer shimmied out of the bodice of her dress, the bright pink linen fabric sliding down to reveal her breasts encased in lace of the same pink.

Fuck me.

I'd missed her breasts almost as much as I'd missed Summer herself. Full and round, her curves highlighted by the tan line left from her bathing suit, the hidden skin of her breasts a creamy white that turned abruptly to a deep tan, her nipples rosy and begging for my mouth.

She shoved the dress down over her hips, a matching pink lace thong coming into view one inch at a time.

I pushed off the couch and fumbled with my belt, shedding my clothes at warp speed. When I was naked, I grabbed the hem of her dress and pulled, stripping it down her long legs before tossing it on the floor next to my own things.

She was gorgeous. Perfect. I stretched out on top of her, her soft curves molding to my body. The roundness of her full breasts, the curve of her belly, the velvet-soft skin of her inner thigh brushing mine as she raised her legs and hooked them around my hips, my cock trapped between us, rubbing the lace of her thong.

Bliss.

Summer, mostly naked in my arms, the heat of her pussy pressed to my cock. So close. I wanted it to last forever, and I needed to be inside her. Right fucking now.

I didn't have a condom.

"Fuck."

Summer nuzzled my ear with her nose, nibbling the lobe before saying, "That's the idea."

"I don't have a condom," I said.

Summer pressed a line of kisses to my jaw, ending at my mouth. She sucked my lower lip between hers, pulling, nibbling before dropping her head back.

"When was the last time you were tested? I had a physical a few months ago, right before we—"

She didn't need to finish the sentence. Right before she'd caught me with her file in my bag and thrown me out of her place. Out of her life.

"I had one done right before you threw me out. I was going to show you the test, see if we could talk about ditching the condoms."

Summer's body shook with laughter.

"What? What's so fucking funny?"

"Do you have any idea what I would have done if you'd showed me that test? That's not something you do with a random hookup. That's girlfriend stuff. Relationship stuff."

"You weren't a random hookup," I growled into her hair. No matter what she thought, she'd never been a random hookup.

"I know that now," she said, still laughing. "I didn't know that then."

"You would have said no." She would have been right to

say no if she thought she was a random hookup, but the idea left me deflated.

"I would have been very confused."

"And what about now? Are you confused now?"

"No. I'm not. And I have an IUD."

She wasn't confused, and she had an IUD.

I was about to ask if that meant what I thought it meant when she reached between us and pulled her thong to the side, taking the length of my cock in her hand and guiding me exactly where she wanted me.

That was answer enough. Her knees pressed to my sides, feet hooked around my legs, she pulled me closer, the head of my cock sinking inside her heat one inch at a time.

Heaven. As I pushed inside, Summer's giggles fell away. This was no joke. This was coming home. I filled her to the hilt and stopped, wanting to stay exactly where I was forever. For always.

My mouth pressed to the side of her head, I whispered, "I missed you so much. So much."

It had been a long dry spell since Summer had kicked me out. My body wanted this first time to be hard and fast. Wanted to fuck her with everything I had until we both exploded, releasing all the built-up lust we'd been storing since we'd been apart.

She was bruised from the night before. We had time for rough and fast and hard later. There was something to be said for slow and long. I drew my hips back until the head of my cock slipped from her pussy.

She moaned in aggravation, her ocean-blue eyes flashing to mine with a glare. I moved my hips in a circle, the head of my cock rubbing her slick, swollen clit. Her legs tightened on my hips, her hips rocking, trying to draw me back inside.

"You want it?" I murmured, letting my lips slide against

the sensitive skin right below her jaw, loving the way she shivered against me.

I'd never appreciated this until Summer. I knew her body. Her pleasure. I knew how to tease her until she was wild. How to give her exactly what she wanted. After a life of one-night stands and meaningless hookups, ruling Summer's body made me feel like a king.

"You know I do," she said, squirming beneath me. "Stop teasing and fuck me already."

I sucked her skin and took a bite from her neck, loving the way she gasped out a laughing moan. I played my mouth over every spot I knew would leave her ticklish but drowning in lust.

We'd always laughed a lot during sex. Not just because I loved the way her pussy tightened on my cock when she laughed. One night, I'd pinned her beneath me and tickled her until her laughter alone had me on the edge of orgasm. So good. Amazing. But we'd always laughed because, with Summer, even sex was new. Fun. An adventure we dove into together. Fuck, I'd missed this.

"You're bruised. I don't want to hurt you," I admitted.

"I don't care about that. You're driving me nuts. Just fuck me already. I feel like I've been waiting forever."

So did I. I stopped sliding my cock against her clit and filled her. "Lift your knees. Open for me and I'll give you what you want."

Summer's fingers tightened on mine, her eyes hot. She was flexible and strong, and as her knees pulled back, her hips tilted up, and I sank deeper inside her.

"Now," she demanded. I wasn't going to tell her no. I began to move, fucking her in long, deep thrusts, her tight pussy sucking at my cock, trying to keep me inside.

In this position, her arms above her head, knees wide,

she could barely move. She didn't need to. I sped up, fucking her harder, eyes locked to hers, her pupils dilated, focus blurred, her breath coming in quick gasps.

Yes. This was my girl. Right where I wanted her.

Teetering on the edge of orgasm, her hot, slick cunt about to explode around my cock. I needed to feel it. Needed it more than air. More than life. I needed to give her this after so long.

Reaching down, I cupped her ass in my palm and tilted her hips just a little more, until the base of my cock ground into her clit. Her surprised gasp of pleasure was all I needed to hear.

"Evers," she breathed. "Oh, God, Evers."

She was about to fall, and I was right there with her. My fingers digging into her hips, I fucked her right over the edge until she screamed out my name, her hand dropping to wrap around my neck, her mouth seeking mine.

I fell into the kiss, swallowing her gasps, feeding her my own moans as the tight squeeze of her pussy pulled me into orgasm along with her.

I couldn't catch my breath. For someone who ran every day, my cardio should be better. Summer's body shuddered against me, and I realized she was laughing again, the clutch of her pussy as she giggled sending painful bolts of pleasure through my too-sensitive cock. I stayed where I was, not ready to leave the tight clasp of her body.

"Are you laughing?"

"I was so—oh, my God—so loud. If anyone was in the hall—"

Her cheeks were pink, flushed with sex and embarrassment and amusement, her eyes sparkling with light for the first time since I'd walked through the door of Rycroft Castle.

"If anyone was in the hall looking for us, they knew better than to interrupt."

"I forgot where we were," she admitted. "I forgot how good you are at that."

"No, you didn't," I said smugly.

"No, I didn't."

"I have a long dry spell to make up for," I said, groaning as she shifted against me. Another few minutes, and I'd be ready to go again, my body eager to make up for lost time.

"So do I. You owe me, oh, at least two months of orgasms before we're even."

"That's a lot of orgasms. I should get started on that right now."

I rocked my hips into hers, grinding into her clit. My cock had missed Summer as much as the rest of me. "Now that the edge is off, let's see if we can make this last a little longer."

Summer lifted her mouth to mine. I kissed her, my eyes sliding shut as I fell into my best-daydream-come-true. Wrapped in Summer, her arms around my neck, her mouth on mine, my cock buried in her heat.

I could stay right here for the rest of my life. I would have if my fucking phone hadn't started to ring. Cooper's tone. I ignored it. So did Summer. The ringing stopped, and I refocused on the task at hand.

Making Summer come again. And again. And again.

The phone started up again, ringing until it hit voice-mail. Then again. And again. *Fuck.*

"Aren't you going to answer that?" Summer gasped, her hands braced against the arm of the couch, back arched, breasts lifted, teasing my mouth. I licked one tight rosy peak.

"It's Cooper. And I don't give a fuck if the entire world is on fire. I'll call him back in a fucking minute."

"K," Summer breathed. My lips closed around her hard, pink nipple and sucked, teeth worrying her flesh, the added stimulation driving her hips to rock harder, faster. I wanted her on top of me, straddling me so I could pull her forward and fill my hands and mouth with those pretty breasts.

Later. Next time. The fucking phone was still ringing, but I wasn't answering it until Summer and I were done. Cooper could fucking wait.

I'd meant for this to last so much longer. Once hadn't been enough to take off the edge. Not even close. Summer twined her legs around my waist, so open, inviting me deep. I gave her everything I had. Reaching between us, I slid a finger along her slick pussy, feeling my cock fill her, the heat of her where we were joined.

This was the core of us fucking. Her body taking me deep inside. Summer giving herself to me. My thumb rubbed her clit, a little hard, a little rough, just the way she liked it when she was this close to coming.

Seconds later, she let out a keening wail, her body tightening on mine in rhythmic pulses. I spilled inside her again and knew nothing had ever been like this before. Not even with Summer. It wasn't just the lack of a condom, though that in itself was fucking amazing.

It was knowing she had my heart, that I'd given it to her completely. I hadn't held back, I wasn't hiding behind a lie. She knew everything, knew how I felt, knew what I wanted. She knew it all, and she took me into her body. Gave herself back to me.

I wanted to fall to the side and hold her. To stay here behind that locked door and let the rest of the world go to hell. Ruining my plan, the couch wasn't big enough, and the goddamn phone was still ringing.

Reading my mind, Summer said, "You'd better answer that."

Reluctantly, I moved off of her, reaching to the side table for a box of tissues. Fucking in the library was not the best plan when it came to the aftermath of sex without a condom.

I pulled on my clothes, turning around to give Summer a second of privacy, and finally answered the phone. "What is it? You could have left a fucking message."

My older brother's voice came through the phone, hard and clipped. "If I left a message, you might not have checked it until later. I need you now. We have a problem."

Chapter Eighteen

SUMMER

I'd never been to the Sinclair Security offices before. Never had a reason to. Evers had covered for me with Cynthia, telling her we both had to leave for a meeting while I ran to my room to clean up.

I have no idea what he said to her, but she told me to go with a knowing smile and a wink. I should have been embarrassed, but I was too happy.

Walking in to see Cynthia's mouth on Evers, her arms around his neck, had been worse than a stab to the heart. It had been agony.

Had I told myself I was over him?

I was a liar.

I was never going to get over Evers.

For the first time, it looked like I wouldn't have to.

He was in love with me?

He said he was in love with me.

In a million years I never saw that coming. Liked me, sure. Wanted to fuck me... that seemed pretty obvious. But love? Evers didn't do love.

I wanted to believe him.

I did believe him. Mostly.

I should have told him how I felt. I wanted to. I'd opened my mouth to say the words, but nothing came out.

Later. I'd think about it later. The problems swirling around us were bigger than what was happening between Evers and me.

Cooper hadn't just told Evers he needed him in the office, he'd insisted Evers bring me. I wasn't sure what that meant, but it couldn't be good.

It was only a short drive to the Sinclair Security offices in Buckhead, a four-story, sleekly-modern office building discreetly placed behind a mixed-use residential complex.

It had the benefit of an ideal location without sitting right on the street. The garage appeared locked up tight until Evers' car slowed at the gate. There must have been some kind of scanner that recognized us because the metal door slid smoothly up just long enough to admit his SUV.

Everything inside the building was stainless and black, splashes of red the only color. It was a little dark and forbidding for my taste, but if they were trying to give off the impression of indomitable strength, they'd nailed it.

Evers' palm print and voice called the elevator that carried us to the main offices. I followed him into the reception area to see a vibrant bouquet of red lilies on the front desk beside a petite dark-haired woman with fifties-style cat's eye reading glasses, a short bob and blunt cut bangs. A wide smile stretched across her mouth.

"Good to see you, Boss. You'd better get back to Cooper's office. I don't know what's up, but he's in a mood."

Her eyes landed on my hand in Evers', but she didn't say a word, only winked at me and waved us down the hall.

"Thanks, Alice. Summer, this is Alice. Alice, Summer."

Evers never stopped moving. I waved at Alice as I tried to keep up.

Evers pulled me down a wide hallway lined with black doors, all closed. At the end of the hall we turned right, then left, and ended up in an open conference room with a long, black lacquered table, shiny chrome and black leather chairs, and a wall of windows that looked out to the court-yard below.

Cooper Sinclair sat at the head of the table, his dark eyes heavy—annoyed when they rested on Evers but softer when they landed on me. Griffen was at his right. At his left was Axel, Evers' brother and my best friend Emma's husband. Axel rose from his seat and came around the table to pull me into a hug.

"Summer, it's good to see you. Emma isn't happy she couldn't make it out this time."

"Work?" I asked. The last time I'd talked to her she hadn't said that Axel was coming, much less why she wasn't joining him.

"Some. Mostly that I don't want her here until we figure out what's going on. Looks like that was a good call."

At my questioning look, he shook his head, then dropped his eyes to my fingers twined with Evers'. He looked back up to take in Evers' stance beside me, too close, too intimate, for a friend or coworker.

In a low voice, Axel said, "You okay?"

I wasn't quite sure what he was getting at. In some ways, I was very okay. In others, like the whole situation with my dad, not so much.

"Okay with..."

Axel spared a glance for his brother, standing beside me. Evers dropped my hand and wrapped his arm around me, pulling me into his side in a claiming gesture that was unmistakable.

Axel gave him a look I couldn't read and said, "With this goon here. Do I need to kill him? You're Emma's best friend, which makes you an honorary sister, and I'm bound by law to kill this asshole if he didn't fix things with you."

Evers grunted in the back of his throat, tightening his arm around my shoulder, and I laughed.

"He groveled appropriately," I said.

Exactly what happened wasn't Axel's business, but it was sweet of him to look out for me. Or maybe it just said something about how much he loved my best friend.

"That's good," Axel said. "He can be an idiot, but you could do a lot worse. You could probably do a lot better, too, but you could do worse."

I laughed again as Evers' left arm shot out, and he punched Axel in the shoulder hard enough to force his older brother back a few steps.

From across the room, Cooper bellowed, "For fuck's sake, no fighting in the office. Sit your asses down."

We were taking our seats when Alice popped her head into the room, shooting a concerned look at Cooper before she flashed a bright smile and asked, "Coffee? Tea?"

"I'd love coffee," Evers said.

"I would, too, if it's no trouble," I added.

"No trouble at all. Be right back. Axel, Knox, Griffen? The usual?" The three of them grunted, nodded, and gave a hand gesture respectively, affirming that they wanted whatever the usual was. Alice disappeared, leaving us alone.

"So, what happened?" Griffen said.

"You don't know?" Evers asked, "You've been here all morning."

"Cooper wouldn't say—"

"I wanted to wait until we were all together. The phones have been busy today. I got this message an hour ago, direct to my private line. I was in a client meeting, so it went to voicemail." Cooper picked up the phone in the middle of the table, hit a few buttons to access his voicemail and sat back as the message played.

"Cooper Sinclair. Your father has something of mine," a man's voice said in an accent I couldn't place. Something Eastern European, maybe. Whatever it was, it sounded exactly like the client I'd turned down a few weeks before.

A chill ran down my spine as he continued.

"Maxwell has been missing for three months. I will wait no longer. Find what your father stole or your mother will die. When I'm done with her, I'll come after each one of his sons until every Sinclair is dead. No one steals from a Tsepov. Return what Maxwell stole and you will live. If you do not, I will end your line."

The call cut off. Axel sat back in his chair, shaking his head. "Fucking Russians. So melodramatic. *I will end your line*," he said, imitating the caller. "Tsepov, Jr. is a pain in the ass. Too much ego, not enough brains. I almost wish Emma hadn't killed his uncle."

"This hit my email at the same time as the call." Cooper tossed a photograph down the middle of the table. It slid, floating on the air before it came to a stop dead center. I looked at it, but I didn't get it.

It showed the front of an apartment building that looked like it was near the beach. Just a building. Nothing else. I knew I was missing something because Evers, Knox, and Axel went still.

Griffen said, "That's your mom's condo, isn't it?"

Cooper affirmed, "It is. There are more, pictures from

179

inside. He's telling us that he knows where she is, and he can get inside her place."

Knox pushed his seat back from the table in a startling burst of motion. He said nothing but paced to the wall of windows and stared into the courtyard, one hand gripping the back of his neck, knuckles flexing until they were white.

Axel, his eyes locked on the picture, said, "I'll go down to Florida. Stay with Mom."

"What about Emma?" Cooper asked. "She'll want to know—"

"I don't want her in Florida if these guys are crawling around. I sure as hell don't want her here. I trust my guys in Vegas. She's got someone on her twenty-four seven. She's close to her family. She'll understand me looking out for my mom." Axel looked at me, one eyebrow raised, and I nodded.

"She will absolutely understand you looking after your mom."

"We don't have a timeline," Evers said. "He wants us to return whatever Dad stole from him or he'll kill us all, but he doesn't say how long we have or what it is we're looking for."

"Sloppy," Cooper commented. "We already had a clue Dad wasn't in his car when it went over the bridge. LeAnne Gates told Chase that Dad had been sending her checks until recently. Hard to sign a check when you're dead. The shell corporation making the payments has been filing its annual reports and taxes right on schedule. Someone's got to be coordinating all that. Dad makes more sense than anyone."

"I'm going to fucking wring his neck when we find him," Knox muttered, still staring into the courtyard.

"You'll have to get in line," Evers said quietly.

I reached out to take his hand. My dad wasn't that great a father. He was self-centered and neglectful, but at least he hadn't faked his death and left me and my mom in danger. Maxwell Sinclair had a lot to answer for.

Alice eased the door open and set a tray on the table. Correctly reading the room, she passed out drinks in silence and left as unobtrusively as she'd entered.

"We don't have a lot of leads to follow," Cooper said. "We've been looking for Dad since LeAnne Gates confirmed he might be alive. So far, I've got nothing. Dad was a lot of things, but stupid isn't one of them. He knew how to hide."

"The only halfway decent clue we have is Summer's father," Axel said

"My father? How is my father a clue?"

"Because we know he was getting money from our dad," Evers explained, "and we know those payments have continued. We also know that something happened recently to send your dad underground. Based on the timing, I'm betting it was our father taking off with whatever belonged to Tsepov."

"Fucking moron," Knox muttered. He shot a look at Cooper and said, "In most ways you're right. Dad was not dumb. But sometimes he had a dangerous blind spot. Women and money always fucked him up."

None of Knox's brothers argued.

"You think my dad knows where your dad is? Knows what he took and where to find it?"

"It's possible he doesn't," Cooper said, "but right now, Smokey Winters is all we have to go on. As far as I can tell, he was living near Asheville, moving between there and Greenville along I-85."

Everyone else in the room had a knowing expression

that told me the information meant more to them than just my dad's driving habits. I sent Evers a questioning look. He pinched the bridge of his nose before saying quietly, "Probably running drugs from Atlanta into the mountains."

"He was dealing drugs?" I asked, wishing I were more surprised.

"Maybe. If not dealing, transporting."

I felt a little sick. I knew my father came back to Atlanta fairly often—though I hadn't known he had a place here—but I'd never wondered why.

Maybe I should have. Something Cooper had said stuck in my head. They didn't know where he'd been. But I knew where he'd been, didn't I? And I'd completely forgotten.

Chapter Nineteen

SUMMER

"**O**h, my God," I said in a rush.

"Summer, what is it?" Evers asked, his eyes worried.

I looked up, stricken with guilt. "I am so sorry. I talked to my mom a few days ago, asked her if she'd seen my dad, and I forgot to tell you. I—"

I bit my lip, raising my hands to press my palms to my suddenly-hot cheeks. I could not admit to this roomful of men that I'd forgotten important information about my father because I'd walked in to see Evers wrapped around my movie-star boss.

How could I have been so stupid? How could I have let my emotions get in the way of something so important?

Lamely, I just repeated, "I forgot. I'm so sorry."

"Summer," Evers said gently, "what did you forget?"

"He was in Maine."

Cooper's head shot up, his eyes intent on me. "Maine? You're sure."

"My mom said about three weeks ago, he called her

from Maine. She recognized the area code. He told her he was coming to see me, but I haven't seen him in months."

"Do you know why he was there? Or how long?" Cooper probed.

I shook my head. "I only know he was there long enough to call my mom."

Cooper sat back in his chair and crossed his arms over his chest, seemingly lost in thought.

"Someone has to go to Maine," Griffen said.

Slowly, Cooper picked up the phone and tapped the buttons. "Interesting you should say that. I got another call this morning. Hit my voicemail just after four A.M."

He hit the button for speakerphone and a woman's voice filled the room. She sounded about my age. Scared. Voice high-pitched, her words came fast, tumbling over each other as she spoke.

"'This is Lily Spencer. I—my husband—my former husband—I'm a widow—uh, told me to call you if there was ever any trouble. I live—we live—I live up in Maine, and we've had some break-ins. Uh, I think. The police haven't found anything, but tonight someone got in. Turned off the alarm. I don't know what to do. I don't know if you can help, but he said if anything ever happened I should call you, so I'm calling. Please, if you could call me back I'd appreciate it. Again, this is Lily Spencer."

She rattled off a phone number, then her name again, and the number a second time before she said a quick goodbye and hung up.

Evers looked at Cooper. "Who the fuck is Lily Spencer?"

Cooper tossed a manila folder in the middle of the conference table. Evers reached over to flip it open, and a woman stared back at us. I'd been right, she was about my age.

Deep, brown, almond-shaped eyes in a face of tawny-gold skin. She wore her dark hair in a long, sleek bob that brushed her shoulders, a prim strand of pearls around her neck, diamond studs in her ears, and what looked like a cashmere twin set.

She stood beside a man about her age with white-blond hair in a dark suit. His arm was around her shoulders, his eyes relaxed and happy. Though she wore a polite smile, her eyes were strained. Worried. The picture had been printed from a newspaper article. The caption below read: *Trey and Lily Spencer at the Literacy Foundation Fundraiser.*

Knox left the window and resumed his seat at the table, reaching out to drag Lily Spencer's file in front of him. He picked up the picture and set it to the side before flipping through the contents of the folder.

"Lily Spencer, recently widowed," Cooper said. "Her husband, Trey Spencer, was tied up with dad in this adoption business. And more. One of the shell companies comes back to him, in part."

"How did he die?" Evers asked, his brow furrowed as he watched Knox scanning Lily Spencer's file, his hand over her husband's face, his fingers grazing her hair.

Something about the picture tugged at me. She looked... trapped.

I don't know why she struck me that way. Why that word jumped into my head. *Trapped.* There was tension in her eyes. Something about the set of her chin.

Cooper answered, "Funny thing, that. Car accident. Almost exactly like Dad's, except this time, they found the body."

"So we're sure Trey Spencer is really dead?" Griffen asked.

"Very sure. And it looks like his widow is in trouble."

"I'll go to Maine," Knox said in a low rumble, his eyes absorbing the file, his hand still on Lily Spencer's picture.

"Fine. Go over anything you need to hand off with Riley before you make arrangements. I'll call Lily Spencer back and tell her we're sending you up."

Cooper laid his hand on the table. He looked at Evers and me. "You two go track down Smokey. We need to find him before we run out of time."

"I can't," I said immediately.

Cooper narrowed his dark eyes on me, and the force of will in them had me halfway to agreeing to do whatever he wanted. It was clear that Cooper Sinclair was not used to refusal.

I kept my mouth shut. He wasn't going to glare me into compliance. I wasn't an employee.

I already had a boss, and she expected me at her side every day for the next few months, not bopping all over the place trying to find my errant father.

"I can't leave Cynthia. I have a job. I promised her I'd be at Rycroft."

"I'll stay with Cynthia," Griffen said as if that were the end of the subject.

"No, it's not the same. You can replace Evers, I guess, but I'm her assistant. You can't do my job. She needs me."

"She's going to have to do without you," Cooper said, obviously considering the subject closed.

"Cooper, I can't just quit my job with Cynthia." I turned to look at Griffen. "Why can't you go looking for my dad?"

"No. Griffen stays here," Cooper said.

This time his tone was so final I snapped my mouth shut, at a loss for what to say.

I was not going to be organized by Cooper Sinclair. I wanted to help, but I wasn't going to torpedo my career and let down my best client just because Cooper said so.

"I'll talk to Cynthia," Evers said. "It'll be okay. I promise."

I was almost willing to believe Evers could charm Cynthia into letting us leave for a few days. But I still didn't understand. "Why can't Griffen—"

"Griffen stays here," Evers said in the same final tone Cooper had used.

I glanced at Griffen, prepared to challenge him again until I saw his teeth grind together, his dark green eyes flat and cold.

Okay, Griffen was staying here.

Again, I was missing the subtext. I'd badger Evers into filling me in later.

"Evers, I need you to fix it with Cynthia. I don't want to run out on her. Partly because I don't want to screw up this job and partly because she's my friend and I won't let her down."

Evers tugged my chair closer to his. The wheels shifted until they aligned, then rolled me easily toward him until we were right next to each other. He hugged an arm around me and kissed my temple. "I promise, I'll handle it. Griffen can do this. I have to go, and I'm not leaving you behind."

"You won't leave me behind, but you'll leave Cynthia with Griffen?"

"I think we proved last night that whoever's been breaking in wasn't after Cynthia. They were after you."

"After my laptop," I corrected, "not that it will do them any good."

"You don't know that," Griffen cut in. "He would have

been a fool to try to take you with the house that crowded. Who knows what would have happened if he'd bumped into you on a late-night kitchen raid? No one else around, the house quiet. Maybe his plan was to take the laptop and phone and run. Or maybe he was going to grab them, hide out in the house somewhere, and come for you later. You should go with Evers. A moving target is harder to catch."

I stared at Griffen, at a complete loss for words. I thought about my father, here and there and everywhere. Atlanta, Maine, Asheville, and who knew where else.

A moving target was harder to catch.

At the idea that the intruder might have hidden in a closet and come out in the dark of night to find me while I slept... I shuddered.

Resigned, I gave Griffen my sternest look and said, "Keep Clive away from her until we get back. I know she said she was going to meet with him, but that does not happen while we're gone. Promise me. You don't know him. He's got a silver tongue, and she's still half in love with him. She's not seeing him without me there."

"I promise. I'll hold him off until you get back."

"And keep her out of trouble."

"Now that, I can't promise," Griffen said with a grin

"Try," I pressed. Griffen sat back in his chair, a laugh in his eyes, the dark look wiped away as if I'd imagined it. "I'll sacrifice myself to the cause if I have to."

"Poor Griffen, trapped in a castle with the closest thing to a princess we have around here. We all weep for you." Cooper said sarcastically.

Griffen laughed again and flicked a coffee stirrer across the table at his boss. Cooper fielded it before it smacked him in the forehead. Pushing back his chair, he said, "All right, let's get moving. Until this jackass gives me a timeline, we have to assume the hammer could come down at any minute. Axel, we'll get you down to Florida this afternoon. Knox, get ready to head to Maine. If Lily Spencer has any information we can use, we don't want whoever is after her to take her out before we get there. And Evers, Summer..." He trailed off, searching for the right words. "Good luck."

Good luck. We were going to need it.

Chapter Twenty

SUMMER

My overnight bag sat on the back seat of the car, stuffed with everything I thought I might need for a few days away. Since I had no clue what we were doing, I might have overpacked. I like to be prepared.

Beside my bag was another, holding a brand-new laptop and phone. Cooper had handed them to me before we'd left the Sinclair offices, saying, "It's our fault you need these. No one should have breached Rycroft. If you don't like them, let Evers know and we'll upgrade."

I'd checked on the drive back to Rycroft. The phone was the newest model and the laptop was a serious improvement on the one that had been stolen the night before.

"Evers, this is too much," I'd protested.

"Don't argue. Cooper was right. It was our fault your things were taken. Replacing them is the least we can do."

"Would you do this for another client?"

A quick, hot glance. "You're not a client, Summer. You're mine. Don't argue."

I was his.

I decided not to argue.

I have no idea what Evers said to Cynthia, but she waved us off, standing at the open front door, her arm looped through Griffen's, smiling widely. A few days before, she'd flipped out at the idea of Evers leaving long enough to take me to the stationery shop. Today, she was perfectly fine with both of us abandoning her.

"What did you say to her?"

"I told her you had a personal problem and we had to sort it out."

I gave him the side eye. There was no way it had been that simple. "What did you have to promise her? You're not sleeping with her. I hope she knows that."

Evers laughed, taking his eyes from the road just long enough to catch my gaze. "You know I'm not sleeping with her."

"I know, but what did you promise her? I know you had to promise something."

"A huge discount," Evers admitted.

"How huge?" I asked, suspiciously. Cynthia liked her luxury, but she was sharp about money.

"Let's just say we'll be taking a loss on the job. And I might have thrown Griffen in her path."

"Newsflash, she already noticed Griffen." Cynthia had an eye for attractive men, and she'd have to be blind to miss Griffen. I was crazy for Evers, and I could still appreciate Griffen's roguish grin and distinctive green eyes. Not to mention his body... Not that I'd looked. Much.

"She's not going to do anything about it, you know," Evers said. "Cynthia, I mean, and Griffen."

"No, she won't," I agreed. "She likes to flirt, but I don't

think she's been with anyone since Clint. I think she would have slept with you. I think having a history made her feel more comfortable."

"Wasn't going to happen," Evers said flatly.

He shot another glance in my direction. He was worried I didn't believe him. I reached out and slid my hand to his thigh, squeezing lightly.

"I know that, Evers."

"As long as we have that straight."

He rested his hand on top of mine, keeping it in place on his leg. I drew circles, figure eights, and little hearts with my fingertip, my knuckles brushing his cock through the fabric of his pants.

"Are you going to tease me the whole drive?"

"Maybe. Do you want me to stop?"

"Fuck, no." He took his eyes off the road and turned his heavy-lidded gaze to me. "I wish all of this wasn't going on," he said. "I wish I could take you somewhere, just the two of us, and forget about the rest of it."

"Later," I promised. "When this is over we'll take a vacation."

"Absolutely." He glanced down at my feet, encased in pink, scrappy wedge sandals. "How's your ankle? Should you be wearing those shoes? I don't want you to trip and make it worse."

I rotated my ankle in a slow circle. It was a little sore, and when I pointed my toe I felt a twinge, but otherwise, it was fine. "It's good. I swear. I felt awful last night, but I think I was more scared than anything."

"You have a bruise on your shoulder," he said, reaching out to run a finger lightly down my shoulder blade.

"It's not that bad."

"It shouldn't have happened. You should have been safe in the house."

I knew where he was going with this. "It wasn't your fault, Evers."

"Of course, it's my fault."

"You can't control everything. I'm fine. Let it go."

The growl in the back of his throat told me that he wasn't going to let it go, but he'd drop the subject. Taking my hand, he watched the road ahead and we let silence fill the SUV.

His thumb rubbed the back of my hand absently, sweetly. This was one of the things I'd always loved about being with Evers. We could talk all night if we wanted to, but the quiet was just as good.

I loved being with him. He filled the space around me with warmth and comfort. With a simmering hint of lust. Sitting beside Evers, I could relax and just be. Daydream about the night to come, anchored by the touch of his hand on mine.

I watched the green hills roll by and finally asked the question that had been bugging me since the meeting at Sinclair Security.

"Why couldn't Griffen make this trip? And don't tell me it's because I'm not safe at the house. The only way that guy got in was because of the party. I know you've got Rycroft Castle on lockdown. You'd never leave Cynthia unprotected, so I don't buy this bullshit about moving targets. What's the real reason?"

Evers sighed. "I'll tell you, but don't bring it up with Griffen. None of us talk about it."

Now I was intrigued. I liked Griffen. He'd saved Emma after Axel had landed her in an ugly situation, and I'd forever be grateful to him for that. Even if he hadn't saved my best friend's life, he was a good guy.

Cooper and Evers had shut down any mention of Griffen making this trip to North Carolina. There was a story there.

"I swear," I promised. "I can keep my mouth shut, but now I'm curious."

"Okay. He told us some of this, some we dug up ourselves. Griffen is from a town outside of Asheville. Sawyers Bend."

"Sawyers Bend as in Griffen Sawyer?" I asked.

"Exactly. Griffen is the oldest of seven. Or maybe it's eight."

I winced. Eight kids? "His poor Mom," I murmured.

"Griffen's mother only had two. His Dad went through wives like most men go through shoes. From the little Griffen let slip and everything we dug up, his father is a real bastard. Playing the kids against each other, writing them in and out of his will depending on who kissed his ass the best. A real piece of work. Griffen's family owns half the town, not to mention real estate all over North Carolina. A logging company. One of the last successful textile manu-facturers and a thriving furniture and design company. The father keeps all of it under his thumb."

"If he's the heir to all of that, what's Griffen doing working for Sinclair Security?"

"We're not exactly sure," Evers said with a laugh. "He's a little older than me. We met in the Army. Rangers. The best I've been able to put together, he was living his life, doing the Sawyer thing, running the family businesses and dancing to his father's tune, and then he just walked away."

"What happened?"

"No clue. He left, and he's never been back. From what we could find out, the father disinherited him completely, tossed him out and told him never to set foot in Sawyers Bend again. I got the feeling Griffen rode out on a giant *fuck you*. He doesn't go anywhere near Sawyers Bend or Western North Carolina. Too close to home. We have an understanding. Work that runs in that direction, we give to someone else. He doesn't want to deal with his family. I'm not going to be the one to make him."

"I'm not sure you could make Griffen do anything," I said quietly. Griffen did easy-going charm as well as Evers, but I'd seen that flat, cold look in his eyes. Like Evers, there was a lot more to him than a handsome smile.

"He wasn't going to touch this one. Your dad's place isn't in Asheville. It's outside the city, not that far from Sawyers Bend. We tracked his credit card receipts—"

"How did you get his credit card receipts?" I asked. Wouldn't they need a court order? They weren't the police.

Evers didn't answer.

"You're not going to tell me?"

Evers cleared his throat. "It's not important how we got them. Your dad deals mostly in cash, but when he runs short, he'll pull out the card. There are a few places in Asheville we should check, charges show up often enough that we might be able to find somebody who's seen him. He doesn't spend a lot of time in Sawyers Bend. Too many tourists, not enough places to find trouble, but Griffen wouldn't have wanted to run the risk of dealing with a case at his family's back door."

"Now I kinda want to see this town." I murmured.

"Maybe you will. We'll see how it goes."

It was after dinner time when we rolled into Asheville, the city busy with tourists eager to try one of the many craft breweries or unique restaurants.

We flashed through downtown on the expressway before driving through Beaucatcher Tunnel and ending up on a crowded street lined with chain restaurants and hotels. If not for the backdrop of the Blue Ridge Mountains, we could have been anywhere in America.

Slowing, Evers pulled into a run-down little strip mall in between a big chain steakhouse and a hotel. The strip mall had a pawnshop, a video game store, a nail salon, and a bar creatively named *The Bar*. The windows were papered over from the inside, and the light above the door was broken.

Evers gave the place a long look. "Maybe we should get a hotel. You can stay in the room. I'll make some stops, see if I can find your dad. We'll go out to dinner first."

"No way in hell. You're not dumping me in some hotel. We're here to find my dad. One look at you and he'll take off running. If he sees me, there's a good chance he'll talk to us. If for nothing else, to try to score some cash."

Evers shook his head "For someone who was getting pretty big payments for his services, your dad seems like he was constantly broke."

My laugh was tired. "That's my dad. Put a dollar in his hand and it's gone a second later. If it hadn't been for my mom, I don't know that I would have had food on the table when I was growing up. He lost money just as easily as he made it."

I scanned Evers in his perfectly-tailored dark suit and crisp white shirt. He was bone meltingly hot, but exactly the kind of man my Dad would run from. Evers radiated command. Control. One look at him and my dad would be gone.

"He's not going to talk to you if he can help it. You'll need me to draw him out."

"All right, fine. You can come in this time."

"Works for me." I unsnapped my seatbelt and opened the door to Evers' SUV before he could change his mind. I was still wearing my hot pink linen sheath dress with matching sandals and clutch, and a filmy, patterned scarf. I had no idea what was behind those papered-over windows, but I was sure it was not the kind of place that called for hot pink sheath dresses and cute matching sandals.

Evers slid his arm around my waist and took the lead, guiding me across the small parking lot to the door. He shook his head as he pulled it open as if asking himself what the hell he was thinking.

The inside of the bar looked as if it had once been a fifties-style diner with naugahyde booths and a long counter. But where in the past there might have been a griddle and cooks working, now there was a bar, the shelves makeshift and rickety.

Conversation ground to a halt as the patrons caught sight of us. I'd been right. Hot pink sheath dresses with cute matching sandals were not the normal attire at The Bar. Neither was Evers' dark suit.

We stuck out like the proverbial thumb, and a flutter of nerves tickled my belly. Most of the patrons were male and a little scary. I hadn't had a lot of run-ins with bikers, but these guys were what I imagined bikers looked like. Grizzled and unshaven, in worn leather jackets, with yellowed teeth and growly voices.

Not sexy growly like Evers' voice could be, but too many cigarettes and cheap alcohol growly. I almost regretted not letting Evers stash me in a hotel. Asheville was a tourist town and an upscale one at that. I'd never visited before, but I knew there were some seriously lush resorts here.

What was I doing in this sketchy, scary little bar when I could be getting a massage and room service?

Oh, yeah, looking for my father. This was exactly the kind of place Smokey Winters would hang out. Squaring my shoulders, I leaned into Evers and nudged him further inside.

We were here. We might as well get this over with.

Chapter Twenty-One

SUMMER

Evers wasn't as creeped out by the bar as I was, but I could tell he was uneasy that I was there. He kept his arm around my waist, guiding me through the dim, smoky room.

I was pretty sure it was illegal to smoke indoors in North Carolina, but no one at The Bar seemed to have gotten the memo. They didn't look too concerned that they were breaking the law, either.

Why did I have a feeling being law-abiding wasn't a big concern for this crowd? We squeezed into a spot at the bar, and Evers pulled out a bill, flashing it at the bartender before setting it down and covering it with his hand.

I didn't see the denomination, but the bartender must have, because he hustled over, his speed belying the suspicious, aggravated look he shot in our direction.

When he was close enough, Evers moved his hand back, and I caught a hundred on the corner of the bill. I doubted there were any drinks served in this place that would add up to a hundred bucks.

Abruptly, I realized Evers wasn't ordering a drink, he was ordering information. One hundred dollars was probably the starting price. Crap. My dad was a money pit even when he wasn't around.

Mentally, I adjusted my budget to reimburse Evers for what he was spending to find my dad. On top of the discount I'd have to offer Cynthia for my time off, my dad was digging into my reserves.

"You two lost? Downtown's up the hill and through the tunnel."

"We're looking for someone—"

"Don't know no one," the bartender shot back before Evers could finish, his small, dark eyes belligerent yet greedy as they tracked the corner of the bill beneath Evers' hand.

"You sure?" Evers asked, easily.

The bartender's eyes lingered on the bill, his longing clear, almost poignant before he straightened and looked away. "Don't know no one. You want to stay, order a drink."

Evers started to reach into his pocket, probably for more money. My expenses racking up in my head, I leaned forward and caught the bartender's eye.

His expression as he looked at me was only marginally softer than the one he'd given Evers. I set my hand on top of Evers', keeping the hundred dollar bill on the bar.

"Hey, we don't mean to bug you. I'm just looking for my dad. Smokey? We have some family stuff going on and he's not returning my calls. I'm worried and I need to find him. Can you at least tell us if you've seen him?"

The bartender studied me. After a long moment, he said, "You Smokey's girl?"

"The one and only," I confirmed. Following instinct, I

held out my hand, gave him my best smile and said "Summer. Summer Winters. You know my dad?"

Reluctant and surprised, the bartender shook my hand, then shot a suspicious look at Evers. "If you're Smokey's girl, who's this guy?"

"He's my boyfriend. He didn't want me to go looking for dad by myself..."

I trailed off, and my instinct had been right. The bartender's suspicion didn't disappear, but it now included a nod of approval in Evers' direction.

He muttered, half to himself, "Good thinking." Looking at me, "Girl, you don't want to go wandering the places your dad gets to. You should go home and wait for him to call."

"I would," I agreed, "but when Smokey's having a good time, who knows how long it'll be before he checks in? You know how it is. I really need to talk to him now."

The bartender looked at the bill under Evers' hand again, the gears turning slowly in his head. "Smokey's got a tab. I'll tell you where you might find him if you pay it off."

I sighed. Of course, he had a tab, and of course, we were going to get stuck paying it. I started to step away from Evers to open my clutch for my credit card.

His arm tightened, holding me still, and he murmured, "Don't even think about it."

"How much?" he demanded of the bartender.

"Five hundred."

The number was bullshit. No bar tab was an even number, plus I doubted this place let its patrons run up a tab that big. How had my dad run up a five hundred dollar tab drinking cheap whiskey? I didn't want to know.

My dad wasn't against alcohol, per se. He liked to drink, and he loved his beer, but drugs had always been his chemical of choice. I could easily see him having a huge tab with his dealer, but not in a crappy bar like this.

"Cash."

Of course, he wanted cash. My new car fund was going to take a hit. This kind of thing was why I understood when my mom divorced my dad. She worked hard, was smart with money, and then he'd pull crap like this and end up frittering away everything she'd worked for.

Evers was more prepared for this whole scene than I was. He didn't even pull out his wallet, reaching into his pocket and producing a money clip from which he peeled off exactly four one-hundred dollar bills to go with the bill already on the bar.

The bartender made a grab for the money, fingers outstretched. Evers slid the cash out of reach.

"When was the last time you saw Smokey?"

"Couple of days. He came in with a friend. Warren."

I knew Warren. I couldn't remember his last name, but he and my dad had been friends for years. I hadn't seen him in a while, and I couldn't remember where he lived, but I could find out.

"That's it? Last time you saw him was a couple of days ago with his friend Warren?"

"That's it. Now give me my money."

"Last name for Warren?"

"Don't got no last name. Always pays cash. That's all I got for you."

"Do you know where else my dad hangs out?"

For the first time, the bartender shifted uncomfortably, eyeing my pink dress and pretty scarf. Almost hesitant, he said, "I do, girl, but let your man here take care of it. Your daddy, he don't pick the best company for a pretty thing like you."

"He's my dad," I said quietly.

The bartender shook his head in sympathy. Sharing a look with Evers that was almost commiserating, he said, "Smokey likes The King's Club. You're not going to want to bring her there."

I had no idea what The King's Club was, but Evers nodded in response. He was going to try to shut me out. I wasn't going to let him.

Evers wouldn't let anything happen to me, and being Smokey's daughter gave us an edge. I looked enough like him that the bartender had dropped his guard to talk to us. Without that, Evers would have had to fork over more cash before we even got to the offer of information.

Leaving me behind might suit Evers' protective impulses, but it would only drag out the search for my dad. We needed to find Smokey and get back to Atlanta. We didn't have time for Evers' caveman tendencies or for me to wimp out and hide in a plush hotel room.

The bartender made another grab for the money. Evers held it out of reach. He pulled a card from his pocket, slipped it between the bills and handed them to the bartender, who snatched the money from his fingers and shoved it in his pocket.

"You see him, you get any information about where he might be, there's more of that in it for you." Evers nodded in the direction of the bartender's pocket, now stuffed with cash.

The bartender gripped the cash in his pocket, shrugged a shoulder. "Sure. I hear anything, I'll let you know."

He wouldn't, and we all knew it.

I climbed into the passenger seat of the SUV and waited while Evers pulled up an address on his phone.

The King's Club.

"You already had the name?" I asked.

Evers started the car and pulled out of the parking space. "It was on his card, but good to know he's been around in the last few days."

The SUV idled, blinker on, but Evers made no effort to turn onto the road. Catching my eye, he said, "Is there any way I can talk you into sitting this one out? There are a lot of places I'd like to bring you. The King's Club is not one of them."

Warning me away wasn't making me any less interested. "Evers, I don't really want to go all over town chasing down my dad in his regular hangouts. I want this over with, and so do you. Let's just do it."

"I could get a room in a hotel," he offered, "order dinner, we could relax, then I'll head out later."

He really didn't want me to go to The King's Club. That only made me more determined. I wouldn't be able to relax and enjoy dinner if I knew he'd leave me tucked into bed and go out searching for my dad.

"I'm coming with you."

"Fine. But I'm kicking your dad's ass when we find him."

"I'm not sure I'll try to stop you."

The King's Club wasn't far from The Bar. We headed another mile away from downtown and turned down a road that ran along the river, dotted with small businesses and warehouses, all of them run down.

Evers slowed as we approached what looked like a purple double wide trailer with a spotlighted sign out front. The paint was chipped and faded, but the illustration of a crown and the words 'The King's Club' identified our destination.

The parking lot didn't have many cars. It was early on Saturday night, and whoever liked to hang out at The

King's Club, they weren't here yet. A few older compacts and a hatchback were parked in the back of the building, along with a jacked-up pickup with huge tires, and a red motorcycle.

Evers pulled into a spot and put the SUV in park. From this angle, I could see that the building wasn't a double wide but two or three boxy trailers connected, the purple paint doing a half decent job of camouflaging the seams. The whole place looked like it would fall down in a stiff wind.

"This is a bad idea," Evers said.

Probably. We were going in anyway. If Evers really thought it was dangerous there was no way we'd be here. He just didn't want me to see what was inside that rickety purple monstrosity.

Perversely, that only made me want to see it more.

"We're here now. Might as well go in and see if we can find my dad."

Not waiting for Evers to try to talk me out of it again, I grabbed my pink clutch and hopped out of the SUV.

He let out a heavy sigh as he joined me, holding out his arm. I took it, smiling up at him brightly.

"So, what is this place?"

Evers shook his head in resignation. "It's a strip club. And based on your father's usual haunts, not a good one."

"There are good ones?" I asked. I was no stranger to bars, but I preferred the wine and martini end of the spectrum. Strip clubs were not in my realm of experience.

Evers shot me an unexpectedly wicked grin. "Oh, yeah, there are good ones. We'll visit Axel in Vegas and I'll show you what a good strip club is like. Places like this are just—"

"Just what?"

"You'll see," was all he would say as he led me to the entrance.

Chapter Twenty-Two

SUMMER

A mountain of a man perched on a stool at the door, his eyes half closed, headphones on, his bulk almost hiding the stool. As we approached, his eyes popped open and he said in a lazy, sleepy drawl, "'Twenty-dollar cover, two drink minimum."

Evers handed over forty dollars, and the big man swung the door open. It was just bright enough outside that, at first, the inside of the club looked like a black hole.

The smells hit me as the door swung shut behind us, cutting off the light. Cigarettes and mildew. Sour alcohol and sweat. I'd never put a lot of thought into strip clubs, only enough to know that guys seemed to like the idea of watching women dance naked.

Naked was sexy, right? I hadn't even seen this place, and just from the smell, I could tell you it was not sexy.

The stage came into focus first. Ten feet wide and three times that in length, it was curved at the end, with two shiny gold poles and seats lined up all the way around. Spotlights were trained on the length of the stage where only one girl danced.

The music was old, a nineties hit I vaguely remembered. The dancer was still mostly dressed. If you could call a red thong and matching bra dressed. I guessed in a strip club that counted.

Her eyes closed, she swayed to the music, twisting her hips in the direction of the few men circled around the end of the stage. One reached up to tuck a bill in her thong and grab a handful of her ass.

I would have jumped and smacked him. She registered the bill but not the grab.

Other girls walked the floor in tiny skirts that didn't quite cover their rear ends and cheap fluorescent push-up bras that showed the top curve of their nipples. Evers led me to a table not far from the stage and gestured for a waitress.

The girl who came to the table barely looked old enough to drive, much less serve alcohol in a strip club. She wore her bright red hair in two ponytails with fluffy bangs, heavy mascara, and bright pink lipstick. I snuck a peek at her clear plastic platform slides. If I'd tried to wear those shoes I would have fallen flat on my face.

I expected the same lazy, half-asleep attitude as the bouncer and the stripper on stage, but she flashed us a bright smile.

"Hey, y'all. What can I get you?" To me, she said, "I love your dress. That pink is so pretty. Did you get it around here?"

"Two gin and tonics," Evers said brusquely. I kicked the side of his foot with my sandal. No need to be rude.

"No," I said, smiling back at the girl. "I got it at Nordstrom's Rack. Summer sale."

"Oh, Nordstrom's. I wish we had one here. Our mall is so lame. Not that I have enough cash to shop. You know how it is."

She rolled her eyes, and I found myself agreeing, even though I wasn't exactly sure I did know how it was.

From across the room, a low voice snapped, "Jade!" The waitress swung her head to the bar where a short, skinny man glowered at her.

She rolled her eyes again and giggled. "I chatter too much, and it drives the boss nuts. I'll be right back with your drinks. Do you wanna run a tab?"

I looked to Evers who said, "No tab, just the drinks."

"Coming right up," she said, gliding across the room in those crazy high heels so smoothly I knew she must wear them for hours every night.

On the stage, the dancer was peeling off her bra, and the patrons' attention had kicked up a notch, hands reaching out as she went to her knees and gyrated, hips thrusting, breasts motionless on her chest. Those were not real. Pretty, but not real.

I tried to keep my eyes on the dancer and not the men crowded around her. I didn't have to guess where the smell of sweat and cigarettes came from. Another place where the no smoking rule didn't seem to be in effect.

If I were up on that stage I wouldn't want any one of those guys reaching out to lay a hand on me. Half of them looked like they hadn't showered in a while, and the other half were just creepy. Hungry and a little angry.

Jade was back a moment later with our drinks. She set them on the table in front of us and said with an oddly inno-cent smile, "Either of you want a lap dance?"

I sucked in a breath, hoping Evers was going to handle her question. I had no clue what to say.

Did I want Evers to get a lap dance? *No.*

Did I want one myself? *Also no.*

Jade was pretty, and unlike The King's Club, she smelled good, but girls aren't my thing. Getting a lap dance in this moldy, dark club was not on the menu.

Smoothly, covering my reaction, Evers said, "Not right now, but can you sit with us for a minute? We're happy to pay you for your time."

Giving us a curious look, Jade thought for a second, then scanned the mostly-empty floor of the club. She made a signal to another waitress and pulled up a chair next to me.

She leaned forward, bracing her arms on the table, showing her breasts to their best advantage, her arm sliding next to mine. She did smell good, and her skin was as soft as it looked. The tacky miniskirt and barely-there bra aside, she didn't look like she belonged here.

"So, you don't want to go into a back room?" she said, raising an eyebrow and giving me an appraising look that brought a flush to my cheeks.

I was completely out of my depth. I'd been shoved on stage in the middle of a play and no one had given me my lines. Evers didn't answer her question, so I forged ahead. "No, I'm looking for my dad."

"I figured it might be something like that. We get couples in here every once in a while who want to walk on the wild side, but they usually don't look like you two. We're not supposed to talk about the customers," she shot a look at the bar where the bartender glowered in her direction, "but I'll tell you what. You tell me your dad's name. If I can help you, I will, for three hundred bucks and your purse."

"My purse?" I looked down at the pink linen clutch in

my hand. It matched my dress and shoes perfectly, but I could find another purse.

"Yeah, your purse. I have a top it would look awesome with." An expectant look in her eyes, she waited.

"Deal," Evers said. "His name is Smokey. Smokey Winters."

Her eyes lit up and she laughed, the bubbles of sound too bright for the dim, grungy room. Quietly enough that she wouldn't be overheard she said, "Oh, I know Smokey."

"Then spill," Evers said coolly. His eyes narrowed as Jade slid her chair closer to mine, draping an arm around my shoulder and leaning in, pressing her breasts against my side.

She caught his look. "I don't want the boss to think we're just having a chat. As far as he knows, I'm trying to talk your girl here into a champagne room. You pay him for the champagne room and once we're there, you're going to give me the three hundred and the purse and I'm gonna tell you everything I know about Smokey. Sound good?"

Her voice was light and friendly but beneath it was steel. If Evers said no she'd get up and walk away, telling us nothing. To me, almost apologetically, she said, "I want to help you, really, but I can't lose my job over it. I've got bills to pay."

Evers nodded. "Be right back," he said in my ear, "don't move from this seat without me."

I just smiled. He had nothing to worry about. There was no chance I was wandering around The King's Club on my own.

Evers got up and stalked to the bar. I took a sip of my gin and tonic, my eyes watering at the strength of the drink. Jade saw and giggled again. "He likes a heavy pour for the first drink," she said in a low voice, "gets the customers to open their wallets faster."

That made sense. I took another sip of the gin and tonic. "Do you guys get busier than this?" I asked, feeling stupid when Jade giggled again.

"Oh, yeah. Not so much on weeknights, but tonight we'll be hopping. We're the only club in town. You want something bigger, better, you have to go all the way to Greenville. This place may look like a dump, but the girls who know how to dance don't do too bad."

I remembered the way Jade had moved in her high, high platform heels and said, the gin loosening my tongue, "I bet you're a good dancer."

Another giggle. "You sure you don't want me to show you? I love dancing for girls. Not as grabby, and you smell better."

"I was just thinking the same thing about you," I said and flushed red, draining the rest of my drink so I couldn't say anything else. I couldn't embarrass myself if I couldn't talk. Jade gave me a squeeze as she laughed again.

"Green Apple glitter lotion," she said. "Looks great under the lights and smells so yummy."

It really did. I didn't think glitter lotion fit into my life, but I'd love something with that green apple scent. I made a mental note to check my favorite lotion store and see if they had anything similar.

Evers appeared beside my chair. Reaching to take my hand, he pulled me from my seat. Jade moved to his other side and looped an arm through his, guiding us to the back of the club, past the long length of the stage to a dark hallway with numbered doors the same purple as the exterior of the club, the numbers in the same flaking gold paint as the sign.

Jade pushed open the door marked 1 and led us inside. I don't know what I'd expected in a champagne room, but it definitely wasn't this.

The word *champagne* conjured a certain image.

The cracked faux leather sofa, stripper pole bolted in the middle of the room, and worn, stained carpet were not it.

I heard myself say, "Where's the champagne?"

Evers huffed out a laugh.

"The champagne is extra in the champagne room," he explained under Jade's giggle. "This little venture is costing enough as it is, and I have no idea what they call champagne here—"

The door closed firmly behind us as Jade said, "You don't want it. Trust me."

"I figured," Evers agreed.

Jade strode to the side of the room, turned on a small stereo and music filled the air. She gestured to the couch.

"There's no audio in here, but there are cameras. We can't just sit down and have a chat. I'm going to dance. You're going to put the money in her purse so I can take it when we're done."

Evers nodded. Jade began to sway to the music, and I busied myself emptying my personal things out of my little pink clutch. There wasn't much. My driver's license, credit card, a few business cards. I left Jade the loose change since my dress didn't have any pockets.

Handing Evers the clutch, I looked up at Jade. My mouth went dry. Jade's hips swayed, her body rubbing the pole behind her, bra already gone. Her very full, very natural breasts swayed with every turn of her hips.

I blinked. I hadn't expected to see that. Kind of dumb,

considering I was sitting in a private room in a strip club and she'd just said she was going to dance.

Still, I hadn't expected breasts. Not up close and personal. On the stage, sure. Not in arms' reach.

I could kind of see where Evers was coming from. I was too sheltered to hang out in a strip club if I was surprised by naked breasts.

The sway of Jade's body mesmerized me—the twist of her hips, the dip of her shoulders, the smile on her lips as her back arched.

My cheeks flushed with heat, and I cleared my throat. Evers slid closer to me on the couch and murmured in my ear," If you keep looking at her like that I am not going to be responsible for what happens."

I swallowed hard and met his eyes. They burned with icy-blue fire. Stark need. Not for Jade. For me.

He reached up and ran his thumb over my flushed cheekbone.

"I'm definitely taking you out on the town in Vegas. Watching you watch her? That's fucking hot."

My cheeks burned. I pressed my knees together, fighting the sudden warmth between my legs. Evers' hot eyes, his thumb stroking my cheek, the sound of his voice, the gin muddling my brain, and Jade, dancing only feet away—all of it had my head swirling.

I looked back to see Jade place her hands high on the pole and effortlessly lift her body until she was upside down, legs wrapped around the dull gold surface. Changing her grip, she parted her legs in a wide V, bracing her feet on the pole, and spun, her red hair flying. Before I could figure out how she did it, she hooked a leg around the pole, bending her other behind her in an arabesque, and spun again, her back arched, full breasts front and center.

My jaw might have dropped just a little. Under his breath, Evers said, "Fuck me."

He wrapped an arm around me, pulling me closer until I was almost plastered to his side, then turned his attention to the middle of the room, fastening his eyes on the ceiling, just above Jade.

Through the mess of thoughts in my head, it struck me as incredibly sweet that Evers wasn't staring at the gorgeous naked woman only a few feet away. And she *was* naked now. Somewhere, somehow, while she'd been on the pole, the thong had hit the floor.

I squeezed my eyes shut for a second then blinked again. Jade was seriously athletic. I'd underestimated the dancing skills required for stripping. Jade had said she did pretty well. Watching her work that pole, I was not surprised.

Once I got past the fact that she was naked, I saw the strength in her legs, the flex of her arms. Dropping from the pole, she landed on the ball of one foot and spun in two quick pirouettes before reaching for the pole again and lifting herself into the air. I'd taken just enough ballet as a girl to recognize a trained dancer.

"You can look," I whispered to Evers, wondering what had gotten into me.

He swallowed hard and shook his head, less in denial than exasperation. "Smokey Winters," he said to Jade. "What do you know?"

"He really your dad?" she asked me, flipping upside down against the pole, eyes on mine, her breasts practically at her chin.

Distracted, my voice frozen in my throat, I nodded.

"I could see that," she said conversationally as if we were having tea and she wasn't stark naked and hanging from a stripper pole. "You look like him. Same eyes. Though yours aren't bloodshot."

Yep, she knew my dad.

"When was he here last?" Evers asked.

"A few days ago. With his friend Warren. You know Warren?"

"I know Warren," I said.

I racked my brain for what I could remember about my dad's friend Warren. I didn't know him well, but I knew Dad and Warren had been tight since long before I was born. I had the vague idea Warren lived somewhere in Alabama, but maybe I had that wrong.

"Is Warren local? I didn't think he lived around here," I said.

"Oh, yeah." Jade flipped right side up and landed on her feet, grinding her ass against the pole and shaking her breasts. "Well, kind of local. He lives south of town a ways. I think almost in Sawyers Bend. I've never been to his place, but I've heard him bitch about the drive."

"You have a last name on Warren?" Evers asked.

"I don't know," Jade said vaguely. She turned around, sending a teasing look over her shoulder at me, then bent over, legs spread, swaying her hips.

My eyes shot to my knees. Jade was completely comfortable putting all of her goodies on full display to strangers sitting five feet away. Her dancing had been mesmerizing. This was too much.

I cleared my throat and snuck a sidelong look at Evers. He smirked at me in amusement. I would have bet my face was the color of a cherry tomato.

Evers leaned in and brushed his lips across my cheek. "You are fucking adorable. If we don't wrap this up so I can get you out of here—"

I cleared my throat. "It would really help if you could give us a last name for Warren. I can't remember. I haven't seen him in a few years."

Jade hummed to herself and finally, blessedly, stood up and turned back around to give us the front view.

I could handle the front view without dying of embarrassment. She really did have very pretty breasts. Pretty breasts and a spectacular body.

A friend of mine took a pole dancing class for exercise. She'd said it was fun but hard as hell. Watching it in real life, I could imagine. I wondered what Evers would think if I took a pole class and danced for him at home. Somehow, I thought he wouldn't mind that at all.

Jade twisted her hips, running her hands over her breasts and humming to herself as she thought. "Warren, Warren, Warren—" she said to herself, over and over. Finally, "Warren Smithfield. I kept thinking Warren Freshfield but that's not it. Warren Smithfield. Freshfields is a grocery store. Warren Smithfield. That's it."

"You're sure," Evers said.

"Oh, yeah, I'm sure. I remember looking at his card and thinking it was an awfully dignified name for a guy like Warren." She looked at me, "You know what I mean."

Sadly, I did. I hadn't seen Warren in a few years, but he was the last guy you'd describe with the word *dignified*.

Evers stood, set my pink clutch on the arm of the sofa, and pulled me to my feet, wrapping his arm around my waist, keeping me glued to his side.

"Thanks for your help, Jade. We can see ourselves out."

"No, thank you. And thanks for the purse. It's going to look awesome with my shirt. I hope you find your dad."

"I put my card in there," Evers said, nodding toward the arm of the couch. "If you see Smokey in the next few days, and you give me a call, tell me where he is, I'll make it worth your time."

Jade winked at us. "Gotcha. I'll keep an eye out."

I gave her a friendly wave as Evers pulled me away. We strode through The King's Club and out the door, the humid summer air delicious after the musty, sweaty smell of the club.

Chapter Twenty-Three

SUMMER

E vers opened the passenger door of the SUV, waiting until I was fastening my seatbelt before closing the door and rounding the hood to get in himself.

As soon as the door was shut, he picked up his phone, tapped the screen, and a moment later said "It's Evers. Run a Warren Smithfield. I need an address. Western North Carolina. Text it to me."

He put the phone in the center console and looked at me with burning eyes. The heat between my legs intensified. My head spun with the utter oddness of the situation.

This whole night had been a big step outside my world. Sleazy bars and strip clubs were not in my universe.

"I never in a million years pictured you in a strip club," Evers said, his voice a low rumble, "but watching you watch that girl dance was the fucking hottest thing I've ever seen."

He'd said that before, in the club. Making sure I understood, I clarified, "Watching me watch her? Don't you mean watching her?"

Slowly, Evers shook his head. "No, baby. I've seen plenty of strippers dance. That girl is nothing next to you. But the look on your face while you watched her dance, your wide eyes and the flush on your cheeks, the way it spread down your neck and across your chest until I wanted to unzip that dress and see how far that pretty pink color went... No, Summer. Watching you watch her. That's what was hot."

Bright light flashed through the windows as a car pulled into the lot, then another. I glanced at the dashboard clock. It was after eight, and Jade had been right, The King's Club was starting to pick up.

Evers noticed, too. "I wish we already had a hotel room. I want you in bed."

He reached across the center console and slid his fingers across my cheek to bury themselves in my hair, curving around the back of my head and pulling me forward until his lips met mine, hungry and impatient.

I shifted in my seat, turning, straining against the seatbelt, trying to get closer. I'd been dead set against that hotel room. Now I was right there with him. We needed a room. A bed.

After almost two months apart, the couch in the library had not been enough.

Evers' phone beeped with a text and he pulled back, breaking our kiss. I let out a short whimper at the loss of contact. At the loss of him.

Checking the screen, he stared at the address for a moment before he said, "I guess you get your wish. We're headed to Griffen's hometown. Your father's friend has a place in the hills outside of Sawyers Bend."

The sun was slowly setting over the mountains as we drove west out of Asheville. The city transitioned quickly to suburbs and then, in the blink of an eye, to nothing but green mountains.

The drive wasn't much more than a half hour, and again, the transition from mountains to civilization was abrupt. No fast food restaurants or big box stores, just the four-lane road moving to two lanes and then Main Street.

Sawyers Bend was a perfect slice of Americana. Main Street was busy, couples strolling hand-in-hand past shops, galleries, restaurants, and the occasional bar. Storefronts had neatly-painted windows, flowerpots by the doors, striped awnings and wrought iron benches.

Evers slowed the SUV to a crawl, held up by tourist traffic and crowded crosswalks, giving me plenty of time to soak in the local flavor. Art galleries showcasing paintings, sculptures and dramatic woodcarvings. Two craft breweries. This area of North Carolina seemed to have as many craft breweries as churches, which is saying something in the Bible Belt.

Not to mention all the restaurants. Based on the dining options, I guessed foodies flocked to Western North Carolina along with the beer and nature lovers.

At the end of Main Street, just after the last of the shops and restaurants, a massive stone and timber building loomed over the street. Evers pulled into the curved drive beneath a dark red awning and parked. A uniformed valet came to his side of the SUV.

"Checking in?" he asked when Evers lowered the window.

"We'd like to, but we don't have a reservation. Do you know if you're full tonight?"

"You'll have to ask inside, but I'm fairly sure we have rooms available. Would you like me to take care of your vehicle? I can pull it to the side and the desk will let me know if you need me to park it."

"That would be great, thanks."

I let myself out of the car, looking through the glass double doors into the lobby. A brass plaque beside the door read *The Inn at Sawyers Bend*.

Evers and I were met at the front desk by a young woman in a dark red jacket similar to the valet's.

"Can I help you?" she asked with a pleasant smile.

"We don't have a reservation," Evers said. "Do you have any rooms available?"

"We do, sir. What are you looking for?"

"I'm open to ideas. What do you have?"

"We have several of our standard rooms, all unique and custom-designed with king size beds, flat-screen televisions, broadband Internet, and luxury baths. Most have beautiful views of the mountains. We have two suites available and one of the cottages. I believe—" she clicked a few buttons on her keyboard. "Yes, the Honeymoon Cottage."

Evers leaned across the desk and flashed his most charming grin. "Tell me about the Honeymoon Cottage," he said with a wink at me.

I opened my mouth to tell him we didn't need anything fancy when he pulled me close, dropped his lips to my ear, and whispered almost inaudibly, "Don't argue and don't say my name."

He kissed my cheek before he straightened, and I gave an internal shrug. If he wanted to pay for the Honeymoon Cottage, I wasn't going to get in his way. After what I owed for the info on my dad, I wasn't in any shape to offer to cover the room. As for the name thing, I'd figure that out later.

Staring at us with polite speculation in her eyes, the clerk said, "Our Honeymoon Cottage is two rooms, a spacious master bedroom and open living room with dining area and kitchen. The bath is imported marble and features a soaking tub built for two. The cottage has a screened-in porch overlooking the river and a stone fireplace, with a fire already laid. The interior design and all furnishings were created specifically for the cottage. It's one of our most luxurious spaces, and its location offers both privacy and beautiful views of the river and the mountains."

"We'll take it." Evers pulled a credit card from his wallet and slid it across the counter.

She picked it up, read the front, and said, "Thank you, Mr. Wilcox. How long will you be staying with us?"

"Only tonight. Is the cottage available for tomorrow night if our plans change?"

"It is. May I ask, have you eaten yet?"

"We haven't. Do you have any recommendations?"

"There are a number of excellent restaurants within walking distance. We also have an award-winning restaurant on site." Giving us an assessing look she offered, "Room service is available if you aren't interested in a crowded dining room."

Evers' eyes gleamed with interest. "Is there a menu available in the room?"

"There is."

"Does that work for you?" he asked.

Alone with Evers? Food or no food, being anywhere alone with Evers worked for me.

"Sounds great," I agreed.

"Our car is out front, the valet said he'd wait—"

"I'll take care of everything." She handed Evers back his card. "One moment and I'll have someone show you to the cottage. If you're interested in dining in, you'll want to look at the menu and order right away. The kitchen closes in an hour and I wouldn't want you to miss it. If you do, there are other options in town, but our restaurant really is exceptional."

"Our bags?"

"They'll be delivered to the cottage, Mr. Wilcox. They'll follow you by a minute or two, not much more." She looked up, catching the eye of a nearby bellhop. He was at our side a moment later. "James, please show our new guests to the Honeymoon Cottage."

"Of course, this way."

Evers and I fell in behind the bellhop, his uniform a match for the rest of the staff. I was impressed. Thanks to my job, I'd stayed in a lot of hotels, from the big and corporate to small, exclusive boutique hotels, some of them among the best in the country.

The Inn at Sawyers Bend had a polish and professionalism I would have expected in a bigger city, not in a small mountain tourist town.

Looking around at the well-managed hustle and bustle of the busy inn and crowded restaurant, the attention to detail was first rate. The main room of the inn was welcoming and majestic, with stone fireplaces on either side tall enough to stand in, a vaulted ceiling with timber beams, and comfortable sitting areas around coffee tables, some of which had game boards set out. Checkers and chess. A puzzle.

A few were being used by guests, gathering in the central area to visit and share the adventures of their day. As we passed I caught snatches of conversation. Someone had been tubing, another couple hiking, and a third had been exploring the local breweries and restaurants.

This was the place that had cast Griffen out. Why? As if my thoughts had conjured him from thin air, Griffen appeared behind the bar at the far end of the restaurant. I stopped, stumbling into Evers, staring. Griffen was in Atlanta with Cynthia. What—?

Evers took my arm, following my gaze. When his eyes landed on the Griffen look-alike, he tugged me back into motion, shifting position so I was on his other side, blocking my view of the bar. Before I could say anything, he shot me a look and gave a short shake of his head.

Okaaay... I remembered what Evers had said in the car. Griffen's family owned half the town. If they owned half the town I'd bet they owned The Inn at Sawyers Bend. That wasn't just a Griffen look-alike, but one of his brothers or cousins. Someone so closely related they looked almost exactly like him.

Weird.

Weird, and not my business. Whatever had sent Griffen from this town, however pretty and quaint it was, it must have been bad. Sawyers Bend was a little spot of paradise dropped in the beauty of the mountains. If Griffen had left, he must have had a good reason.

Part of me was dying to know what that reason was, but if the Sinclairs hadn't been able to ferret out the information, I was out of luck.

Leaving the restaurant behind, we followed the bellhop across the rear terrace and down a stone path, past a series of cottages built in the same stone-and-timber style as the inn itself, accented with dark red awnings at the windows that matched the employees' jackets and the awning over the front entrance.

At the end of the path, the sounds of the Inn and Main Street faded away, replaced by the babble of the river. The Honeymoon Cottage looked like the others but was set a little apart, just as private as advertised.

The bellhop opened the door and stepped inside, flicking on the lights. In contrast to the stone and timber of the exterior, the inside of the cottage was bright white, fresh and crisp, from the fluffy white couches flanking the pale gray stone fireplace to the crystal chandelier.

Through an open door, I spotted the bedroom with its wide king size bed and more white—a thick duvet and mounds of pillows. The bellhop walked us through the small cottage pointing out the bathroom, an expanse of white marble, and the bedroom with its white-beamed vaulted ceiling and oversized bed. He opened the French doors beside the fireplace and flicked on the light in the screened-in porch overlooking the river.

Main Street wasn't far away, but here on the porch of the honeymoon cottage, we might have been in the middle of nowhere. The bellhop handed us the room service menu before he helped a newly-arrived bellhop deliver the bags we'd left in the back of the SUV. Evers slipped them both a discreet tip and they disappeared, leaving us alone.

Evers crossed the room and wrapped his arm around my waist, pulling me flush to his body.

"I want to forget about dinner and take you to bed right now, but we'll regret it when the restaurant closes and we're starving. This is a small town. I doubt they have a twenty-four-hour grocery store."

"Good point," I said, tugging at his shirt, pulling it free to slide my hand beneath and press my palm to his warm skin.

I was starving. Even upside down from my crazy day I knew that I needed food, but my deepest hunger was for Evers.

I took the menu from his hand and scanned it quickly before handing it back. "Steak, medium rare. Loaded baked potato. Chocolate cheesecake."

Evers pressed a hard kiss to my mouth. "That sounds like heaven."

Releasing me, he went to the phone in the kitchen and placed our order, two of the same except for the dessert. Evers ordered himself raspberry cheesecake. I hoped he planned on sharing.

I heard him say, "About how long do you think you'll be?" Then, "Perfect."

He hung up the phone and stalked across the room toward me, his eyes hot and determined.

"They said twenty minutes. What do you think we can do with twenty minutes?"

We could do a hell of a lot with twenty minutes.

I reached under my arm for the zipper of my dress and whipped it down. Evers' eyes flared. I turned to dash into the bedroom, yanking the dress over my head and letting it fly.

Without warning, he lifted me off my feet and tossed me onto the bed. I bounced, landing legs splayed, one sandal hanging off my toe, my breasts spilling out of my bra.

Evers stood at the foot of the bed, rapidly shedding his clothes. It didn't take me long to get rid of my underwear and toss off my sandals. I hadn't been naked with Evers in so long. Almost two months. A lifetime.

The library didn't count. Evers had managed to get all of his clothes off, but I'd just pushed mine out of the way. Not that I was complaining about spur of the moment library sex with Evers, but this—a big, wide bed and total privacy—was so much better.

Rushed library sex hadn't come close to banking the heat between us.

The whole strip club thing had only fanned the flames.

Evers was hard before his pants hit the floor. I expected

him to pounce, but he reached out and closed his hands around my calves, sliding me to the end of the bed.

Bending over, he leaned in, his shoulders spreading my legs, baring me completely. If it hadn't been so long, if I hadn't wanted him so much, I might have been embarrassed.

I had no room for that now. Evers traced a finger from one hipbone to the other, then down between my legs and up again, stopping to drawing a circle around my clit, his touch so light my hips moved of their own volition, seeking out more.

"Tease," I accused. His ice-blue eyes lit with devilish amusement as he flicked his tongue across my clit, his fingers dropping to slide the tiniest bit inside. His touch set every nerve in my body alight.

I needed more. Not the slow long buildup—I'd already had that over the last two months. The last few days. The last few hours.

I wanted Evers, hard and hungry and inside me. Right now.

Shifting my legs, I wrapped them around his back and pulled.

His eyes flared in surprise.

I wasn't passive during sex, but I wasn't usually aggressive either.

The clock was ticking. We were running out of time before someone would knock on the door of our hideaway. I didn't want to wait.

Evers placed his palms on my inner thighs, pressing them open. His lips feathering against my most sensitive skin he said, "You don't like that? You just want me to fuck you? Right now?"

He punctuated his question with a hard suck to my clit,

sending a bolt of white-hot ecstasy up my spine to detonate in my brain.

All I could say was, "Yes. Please, yes. I want you to fuck me. Right now. You can tease me later."

Evers didn't answer with words.

Evers answered with his mouth, but he didn't use words.

He sucked again, driving one finger and then two in my pussy as he worked my clit, sending me from hot and aroused to trembling and begging in seconds.

My hips rocked into his mouth and fingers, short, choppy moans coming from my throat. I teetered on the edge of orgasm, almost falling over. He rose above me. His cock pressed slowly inside, filling me until I wanted to cry with the sheer pleasure of Evers joined to me. A part of me.

I wrapped my legs around his waist and held on, eyes closed tight at the stretch and pressure, the exquisite slide as he pulled back and slammed in, driving me over the edge.

He did exactly as I asked and fucked me hard, riding me through my orgasm, my nails digging grooves into his shoulders, my mouth pressed to his neck. The pulses of pleasure went on until it was too much, my body too sensitive for more.

Just when I thought my brain would short out from the overload of sensation, Evers stiffened as the wave took him under, too.

Just in time.

Only moments after we separated, the expected knock fell on the door. I scrambled for the bathroom while Evers grabbed a robe and answered the door.

I could take a break for food. As long as I could have Evers for dessert.

Chapter Twenty-Four

SUMMER

We ate dinner on the screened-in porch overlooking the river. Wearing the fluffy white robes provided by the inn, we moaned over the amazing steak and twice-baked potatoes, fed each other bites of chocolate and raspberry cheesecake, and sipped the champagne that was part of the Honeymoon Cottage package.

Surrounded by so much pristine luxury, it was hard to believe we'd spent the first part of the evening in a dingy biker bar and musty strip club. Our stomachs full, we filled the massive soaking tub and climbed in, Evers pulling me into his lap, my back to his front, our legs entwined.

There, immersed in steaming, scented water, he fulfilled his promise to tease.

I rolled my head back on his shoulder, my lips grazing the side of his neck, his ear, his jaw, as his hands slid along my soapy skin, cupping my breasts, squeezing my nipples, dropping between my legs and sliding up over my belly, my ribs.

He was everywhere and nowhere, his cock between my legs, not seeking entry, just there, its hard length a tease in and of itself. I lay still as long as I could, reveling in his undivided attention until I couldn't stay still any longer.

When his roaming hands had me on the edge of insanity, I flipped over, splashing water over the sides of the tub, and settled myself on top of him, reaching between us to guide his cock where I needed it most.

It was my turn to tease. I rode him slowly, offering my breasts to his mouth, letting him feast before leaning back, grinding my hips down, playing until he lost patience and clasped his hands around my waist, holding me still and thrusting hard, driving me over the edge, following a moment later.

He helped me from the tub, drying me carefully, reverently, before lifting me into his arms and carrying me to the bed. We lay there beneath the fluffy white duvet, arms and legs tangled, kissing and touching. Murmuring nothing and everything until sleep pulled us under.

Waking up in the honeymoon cottage, sunlight streaming through the tall windows, it seemed like no darkness could touch my life again.

Evers slept beside me, his face relaxed, looking younger than I'd ever seen him. His thick dark hair fell over his forehead, his tanned skin warm and soft as silk. I slid a hand down his chest, fingertips absorbing the ridges of muscle, the lines of his abdomen narrowing into a V pointing straight to my destination.

I woke him with a kiss before taking his already-hardening cock between my lips and tasting him, teasing him awake. I owed him one after the night before in the tub.

Evers' hand sank into my sleep-tousled curls, holding on

as I worked my mouth over his length, sucking and licking, my mouth watering and so full of him.

Evers was a lot to handle, but I had enthusiasm on my side. I'd always loved his taste, the way he filled my mouth, the sounds he made when I squeezed the base of his cock and sucked hard.

I loved his voice, rough with sleep and heat, saying, "Summer. Oh, God, Summer."

I thought about climbing up, riding him until we both came. Later. There'd be time for that later. Right now, I wanted his pleasure for myself. I wanted to bring him to the edge and send him over, just like this.

When he said, "Summer, I'm going to... I can't...," and tugged my hair, I didn't move. I couldn't quite take all of him, but I tried, squeezing the base of his cock and sliding my hand in rhythm with my mouth until he shook beneath me, his hips thrusting, giving me his pleasure. Giving me everything.

When he caught his breath, he hooked his hands under my arms and hauled me up the bed. Rolling to pin me down, he kissed me hard and deep before pinning my hands above my head and tasting every inch of my body until I was limp with satisfaction.

I was half dozing when he threw on a robe and ordered breakfast.

"I should get up," I said, "take a shower." That big, lush bathroom with the oversize shower and Evers. I'd get out of bed for that.

"No, you shouldn't. You should stay right there. We can take a shower after breakfast. We don't have to go anywhere yet."

Still in his robe, Evers crawled back into bed. I rolled into him, pushing the lapel of the robe back so I could rest my head on his chest. He stroked his fingers through my hair.

"I could stay here forever," I said.

"Here is nice," he agreed, "but as long as I have you, I can go anywhere."

His sweetness struck me dumb. I couldn't think of what to say. I believed him. It wasn't that.

A voice in my head was saying, *I love you*.

I love you.

The words wouldn't come out of my mouth.

I believed that Evers loved me.

I did.

I wanted to believe he did.

I wanted to give him those words, but they were stuck.

All I could say was, "I missed you so much."

That was the truth.

Evers craned his neck to kiss the top of my head. "Me too. I missed you like crazy."

Evers wanted me. I wanted him.

We'd messed it up—mostly he'd messed it up—but we'd figured it out and we were together. That's what was important.

And still, those three little words stuck in my throat.

Evers didn't seem to notice. I was relieved. Once I got used to having him, I'd be able to say them. I knew I would. I just needed a little more time.

Now that we were together again, we had all the time in the world.

We lay there, me listening to his heartbeat while he ran his fingers through my hair until a knock sounded on the door. Breakfast.

After we ate, we showered, got dressed and packed our

bags. Evers was quiet as we checked out, making no mention of the possibility of returning for a second night.

Fun time was over. We were back to work.

We drove straight to the address Evers had for Warren Smithfield. Funny that I'd never known his last name until now. A thought occurred to me as Sawyers Bend disappeared in the rearview mirror.

"Why are we going to Warren's? Why aren't we going to my Dad's place? I thought he lived around here?"

Evers didn't answer right away. Sending me a cautious look, he said finally, "We have cameras in his place. It's empty."

"You had cameras in his place in Atlanta and you took me there."

"His place in Atlanta had been tossed. Harder to tell if anything was out of place." He pressed his lips together before flashing a quick, embarrassed smile. "And I wanted you alone. Away from Rycroft. You wouldn't talk to me, but you wanted to help your dad."

"Hmmph." I didn't know what to say to that. Sweet and sneaky. That was Evers. I wasn't going to complain. "If you have cameras on his place here, you know when he was home last."

"Three months," Evers said, the embarrassed smile replaced with a tight jaw.

"What? If he hasn't been home, where has he been?"

"A lot of people would like the answer to that question."

Our problem in a nutshell.

Warren didn't live in Sawyers Bend proper. We drove back toward Asheville before turning on to a narrow country road that transitioned from pavement to gravel to dirt, barely wide enough for two cars to pass. We must have bumped along the dirt road for over a mile, never seeing another soul. The only sign of inhabitants were the rusted mailboxes that popped up here and there, drunkenly leaning in every direction, looking as if the postman hadn't touched them in decades.

Evers slowed as we reached a hunter green mailbox with the number 48 drawn on the side in black marker. He turned down the rutted drive, his SUV bouncing and jolting. I grabbed the handle above the door to steady myself before I bounced right off the seat.

At first glance, the house at the end of the drive looked abandoned. Cracked windows had been repaired with frayed duct tape. Sagging cardboard boxes were stacked haphazardly on the porch. A washing machine that could have been from the fifties sat in the center of the front yard.

There wasn't much grass. Definitely no landscaping. The front steps were cinderblocks tilting in the dirt, the storm door sagging on its hinges.

Evers gave me a forbidding look. "You stay in the car."

"No." Before he could argue, I explained, "Warren knows me. I haven't seen him in a while, but he knows me. He takes one look at you—"

I scanned Evers' charcoal suit and crisp blue-and-white striped shirt. He'd left off the tie, but that didn't make him look any less like a wealthy, successful businessman.

Looking at him, no one would guess he was an excellent shot who could handle himself in a fight. To a man like Warren, anyone dressed like Evers meant one thing. Trouble.

One look at Evers and Warren would barricade the door.

"You need me. Warren wouldn't hurt me. He's not dangerous."

"You don't know that. You said yourself you haven't seen him in a while. He's friends with your father, and your father is in deep shit. You don't know what's behind that door."

"I know we have to talk to Warren. We're here now. I'm coming with you."

Evers sat for a long moment, his eyes on mine, thinking. Finally, he opened his door. "Stay behind me."

That I could do. Mostly.

Evers tried knocking on the door and calling out Warren's name. As I'd expected, no response.

I had a feeling if I hadn't been there Evers might have used a less conventional method of gaining entry. Something along the lines of putting his foot through the door.

I called out, "Warren? Hey, it's Summer. Smokey's girl. Listen, I'm looking for my daddy, I just want to talk to you for a minute. Don't mind the guy with me. I know he's a suit, but he's okay. Could you open the door? I promise we're not here to give you any trouble. I just want to talk to you about my dad."

The house remained silent. I tried again. "Warren? Please? I really don't want to bother you, but we came all the way out here, and I can't leave until I talk to you. If you could open the door—"

A shuffle from inside and the door creaked open. Warren stood there, thinner than I remembered. He was a few inches shorter than me, and he'd always been round. Wide. Now his skin hung loose, and beneath his weathered tan he was gray. If I passed him on the street I might not have recognized him.

He looked past Evers, his eyes coming to rest on me. A smile cracked across his face, and he pulled the door open more.

"Summer, what are you doing here? I thought you were living in Atlanta."

"I am, Warren. I've been looking for my dad. I need to find him. He's not returning my calls."

"You came all the way out here?"

"I didn't know where else to go," I said. "Can we come in and talk?"

Warren shot a nervous glance over his shoulder and shook his head. "I wasn't expecting visitors, if you know what I mean."

"I don't think we do," Evers said, craning his neck to look over Warren's shoulder into the dim interior of the house. "Let us in. We won't take much of your time."

"We can talk out here—"

I shook my head. "Warren, just five minutes? Please."

He shot another look over his shoulder. When he stepped back to let us in, I fully expected to see someone else in the room. Maybe my father.

The house appeared to be empty, but I quickly realized why Warren hadn't wanted company. The place was a bizarre combination of messy and organized. I hadn't known Warren was a hoarder.

In the corner of the room, stacks of newspapers rose to tower above my head. Beside them, a wooden crate overflowed with old-fashioned alarm clocks, at least twenty or thirty of them. Another crate held toasters; toaster ovens, slot toasters—some of them older than me.

Rocking chairs were crammed along one wall, the seats filled with stacks of boxes. Electrical cords spilled from one. Old clothes from another.

Layers of filth had accumulated beneath Warren's haphazard collection of belongings. I doubted his house had seen a bottle of cleaning spray or a rag in decades.

On the coffee table, I spotted a glass pipe, a lighter, and a small plastic baggie filled with a white powder interspersed with small whitish crystal shards. Shit.

I don't do drugs. Growing up with my father and his ubiquitous pot smoking had been enough for me. I like a glass of wine or mixed drink now and then, and beer is okay, but drugs are not my thing.

Still, you didn't grow up with Smokey Winters for a dad and not learn more than you wanted to about the tools of the trade. I knew pretty much every device you could use to smoke pot, from a glass pipe to a bong. I even knew how to carve an apple into a pipe and how to make a gravity bong from a soda bottle. Thanks, Dad.

Despite my extensive education in pot smoking, I was pretty sure nothing on that table had anything to do with pot. Warren had moved on to meth. Shit. I closed my eyes and sent a prayer to the heavens that my dad hadn't made the move with him. Pot was one thing, but meth...

Meth was an entirely different problem.

Evers saw everything I did, probably more. He positioned himself in the room between me and Warren. Time to get this over with. I didn't want to hang out in Warren's place any longer than we had to.

"When's the last time you saw my dad, Warren?"

"Oh, it's been a while," Warren said vaguely, shooting another glance over his shoulder.

I couldn't figure out what he was looking at. His house wasn't more than one big room. There were a bedroom and bathroom off to the side, nowhere near where he kept looking. The kitchen was behind him, but it, too, was empty. Behind that, there was just the backyard and more trees.

"Okay," I said, not wanting to push too hard and scare

him off, "Do you remember more specifically? Did you see him here or in town? Did he tell you what his plans were?"

"No. I'm sorry Summer. I want to help you. I do. But your daddy didn't say anything. He's just—"

Warren wrung his hands together, his fingers twisting, clenching until the knuckles were almost white. He shifted his weight and shot another look over his shoulder. This time I saw he was looking through the main room, through the window in the kitchen to the backyard.

Something in the yard had him on edge.

"What about my dad, Warren? You can tell me. I love him, but I know he's not perfect."

"Summer, girl, you should go back to Atlanta. Take your man with you. Your daddy, he's been messing with some people, you don't want them to know about you. You let Smokey deal with his own troubles. He wouldn't want you here."

Shit. Evers had told me it was bad. I'd believed him. Mostly. But this? Warren, like my dad, was generally too stoned to get scared. A warning from Warren was not comforting.

"You can't tell us anything about when you last saw Smokey Winters or where he might have been heading?" Evers asked in a hard voice. Either he'd learned what he needed to know, or he was out of patience.

Warren shrugged his shoulders helplessly, and with another nervous glance over his shoulder said, "I wish I could be more help. I really do."

"Thank you for your time," Evers said, backing me towards the door. If I thought there was any chance we'd get more out of Warren, I might have argued or offered a bribe. Unlike the bartender and Jade, Warren was too scared to be useful.

Fear shimmered in his normally dull, bloodshot eyes. I would have expected him to be nervous about the meth paraphernalia on the table, but he hadn't spared it a glance.

He wasn't afraid we'd catch him with drugs.

He was afraid we'd catch him with something else.

Evers jumped off the porch, turning to lift me over the ramshackle concrete block steps. Instead of heading to his SUV, he took my arm and led me at a brisk pace around the side of the house.

Warren, his voice high and desperate, called out behind us, "What are y'all doing? You can't go back there. This is private property."

We ignored him. Following Evers into the backyard, I saw what he'd spotted and I'd missed. Across the rough dirt of the backyard, hidden in the trees, was a tiny, ancient camper.

Smoke leaked from the cracked window. As we drew closer, I recognized the smell of it. Evers reached for the handle and yanked open the door.

My father stood there, his hair straggly and badly in need of a cut, wearing an ancient Grateful Dead t-shirt and a pair of jeans faded white at the seams. His Winters-blue eyes, bloodshot and hazy, lit up the moment they fell on me.

He broke into a wide grin and stumbled through the door, arms wide. Pulling me into his embrace, he rocked me back and forth, the familiar scent of patchouli and pot filling my nose.

"Baby girl, baby girl. You're a sight for sore eyes. Your old dad is glad to see you."

I didn't believe that for a minute.

And yet, for all his faults, I relaxed into my dad's arms, relieved to have found him alive and in one piece.

Chapter Twenty-Five

SUMMER

"Baby girl, you have landed a seriously nice gig," my dad said, lounging on the back terrace of Rycroft Castle.

Seeing my dad in these surroundings was bizarre. His worn jeans, tie-dyed t-shirt, and scraggly hair did not fit in with the splendor of Rycroft Castle.

He'd been quiet on the ride back to Atlanta, stonewalling all of Evers' attempts to get information. Evers asked about Maxwell Sinclair. Who they'd been working for. Exactly what Smokey had been doing for Maxwell and William Davis.

Smokey had ignored him, pretending to nap. Evers grew progressively more irritated as each mile sped by, his jaw tight, eyes hard. By the time we reached Atlanta, he could barely grind out a word.

I wanted to step in and bridge the gap, but what was there to say? Evers had his own agenda, and Smokey didn't want to play along.

I had never in my life been able to get Smokey to do anything he didn't want to do. Smokey went his own way.

Neither of us wanted him at Rycroft. For one thing, he didn't have the right to be there. It was Cynthia's house for the time being, and he was an uninvited guest.

Evers didn't want Smokey unsupervised in my condo. To be honest, *I* didn't want Smokey unsupervised in my condo. I didn't need much imagination to picture all the trouble he could get into.

The only other acceptable location was the safe room at Sinclair Security.

The safe room. Such a friendly name for what I suspected amounted to little more than a locked cell. Of course, Smokey refused that option. I hadn't liked it much myself.

My dad was in some trouble. I knew that. If he'd been working with Maxwell Sinclair, he'd been up to no good.

But he was my dad. The idea of dropping him off at the Sinclair building to be locked away until he did what they wanted didn't sit right.

He wasn't a good guy all the time, but he wasn't a criminal. Well, okay, he was a criminal. Kind of. He definitely broke the law when it came to drugs.

If half of what Evers and his brothers suspected about their father was true and Smokey had been working for him, then he'd stepped well beyond misdemeanor possession.

Why didn't that matter? Why couldn't I push him out the door let the Sinclairs deal with him? Their mother had been threatened. They had a right to be worried. If my dad had anything to do with putting their mother in danger, he should fix it.

I was Team Evers, right?

Right?

Every time I wondered, all I could think was *he's my dad*. He'd never been a great father, but he was the only one I had.

I wanted him to do the right thing, but I didn't want him hurt in the process.

We pulled into Rycroft Castle intending to get rid of Smokey as soon as we could. Cynthia met us at the door and invited him to stay.

Simple as that.

Not simple at all and a terrible idea.

We didn't have a better solution. Smokey and I were dead set against the safe room option. Evers wouldn't consider my condo or a hotel.

Rycroft Castle was crawling with security. No one could get in and Smokey couldn't get out.

Evers had confiscated Smokey's phone before we'd left Warren's house and refused to give it back. Smokey begged me to intercede, but one look at Evers and I'd kept my mouth shut.

Sitting beside me, a whiskey in his hand, Smokey took a long drag on his cigarette, tapping the ash onto the flagstone terrace. I winced. "I'm sure we have an ashtray around here somewhere."

Smokey shrugged. What did he care about an ashtray? Someone else would clean up the mess.

"Look," I said, "Cynthia said it was okay for you to stay, but this is her place. You need to treat it with respect. You're a guest here."

Smokey took another drag off his cigarette, blowing the air out in a thin stream. "You look good, Summer girl. Doing well. Happy. I don't want to mess that up for you. I don't have to. You could just open the door and let me walk away. I can't help your boy anyway. I don't know a thing."

"They don't believe that. I'm not sure I do either."

My dad gave me an entreating look. His eyes, so like mine, betrayed nothing but wounded innocence. "Summer, I know I'm not the best dad. I know I like my weed and whiskey too much. Know I wasn't always there for you. But do you really think I'm mixed up in some sort of real trouble? You know that's not me."

He was saying everything I'd been thinking.

And yet, behind his practiced expression, there was something else. Something canny and hard.

"I can't believe you'd treat your dad like this. You don't have the right to take me prisoner."

"You have free room and board in a castle," I said wryly. "I saw where you were staying with Warren."

I shuddered a little at the thought of the ancient camper, almost as filthy as Warren's house had been. Whatever my father had done, he must have been scared to hide out there.

With a sinking heart, I said, "Dad, don't lie to me. I know you're in trouble, and I know you can help the Sinclairs. I don't understand why you won't tell them what you know."

"Because it's none of their goddamn business," Smokey said, taking a final drag on his cigarette before grinding it out on the bottom of his shoe and flicking the butt into the flower bed at the edge of the terrace.

I made a mental note to pick it up and throw it out before I went in. I'd have to apologize to the cleaning staff and make sure they got a bonus, even if I had to pay for it out of my own pocket. My father was becoming a strain on my budget.

"You need to stay out of my business, Summer. Safer for everyone that way."

"How can you say that? I saw your place. I know someone broke in looking for something. I'm worried. You're my Dad."

"Then act like it and do what you're told. Your boyfriend made me leave my stash at the trailer. Give me your phone so I can make a call."

"No," I said, shooting to my feet. "I am not giving you my phone, especially not so you can call a drug dealer to come to Cynthia Stevens' house. Are you crazy? I don't care if she said you can stay here. This is ridiculous—"

Smokey waved a hand telling me to sit back down, not the least bit disturbed by my outburst. I sank back into my chair, a familiar impotent frustration rising in my chest.

I wanted to shout, to make demands, and I knew it wouldn't do any good with my father. He'd just give me the same lazy look and wait for me to burn myself out. Then he'd do whatever he'd planned in the first place.

He shook his head at me in regret and said, "I don't know how your mother and I had such a boring kid. She was too together for me, but at least she had a spark. She had fire. You're all about rules and doing the right thing. Like a little hall monitor. Never any fun."

Evers' voice came from behind us, tight and angry. "You need to shut the fuck up right now."

His hand dropped to my shoulder, giving me a squeeze. He ran his knuckles across my cheek before moving to stand in front of us, arms crossed over his chest.

He'd changed when we got back to Rycroft, but even in jeans and a T-shirt he was intimidating. Smokey blew me off without a second thought, but one look at Evers and he cringed.

Proving he wasn't the sharpest tack in the box, he raised his chin in defiance. "Don't tell me how I can talk to my own daughter."

"I will if you speak to her with anything less than respect. Your daughter is smart and successful. She works hard. She's fun. She's a great friend and everyone loves her. You? Haven't heard many people say that about you. If it weren't for your daughter you'd be locked up right now, so if you've got a brain in your head—which I doubt—I'd suggest treating her better."

Smokey's eyes shifted away, and he declined to answer. Evers ignored him.

To me, he said, "I have no idea what's gotten into her, but Cynthia insists that Smokey stay here. Says he's family. We'll stick with that for now."

To Smokey, who still refused to meet his eyes, he said, "Security has you on their radar. They're watching you, stay away from the phones and behave yourself."

Still no comment from my father. Again to me, Evers said, "Cynthia is looking for you."

I met his worried eyes and tried to give him a reassuring smile, but I couldn't pull it off. "I'll go find her in a minute. Thanks."

Evers nodded and left. So much energy trying to find my father, and now that he was here... I let out a long sigh.

"Summer, girl, I get what you see in him. I'm not blind, and I know the Sinclairs. Rich as hell. He's a good score, but he is not looking out for you."

Smokey lit another cigarette, taking a deep drag. When he spoke again, it was through a cloud of smoke. "He's got problems with his father, he's gotta watch out for his mama. You are not at the top of his list, you get me?"

I gritted my teeth against the brush of fear at my father's

words. Quietly, I said, "You're wrong."

He was wrong. Evers said he loved me. He might have lied before and played me to keep me away from his friends, but he wouldn't lie about love. He wouldn't.

Sensing weakness, my father dug deeper. "I know you can get around the security. You and I should just go. We can go back to your place or take off somewhere. You've got cash. Let's just get the hell out of here. He's using both of us. He used you to get to me and now he's only biding his time, thinking I'll give in. I can't help him find his father."

"You knew Maxwell was alive, didn't you?" I was getting tired of his protests of innocence. Maybe I wasn't entirely sure of Evers, but I knew my dad wasn't on the level.

"Hell, they already know he's not dead. It isn't exactly news," he said, dismissing Maxwell's return to life as if it were no big deal.

"It was news to them," I snapped. "Having it confirmed would be helpful. Anything would be helpful. Anything other than sitting out here drinking and chain-smoking."

"Summer, you're wasting your time. I can't help you. I can't help your boy. The longer you hang around thinking he's going to come through for you, the harder the fall will be when he walks away. Trust me. I'm your dad. I'm looking out for you."

I pushed myself out of the chair and walked down the steps of the terrace to pick up the cigarette butt he'd flipped in the flower bed. He hadn't changed, and he never would. If I could have thought of a better place to stash him than Rycroft Castle, I would have taken it.

Instead, I said, "I have to find Cynthia and see what she needs. Dinner is at seven. Try to stay out of trouble."

Chapter Twenty-Six

SUMMER

Smokey staying out of trouble wasn't likely, but I could hope. Cynthia kept me busy for the rest of the afternoon, going over social media accounts, approving scheduled posts, editing video showing her training for the upcoming movie. Her phone rang repeatedly, but she didn't answer.

Usually, when she had a call she didn't want to deal with she passed the phone off to me, but she didn't do that either. I was curious, but I couldn't think of a good reason to take a look at her phone.

I kept my curiosity buttoned-down and focused on work. When we were done, I said, "Are you sure it's okay if my dad stays here? We can make other arrangements. It's totally inappropriate—"

"Summer, it's fine. Evers is making up for any inconvenience, and I know if your father goes somewhere else, so will Evers. I don't know the details, and I'm not asking you to tell me, but whatever's going on has his attention. I feel better if he's running security here, so if that means your father stays, your father stays. If he were dangerous, Evers wouldn't have let him through the door."

"He's not dangerous," I said immediately. Reconsidering, I added, "Unless you have a bag of weed somewhere in the house, because if you do, I guarantee he will sniff it out."

Cynthia laughed, the sound light and clear as a bell, reminding me how little I'd heard it from her lately. "No weed for me. Smoking is hell on the skin, and I haven't been a stupid young starlet for a lot of years. But don't remind me how many."

"I don't know what you're talking about," I said with a smile. "You were an ingénue yesterday."

"You're a good friend, Summer," Cynthia said, suddenly serious, "so I'm going to give you some advice. Keep an eye out for your father. I know guys like him."

"Stoners?" I asked, trying to lighten the mood. Cynthia wouldn't be diverted.

"He's the guy who's always working an angle. The guy who causes trouble and leaves everyone else holding the bag."

I sighed.

"Am I wrong?" she asked. I shook my head. Cynthia went on, "You have a good thing going with Evers."

I glanced at her in surprise. I knew she'd set up their kiss, but we hadn't talked about it. Evers and I had left not long after to look for my father, and it hadn't come up since I'd been back.

"Evers is a good man, Summer. A really good man. And he's got it bad for you. He's hooked. I threw myself at him, and he wasn't even tempted. You and I both know that does not happen often."

She wasn't being arrogant. It was a fact.

Cynthia Stevens did not get turned down.

What man would say no to a screen goddess who was perfection from head to toe?

Only a man in love.

I didn't say anything, thinking about my father and Evers. About loyalty and love and stupid mistakes.

Cynthia said, "I don't mind if your dad stays here for now until you and Evers sort out what to do with him. But stay sharp. There are two men in this house who claim to have your best interests at heart, and only one of them really does."

"You barely know my dad," I protested, feeling like I had to stick up for my family.

"Honey, I know better than anyone how family can mess you up. You're loyal and you have a big heart. You want to see the good in the people you care about. It's one of your best qualities. Don't let it blind you. Be smart."

I let out a short sigh. I didn't want to admit she might be right. It was a hard thing to accept about my own dad.

Her phone rang again. Trying to change the subject, I said, "Is Clint trying to set up a meeting?"

"I'm putting him off," Cynthia said, pushing the phone across the table. "I promised I'd talk to him, and I will, but I need a few more days."

"He isn't taking it well?"

She looked at her phone wistfully. "Not exactly."

I couldn't think of anything to say except, "I'm sorry."

***

I WAS DREADING DINNER, SITTING AROUND THE TABLE with my father, Cynthia, Angie, Viggo, Evers, and Griffen. It wasn't the nightmare I anticipated. My dad managed to behave himself, telling only slightly off-color stories, mainly keeping the attention on me by recounting all of my embarrassing memories from childhood.

Thanks, Dad. I really needed my boss and my boyfriend to hear about the time I threw up backstage at the second grade spelling bee.

After dinner, Cynthia announced she was watching a movie in the theater and going to bed early. She claimed to be exhausted from training with Viggo, but the way she clutched her phone in her hand had me suspicious.

She'd said Clint was calling. She hadn't said if she'd answered. If they were talking. I looked between Evers and my dad. I knew who I wanted to spend the evening with, I just didn't know if I could.

"I want to check out this theater," Smokey said, making my decision easy. Cynthia smiled at him, an open, friendly smile that gave no hint of her reservations about my dad. Then again, Cynthia was an excellent actress. The best.

Sending me a quick look that told me I owed her one, she hooked her arm through Smokey's and led him from the dining room saying, "Why don't we order up some popcorn and snacks, make a night of it?"

Angie disappeared upstairs and Viggo trailed behind, an annoyed expression on his face. I could sympathize. I didn't know what he had going on with Cynthia, if anything, but I was pretty sure I knew what he'd hoped he'd have going on.

Smokey was in his way. Smokey was in everyone's way.

I sighed. Evers came up behind me and wrapped his arm around my waist, pulling me against him, resting his chin on the top of my head.

"You sure you don't want me to lock him in the safe room?"

"Am I a horrible person if I say I kinda do?"

"No. You're really not. One phone call and—"

"I can't lock my father up in your safe room, Evers," I said, hearing the edge in my voice and hating it. Evers' arm tightened around my waist and he let out a short sigh of his own.

"Let's not think about your dad right now. Let's go swimming."

I turned in his arms and wound my arms around his neck. "Swimming? I could go swimming."

"I need to check in with the control room, make sure the shift change went well and everything's quiet. I'll meet you there."

We walked together down the hall to our rooms, my hand closed in his. I could almost pretend things were normal. Evers left me at the door to my room with a kiss and a promise to see me soon.

I stood in front of my dresser, thinking. I'd packed three bathing suits for my stay in Rycroft Castle. I liked to swim and had known the pool would be spectacular.

One suit was utilitarian, a racerback designed for swimming laps. The pool wasn't quite long enough for laps but almost. Close enough. The second suit was a striped tankini. Cute, but modest. Appropriate for swimming around my employer and her staff.

And the third... The third was that bathing suit every woman has that she buys on impulse and then wonders what the hell she was thinking. The deep raspberry-pink bikini had a lot less fabric than any other bathing suit I'd ever worn. I'd bought it on a shopping trip with Julie after a two-margarita lunch at the mall.

Julie talked me into it, telling me I'd get every guy at the beach. We never found out because by the time we'd hit the beach later that summer, I'd taken one look at that bikini and shut it away in the drawer.

I'd never had the nerve to wear it. Rycroft Castle was probably the only place I'd ever swim in privacy. I didn't have my own pool. This was as close as I'd get. I'd thrown it in my bag thinking maybe I'd finally use it and justify buying it in the first place.

I snatched the bikini out of the drawer and told myself to stop thinking so much. Twisting my hair in a knot on the top of my head, I threw on the bikini and grabbed a short robe I'd packed exactly for this purpose. I wasn't shy, but I wasn't strolling through the castle in a bathing suit either.

I pushed open the doors to the pool to find the lights on but the room empty. Dropping my robe on a nearby lounge chair, I stuck a toe in the water. I hadn't had a chance to swim yet between the chaos of putting together the party, the break-in, and then going after my dad. For what was supposed to be a leisurely few months pampering Cynthia, this job was turning out to be anything but.

The pool was heated to the perfect temperature. I waded in and swam the length breaststroke, looking around. If I ignored the lounge chairs and the kitchen against the far wall, it wasn't hard to imagine I was in an ancient Roman spa.

The spacious room was fashioned from the same limestone as the exterior of Rycroft castle, the pool a long, cerulean rectangle, the blue of the water vibrant against all that creamy stone.

Wide, round pillars held up the ceiling which curved into a dome above the pool, painted with a mural of the night sky. I floated on my back and looked up into the stars, some of which were lit with tiny LED lights, sparkling against the deep midnight mural of the sky.

The pool was saltwater, filling the spa with the faint, fresh scent of the sea. Forget the rest of Rycroft Castle, I could live right here.

The door pushed open. Evers walked in wearing dark green swim trunks and nothing else. My heart beat faster as I took in all that smooth, tanned skin, the sprinkle of dark hairs on his chest, the ridges along his abdomen, the swell of his biceps.

I wanted to slide out of the pool and bite one of those firm calves, to work my way up every inch of that strong body until he was begging for more.

He came to a stop at the edge of the pool and said, "My own personal mermaid. Where the fuck has that bikini been my entire life?"

"In the back of my sock drawer, hidden away because I was too shy to wear it," I admitted.

Evers executed a perfect shallow dive off the side of the pool, skimming along the surface and coming to stop right in front of me.

I set my feet on the bottom and stood, reaching up to smooth his wet hair off his face, lost in the sparkle of water droplets on his thick dark eyelashes, the way his icy eyes picked up the blue of the pool.

He was so beautiful it was almost unreal. I traced a thumb along his cheekbone, the lush curve of his lower lip.

"Hi," I said, a little breathless.

Evers ran two fingers along my collarbone, reaching the hollow of my throat and dropping straight down between my breasts, tracing the curves almost spilling out of the raspberry bikini top.

"It's a good thing I have my own pool," he said, "because I could see you in this bathing suit every day, but if anyone else sees you in it I'll have to kill them."

"What about the security cameras?" I asked, suddenly remembering that every public space in Rycroft was monitored.

Evers shook his head. "Turned off in here. Just for now."

"Oh," was all I could say. Then his words registered. "You have a pool?"

Regret shadowed his eyes. "I should have brought you to my place before. Yeah, I have a pool. I like to swim. I think you'll like my house. It's no Rycroft Castle, but it's not bad. It's private." His hand dropped to cup one breast. I shifted closer. His erection brushed the front of my thigh. Heat spiked through my body.

"Private?" I breathed, my head swirling with all the things we could do with privacy and a pool.

Evers dipped his head, his lips on the curve of my ear. "Private," he promised. "Not too far from here. Set back in the woods. The house needs a little work."

He skimmed his lips along my jaw. I tilted my head to the side, giving him access to that spot below my ear that only Evers knew about. His mouth found its target, sending shivers rippling across my skin, the brush of his lips almost unbearably sweet as he repeated, "The house needs work, but the pool is fantastic."

"Sounds nice," I breathed.

He moved his mouth to the other side of my neck, nibbling, sucking lightly. I melted in his arms, my hand stroking over all of that smooth, warm, water-slick skin.

"When this is over, when we have time, I want you there. I want you in my pool in this bathing suit." He slid a finger under one of the narrow straps and tugged, sliding it off my shoulder. His lips on my neck, he mouthed, "In the suit and then in nothing at all."

"Skinny dipping?" I asked, intrigued. I'd never been skinny-dipping.

Evers smiled, his lips curving against my skin, and confirmed, "Definitely skinny-dipping."

He kissed me, and I forgot all about swimming.

Evers had me wound up with just a few words.

A few touches.

That, and all of his bare, water-slick skin.

Chapter Twenty-Seven

SUMMER

Dizzy from his mouth on mine, the fantasies swirling in my head, I slipped my hand through the waistband of his trunks and gripped his cock. The hard length flexed in my grip. His kiss turned hungry.

My hand slid from his cock as he lifted me, backing me into the side of the pool. My legs twining around his hips, I braced my elbows on the edge, the arch of my back pressing my breasts into my bikini top, straining the thin fabric. Evers lifted one finger and hooked it in the narrow string between the cups. With a tug, my breasts spilled free.

Cool air rushed against my suddenly-hot skin. Evers' mouth dropped to my nipple, feasting with liquid, sucking pulls, drawing every bit of tension and pleasure to a tight, hot point, the echo pulsing in my clit.

My hips rolled, only two scraps of fabric between us. All he had to do was shove his trunks down, tug my bikini bottom to the side and—

I couldn't think. My fingers sank into his shoulders. He moved from one breast to the other, playing. Tasting. It felt so good. It all felt so fucking good. Slick heat built between my legs. I'd heard pool sex could be uncomfortable, but I was willing to give it a shot.

The idea of waiting one second longer to have Evers inside me was not going to work. I ground my pussy against the length of his cock, trying to reach his trunks so I could drag them down and free him.

He must have gotten the message. Without moving his mouth from my breast, he shoved his trunks down just enough, yanked the gusset of my bikini to the side, and nudged the head of his cock against my pussy, sliding and pressing, making sure I was ready before he drove himself home.

He thrust once hard, pushing me back, my elbow scraping the edge of the pool. At my quick intake of breath, Evers went still.

Lifting his head, the fog of lust clearing from his eyes, he muttered "Fuck."

"I'm okay. Don't stop."

To my grave disappointment, Evers withdrew from my body, sliding his trunks and my bathing suit back into place.

I felt the pout form on my face. I would happily take a few scrapes if it meant Evers would never stop fucking me.

"You look like someone just took her favorite toy," he said before sucking on my lower lip. I didn't have to see my face to know I looked sulky. I *felt* sulky.

"Someone did take my favorite toy."

"The doors are unlocked. I lost my head there for a second, but the doors are unlocked."

How could I have forgotten that the doors were unlocked?

The doors to the spa didn't have locks, probably for

safety reasons. Short of shoving the pool skimmer through the handles, there was no way to secure them closed.

Well, crap. That put a damper on my plans.

I was wrong.

Evers scooped me up into his arms and pushed through the water until we reached the stairs. Once we were out of the water, he headed straight for the changing room.

Such a smart man. The changing rooms *did* have locks.

Locks and a nicely padded divan. Why anyone would put a couch in a glorified bathroom was beyond me, but I wasn't going to complain. Somewhere between turning the locks and setting me on the divan, Evers lost his trunks. I was reaching for my bottoms when he dragged them down my legs, tossing them on the floor.

A heartbeat later he was filling me again, and I was whole. Nothing in my life had ever felt as good as Evers inside me. His long, strong body against mine. Surrounding me. A part of me.

That morning in the honeymoon cottage might have been a million years ago. My body was desperate for his. Evers rocked against me, my breasts pressed to his chest, the scratch of hair against my nipples sending fireworks sparking through my body, building the heat between my legs until my head was spinning.

I clutched Evers, my fingers wrapped around his biceps, my mouth on his neck, kissing, sucking, needing to taste him. To feel him everywhere.

There was so much I wasn't sure of, so much about him that scared the hell out of me, but not this. My heart wavered, afraid to trust, but my body had no such reservations. My most basic instincts shouted that Evers was mine.

I bit down on the cord of his neck as I came, sharp-edged bliss shattering, a keening wail torn from my chest, my thighs tight around him, trembling. It was all too much.

Pleasure, love, need. Such need I couldn't contain it. I embraced it and feared it, holding tight to everything I wanted, my forehead pressed to Evers' damp skin, my body pulsing around him.

Evers' arms locked around me, his hips moving in tight, fast jerks, he breathed my name as he came.

After, neither of us moved, struggling for breath. Finally, he said, "You're shaking," and I realized that I was.

Not shivering. How could I be cold with Evers stretched out on top of me?

No, my body shook with a fine tremble I didn't understand. My heart was too full, felt too much. I wanted to bury my face in his neck and cry. This was so right. So good, and I wanted him so much.

I didn't know what to say. I knew what I wanted to say. "I—"

The words were stuck. In my head, I spoke them loud and strong.

I love you.

I love you so much.

My lips, my voice, couldn't form them. Couldn't give them substance. I pressed my mouth to his, trying to outrun all my uncertainties. Trying to show him what I couldn't say, to give him what was in my heart the only way I could.

He kissed me back, turning to his side and taking me with him, tangling his legs with mine as if we had all the time in the world.

Eventually, we got up and made use of the shower. Soap in my hands, I washed Evers' back, thoroughly exploring every curve of his amazing ass. It wasn't long before I found myself pinned against the white limestone wall, legs spread, holding on for dear life as Evers fucked me to another blinding orgasm.

My legs were wobbly when he set me back down. He whispered in my ear, "When we fix up my house, we're putting a shower next to the pool. A big one."

"I'm in favor of that," I agreed. I was boneless, every joint liquid as I pulled my wet bikini back on and shrugged into my robe. Evers had to check in with the control room again, and I needed to comb my hair or I'd wake up with a rat's nest in the morning.

"I'll walk you to the control room." I threaded my fingers through his and strolled down the hall, a sleepy, smug smile on my face.

We were passing one of the storage closets when I caught a familiar scent in the air and came to an abrupt halt.

I wasn't the only one. Evers smelled it, too.

On a surge of anger, I wrenched open the door to the closet and found my father, a joint in his hand, pungent smoke wreathing his head.

"Are you kidding me?" I planted my hands on my hips and stared him down. My father looked back with a slightly befuddled, completely unrepentant gaze.

Of course, he didn't care that he was smoking pot in my boss' house. Caring about someone else would be inconvenient.

"Where the hell did you get that?" I demanded.

"Relax, baby girl. It's just a joint. I had it in my pocket. Don't be so uptight."

"I am not uptight!" My voice was rising to a screech. Not only was security just down the hall, the theater was at the other end. I did not want Cynthia coming to investigate. Searching for control, I said, "You cannot smoke that here."

Evers reached out and plucked the joint from Smokey's

hand. He ground it out against the concrete floor of the storage closet. "I'll be right back."

He disappeared down the hall toward the spa, the rest of the joint in his hand.

Smokey leaned out of the closet, watching him with a yearning I imagine he'd never expressed toward any of the people in his life. His spine sagged, and he stared at his feet forlornly.

"He didn't have to take it," he muttered.

"He did have to take it," I hissed, leaning in. "I already told you. You can't do drugs in this house. This is Cynthia's place. If anyone found out—"

"All those Hollywood types do drugs. She's probably got a stash in her room upstairs." At that thought, his eyes lit up.

"Oh, no. No way. Maybe other people are like that, but Cynthia is not. She doesn't do drugs. She doesn't even like prescriptions, and she rarely drinks. Unless it's champagne," I corrected. Cynthia did like her champagne.

"This is her home. She kindly invited you to stay for a few days. Your other option is the Sinclair Security safe room, and I don't think you want to stay there."

"I can't believe you'd let them lock me up. You know what they'd do to me if they had me in there. Maxwell told me about his boys. They're all ex-military. Hard-asses. Are you really gonna let your boyfriend hurt your dad?"

I stared at Smokey, speechless. I honestly hadn't considered what the Sinclairs might do with Smokey if they had him under their control. He had information they needed, and he wasn't talking. Unease spiraled through me.

My dad made me so furious I thought my head would explode.

Smoking pot in Cynthia's house? How could he be so rude? How could he endanger my job this way?

And why did I still want to protect him? Why did I feel responsible for him? When had he ever protected me?

Evers returned with a wet paper towel. He shoved it in Smokey's hand and pointed at the dark smear on the concrete floor where he'd put out the joint.

"Clean it up." When Smokey looked as if he would argue, Evers only said, "Now."

Smokey dropped to his knees and started to scrub.

I couldn't look at Evers. My stomach was tight, sick with humiliation.

There was nothing I could say to excuse my dad's behavior. Nothing I could say that would make it okay.

We watched my father clean the floor in stiff silence. When he'd wiped away the evidence, he stood, the wet paper towel clutched in one hand, the other shoved in a back pocket, his chin jutting up, looking more like a rebellious teenager than a fully-grown adult.

Faking bravado, or maybe he really was that stupid, he attempted to shoulder past Evers, saying, "Might as well go finish watching the movie."

Evers' hand closed over his shoulder in a grip so tight Smokey and I flinched simultaneously.

"You're going to your room. I'm posting a guard on the door. You don't come out until breakfast." I'd never heard his voice so hard. So cold.

"What if I get hungry? Or thirsty?" Smokey whined as Evers half led, half dragged him down the hall, his hand still clamped on my dad's shoulder, me trailing behind.

Disgusted with my father, he said, "Drink out of the tap. You get food at breakfast."

The walk to our rooms was endless. Smokey's temporary quarters were at the end of the hall, beside Angie and across from Viggo. Evers shoved him into the room, following. Over his shoulder, he said to me, "Go to your room. I'll stay on his door until someone gets here."

I nodded and walked blindly down the hall to my own room. I needed to comb out my hair and dry it, to rinse out my bathing suit, and wash my face. I did it all mechanically.

I lay my head on my pillow in the dark, too wound up to sleep, reeling from the whiplash. One moment I'd been blissfully happy. Boneless with pleasure. A blink later I was drowning in humiliation, regret and fear freezing my heart and turning my stomach.

The Evers in the pool, in the dressing room, in the honeymoon cottage—that Evers I loved. I trusted. I'd do anything for that Evers.

The Evers who locked my dad in his room?

I loved him, too, but I didn't trust him. My dad was right. Evers had his own agenda. I couldn't blame him for that. He was looking out for his family. Just like I was.

My dad was irresponsible and thoughtless, but he was mine. He'd been my father for twenty-six years. Evers had been in my life for two years, and for more than half of that he'd been lying to me. Using me.

How could I put him before my own father? My father had never particularly looked out for me.

Neither had Evers. At least my Dad never set out to use me for his own ends.

My brain and my heart at odds, I fell into an uneasy sleep, my dreams flashes of being chased. Of wandering in the dark, lost. Alone.

I woke sometime later to feel Evers stretched out beside me, his chest pressed to my back, his arm around my waist, his hand curved around my breast. I drifted back to sleep, suffused with a sense of safety, and knowing that safety was an illusion.

Chapter Twenty-Eight

EVERS

M y phone rang, dragging me out of sleep. My eyes blinked open and my brain clicked online. Axel's ringtone.

I grabbed my phone off the nightstand.

4:12 AM.

"What happened?"

"Attempted break-in at the condo. Through the window of Mom's bedroom."

My gut clutched. "Is she okay?"

"Yeah. She twisted an ankle trying to get out of bed. Got tangled in the quilt. He set off the alarm and bailed, but he managed to get the window open. If he'd wanted to, he could have taken a shot."

"Did you get him?"

"No," Axel said, sounding annoyed and resigned. "I thought she'd broken her foot and I didn't want to leave her alone long enough to go after him."

"Fuck." Beside me Summer stirred, rolling over and looking at me with questioning eyes. I reached out to take her hand, running my thumb over her knuckles. "Did you talk to Cooper yet?"

"A minute ago. Mom and I are headed to Vegas as soon as I get her ankle checked out."

"I thought you said it's a sprain."

Axel sighed, and I had a moment of gratitude that I was in Atlanta, in bed with Summer, while he was stuck in Florida with our mom.

"It *is* a sprain. If she hadn't had a supersized gin and tonic before bed, she wouldn't have fallen in the first place. She's insisting she see her own doctor. Actually, she's refusing to budge from the condo."

"What are you going to do?" I wasn't sure I wanted to know.

"Take her to the doctor and then go straight to the airport. I'll carry her onto the fucking plane if I have to."

"Fuck," I said again, torn between guilt that Axel and Emma were saddled with our mom and rising fury that Tsepov had gone after her so directly.

I couldn't shake the mental image of her waking in the night, afraid, struggling with her blankets while one of Tsepov's goons aimed a gun at her head. Our fucking father had a lot to answer for.

Axel interrupted my thoughts. "Cooper said you picked up Smokey Winters."

"Yesterday," I affirmed.

"He's not talking?"

"Not yet. Claims he doesn't know anything."

"That's bullshit," Axel burst out, worry simmering beneath his anger.

I was pretty fucking pissed myself. We knew Smokey had information that would help get Tsepov off our backs, and he was sitting around sponging off Cynthia and

Summer, taking care of number one and leaving the rest of us blowing in the wind.

"Make him fucking talk," Axel said.

Summer went stiff, and I knew she'd heard.

I didn't look at her.

I couldn't.

I knew what I'd see in her eyes. Worry. Distrust. Fear.

She wanted to look out for her dad. She wanted us to go easy on him.

Easy was done.

I had another flash of my Mom, alone in her bed, one of Tsepov's men coming through the window. Not again. We'd tried it Summer's way. Now it was my turn.

Axel pulled my attention back to our conversation. "Cooper wants you and Smokey in the office. Now. He was going to call, but I told him I'd pass along the message."

"Understood," I said. "We'll call you back when we're done. Give Mom my love, okay? Tell her we're going to fix this."

"Yeah, I will. And you fucking better."

Axel ended the call.

"Is your mom okay?" Summer asked. I rolled out of bed and looked past her, unable to stomach the reproach I'd see in her eyes when I told her what was about to happen.

"She is for now. Someone tried to get into her condo. She's a little banged up. Scared. I'm bringing your dad in."

"In for what?" she asked, voice tight with fear. She didn't need my answer. She already knew.

"For questioning," I said, shortly. "We don't have time for his bullshit, Summer. It would be different if they were coming after me or my brothers, but my mom deserves better than this. He's going to fucking talk, whether he wants to or not."

I was through the door before she could respond, heading for my room to get dressed. Ready to go, I went for Smokey, swinging his door wide, the room flooding with light from the hall.

Smokey was so deeply asleep I'd pulled him to a sitting position before his eyes opened. "What the hell? What's going on?"

"Get your ass out of bed. You're coming with me." I pulled him to his feet, pushing him in the direction of his dresser.

"Hey, man, back off. You can't make me—"

I dropped Smokey's arm and stepped back, drawing my gun from the holster at the small of my back and leveling it on Smokey.

"I can do whatever I fucking want. Get out of the goddamn bed and put your clothes on."

Smokey's face paled as he took in the gun. He was a weasel, but he knew I wasn't. I'd learned early—never pull a weapon I'm not prepared to use.

Smokey saw the intent in my eyes. Moving faster than I'd ever seen him, he pulled on jeans and a T-shirt, shoving his feet into a pair of worn flip-flops.

"Face the wall and put your hands up."

He did. I holstered my gun and pulled a pair of handcuffs from my pocket. I had him cuffed and was shoving him into the hall when we almost bumped into Summer, pacing outside Smokey's door, her hair in a loose ponytail, wearing the bright yellow sundress she'd discarded last night in favor of that pink bikini.

I couldn't think of Summer in that bikini, of peeling it off her. Not now. Not if I was going to look after my family.

"I'm coming with you," she announced, dismay darkening her eyes at the sight of her father with his hands cuffed behind his back.

"Summer," Smokey said, sensing an advantage, "baby girl, tell him to let me go. Call the police or something. He can't do this. It's unconstitutional—"

"Shut up, Dad," she said, glaring at her father. To me, she said again, "I'm coming with you. I'm not letting you take my dad away. I'm coming with you."

"Summer," I started, but she cut me off.

"I'm coming with you or I'll report you for kidnapping. You can't just lock him up until he tells you what you want to know."

I could do exactly that. And I would. If I had to, I'd stop Summer from calling the police, too. I hoped it didn't come to that.

"Summer," I tried again. I risked a look at her face and knew she wasn't going to back down. Might as well let her come. At least I'd know where she was. "Fine, but stay out of our way."

Summer fell in line beside us, glaring at her dad and refusing to look at me.

I was fucking up again. I knew it, and I couldn't stop myself.

I was done babying her father. Maybe she wanted to lie to herself about dear old Dad, but I had to face reality.

Smokey Winters was a criminal who didn't deserve our consideration.

He had information we needed, and he was going to give it to us.

That was reality. Anything else was Summer fooling herself.

I'd fix things with her later. I had to believe I could.

For now, Cooper and I had one job. Get Smokey

Winters to talk.

Cooper was waiting in the safe room when we got there. Lucas Jackson was with him. If I'd wondered about Cooper's plan, seeing Lucas answered my questions.

Torture wasn't our go-to when it came to extracting information, but Smokey Winters didn't know that.

Lucas Jackson is a good guy. A marshmallow when it comes to his wife. At 6'6", with shoulders as broad as a barn door, he made for an intimidating threat. He looked like a brawler, had spent some time undercover in a biker club, but at heart, Lucas preferred peace to war.

We'd brought him on knowing his military and civilian files had blank spots. A lot of blank spots. He'd done things he didn't like to think about, and he worked with us because we rarely asked him to access the darker side of his skill set.

He ran our division of computer experts. If you didn't know better, you'd never guess Lucas was happiest in front of a keyboard. He looked like the furthest thing from a computer geek, which just went to show that appearances are deceiving.

Smokey took one look at Lucas, and his eyes flashed wide with fear.

Good.

Maybe a little fear would loosen his tongue.

A table sat in the middle of the safe room, a chair on either side. I shoved Smokey toward one of the chairs.

"Sit."

Cooper took the other chair. Lucas stood behind him, arms crossed over his chest, his green eyes flat, dangerous, and trained on Smokey.

Smokey squirmed. Summer started forward, moving to

her father. I closed my hand over her elbow and pulled her back.

"Stay out of it."

Smokey shot her a pleading glance, but she stayed where she was. Her quiescence wouldn't last.

She was thinking, trying to figure a way out for her father. There wasn't one. This wasn't a game. Not with my mom's life at stake. Smokey wasn't leaving this room until he told us what we wanted to know.

If it got ugly along the way, we were all going to have to live with that.

"How long did you work with my father?" Cooper said, starting with the easy question.

I could see the gears turning in Smokey's mind. Saw him consider a smartass response. His eyes, so like Summer's, flicked up to Lucas. He took in Cooper's resolve, his silent daughter beside me, and decided to give a little something before it was dragged from him by force.

"Off and on since 2003."

"What happened in 2003? Why then?" Cooper asked.

Smokey shot a look at Summer. "You don't need to be here, girl. Let your man take you home."

Summer went stiff. "What happened in 2003, Dad?" she asked, the suspicion in her voice telling me she knew she wouldn't like his answer.

Smokey was a mostly-absent father, but he knew his daughter well enough to tell when she wouldn't be budged. He held his breath for a long moment before it rushed out in a gusty sigh, carrying with it a flood of words.

"It was when Hugh died. I called. I wanted to come see my second cousins, or whatever they are. I wanted to see the kids."

"First cousins once removed," Cooper murmured.

"Whatever. Hugh and James were gone, I wanted to see—"

It hit all of us at the same time. Summer made a sound somewhere between a gasp and a wail. "You wanted to see if you could get any money out of them, didn't you?" she asked, her voice rough with pain. "That's why you called them."

"No, I wanted to see if they were okay. That was all, but—"

"Of course, they weren't okay." Cooper looked at Smokey with disgust, his face mirroring the expression on my own and Summer's.

"I never talked to any of them," Smokey said defensively. "Davis picked up the phone. Invited me to meet them, but when I got there, it wasn't the family. It was just Davis. He told me he knew who I was, and he wanted me to stay away from the kids. He, uh, he—"

"He offered to cut you in on some cash if you'd promise to stay away from the Winters kids," I finished for him.

Chapter Twenty-Nine

EVERS

"Dad," Summer said, her words caught in her throat, arms wrapped around her chest, hugging herself.

Not thinking, I reached for her. She looked so alone, betrayed and devastated as she stared at her father like he was a stranger.

At my touch she jerked, stepping out of reach. My gut turned to ice at the look in her eyes.

It wasn't just her father. She looked at me as if she'd never seen me before. As if I were the enemy.

"Is that why you told me never to contact them?" she demanded of Smokey. "You traded family for money?"

"They aren't your family, Summer," Smokey said, "and it was a lot of money."

"They are my family, and we could have been there for them. You're obviously useless, but Mom and I, we could have been there when they needed us. You gave up our family for nothing."

Smokey jerked in his chair, trying to stand, but he was

off balance with his hands cuffed. His thighs hit the underside of the table and he fell back into the chair, staying where he was.

He looked at his daughter with a desperate anger. "Not for nothing. I kept a roof over your head—"

"Mom kept a roof over my head. Mom worked her butt off. For us. For me. You just bummed around from job to job, forgetting to buy groceries or pick me up from school. What were you doing for William Davis and Maxwell Sinclair? What do you know about Maxwell? About what these Russians want?"

Smokey shook his head. "You don't understand, girl. I was nothing more than an errand boy for them. They gave me a job and I did what I was told."

"And what did they tell you to do?" Cooper asked evenly, holding an iron control on his temper.

Smokey shifted in his chair and shrugged one shoulder with a jerk. "Drive, mostly."

"Drive what? Where?" Cooper asked. Cooper's control wouldn't last long. One finger tapped the surface of the table in a steady rhythm. It was his tell, a gauge of the fury building inside him.

This was going to devolve fast if Smokey didn't start talking. Summer stood out of reach, tears shimmering in her eyes, looking as if she'd lost her puppy, her best friend, and found out the truth about Santa Claus in one fell swoop.

"Half the time I didn't even know," Smokey hedged. "I moved product. I got paid. That was all."

Through gritted teeth, Cooper asked, "What product?"

No one in the room really wanted the answer. Anything Smokey said would only reveal deeper levels of the filth painting our father and Summer's.

If it weren't for my mother and Tsepov's threats, I would

have shoved Smokey out the door and washed my hands of him. Of all of it.

My father might be dead. He was probably alive. Either way, right now I didn't fucking care. He'd caused enough trouble, broken enough hearts, shattered enough lives.

If it weren't for my mother and Tsepov I would have been done, but I couldn't walk away. None of us could, and we needed the answers.

Cooper's finger tapped faster on the table.

"What product?" Cooper repeated.

Shifting uneasily, Smokey said, "Drugs, mostly, okay? A few times, sometimes guns. Stuff like that. And uh... sometimes it was... I'd drive the van and it was, uh..."

"Women or children," Lucas finished, in a gravelly, deadly voice.

The blood drained from Smokey's face. His eyes locked on Lucas, he nodded slowly. "Sometimes, it was."

Summer let out a whimper of distress.

I couldn't stop myself. I crossed the room and pulled her into my arms. She let me, burying her head against my chest, the heat of her tears leaking through my shirt.

I could do this. If she was here, letting me take the burden, letting me hold her, comfort her—I could do anything as long as she was in my arms. As long as there wasn't that distance in her eyes. As long as she wasn't making me the enemy.

No one spoke, the sound of Summer's harsh breathing filling the room. Smokey shot a look at her that was half apology and half disgust.

Cooper pushed harder. "What does Tsepov want from us? What did my father take?"

"I don't know, man. I don't have a fucking clue. I didn't

even know Davis was dead until a week ago. I'm telling you, I was a driver."

Cooper glanced at Lucas. Lucas nodded.

Rounding the table, he moved to stand behind Smokey and bent to unlock the handcuffs. Smokey barely had a chance to say, "What—", before Lucas had one hand free, the other re-cuffed to the side of the metal chair.

Lucas grabbed Smokey's free hand and slammed it down on the stainless steel table. Smokey jerked his arm back, trying to get free. His hand didn't budge under Lucas' grip.

Leaning one hip against the table, Lucas pulled a shiny, steel butterfly knife from his pocket. He didn't say a word, didn't even look at Smokey, only flicked the knife open and flipped the blade back and forth in a mesmerizing pattern.

In. Out. Circling around, the metal clicking and sliding, the sharp blade flashing in the harsh overhead light.

Smokey started to shake. Then he started to beg.

"I don't know anything. I swear. I swear. I swear. I don't know anything. Please, look, man, look at me. I'm a stoner, man, I'm a mess. You think they're going to trust me with anything important?"

Lucas' hand tightened on Smokey's wrist. Smokey's words came faster. "I did what I was told, and I took the cash. That's all. That's all I did. I swear." The acrid scent of urine filled the air as Smokey pissed himself in terror.

At the desperation in her father's voice, Summer lifted her head, turning in my arms. Every muscle in her body locked tight as she took in the scene in front of her. For one disorienting moment, I saw the room through her eyes.

The concrete floor tilting down to a drain. The spare metal bed frame in the corner. The stainless steel table.

That sharp, shining blade in Lucas' hand. We called it the safe room. There was no hiding that it had other uses.

Before I could say anything, Summer looked up at me, the plea in her eyes tearing at my heart.

I wanted to promise her Lucas wouldn't hurt her father. To swear this was just a threat to scare Smokey into talking.

I couldn't do it.

It was probably true. *Probably.*

If our mom hadn't been threatened hours before, I would have bet my life that the blade in Lucas' hand was just for show.

Looking at Cooper, I wasn't entirely sure myself.

I wanted to believe my brother wouldn't torture an innocent man.

Except Smokey Winters wasn't all that innocent.

I wanted to believe Lucas wouldn't use that knife. In another situation, maybe he wouldn't. Watching him look down at Smokey, a man who'd just admitted to not only running guns and drugs but trafficking women and children, I wasn't sure what Lucas would do.

This wasn't just about Smokey or my dad. Not anymore. I could believe that the guns and drugs were my Dad's work. I didn't want to, but I could see it. Trafficking? That was Tsepov, all the way.

If my dad and William Davis had been that deep with Tsepov, we had a bigger problem. We didn't just need to get Tsepov off our backs, we needed to shut the whole thing down.

My father always hated our connection to Matt Holley, the SAC of the Atlanta field office of the FBI. Now we knew why. Holley had stepped in to help Emma when she'd uncovered the elder Tsepov's dealings with her boss. When she shot Tsepov to save Axel's life, Holley said it wasn't over. He'd been right.

Summer began to shake in my arms, her teeth chattering from the rush of adrenaline-fueled fear. Whatever I believed, whatever Cooper and Lucas might have planned, Summer was terrified to her bones.

She squeezed her eyes shut and said, "Please, Evers. Please don't hurt him. I know he's—" She cut off with a sob.

I tightened my arms around her, pressing my chin to her head, trying to stop her shaking. Trying to figure out what the fuck to say.

Cooper, his dark eyes hard as granite, said, "Lucas."

Lucas moved the knife, drawing closer to Smokey Winters' outstretched hand. Smokey struggled, jerking his body away, but Lucas' grip was too strong. The knife flashed —snick, click—as he flipped it in and out of its case, twirling his wrist, bringing it closer and closer.

Summer whimpered again. "Please. Evers, please—"

I was out of time, and I knew what I had to do. Cooper was too angry, Lucas blinded by loyalty.

"Stop," I said. "Stop. He doesn't know anything."

Lucas froze, the knife dangling from his fingers, the faintest hint of relief in the shadows of his eyes. I knew what Lucas could do with that knife. I also knew he didn't want to use it. Not on Smokey. Not on anyone. Not anymore.

Finger tapping faster, his voice deceptively even, Cooper said, "Stay out of it, Evers. Take Summer and get out if you can't handle it."

Summer dug in her heels, trying to pull out of my arms. I held her where she was. "No," I said, shaking my head. "I'm not walking out. I'm not leaving him here with you. He's an asshole, a criminal, and I'm not sure he has a fucking conscience, but he can't tell us anything."

"You don't know that," Cooper growled in frustrated anger.

"Come on, I do know that. You know that." I nodded towards the chair where Smokey sat, hand still pinned to the table, stewing in his own urine. "He pissed himself out of fear. You really think this guy wouldn't talk? He'd talk. He sold out his family for a buck, he'd throw his daughter under the bus if he thought it would save him. If he had anything to tell, he would have spilled it already. We're going to have to find it another way."

"We're running out of time," Cooper said.

"I know."

Maybe I was making a mistake. Maybe Smokey was that good a liar and I was letting him slide. I didn't know. I couldn't read my gut on this one. My emotions were too tangled up. Fear for my mom. Love for Summer. Agony at her pain.

I didn't know if I was doing the right thing.

I only knew that if I had to choose between finding what Tsepov wanted or protecting Summer, I chose Summer.

I wasn't going to fuck things up with Summer over my father's bullshit and some Russian mobster who couldn't fucking tell us what he wanted before he threatened to kill us all.

I knew to the marrow of my bones that if Lucas' knife touched Smokey Winters, I would lose Summer forever. She might be disappointed by her father's failures, but if we drew his blood, that would be it. She'd never forgive me. I wasn't sure I'd blame her.

I wasn't going to lose her over this. Not over anything.

Lucas flicked the knife one more time, sending it back into the handle before he shoved it in his pocket and stepped away, releasing Smokey's hand. Summer's arms tightened around me, her tears of relief soaking my shirt.

I stroked her back and murmured into her hair, "It's going to be okay. I promise it's going to be okay."

I thought I spoke the truth.

I'd never been more wrong.

Chapter Thirty

EVERS

"What do we do with him now?" Summer asked, glancing at her father in the rearview mirror. He sat in the back, leaning against the door, staring out of the window and ignoring us.

Fine with me. Just because I'd gotten him out of the safe room didn't mean I was on his side. Far from it.

"I don't know," I said. "We could take him back to his place. He's got a lot of cleaning up to do. Might as well get started."

At that, Smokey came to life. "No way, man, you can't just drop me off and get rid of me."

"Why not?" Summer asked. She'd begged for her father's life, but she still stared at him as if he were a stranger. In a way, he was.

She had a mental image of Smokey as a ne'er-do-well stoner.

I didn't have to imagine her shock at finding out he was anything but.

I knew exactly how she felt. I'd been there. I'd grown up thinking my dad was a hero. He kept people safe. Rescued them from danger. He was one of the good guys. Tough, sure. Kind of a jerk to my mom, yeah.

With the blind love of a child, I'd worshiped the good and brushed aside the bad. Even as I'd gotten older and his praise felt hollow, his casual cruelties more distinct, he was my father. A tarnished hero, but still high on that pedestal.

When it all came crashing down, when we'd realized who he really was, the past had come into focus. Maxwell Sinclair was no hero. Expecting us to live up to his bullshit ideals, treating my mother like crap, and turning into a criminal when he was bored with a normal life.

Success, wealth, and a family who loved him hadn't been enough. He had to have more. Always more.

I thought of Hugh Winters. Aiden's dad had been like a second father growing up. *Hugh* was a hero. He loved his kids, worshipped his wife. Worked hard and still managed to make every game, every recital. He never cut corners. Never failed to tell his kids he was proud of them.

Hugh had deserved his pedestal.

My father was a fraud.

On the surface, Smokey was a hippie stoner, while my father had country club written all over him, but under the skin, they weren't that different. Corrupt and greedy. Selfish.

I knew exactly how much it hurt to learn that the person who was supposed to look out for you had only been looking out for themselves.

I reached across the seat and took Summer's hand. She squeezed my fingers and stared out the window.

Finally, quietly, she said, "I think we should drop Smokey off at his house."

"Summer! What the hell? I'm your father, for Christ's sake. You can't just throw me to the wolves. You guys saw what they did to my place. What do you think would have happened if I'd been there? There's a reason I was hiding out with Warren, you know."

"And now you expect us to clean up your mess?" she challenged, her eyes tired.

"There's nothing to clean up. I just need a safe place to stay for a while. Cynthia said I could stay at the castle. It's her house. She said—"

"She only said you could stay as a favor to me," Summer cut in. "And I don't want you there. I can barely look at you right now."

Summer's words sank in. For the first time since I'd pulled him out of the safe room, panic worked its way into Smokey's consciousness. Talking fast, he said, "Just for a few days, Summer. I'll figure something else out. Just for a few days. I'll stay in my room, I swear. I won't be any trouble."

Summer looked over at me, one eyebrow raised.

Shit.

I wanted to say *fuck, no.*

I wanted to slow down at the curb in front of his house and shove him out of the SUV. I wanted him out of Summer's life. Out of my life.

We'd get there eventually. Another day or two wouldn't change anything.

Ignoring Smokey, I said to Summer, "It's up to you."

Summer tilted her head back and closed her eyes. After a long moment, she said, "Three days. That's it. Three days and either you leave on your own or I'll have security dump you outside the gates. If you try to get back in, I'll call the police."

Smokey pressed his lips together and said nothing. I

already knew he wouldn't bother to thank her. Odds were an insult hovered on the tip of his tongue. I hoped he'd be smart enough to keep his mouth shut. He was. Barely.

When we got back to Rycroft, Smokey slammed out of the SUV and headed straight to his room. If he wanted to hide out up there, it was fine with me. The longer I went without seeing his face the better I'd feel.

Exhausted from the early wake-up and everything that had happened since, Summer and I needed food. It felt like an entire day had passed since we'd left Rycroft, but breakfast was still being served in the dining room.

Tired to my bones, I wanted nothing more than to pack Summer up and take off. Go somewhere we could be alone. Somewhere we could leave this mess behind. So many options. Hell, we could be in Vegas in a few hours. Get a suite at the Delecta, and then I could show Summer what a good strip club was really like.

Already imagining the way her blush would spread down her neck and across her luscious cleavage, I was distracted when Cynthia said my name.

Fuck. *Get your head on the job, Evers.* "Sorry what?"

"Where did you two go so early? Is everything okay?" Cynthia's worried glance took in Summer and myself.

"There was a problem with my mom. She's all right, but we thought Smokey might know something. We brought him into the office to find out."

"Did he?"

"No," I answered.

"And your mom's okay?"

"She is. Axel's in Florida with her. He's taking her to Vegas, but if we don't wrap this up soon, we might have to bring her to Atlanta."

"If I recall, your mother hates Atlanta," Cynthia said with a small smile.

"She wouldn't be happy," I agreed, "but we'll do what we have to do."

"If you want Smokey to leave," Summer offered, "he will. This is all a little more complicated than we anticipated. You shouldn't have to deal with any of it."

"Summer, honey, Evers and his guys have this place so locked down no one is getting in or out without them knowing. Seems like the safest place to keep him is here. Right?"

"It is," I agreed, "but this is your show. It's your house, and we're your team. You call the shots. If you want us to move him somewhere else, consider it done. We appreciate your patience—"

"—but we don't want to take advantage," Summer finished.

Cynthia's phone chirped with a text. She dropped her eyes to the screen, brow furrowed. As if we hadn't been in the middle of a conversation, she picked up the phone and tapped to text back.

"Cynthia?" I prompted.

She looked up, biting her lip, one eyebrow raised. "Oh, no, it's fine. Smokey can stay. Don't worry about it."

Summer watched her employer, eyes narrowed. "Who are you texting?"

I was surprised at her tone. She was usually deferential to Cynthia. A smart move considering that Cynthia was used to the world fawning over her. She did not enjoy being challenged.

For once, Summer didn't seem to care. Cynthia turned her phone upside down and shoved it half under the side of her plate. "Nobody. Nobody you need to worry about. It's nothing."

For an Oscar-winning actress, she'd suddenly turned into a terrible liar. Summer appeared to agree. "Bullshit. Who are you texting?" When Cynthia opened her mouth to dismiss Summer's question again, Summer leaned forward and said, "Don't make me come over there."

Cynthia sighed. "Clint, okay? I've been texting with Clint."

"Is he trying to set up a meet?" I asked. Cynthia had been putting him off since the party. He had to be getting impatient. He hadn't attempted to get through the gates again, but eventually, he would.

"No. Well, yes, but he's trying to convince me that all the rumors are just rumors. That there was nothing going on in that picture with the girl, that he hasn't touched a drop of alcohol or anything since he left rehab. He said someone is spreading lies. Trying to drive us apart."

"And you believe him?" Summer asked.

Summer knew Clint Perry, had known him when he and Cynthia were happy together. Until he'd started drinking and cheating on Cynthia, she'd liked him.

Cynthia's shoulders slumped. She rubbed her thumb along the rim of her coffee cup, staring at the dregs staining the white china.

"I've believed him so many times. I'm tired of feeling like a fool. But when I talk to him—"

"He's been calling, too?"

Cynthia shot Summer a quelling look. Summer dropped it. She knew her limits.

"When I talk to him," Cynthia continued, her words wistful and sad, "he doesn't sound like he's lying. I don't know. I don't know what to do." She looked at me, entreating, "Can you find out if someone's spreading these rumors? If it's true?"

I was torn. Axel had an office in LA, and his team there knew the scene. Knew the players. Tracking down whoever was spreading these rumors—if they were rumors—wouldn't be too hard.

We're talking about celebrities, not super-spies.

If I was going to leave town for a few days, now was the time. Smokey wasn't going anywhere for seventy-two hours. My mother was safe, headed to Vegas with Axel. He had a lock on his city, and his place was a fortress. No one would get to her there.

We had Tsepov's unknown deadline bearing down on us. A deadline with no date to find an unidentified prize. The elder Tsepov, the one Emma had shot, never would have been so sloppy.

If the Russian actually wanted us to find what my father took, he might have told us what it was. And when he wanted it.

Fucking amateur.

That didn't mean he didn't have an army at his disposal. An amateur heading an army was more dangerous than a professional. We could have negotiated with his uncle. Worked something out. This guy—this guy was all bravado and ego. There was no negotiating with someone like him.

He was dangerous, but not so much that we had to hide in the castle until we neutralized him. I wouldn't let him cage us with his open-ended deadline.

On the other hand, Cynthia's planned visits with family and friends, the visits the party was supposed to spark, had never happened. With Clint lurking around, she'd stayed close to home. Isolated.

She'd come to Atlanta for peace, but the Cynthia I knew was social. If she resolved things with Clint once and for all, maybe she'd feel free to live her life again.

"This isn't the best time to leave town," I hedged.

Cynthia, sensing an opportunity, gave me a pleading look that would have been affecting if it weren't so practiced. "Evers, it would mean the world to me if you could do this. Really. The world."

"Define *the world*," I countered.

The sweetly pleading look melted away. Deadly serious, Cynthia said, "It means that if you can give me an answer, one way or another, I'll pay the original fee despite all of these interruptions in service."

Well, damn. She really wanted to know if Clint was telling the truth. After the break-in at the party and our trip to North Carolina, she'd negotiated me into taking a bath on the job. Going back to the contract price was a big swing.

We'd originally been on track to make a sweet profit. You don't get to be the premier security agency in the country by ignoring business. This job had gone sideways, but if a quick day or two in L.A. could salvage it from a red line item back to black it would be worth it.

Summer watched me with hopeful eyes. I didn't need to ask what she wanted me to do. I did anyway. "Are you okay if I go to L.A. for a few days?"

Below the tablecloth, she slid her hand up my leg, her pinky grazing my cock. "I'll miss you, but if you can find out what's going on with Clint it really would mean a lot."

My body at attention, I leaned over and pressed a kiss to her cheek. "Thanks," I said softly, my lips brushing her smooth skin.

"You two are so sweet I have a toothache. You know you owe me, right?"

Summer rolled her eyes at Cynthia. "Maybe. But I still remember you kissing him, so..."

Cynthia cocked an eyebrow. "Well, you weren't kissing him, and it's a crime to let a man like that go un-kissed."

Beside me, Summer let out a harrumph. Shooting me a dark look, she said, "He didn't deserve to be kissed."

I didn't like where this conversation was going. I stopped her mouth with mine. When her cheeks were flushed and she'd forgotten why I didn't deserve her kisses, I picked up my fork and dug into breakfast. I filled my stomach while I went over logistics in my head.

"Let me call Axel, see who he can set me up with out there. I can't be gone long, but I should be able to find something out and come back in a few days."

"Thanks, Evers," Cynthia said, relief easing the tension in her eyes. She turned to Summer, going over some video she wanted to shoot for her social media. Summer pulled out her phone, taking notes with one hand while she ate with the other.

I was going to miss breakfasts at Rycroft Castle over the next few days. Plate clean, I stood, telling Cynthia, "I'll get Alice working on a flight. I'll let you know what's going on as soon as I'm done."

Chapter Thirty-One

EVERS

As I'd expected, Axel had exactly the right guy to help me out. His team in L.A. focused on celebrity protection details, and they knew everyone. Who was up-and-coming. Who was on their way out. Who had a secret drug problem. Who was sleeping with whose husband, or wife, or lover. Who was in the closet, and who was about to come out of the closet.

If there was a secret in Hollywood, Axel's guys knew it.

He offered to have them handle the investigation without me, but I'd promised Cynthia I'd do it personally. Griffen would stay at Rycroft in my place. With Axel in Las Vegas and Cooper holding down the fort in the office, Griffen was the only other person I trusted to keep the job under control and watch out for Summer.

An hour later, I was kissing Summer good bye and heading for the plane. Leaving Summer behind felt like cutting off a limb. We'd only just found one another again. I didn't want to go anywhere without her.

It would fade eventually, this feeling that I had to have

her in arms' reach. The faint, nagging fear that I was going to fuck it all up and lose her again. When we were together, I could fool myself into thinking we were solid. That we'd made it out the other side.

When I was alone, I remembered the way she'd thrown me out. The distance in her eyes in the safe room.

When I was alone, I remembered that I'd told her I loved her, and she'd never said it back.

I'd make it a quick few days. If it took more than that, I was passing the job off and coming home.

I'd planned on no more than seventy-two hours. Not counting travel time, it took less then forty-eight.

Cynthia's rival for her upcoming film hadn't taken her loss of the lead role very well. She'd tried spreading rumors that Cynthia was old, washed up, and had a drug problem.

None of those had gained any traction.

When her attacks on Cynthia didn't work, she decided to go after Clint. With his history of addiction and infidelity, he was an easy target. It didn't take us long to track down the ingénue crawling all over him in those infamous pictures. A little persuasion and she'd spilled everything.

The life of an up-and-coming actress in L.A is expensive. Fake-it-until-you-make-it is tough when parts are thin on the ground. She needed the visibility to get cast, and without the right roles, her bank account had been running dry.

I didn't need the hint. Enough of a bribe—one I'd bill to Cynthia—and she was more than happy to go on record with the whole story. I promised her the recording would stay between us. She'd been desperate enough to take the risk.

Between her video confession and an audio recording of Cynthia's rival drunkenly admitting what she'd done, we had everything we needed. I was on a plane headed east an hour later, more than ready to leave LaLa land for home. For Summer.

We'd talked on the phone a few times while I'd been gone. Rycroft Castle had been quiet. Smokey was bitching and moaning about all the rules. No drugs. No getting drunk. Summer was at her wit's end. He had less than twenty-four hours before I was throwing him out, and she was counting every minute.

When I got to Rycroft, I should have gone straight to Cynthia. She was the client, and I'd been in LA for her. Instead, I went hunting for Summer. Cynthia could wait.

As luck would have it, she and Summer were working together in the library. I stepped into the room, my greeting caught in my throat as my eyes fell on Summer. Two days and it felt like a lifetime.

The scuff of my shoe on the floor caught her attention, her blue eyes lighting with joy. She leapt out of her chair and threw herself into my arms. I didn't like being away from her, but if this was what I got on return, maybe it had been worth it.

Cynthia gave a sigh of impatience at our reunion and said, "Well?"

I released Summer and took the chair beside Cynthia, pulling my phone from my pocket. "I can't give you this video. I promised Annette I'd delete it as soon as you saw it, but she admitted that Meredith Porter bribed her to go after Clint. Meredith staged the whole picture, fed it to the paps, everything. Annette said she's also behind the rumors that Clint's been drinking again."

"That bitch. It's not my fault she wasn't good enough to get the part. What—"

"Do you want to see the video?" I asked, interrupting the tirade to come.

"Yes, I want to see the fucking video," Cynthia snapped.

I held up my phone and hit play. We were treated to a five-minute recording of Annette Hunt looking less than red-carpet-ready as she blubbered through her confession.

In photographs, she looked so sophisticated. Mature. On the video, it was easy to remember that she was barely more than a teenager. Still a kid, and in over her head with the far more savvy and experienced Meredith Porter.

I played the recording of Meredith's confession, lubricated by vodka, watching Cynthia's limpid green eyes grow shadowed and thoughtful. When the recording ended, Cynthia sat back. More to herself than to us, she said, "I need to talk to Clint."

Summer studied her with concern. "Are you going to give him another chance?"

Cynthia shook her head *No* but said, "Maybe. I don't know. I need to talk to him. I'm calling him now. When he gets here, I want the two of you nearby. Not in the room, but don't go far, okay?"

I couldn't remember the last time I'd seen Cynthia Stevens this uncertain. Even when she was young, before she'd left home to find fame and fortune, she'd been brimming with confidence. Determination.

I shook my head. "I'd rather be in the room, just in case—"

"No. Clint's not dangerous."

"Cynthia," I started, prepared to argue. She cut me off with a sharp shake of her head.

"No. Outside the door is fine. Not in the room. This

whole situation has been embarrassing enough, I'm not having this conversation with an audience."

Clint must have been waiting for Cynthia's call. He had a room at The Intercontinental, not far away. Ten minutes later he was rolling through the gates in his rented sports car.

Now that he had the meeting he wanted, I expected him to be brash. Aggressive and demanding. He was none of that, thanking me for letting him in and staring at Cynthia the way a man dying of thirst looks at water. As if he were parched for her and only her.

Summer and I followed them to the parlor where Cynthia firmly shut the doors.

"Do you think—" I started.

"Shhh." She shushed me, holding up a finger. "I want to see if I can hear what they're saying."

I could have told her the doors were too thick for that unless they started yelling, in which case we'd be through them in a second. I didn't bother. Instead, I moved to stand beside her, sliding an arm around her waist.

I would have preferred Cynthia allow us in the room for security reasons, but I didn't mind a little time alone with Summer. I tried not to laugh as she pressed her ear to the door. Nothing. With a little grunt of annoyance, she pushed away from the door, whispering, "Be right back," over her shoulder as she disappeared down the hall. She came back a minute later with an old-fashioned crystal glass she must have grabbed from the bar. Pressing it to the thick door, she strained for a hint of sound.

Doing my best to keep the laugh from my voice, I said, "Nothing?"

She straightened, dropping the hand with the glass to her side. "Nothing."

Wandering to the terrace doors, she set the glass on a side table and stared out the window to the garden. I came up behind her, my arms sliding around her waist, my heart settling when she leaned into me, giving a low hum of pleasure.

"I missed you," she said under her breath. "I know you were barely gone, but I missed you."

"Me too. I didn't want to go."

"I'm glad you did, though. No matter what happens with Clint, she needed to know the truth."

Not sure it was the right time to get into it, I said slowly, "I don't travel for work as much as I used to, but I do travel. Sometimes I can take you with me, but—"

"I travel here and there, too," she said, turning in my arms and raising her face to mine. "We'll figure it out."

"Most of the time I can't talk about my work," I said, not knowing why I felt the need to lay it all out, show her all the pitfalls of being with me.

Summer shook with silent laughter. "I already know that, Evers. Considering my clients, sometimes I can't talk either." She reached up, taking my face between her palms. "Stop worrying. I know all the bad stuff. We're past it. Aren't we? Are there any other secrets you're hiding?"

"No more secrets," I promised, letting her draw my face to hers, my eyes sliding shut as she pressed her lips to mine. This was what I'd missed. Summer, her flowers and lemon scent, her gentle hands, her sweet mouth. Her open heart.

I kissed her, savoring her taste, the slow slide of her tongue as it danced with mine, the low sounds of pleasure humming in her throat.

I needed to keep one ear on the parlor door. There was staff wandering around, both Cynthia's and my own.

I didn't care.

I was a second away from tossing Summer over my shoulder and carrying her to my room when the sounds of footsteps and giggles reminded me where we were.

Two of the day maids crossed the hall carrying a vacuum and a bucket of cleaning supplies, both sets of eyes glued to Summer and me. Reluctantly, I released Summer, shifting to block her from their view as she swiped a thumb beneath her lip to clean up her smudged lip gloss.

"Oops," she said with an embarrassed giggle. Rising on her toes, she kissed the side of my jaw as she said, "I'll save it for later."

At the thought of what she was saving for later, I groaned. Two days had never seemed so long. I'd gone far longer without sex, but going without sex with Summer was a whole other ball game.

Putting a little space between us, she stepped to the doors, looking out into the garden again. I burned to close the distance but stayed where I was, willing my body to stand down. As much as I wished it were, this was not the time. We were both working, even if, for now, that meant standing and waiting.

Summer's eyes scanned the garden behind Rycroft with its manicured beds and bright flowers. "I kind of miss having a garden. It's the downside of a condo. No maintenance, but no yard for a garden."

I thought about the land around my house. It wasn't a ton. I lived in Buckhead, not in the country, but it was enough for a garden. I didn't say anything about that to Summer. I'd only just gotten her back. I didn't need to scare her off by asking her to move in. Yet.

There was time. Now that I had her back, we had time. Summer was studying the garden, lost in thought, and I was studying her—the swoop of her cheek, the curve of her ear, the shades of blonde threading her curls—when she stiffened, her eyes narrowing.

"Is that Smokey?" she asked, raising a hand to point through the glass at a figure moving along the wall on the west side of the property, coming through the trees, back toward the house. "What the hell is he doing?"

"I don't know, but we're going to find out." Keeping an eye on Smokey, I eased the terrace doors open and led Summer outside. We kept tight to the back of the house, staying mostly out of Smokey's range of vision. He kept moving until he reached the door set in the wall by the garage and began to tinker with the lock.

"Is he trying to get out?" Summer hissed. "I swear, I'm done. I am just done. All that stuff he admitted in the safe room was bad enough, but we offer to help him, and now he's trying to sneak out?"

"Or let someone in," I said, darkly. If that was his plan, there would be hell to pay. Before I could stop her, Summer, driven by betrayal and rage, called out, "Dad! What are you doing?"

Smokey jumped and turned around, letting go of the handle, pressing his back to the locked door in the wall. "Nothing. Nothing, baby girl, I'm not doing anything. I just wanted some fresh air."

"Then what are you doing messing around with the door? It's locked. It's supposed to be locked."

"I'm not messing with the door," he said despite the fact that he'd been doing exactly that, and we all knew it. I was an arm's length away, and I could feel Summer's temper boiling over. I rested a hand on her back, thinking to calm her. It didn't work.

"I swear to God, Dad. I've had enough. I know we said three days, but you need to go."

"I have one more day. I don't have anywhere to go yet. I'm working something out. Tomorrow. I swear I'll go tomorrow. I promise. Cross my heart."

"One more day won't hurt," I said to Summer.

She sighed. "It might. I might kill him in his sleep."

She might have to get in line. Smokey stared at his feet, shuffling them, looking like he was about to bolt past us into the house. I sighed.

"One more day," I repeated. "Then I'm driving you home and leaving you there. Got it?"

Morphing back into a sulky kid, he scuffed the dirt with his shoe and said, "Yeah, sure. I got it." He walked past us, bumping Summer with his shoulder. It took everything I had not to take a swing at him.

Less than a day, I told myself. *Less than a day and he'll be out of our hair.*

We followed Smokey back into the house, watching as he went down the hall and climbed the stairs to his room.

Summer and I returned to our positions outside the parlor doors. We didn't have to wait long. Cynthia opened the door, eyes puffy from tears, eye make-up smudged, lipstick smeared, her hand in Clint's.

Regal as a queen, she announced, "Clint and I are back together. He'll be moving in."

They swept past us down the hall and up the main stairs, headed to Cynthia's suite to make up for lost time. Summer watched them go with a furrowed brow. "I hope she knows what she's doing."

"Sometimes a guy deserves a second chance," I said quietly.

She turned and smiled up at me. "That's true. Sometimes a guy does deserve a second chance. And do you know what I just realized?"

"What?"

"If Cynthia is in her room giving Clint his second chance, then I don't have anything to do."

"That's a shame," I said, "I'd hate for you to be bored."

"Do you want to come upstairs and entertain me?" she asked.

I kissed the grin from her mouth before I answered, "Absolutely."

Chapter Thirty-Two

SUMMER

The sounds woke me, muffled and indistinct, flowing around my head in a swirl of noise. Voices. Grunts. The slide of something on wood. I came awake slowly, my brain sluggish. Confused. The sour taste in my mouth made my stomach roll.

Something was off, but I couldn't seem to figure out what it was. Why was I sitting up? Why wasn't I in my room? Where was Evers? My eyes creaked open, lids heavy as concrete.

The sounds in the room were clearer. Voices. A thump. A furious grunt.

Vaguely, I was aware something was wrong.

I shouldn't be here. I was in my nightgown. I should be in bed.

I couldn't move my arms or legs. I sat slumped, head fallen forward, my hair brushing my face.

Concentrating hard, I forced my eyes to open all the way, peering through the curtain of my sleep-tangled hair.

The room swam into focus, the scene before me so bizarre that, at first, I was sure I was still asleep.

I was in the bar at Rycroft Castle. I recognized the dark wood paneling, the thick oak bar top the owner had imported from a pub in Ireland, the heavy chair to which my arms and legs were zip tied.

Zip ties? The thin plastic strips were pulled tight, cutting into my wrists and ankles, securing me firmly to the solid oak chair.

A tall, slender man in a dark suit stood before me, a gun in one hand. Three other men, larger and broader, their faces blank, eyes cold, stood arrayed behind him. They also held guns.

As the strangers and all those weapons registered in my sluggish mind, a surge of panicked adrenaline hit me, sending my heart pounding, every instinct telling me to run.

I twitched against my bonds, my brain unable to override my need to bolt for safety. I didn't think the four men had seen my eyes open, the thick fall of my hair giving me some camouflage.

Sliding my gaze to my right, my heart sank as I saw Evers, tied to one of the heavy leather club chairs, zip ties securing his arms and legs to the chair, a wide strip of duct tape covering his mouth. His face was flushed with strain, his eyes blue flames of fury. Behind the crude gag, he emitted muffled sounds of rage.

His eyes were drawn to mine like a magnet. I needed no words to understand the message in his furious gaze. *Be careful. Do nothing.*

I blinked, the only message I could send without giving myself away. To my left, I caught a glimpse of my father, zip tied to another of the club chairs. Unlike Evers, he sat calmly, his mouth free of tape.

I drew in a breath, mind racing, panic clearing the last of the fog, leaving me with a dull headache. We were waiting. For what?

I snuck another look at my father. Something about him felt off. Wrong. Smokey didn't look scared. Not really.

Evers was too angry to be afraid. I didn't have that problem. My heart raced in my chest, thumping in my ears, my lungs cranking down tight until I could barely draw a breath.

But Smokey just looked nervous. Wary. And he wasn't wearing a gag.

I wasn't gagged either, so maybe it didn't mean anything. I kept my eyes down, off of the men watching us, not wanting to draw attention to the fact that I was conscious. My stomach, queasy and sour, twisted hard, sending bile into my throat. I swallowed it back.

Think, Summer. What the hell is going on? Evers, Smokey, and I appeared to be the only ones in the room. Assuming it was the middle of the night, the day staff was gone, leaving Cynthia, Clint, Angie, Viggo, and all of the security staff unaccounted for.

Fear surged in a wave. I struggled to shut it down. No time to worry about them. If they were in trouble, I couldn't help them until I helped myself. I could only hope they were okay.

All at once, it came to me.

Drugged. We'd been drugged.

That thick, cotton wool fog in my head, my sluggish limbs, the twist of my stomach, and the sour taste in my mouth. We'd been drugged.

It didn't take me long to figure out when. Or who.

Dinner and the wine. Flashes of memory flitted through my mind. Smokey lingering in the dining room before the meal. Talking up the wine until we'd all had a glass.

But the guards? How did he get to security? They ate separately, and they wouldn't have had the wine. I hoped they were still alive. I hoped I lived long enough to find out.

Smokey, Evers, and I were here, tied to these chairs because the man in front of us wanted something. I didn't need to know how we got here to understand that much.

The security team, Cynthia, Clint, Angie, and Viggo must be unnecessary, which might mean they'd been taken care of. Permanently. I squeezed my eyes shut at the thought.

Cynthia. Oh, God, Cynthia. And Clint. They'd only just... No. You're not going to help them by getting hysterical. Get your shit together and think.

I recognized the voice that cut through my rising hysteria. "Miss Winters. You've joined us. I was beginning to worry your father got your dose wrong."

He sent a derisive look at Smokey, who shrugged a shoulder and said, "I told you I didn't."

Nausea swelled in my stomach at my father's casual acknowledgment of guilt, at his lack of worry that I hadn't woken. I swallowed hard, fighting the urge to throw up, and raised my head, tossing my hair out of my eyes. The abrupt movement sent my head throbbing.

"You did this," I hissed at Smokey, ignoring Evers' grunt of warning from beside me. Staring at my father, wondering how, after all I'd learned, I could still have hoped he cared about me.

"You did this. You drugged us. You let them in."

"He did," agreed the man in the suit in an accent I recognized.

He was the one who'd called and left that message at

Sinclair Security. The man who'd threatened Evers' mother, promised to come after Evers and his brothers.

This was Andrei Tsepov. My father had betrayed us to Andrei Tsepov.

"His help is the only reason your father is still alive." Tsepov raised his gun and pointed it at Smokey, who, for the first time, betrayed a glimmer of fear in his wide eyes.

"Why are you pointing that gun at me? I'm on your side. I helped. I did what you asked. I did everything you asked."

"Not precisely. I asked you to find what Maxwell stole. In that, you have failed. Again."

Smokey shifted, testing his bonds, moving restlessly. His words stuttering, begging, he said, "I don't know. I don't know what he stole. He didn't tell me anything. I don't know what he took. Man, if you just tell me what it is, I'll find it and give it back. I swear."

An amused chuckle rumbled in Tsepov's throat. "There truly is no honor among thieves. And you, Smokey, have never had even a hint of honor. You're a fool and an addict."

He shook his head as if he were disappointed in my father, but beneath the act was a black hole of emotion. Tsepov was playing at being human, acting out his feelings, manufacturing the drama. This was a game to him.

We were pieces on a chess board, either tools or obstacles. He knew what he wanted. We could help, or he would move us out of his way. I saw it in his dark eyes. The calculation. The deliberation.

We were on our own, outnumbered, and Tsepov was determined to win.

My father opened his mouth to speak, but I got there first.

Evers wanted me to be careful. To be quiet.

I would have. I wanted to. But I knew without a doubt

that whatever words were about to come out of my father's mouth, they would only make things worse.

I wasn't going to die because Smokey was a fucking idiot, and I wouldn't let him get Evers killed.

"He doesn't know," I cut in, meeting Tsepov's dark eyes. "Neither do the Sinclairs. They questioned Smokey already, scared the hell out of him. If he knew, he would have told them. No one knows what Maxwell took. They'll find it if you tell them."

Tsepov stared at me nonplussed, eyes blank and a shade confused. He regrouped and gave a wry shake of his head. "Is it really possible? Maxwell left his boys out of his business? I'm not surprised about this one," he said, nodding his head in my father's direction. "He's an idiot. But I always thought Maxwell's boys were in the game despite his protests they were clean."

Leveling his dark, curious eyes on Evers, he said, "It is true you know nothing of your father's business?"

Evers stared at Tsepov with a glare so hot, so furious, I half expected laser beams to shoot from his eyes. But this was no superhero movie. Instead of being incinerated by the force of Evers' rage, Tsepov shrugged a shoulder, dismissing him.

"I see I may have misjudged the situation. I would have saved some time if I'd been more forthcoming. What's done is done." Shifting from the philosophical to business, he said, "Account numbers. Maxwell transferred money he owed my uncle into new accounts. I want the numbers. I want the money."

His eyes locked on my father, he trained the gun on Smokey's chest. Conversationally, pleasantly, he said, "Now that we have that out in the open, where are the numbers?"

Smokey, finally realizing that Tsepov did not consider

him an ally, pulled frantically at his bonds, whimpering, "I don't know, man. I don't know anything about any numbers. If I had them, I'd give them to you. Didn't I do everything else you wanted?"

Another offhand shrug. "Some of it. Most of it. But drugging the guards and the wine doesn't wipe the slate clean, Clive Winters. You are only necessary so long as you are of use. And if you don't know anything about those account numbers—"

"I—I—I—" Smokey flailed for something, anything, that would justify his continued existence. It seemed obvious to me that he didn't know a thing about any account numbers, but Tsepov wasn't willing to work on assumptions.

"Maybe this will clarify your thoughts," he said. Lowering the gun a few inches, he pulled the trigger.

It was loud. On TV, guns sound more like a sharp *pop*. Not this one. The shot echoed in the room, my ears ringing from the sound until Smokey's wail of agony drowned it out.

A hole had opened in his upper thigh, frayed edges of denim circling a black pit that bubbled and flowed with the gleam of red blood. He'd shot my dad.

A sound reached my ears, plaintive and thin. I realized it was coming from me. I sucked in a breath. Evers growled beside me. I needed to keep it together. I could not fall apart. Smokey was falling apart, and he had a bullet in his leg to show for it.

Smokey wept, tears streaming down his cheeks, snot bubbling from his nose, dripping on his shirt as he sobbed, "I don't know I don't know I don't know oh God oh God please I don't know," the words running together in a mumbled rush until he was no more than a wounded animal whining from the pain.

Tsepov, unbothered by what he'd done to my father,

turned his attention to Evers. "And you," he said, easily, "I regret wasting all of our time. I should not have assumed your father's business was family business. But, now that you know, where are the account numbers?"

Evers, the tape still firmly across his mouth, shook his head in a negative. Tsepov raised the gun, training it on Evers' chest.

"No," I shouted, terror driving the words from my mouth. "No, no, he can't find them if you shoot him. He can find them, they just didn't know what you were looking for. Please. He can't help if you shoot him."

The sound coming from Evers was somewhere between a growl and a moan of despair. I couldn't bring myself to look at him, to see his fury aimed at me. I knew he wanted me to be quiet, to let him handle this.

Too bad. I was not going to sit there with my mouth shut while Tsepov shot him no matter what he wanted me to do. Tsepov lowered the gun to his side and looked at me consideringly. To the goon on his right, he said, "Yanev, release her. Bring her here."

The man holstered his weapon and circled the room to stand behind me. The snick of the knife opening was loud in the suddenly-quiet room, my father's noise reduced to whimpers and occasional sobs. The plastic ties on my wrists and ankles pulled tight as Tsepov's man knelt by my side, smelling of onions and too-strong cologne.

One by one, the ties fell away. He closed a meaty hand around my arm and yanked me to my feet. My arms still secured behind my back, I stumbled as he dragged me across the room to Tsepov. Coming to a jerking halt, I was turned until I stood side-by-side with my captor.

Reaching out a hand, he stroked a finger across my cheek. At my instinctive recoil, his eyes narrowed. "Who would have thought Smokey Winters would have such a beautiful daughter? I've seen pictures, but they didn't do you justice."

His finger pressed up on my chin, lifting my face to his. "If we can't come to an arrangement for the account numbers, I can make use of you. You look like a cheerleader. All this blond hair. Those blue eyes. Still young enough to have a tight little body. Very popular overseas."

Dark, soulless eyes trailed down to my toes, taking in every inch of skin exposed by my silky nightgown. My stomach clenched hard, saliva pooling in my mouth. I could not throw up on this man. Knowing what he was implying, what use he planned to make of me, I wasn't sure I could stop myself.

Across the room, Evers let out a sound of such rage, such frustration I wanted to weep. Instantly, my nausea slid away. I had to hold on. Evers was going to lose it, tied to that chair, temporarily helpless.

I wasn't going to make it worse. He wouldn't let anything happen to me. A ridiculous thought, considering that he was unarmed and zip tied to a chair. It didn't matter. Evers wouldn't let anything happen to me. I just had to hang in there, keep Tespov from shooting anyone else, and we'd figure out the rest.

Tsepov dropped his hand from my face. As if we were friends, he slipped an arm around my waist, turning me to face my father and Evers.

"Here we are, the two men in your life before us. Your father and your lover. You're a smart girl. What do you think? Is your father lying? I find it hard to believe he has the mental discipline to withstand pain, but you'd be surprised what people will do for money."

He flicked the gun in Evers' direction, sending a shaft of

ice into my heart. I wanted that gun pointed anywhere but at Evers. "Maxwell's boy, well, if he wasn't working with his father, then I'll believe he doesn't know where the numbers are. But he's resourceful. Useful. I only need one of them. You tell me, which one can solve my problem?"

Tsepov lifted the gun and pointed it at Evers, then slid it past my empty seat to settle on Smokey, who flinched and whimpered. Then back to Evers, who leaned into the room, his eyes on fire with rage, cold with fear, arms straining so hard on the plastic ties blood trickled down his wrists. The fear wasn't for himself. It was for me.

Tsepov swung the gun back and forth, a faint smile on his face, waiting for my answer. I spared my father a look, saw his fear, his weakness, and beneath both, love. Somewhere in his heart, my father loved me.

I knew to the depths of my soul that he'd never imagined his actions would put me in so much danger. He was stupid and foolish and selfish, but he wasn't malicious.

I didn't have to think.

Maybe I should have.

Maybe I'm a horrible person for making my choice so quickly. So easily.

I didn't care. My head and my heart knew exactly what to say.

My eyes locked to Evers, hoping he could read in them the words I'd never spoken aloud, I gave Tsepov my answer.

"Evers. You need Evers. He'll get you what you want."

Warm breath brushed my ear. "Good girl. That wasn't so hard, was it?" Then, turning his head, "Yanev."

Black fabric dropped over my head, cutting off my vision, trapping my sour, humid breath, the sound of my panting breaths filling my ears. A cold hand closed over my breast, squeezing hard enough to draw a gasp of pain from my tight lungs.

Evers bellowed with rage behind the layers of tape, wood banging as if he'd lurched in his chair.

His hand kneading my breast, voice pleased, Tsepov said in my ear, "Now we'll see how good a girl you really are."

I trembled with the effort to stay still, terrified that any show of resistance would bring that gun back to Evers. Another muffled roar. Squeezing my eyes shut, I prayed. *Please. Please.*

Abruptly, the clutching hand dropped away. The sack over my head tightened around my neck and I was dragged back, almost losing my footing. Big hands, not Tsepov's, grabbed me under my armpits, pulling me away from Tsepov. Away from Evers.

Through the thick fabric over my head, I couldn't make out Tsepov's next words. The only thing I heard clearly was the gun. It fired, two shots in rapid succession. My knees buckled, legs giving way. Strong arms swept me off my feet, tossing me over a wide shoulder. I couldn't see, couldn't hear, and then we were gone, the ring of gunshots echoing in my ears.

Chapter Thirty-Three

EVERS

His words ran on a loop in my head. "I'm keeping the girl. Consider her your incentive. Get me what I want, or she disappears."

Get me what I want, or she disappears.

I squeezed my eyes shut, trying to stem my rising panic, to block the memory of his hands on her, her eyes, wide and terrified until they hooded her and dragged her from the room.

I knew what *disappear* meant, what he might be doing to her even now.

When I found Summer, when she was safe, I was going to rip him to fucking pieces. Fucking pieces.

"Oh, God. Oh, God, it hurts. It hurts. Oh, God, someone help me." Smokey moaned and cried, slumped in his chair, his body held up by the zip ties securing him.

When I got free, I was going to fucking kill him, too. He'd handed his only child over to a monster, served her up on a fucking platter.

"I'm dying. You have to help me," he sobbed.

Fuck him. He could bleed to death for all I cared. The second I got free of this goddamn chair I was going straight for Summer. Anything that got in my fucking way would burn to ash.

Only one thing mattered now.

Getting her back. Saving her from—.

No.

I could not fucking think about what I'd be saving her from. Couldn't think about his hands on her and the fear in her eyes.

In all my life, I never imagined I would love anyone the way I love Summer.

I would have sold my soul to keep from failing her. And yet, I had. I'd failed her so completely she might be lost forever.

No.

I would get her back or die trying. That was it. Summer was all that mattered.

Ignoring Smokey's fading whimpers, I rocked the chair from side to side, trying to break it apart. Normally, getting out of zip ties wouldn't be that much of a problem.

If they'd just secured my hands together, I would have been fine, but they'd strapped my arms to the sides of the chair, forearm and bicep, preventing me from getting any leverage. Ditto for my legs. Zip ties were pulled tight at my ankles and shins, and this goddamn fucking chair might as well have been made of iron.

Solid oak. Hand carved joints. The fucking thing weighed more than I did, and so far, nothing could break it apart. I could barely rock it from leg to leg it was so heavy. With my legs tied to the chair from ankle to knee, I was close to immobile. Immobile and unarmed. Trapped.

I needed help.

I needed my team. My brothers. Anyone.

Anyone but the useless, dying traitor beside me.

Sitting there, unable to move, unable to speak, unable to save the woman I loved... Every inch of me burned with rage and frustration, and determination to make this right. Whatever she needed to erase what he was—

I threw my head to the side as if I could fling the image from my brain. Her eyes. Her hands shaking as she tried so hard to be brave. Fuck that, she didn't *try,* she *was* brave. She'd saved my life.

Maybe I could have talked my way out of it. Or maybe I'd be like Smokey, slumped in my chair, counting the remains of my life to the tick of the clock on the mantle.

Summer had saved me. She hadn't just saved me, she'd looked me in the eyes and chosen me over her father. She knew what she was doing. She knew what would happen, and she'd chosen me.

All this time she'd never told me she loved me. Not until today. She hadn't said the words, but next to the sacrifice she'd made, how could I doubt? She'd chosen me, saved my life and sacrificed herself.

If she hadn't drawn Tsepov's attention, if she'd stayed quiet, he wouldn't have taken her. She'd jumped into the fray to get his gun off me and now she was gone.

I couldn't live with it. I wouldn't live with it. I would get free from this motherfucking chair, and I would find her, and I would fix—

Fucking stop thinking about it, I ordered myself.

I had to save my girl, not go off like a fucking loose cannon.

Easier said than done.

This wasn't a mission.

It wasn't a job.

I wasn't a Ranger or a Sinclair.

I was a man desperately in love with a woman in the hands of a monster.

My head throbbed from the drugs. A sour taste coated my tongue. Blood ran down my hands from the zip ties cutting into my wrists. They were too tight to slip off even with the lubrication of blood.

Fuck them for being smart enough to secure my arms. And fuck the owner of Rycroft for buying this goddamn indestructible chair. I rocked it again, trying to hop from the front legs to the back and only getting it a few inches off the floor. Not enough to tip over. The thing weighed a fucking ton.

The silence in the house was deafening, the tick of the clock on the mantle loud as a church bell.

Where the fuck was everyone? Were they still unconscious? Or dead?

Tsepov's men had strolled into the house like they owned it. Had they found the control room and taken out the guards?

There was no way Smokey could have drugged everyone. The team guarding the wall hadn't eaten dinner in the house. Unless they'd hit the control room for coffee when they checked in with Griffen during the shift change. Hopefully, that was it. Drugged was better than dead.

It didn't matter. There wasn't a fucking thing I could do for them strapped to this fucking chair. I could only sit there, yanking on my bonds, rocking the chair, my ears straining for any movement in the house.

An eternity passed. Smokey's whimpers had died down to vague intermittent moans. He was alive. For now. He had three bullets in him, one in the leg and two in the chest.

I was surprised he wasn't dead yet. He should have been. If someone didn't get here soon, he would be.

Lights flashed through the room, sweeping past the windows as a car—thank fucking God, a car—pulled up in front of the house. Doors slammed, feet pounded, and a voice called my name.

Cooper.

Tears of sheer relief welled in my eyes.

Thank fuck.

I blinked them away and called his name from behind the duct tape, doing my best to make some noise. He must have heard me because he came tearing through the doorway before skidding to a stop.

"Fucking hell," he said, taking in the scene in a glance. Over his shoulder, he said, "Smokey's been shot. Call an ambulance. And call Whitmore. Get him here."

Cooper strode into the room, pulling a knife from his pocket and flicking it open. Crouching in front of me, he said, "This is going to hurt."

Scraping a fingernail across my cheek, he pulled up the edge of the duct tape, then ripped his hand down, taking off the tape and more than a few layers of skin.

"Tsepov has Summer," I said in a rush. "Get me off this fucking chair. We have to go. Now."

Cooper stared at me for a long moment before standing and closing the knife.

"What the fuck are you doing? Cut me loose. Did you hear me? Tsepov has Summer. He's got her and he's going to—"

I couldn't force words past the lump in my throat. I couldn't say it out loud. I jerked against my bonds, dragging the chair inches off the ground before it slammed back down.

"Tell me what happened first," Cooper said.

"Cut me loose, you fucking bastard."

"No. You're an inch from completely losing it, and you know it. I cut you off that chair, you're out the door, and we still have no fucking clue what's going on. Sit there for a fucking minute and get your shit together. We'll find Summer. I swear it, but I need to understand what happened."

I knew my brother. Knew that tone in his voice. He meant what he said. He was leaving me exactly where I was until I brought him up to speed.

And he knew me. One look and he knew exactly how close I was to the edge. He had no idea how willing I was to dive over the side.

Anything. I would do anything to get her back. To see her safe. Nothing else mattered. Not anymore.

Sucking in a quick breath, I forced my scattered thoughts into order.

"Evers. SITREP. Now."

My mouth opened, and I spoke. "Smokey drugged us. I don't know how yet, probably the wine."

"Griffen? The team?"

I shook my head. "I don't know. I can only assume they're down. Tsepov wants account numbers. Dad stole money, transferred it into accounts, and Tsepov wants the numbers."

"Then why the fuck didn't he just tell us that?" Cooper asked, shaking his head in exasperation.

"He thought we were working with Dad. Thought we knew. Were in on it."

"I'm going to fucking kill Dad when we find him."

"He'd better hope someone else gets there first," I said. The moment Tsepov's hands had touched Summer, the moment that bag dropped over her head and Tsepov's goon dragged her from the room, I said goodbye to the last shred of love I had for my father.

Smokey sold us out, but my father was the one who put us here in the first place. My father opened the door to darkness and let it infect our lives. He was the reason Tsepov had Summer.

"He took Summer as incentive," I said, struggling to keep my voice flat and emotionless. I needed Cooper to believe I had my shit together or he'd never let me off this fucking chair. "The longer we leave her with him—"

"I know, Evers. I know who we're dealing with."

"Then let me off this goddamn chair," I roared, my control snapping.

Chapter Thirty-Four

EVERS

Cooper ignored me, turning to the open doorway. Lucas Jackson paced through, his rough-hewn face serious, eyes shadowed.

"Cynthia and the rest of them are upstairs," he said. "Still out. Whitmore's on the way. He can examine them."

"We don't let the paramedics know who else is in the house," Cooper said.

"The inside team is still unconscious. I don't know if he dosed them harder or it's coincidence. Everyone's secured with zip ties. Griffen was just starting to come around. Where's Summer?"

At Lucas' question, I snarled, throwing the chair forward, the zip ties cutting deeper into my arms.

Cooper sent me a cautious look before he said to Lucas, "Tsepov has Summer."

Lucas nodded once, and the sympathy in his eyes almost broke me. Lucas could be a scary motherfucker. The parts of his file that hadn't been blacked out were scary. The blank spots hid worse.

He'd left that life behind, but it lived inside him. He knew exactly how I felt. If it had been Charlie, he would have torn the world apart to get to her.

"We'll find her, Ev. I fucking swear it. We'll find her." Lucas gave Cooper a sideways glance. "I'm cutting him loose."

"No," Cooper said. "You cut him loose and he'll be out the door. He's not thinking straight. He's going to get himself fucking killed."

"Fuck you, Cooper," I said. Cooper was on my fucking list of people to kill, right after Tsepov, Smokey, the goon who'd dragged Summer from the room, and my fucking father.

"He's not going to bolt. I've got him," Lucas said, kneeling at my side, the flash of his knife making quick work of the zip ties.

The second the last zip tie fell to the floor I lunged out of the chair, already planning my next move.

My gun.

My backup weapon.

Car keys.

Hit the arsenal at Sinclair Security.

Head for—

An arm closed around my neck, yanking me off my feet. For a second, I dangled in midair before my shoulders hit a chest as solid as a brick wall.

Lucas' bicep flexed against my neck, cutting off my air. Sometimes I forgot how fucking big the guy was.

He set me on my feet, his arm cranked tight, the lack of oxygen slowing me down. His voice rumbled from behind me.

"I know. I know you're half-crazy and all you can think is

that you have to get to her. I know. You need to listen to me. You're going to get both of you killed if you leave this house the way you are right now. Lock that shit down, Ev. I swear to you, we will get her back. I swear it. Another twenty minutes won't make a difference. If I let you go are you going to run?"

I shook my head as much as I could. Lucas rumbled in my ear, "Liar."

Changing his grip, he released my neck but had my arm twisted behind my back an instant later. I won't dwell on how humiliating it was to be fucking frog-marched out of the room by my own employee.

Never mind the fact that he was half-giant and built of solid muscle. I let him shove me into the hall as the wail of sirens sounded outside.

Rycroft's bar was about to be flooded with paramedics. We needed to move the party anyway. We headed for the library. Lucas pushed me at a chair. I sat, every muscle in my body itching to move. To do something. Anything other than sit around and talk.

I knew Lucas and Cooper were right. Knew I was scared stupid and riding an adrenaline high. Bad for decision making. Bad for Summer. As much as it killed me to sit and wait, I'd do it. I'd do whatever I had to as long as it meant I could bring her home.

Cooper followed us into the library. He'd brought a team, and I could hear one of them opening the door to the paramedics, leading them to Smokey.

I looked at Lucas. "What the hell are you doing here anyway?"

"I was pulling into the garage when I saw Cooper fly out of the elevator like his feet were on fire. I grabbed him, he told me what was up, and here I am."

"What the fuck were you doing in the garage in the middle of the night?" I asked, momentarily baffled.

Lucas' face transformed from craggy and brooding to sheepish. Was I imagining the flush in his cheeks? I had to be. He jerked one shoulder in a rough shrug.

"I haven't seen my wife in four days. Didn't want to wait until tomorrow."

Cooper mumbled under his breath, "Pussy."

Lucas didn't respond. I wasn't going to tease. I might have before Summer. Before I knew what it was to have her at home waiting for me.

Finishing the explanation, Cooper said, "Hendrix called Franklin to give him shit about that bet on the Braves. When Franklin didn't answer, Hendrix pulled up the cameras, saw him passed out at the desk. Called me."

Thank fucking God he did. Thank God for that stupid bet. Hendrix and Franklin were about even this year. I didn't want to think about what would have happened if Hendrix hadn't gotten bored enough to waste some time needling his buddy.

Movement at the door caught my eye. Griffen, wobbling a little on his feet, holding one hand to his head. I imagined he had the same headache I did. His eyes scanned the room, and the first thing he said was, "Where's Summer? She's not upstairs."

"Tsepov has her," Cooper said in a low voice, sending me a cautious glance. "Go get the paramedics to take a look at you."

"Fuck that. I'm fine."

"Griffen," Cooper started.

Griffen shook his head, wincing as it throbbed with the

motion. I knew the feeling. "Save it, Cooper. I'm fine." He looked to me. "How long? What the fuck happened?"

The front door slammed open with a crash. A voice bellowed, "COOPER!"

"Oh, shit," Griffen said under his breath.

Cooper's eyes shot to Lucas in accusation. "You fucking called Aiden? It's the middle of the goddamn night!"

"Yeah, I fucking called Aiden. Clive Winters is the next thing to dead. If he makes it through the night, it'll be a goddamn miracle. His daughter's not here, and Aiden is the closest thing he has to family. There was no time to wait until morning. Aiden would want to know."

Aiden strode into the room, his dark auburn hair standing straight up. I couldn't remember the last time I'd seen Aiden anything but perfectly dressed. Even when we played basketball, I'd swear his T-shirts were designer.

Tonight, he wore a faded Emory sweatshirt and a pair of jeans with a jagged hole at the knee. I'd forgotten Aiden owned jeans.

"What the fuck is going on, Cooper? They're loading Smokey into an ambulance. How could you let this happen? Where the hell is Summer?"

Cooper glared at Lucas, who said quietly, "Tsepov took Summer."

Aiden's eyes went so wide they almost bugged out of his head. In any other circumstances, I would have laughed my ass off. Instead, I was fucking grateful someone finally seemed to be taking Summer's loss as seriously as I was.

"How the fuck did he take her from this house? You said it was safe, Cooper. Tsepov can't just take her. Does he have any idea who she is?"

Cooper waited patiently while Aiden ranted. Aiden

didn't rant often. Pretty much never. His control was as good as mine. Usually.

But Aiden took his role as the head of the family seriously. He'd waited to establish contact, but he considered Summer one of his. She was a Winters, and no one fucked with a Winters. Especially not some two-bit Russian mobster.

And then it clicked.

I knew exactly how we were going to get Summer back.

"Aiden, shut it," I said.

He rounded on me, ready to unleash his fury, when he saw something in my face and fell silent.

I looked to Cooper. "Call Tsepov. Tell him he needs to trade me for Summer, and he needs to do it now. Otherwise, Aiden Winters is going to start a shit storm he won't survive."

Cooper stared at me, mouth hanging open before he shook his head. "No. Not that way. We'll—"

"Yes, that way," Griffen interrupted. "If you want to get her back before he has a chance to—."

Shooting a cautious glance at me, Griffen skipped ahead. "We need to get her back. Now. We don't have time to figure out another way. If it was anyone else, maybe. But not him. He could change his mind about holding her." Another cautious glance at me.

I drilled Cooper with my eyes, willing him to understand. Cooper said, "He's not going to kill her."

"I know that," I ground out. "There are things worse than death. It would take nothing for him to move her. To sell her—" The words stuck in my throat.

I could not say it out loud. I couldn't stand to think it, but I needed Cooper to get that this was not a fucking game.

Lucas stepped in. "Cooper, we have to make him understand that she's too hot to keep and too hot to move. He has to know that every second he has her, he's a target. He wants leverage? Let him have Evers. Evers is leverage. You and Knox will do anything to keep your brother safe, and Evers can handle himself."

Cooper shook his head again "No fucking way am I turning my brother over to Tsepov."

"I'm not asking," I said, "I'm telling you. Call Tsepov. Do it now. Tell him we want to make a trade. Tell him if a single hair on her head is harmed, Aiden will be on the phone with the Deputy Director of the FBI."

"Fuck that. I'll be on the phone with the goddamned president," Aiden spat out.

It wasn't a bluff. Aiden had the personal number of the president, a Supreme Court justice, fuck, probably half the members of Congress, not to mention the Deputy Director of the FBI and a handful of key players at the NSA and the CIA.

When your multi-billion dollar business spans the globe, you develop some pretty extensive connections. Aiden would use every one to protect his family, even an estranged cousin.

"This isn't the way," Cooper said. He wasn't thinking. In his mind, Summer was collateral damage.

"You don't get it," Lucas said. "Call Tsepov. Make the trade."

"You want me to just hand him over?" Cooper demanded, throwing out his hand in my direction, frustration etched in every line on his face.

"Evers would die for her," Lucas said in a low rumble. "He'd do it gladly if it would mean she was safe. They're right. Once Tsepov realizes what he's done, he'll hand her over for Evers. He's not going to want that kind of attention.

Aiden will rain hell down on him if he doesn't give Summer back."

"Damn right I will," Aiden agreed, staring Cooper down. Cooper reared back.

"What the fuck, Aiden? You've known Evers since you were born. You just met this girl—"

"She's my fucking family," Aiden said. "And yeah I've known Evers since I was born. That's why I'm telling you to make the fucking call. Because if you don't get her back, you'll lose him. Fucking look at him, Cooper. You have no fucking clue what's going through his head right now."

"And you do? What the fuck do you know about it?"

"He knows because he has a woman he would die for," Lucas said, his voice like gravel. I knew he was thinking of Charlie, of how far he would go to keep his wife safe.

I shuddered to think what would happen to anyone who caused Charlie a second of pain.

"No, you're right," Cooper said, "I don't know. You're all fucking nuts. Thinking with your dicks instead of your heads."

Cooper was full of shit. I never pushed him on this, but I was running out of time. "You do know, Cooper. We both know, there's one person—"

Cooper pointed a finger at me, stabbing through the air as if he could puncture my words like a balloon. "Shut the fuck up."

"—and if you weren't such a fucking pussy, you'd really know what we're talking about."

"Yeah, you're one to call me a pussy considering all the time you wasted lying to Summer—"

Cooper fell abruptly silent as he realized what he'd said. His face blanched. He ground his teeth together, staring at the carpet between his feet.

After a long moment, he said, "Find another way."

"There isn't another way. Give me the phone, Cooper," I said, holding out my hand. He shot me a disgusted look.

"No. You're a fucking mess. I'm not letting you get on the phone with him. You'll threaten to eviscerate him if he touches her, and the whole thing will go to shit. I'll make the call."

He activated the screen, looking for the number he'd jotted down from Tsepov's voicemail. When he pulled it up, he put the phone to his ear and paced to the door.

"Do it here, Cooper. I want to hear what you say."

Cooper scowled but stopped just inside the door. Tsepov answered the second time Cooper put the call through.

Their exchange was blessedly short. Tsepov, while nowhere near as savvy as his uncle, was not a complete fool. He'd taken Summer thinking she wasn't a real Winters, that Aiden wouldn't care one way or another if something happened to her.

Once he realized she was a liability, he was eager to trade her for me, promising that she was fine, and demanding that Aiden do nothing until he confirmed that Summer was unharmed.

Cooper arranged a meet at Smokey's place in an hour. Tsepov didn't want us knowing where he was holed up, and he didn't trust us enough to come here.

See, not entirely stupid. Smokey's place was empty, temporarily abandoned, and isolated enough to avoid prying eyes.

Cooper hung up and slid the phone in his pocket. "I hope you know what you're doing," he said.

"You know I do." Cooper shook his head in resignation.

335

Already thinking ahead to Summer's rescue, I said, "I'll be right back. Get to work on the plan."

I left the library, heading for the stairs to our rooms. Aiden said something about going to the hospital. All I could think of was Summer in her thin silk nightgown, so short it barely covered the curve of her ass.

She'd be cold. Never mind that it was fucking July, she'd be cold, and she wouldn't want to be the next thing to naked after what she'd been through.

I pushed open her door, my eyes on the robe tossed over the chair in the corner. My fingers closed around the lush cotton, the scent of lemon and flowers and saltwater drifting up, reminding me of that night in the pool. Of her raspberry bikini.

Bundling the robe in my arms, I jogged back down the stairs, buoyed by hope. Tsepov had agreed to give her back. She was unharmed. Now that he knew we were coming for her, she was as safe as I could make her.

In an hour, she'd be with my brothers. I didn't spare a thought for what might happen to me.

Any risk was acceptable if Summer was safe. Any risk.

I would protect her with my life. If that meant I wasn't coming home, that was fine. As long as she did.

Chapter Thirty-Five

SUMMER

The bag over my head was making my face itch. I had bigger concerns than an itchy face, but that was the only one I was willing to think about. Everything else was too terrifying to contemplate.

I was not going to think about the ride from Rycroft to wherever we were now. I was not going to think about sitting in the back of the limo next to Tsepov, his cold, slender hand wrapped around my arm—

I ground my teeth together.

Nothing happened. Nothing fucking happened, Summer. Stop thinking about it.

I shivered. They had the AC cranked up, and it felt like fucking January in here.

When we got here, someone had carried me inside, dumped me into a chair, and wrapped something around the bag on my head, pressing it into my eyes and over my ears until I could barely hear or breathe.

They'd carried me again, up a flight of stairs, and

dropped me onto a mattress. I was alone, my arms and legs bound, blind and deaf and scared out of my mind.

All I could think about was Evers. He would come after me. I had no doubt. His eyes were the last thing I saw before the bag dropped over my head, filled with desperate anger. Guilt. And love.

He would find me. I just had to hold on. Hold on and pray to whatever gods were listening that Evers didn't do anything reckless. I couldn't stand it if anything happened to him.

In another situation, I'd trust Evers' judgment.

Right now?

Right now, I didn't trust anything.

I refused to consider the gunshots. They echoed in my head, ricocheting back and forth until they multiplied into a barrage of gunfire.

It hadn't been a barrage. It had been two distinct shots. Two shots and I had no idea where they'd landed.

Not in Evers. It couldn't be Evers. Hadn't I told Tsepov he needed Evers? Which meant—

Don't think about it, I told myself. *Don't think about your father. Don't think about pretty much telling the guy with the gun to kill him.*

My father was the reason I was here. He'd put us all in danger, and for what? For more money?

I'd seen the numbers on those bank transfers. Where had it all gone? He'd had enough. He'd had more than most people saw in a lifetime, and I was here, half-naked, tied up, and blindfolded in the hands of a man who trafficked women. Because of my father.

I knew from Emma what kind of business the Tsepovs ran. I knew what would happen to me when I was no longer useful.

Worse, my father knew. My father knew exactly what Tsepov would do with me, and he'd betrayed us all anyway.

If begging for Evers' life at my father's expense made me a bad person, I could live with that. As long as Evers hadn't been on the other end of that gun, I thought I could live with just about anything.

I didn't sleep. I wasn't sure I'd ever sleep again, but I drifted. Maybe I was lightheaded from lack of oxygen. Maybe it was the stress or adrenaline. Everything started to seem like a dream.

When the door to the bedroom banged open, it took me a minute to realize someone had come into the room. Rough hands pulled me off the mattress and threw me over a shoulder.

Onions and cologne. The one who'd carried me out of Rycroft. I was on the move. No. It was too soon. Evers needed time. To get free. To find me. If Tsepov moved me, sold me—

HE DROPPED ME ONTO A SEAT. SOFT. A COUCH? No, a car. Maybe the same one as before. Leather upholstery sticking to my bare thighs. A hand closing around my arm, dragging me across the seat, pushing me down.

Fine wool under my cheek. A hand on my shoulder, fingers curled, holding tight. My nightgown was twisted around my hips. Men's voices. Where were they taking me? How was Evers going to find me if they moved me? I'd vanish and—

I shook with the effort to hold back my nausea. The bag over my head was strapped tight to my mouth. I could not throw up like this. I swallowed hard. *Oh, please, please don't let me throw up.*

I was so focused on holding back the need to puke, I barely registered the hand on my hip. I squirmed, trying to get away. It was fruitless. I was bound. I couldn't see. An arm came down over my chest, pinning me in place.

I went still, my lungs heaving, desperate for more than the muffled hot air I pulled through the bag over my head. Not enough oxygen.

Instinct told me to fight, to move, to do anything I could to get those fucking hands off me. Logic said that was only going to make it worse.

I needed to calm down. I could barely breathe. My head was spinning. Fighting would only make me weaker.

I stayed still, praying the ride would be over soon. If they took off the hood, untied me, I might have a chance to get away.

As long as I was alive there was hope.

Whatever they did to me, whatever happened, I had to stay alive.

Evers would find me. If I could just stay alive, Evers would—

The gunshots hadn't been for him. They couldn't have been. Tsepov had no reason to shoot Evers.

Evers would come for me.

Tears leaked from my eyes, absorbed by the bag tied so tightly around my face.

Evers was coming for me.

Whatever happened, I just had to stay alive.

It was all I could think. Everything else—the car, those hands on my body, my burning lungs and spinning head—everything else was too horrifying.

The car came to a stop, and the lap beneath my head slid away. The door at my feet opened, and I was pulled across the seat, my nightgown riding up over my hips, baring my flimsy bikini panties. I didn't have time to cringe before I was airborne, tossed over that now familiar wide shoulder, assailed by the stench of onions and cologne.

For a minute, the smell of wet grass joined the onions and cologne. Then it was pot. Why did it smell like pot?

The air on my skin had changed, the dew of early morning traded for stale heat, like a house that had been shut up for too long. I took another breath, and through the hood, I caught mildew and marijuana.

I knew that smell. Why did I know that smell? I was dropped on something soft. A bed? A couch?

I thought about trying to stand but tossed it out immediately. My hands were secured behind my back, ankles bound so tightly the bones rubbed. What was I going to do, hop? Hop right into a wall was more like it.

I hated being this helpless. I wasn't much better than a sack of potatoes, hauled around, unable to speak, unable to protect myself.

It was quiet, as far as I could tell, but I didn't think I was alone. Before, laying on the bed, I'd known the room was empty even without being able to see. The air had been flat. Still.

Here, wherever I was, I heard nothing, but I felt people. Movement.

I tried talking, begging, but no coherent sound got through the hood. Only desperate mumbling that stopped when a fist cuffed the back of my head, and a muffled, accented voice said, "Shut up."

I was lifted again, this time cradled like a child tucked against a solid chest, the reek of onions and cologne making its way through the hood. Him again. Someone should tell him about his cologne. And the onions.

Steps down and cool air on my skin. Voices. New arms, and I was tossed onto something soft. A car seat. Leather.

Before I could get my bearings, a body fell half on top of mine. Car doors slammed. There was a jolt of movement, tires squealing, and we slid, almost falling off the bench seat.

Hands closed over my arms, pulling me up, and I snapped.

It was the hands. More hands, grabbing, touching my bare skin, pulling at me, dragging me onto the seat.

No more.

They'd sold me, traded me away, and Evers wouldn't be able to find me. Despair and terror drowned out everything else. I fought, the sounds in my throat feral and panicked.

I tried to pull my knees up to my chest, to duck my head down, do whatever I could to block any access to my body. I twisted and burrowed into the footwell to get away from the hands reaching for me.

Voices, indistinct and urgent, filtered through the hood. Hands yanking on the fabric, and the constriction around my mouth and ears fell away.

My name.

I heard my name.

"Summer. Summer, for fuck's sake, stop screaming. It's Griffen. Cooper and Lucas are here. We've got you. We've got you, Summer. It's okay. It's okay now."

Griffen?

I knew that voice. Griffen.

The fight drained away, and I fell limp, breath heaving in my chest, clearing my head. Griffen's hands hooked under my armpits and dragged me up on the seat.

"Don't move. Let me get you out of this thing."

My wrists were free, and he was feeding my hand into a

sleeve. Thick, soft cotton. The smell of my body cream. Lemon and flowers. My robe.

Fabric draped around my body, shielding me, and some of the ice in my bones began to melt. A tear ran down my cheek. I never thought I'd be so grateful just to be covered.

I pulled the robe tight and sat back in the seat, drawing my knees to my chest as Griffen pulled the bag all the way off my head, and I sucked in a sweet, clean breath of air.

My eyes darted around the interior of the vehicle. One of the Sinclair Security SUVs.

Cooper was driving. Lucas sat in the passenger seat, and Griffen was in the back with me.

But where was Evers? Where the hell was Evers?

Chapter Thirty-Six

SUMMER

I asked the only thing I cared about.

"Where's Evers?"

Silence stretched, the men sneaking glances at each other, none of them talking.

Hating the thread of hysteria in my voice, I demanded, "Where is Evers?"

Griffen reached out a placating hand. "Summer, calm down, honey. Everything's okay. Are you hurt? Did they hurt you?"

He shot a dark look to the front of the car. Cooper met my eyes in the rearview, assessing and cool. Lucas stared at me, searching for something in my face.

I pulled the robe tightly around me, tying a knot in the belt, and shook my head. "I'm fine. They didn't do anything, just—"

I couldn't say it. The words *grope* and *touch* didn't describe the violation of those hands, the way my skin crawled beneath them. The fear.

I shook my head again.

"I'm fine. Tell me where Evers is."

"He's—" Griffen started.

"Did he get shot?" A sob choked my voice. "Was it Evers?" My words squeaked out, squeezed by tears and panic. No. He was supposed to be here. He was going to save me, and then he would be here. Where was he?

"He didn't get shot," Griffen said, in a rush.

If those bullets hadn't been for Evers, that meant they'd hit my dad. I'd deal with that later. "Just tell me. Is he okay?"

Cooper's eyes, hard and angry, flashed up to meet mine in the rearview. "I guess that depends. We traded him for you."

My head reeled. What? Why? I couldn't take Cooper's accusing glare. I looked to Lucas and Griffen. "Why? Why would you do that? What if they hurt him?"

"They're not going to hurt him," Lucas rumbled. "Evers was a Ranger. He's tough as hell. These guys," Lucas shook his head in derision, "he can handle these guys, Summer. You couldn't."

"You were in a lot more danger with them than Evers," Griffen said. "And honestly, he was no use to us as long as they had you. He was half crazed. The only thing he cared about was getting you back."

I wrapped my arms around my chest and settled back into the seat, trying to put the pieces together in my head. They had Evers.

I won't lie. I was grateful to be away from Tsepov, away from those hands and that hood. I wanted to go home and take a shower. A long, hot shower. I wanted clothes. A lot of them. I wanted every inch of my skin clean and behind thick layers of fabric.

I didn't want any of that without Evers.

"When are you going to get him back?" I demanded. "Don't tell me you're going to let them keep him. Tell me you have a plan."

"We have a plan," Cooper confirmed. "We're meeting with the FBI in two hours. At Rycroft. Evers has a tracking device built into his clothes."

"What if they find it?" I interrupted.

Griffen gave me a gentle smile. "He has more than one. I guarantee you they won't find them all."

"So, you'll figure out where they have him, and you'll go in and get him?"

"Something like that. Trust me, Evers can get out of almost any restraint. If these guys were more sophisticated, a different kind of criminal, I might worry," Griffen said, "but he'll be okay. If he can't, at least we'll know where he is."

I didn't share Griffen's confidence. "I don't like this. He shouldn't have done it."

"We couldn't talk him out of it," Cooper said in a flat voice. "He was determined. I hope you're worth it."

Cooper's words stung. Not because I thought he was right to doubt me. I *was* worth it. I knew I was. I was worth it because I loved Evers. I loved him more than anything. More than my father. More than myself.

If I'd had any idea what his plan was I never would have let him go through with it. What good was my freedom if he was a captive?

No, Cooper's words stung because I never had the chance to tell him I loved him. All those days I wanted to, and I couldn't get the words out, my fear holding me back. Now he was gone, at the mercy of the man who'd shot my father so carelessly. Easily.

That man had Evers, and Evers didn't know I loved him.

A hot tear streaked down my cheek. I brushed it away with the back of my hand, furious with myself.

"Hey, we're going to bring him home," Lucas said, his green eyes serious and kind. "I swear to you, we're going to bring him home."

I stared out the window in silence, watching the road flash by. Suddenly realizing I never asked, I said, "Is my dad alive? He got shot, didn't he?"

Cooper answered. "He's in intensive care. In surgery, last I heard. Aiden's with him. I think he called your mother, said she was on her way."

"Do they think he's going to make it?"

I didn't think I wanted to know the answer.

I was right.

"It's hard to say," Cooper said gently. "His chances aren't great. He lost a lot of blood by the time he got to the hospital. Do you want us to take you to see him?"

I thought about that. Did I? I should. I should be waiting in the hospital for him to come out of surgery.

I shook my head. "No. I'm not going anywhere until Evers comes home."

Cooper's eyes lit with approval for the first time. He didn't say anything, just gave a brisk nod and turned his attention back to the road.

Tsepov had Evers. That was as much my father's fault as the rest of it. There was nothing I could do for my dad now. His life was in the doctor's hands. There wasn't much I could do for Evers either, but I couldn't bear the thought of leaving Rycroft, of missing the meeting with the FBI.

I couldn't stand not knowing what was happening, not

knowing how close he was to coming home. If I went to the hospital, I'd be out of the loop. An afterthought. That wasn't going to happen.

Rycroft Castle was oddly silent when we arrived. Aside from the cook, the staff had been turned away for the day. Cynthia, Clint, Angie, and Viggo were restricted to their rooms, under guard until the situation with Tsepov stabilized.

Griffen pointed me at the hall that led to my room. "I'm going to ask the cook to make breakfast. Do you need any help getting cleaned up? Do you want me to get Cynthia? Or Angie?"

"No. I'm okay. I won't be long."

I couldn't say anything else. I knew Griffen was worried, and I didn't want to think about it. I just wanted a hot shower.

The water stung the skin at my wrists and ankles where the zip ties had been pulled tight. I turned it as hot as I could stand and let it stream over me.

Everything was wrong.

Everything was upside down.

I'd known Evers would save me. I'd believed it with every cell in my body and every part of my heart. Never in all that hope and faith had I imagined he'd save me by sacrificing himself.

I was going to kick his ass when he came home, kick it so hard he'd never do something that stupid again. I scrubbed my skin three times, shaved, and washed and conditioned my hair.

When I was done, I still didn't feel clean. The stain was on the inside, and no amount of soap could wash it away.

I was exhausted and hungry and still scared out of my

mind. Another half-hour under the hot water wasn't going to fix any of that. Food might. It couldn't hurt.

I combed my hair and pulled it into a loose bun at the nape of my neck. Remembering the FBI was coming, I took a few minutes to swipe on some mascara and eyeliner. We were going to get Evers back, and when I saw him, I didn't want to look like a puffy, weeping mess.

I was strong. I had my shit together. I'd survived, and I was not going to fall apart now. I stood in front of my closet, thinking. My dresses reminded me too much of my discarded nightgown.

I knew I was safe. I knew no one in this house would touch me in a way I didn't want, and yet I couldn't bear to feel so uncovered. I couldn't wear the robe all day either. Not without convincing everyone that I was very much *not* okay.

If they thought I was going to fall apart, they'd stash me in my room under guard like the others, and I'd be cut off from what was happening with Evers.

I ended up pulling on a navy maxi dress and white cardigan. The cardigan was too warm for July in Atlanta, but the AC in the house made it almost acceptable. I'd have preferred jeans, but I hadn't brought any. At least the maxi dress covered me from shoulders to ankles. It wasn't my most flattering outfit, but it wasn't horrible, and it made me feel safe. That was the best I could do for now.

The FBI had joined Lucas, Cooper, and Griffen at the dining room table.

A tall, lanky man with kind eyes rose to shake my hand when I entered the room.

"I'm agent Holley. It's good to see you safe and well," he said. "We're going to get Evers home as soon as possible."

"Thank you," I murmured as I took my seat. Holley introduced the two agents with him. Their names floated in and out of my brain, my nerves wound too tight for good manners.

I nodded in their direction, quickly getting lost as everyone else resumed their discussion of Tsepov and the case they were building against him.

None of them mentioned my father, and for that I was grateful. I was aware that if my dad survived, he was probably going to jail. I had no doubt Cooper had recorded my dad's confession in their safe room.

The cook brought me a plate and a steaming cup of coffee a few minutes after I seated myself at the table. I ate, trying to follow the conversation. Griffen leaned over and whispered, "We picked up Evers' signal. We know where they're holding him, and his vital signs are good."

"How do you know his vitals?" I whispered back.

Griffen winked at me. "Oh, we've got lots of toys."

"I bet you do," I murmured.

I ate mechanically, reassured only slightly by the calm assurance of the FBI, Cooper, Lucas, and Griffen. Cooper's anger at me seemed to have faded now that he knew Evers was okay.

Despite his façade, I knew he wasn't as confident as he wanted me to believe. He tapped his finger on the table in a fast beat, the same way he had when he'd been on the brink of torturing my father in the safe room.

Cooper might look calm. Inside, he was anything but. If Cooper was that on edge, getting Evers back wasn't the sure thing they were pretending it was.

They had a plan. Kind of. I'm no expert, but it sounded to me like most of the plan boiled down to waiting around for Evers to make a move.

I didn't like that.

I liked the *storm the house and get Evers out* kind of plan. I didn't want to wait. I'd spent half the night waiting. I wanted Evers home. Now.

It sounded like I wasn't going to get my wish.

Cooper pushed his chair back from the table. "So, that's it. We'll hit the office, then meet you at the rendezvous, get in position."

"Sounds good," agent Holley said, also standing. The two agents he brought with him stood as well. To me, he said, "Miss Winters, it was nice to meet you. Hopefully, the next time will be under better circumstances."

Considering the next time would probably be when he arrested my father, I didn't think so. I managed a smile. "Nice to meet you, too. You're going to bring Evers home?"

"We're going to do everything we can," he reassured me.

Cooper rounded the table and stopped by my chair. Laying a heavy hand on my shoulder, he looked down into my eyes. "We'll bring him home. I promise."

I started to push my chair back, saying, "I want to come with you."

Every man in the room said, "No," their voices overlapping in a chorus of male affront and exasperation.

Cooper's hand on my shoulder became an iron clamp holding me in place. "Not happening. You'd be in the way."

"Charlie is coming over," Lucas said from across the table. "I figured you wouldn't want to wait on your own, and she's too keyed up to work. She'll be here in a few minutes, and she'll probably be starving. You two can keep each other company because there is no fucking way you're coming with us."

I wanted to argue, but I kept my mouth shut. I wasn't going to win against so much opposition, especially when they were right. I would be in the way. I just hated the idea of sitting around eating biscuits and scrambled eggs when Evers was in danger. When he'd put himself there for me.

I stared down at my plate. "Fine."

Cooper gave my shoulder a squeeze and then a pat. "Just hang in there. Evers knows what he's doing."

Chapter Thirty-Seven

EVERS

I had no idea what I was doing.

My plan was simple.

Trade me for Summer.

Get Summer somewhere safe.

Then get free, go after Tsepov, and alert the team it was time to move.

The first part was easy.

The rest was anything but.

They checked me for weapons and electronics. A wire, GPS tracker, anything that could give them away or come back to bite them in the ass. They found two of the tiny GPS trackers sewn into my clothes.

I wasn't wearing a wire, but they searched. Thoroughly. I couldn't help but imagine them searching Summer the same way. The thought of it made my blood boil.

I'd never had a problem keeping my head on the job. Summer was fucking with that big time.

She was safe, with my brothers and out of danger.

That should have been enough.

It wasn't.

I wouldn't be able to settle down until I saw her with my own eyes. Not a glimpse of her, hooded and in a torn nightgown. I needed to hold her in my arms, to look into her eyes and see all the way to her heart. I needed to know she was okay, know this disaster hadn't left permanent scars.

I'd never find out if I didn't get out of this fucking room. So far, they'd searched me, hogtied me, and left me in a room on the second floor of Tsepov's temporary headquarters. It might have been the same room where they'd held Summer. I imagined I caught a faint trace of her lemon and flowers shampoo on the bedspread.

They hadn't bothered with a hood, shoving me face down in the back seat so I couldn't see where we were going. I got a glimpse of the neighborhood as the garage door closed behind us. Tightly packed McMansions on a cul-de-sac. Not exactly hidden away. Andrei Tsepov didn't do subtle.

Now that the first part of the plan was out of the way, on to the next step. Getting free. It had been a while since someone had restrained me, but in my line of business, it pays to be prepared. I could pick a set of handcuffs behind my back and break through zip tie cuffs in a flash.

They'd had a stroke of luck with that indestructible chair at Rycroft, especially considering the way they'd strapped me down, but they hadn't been as thorough here.

They'd used zip ties to secure my hands behind my back, then more to strap them to my ankles. Once that was done, they'd wrapped the whole mess with duct tape and waltzed out of the room thinking I wasn't a threat.

They were wrong about that. And they were wrong in

thinking that a few zip ties and some duct tape would keep me immobilized.

First on the agenda, strip off the duct tape.

Duct tape is a funny thing. It's strong in its own way but designed to be torn easily. Ironically, the more expensive the brand of duct tape, the easier it is to tear a strip off the roll, making it very handy for jobs around the house but not a great option for securing someone's hands together.

Only people who watched too many movies thought duct tape worked like handcuffs. Fucking amateurs. Sergey Tsepov's crew never would have made this kind of mistake. Had Sergey's guys walked away when his far less competent nephew took over? That was a question for another day.

A little twisting and tugging on my wrists and I had a short tear in the tape. Once the duct tape was split, it was simply a matter of working at it until it fell apart. Strip by strip, I uncovered my wrists, then my ankles.

A few minutes later, I was surrounded by shreds of silver duct tape, leaving me the zip ties to deal with. There are a few ways to break out of zip ties, and I'm an expert in all of them. All of the methods boil down to one of two things: manipulating the connector of the zip tie or breaking the plastic itself.

I hadn't been able to do either when I was strapped to the chair at Rycroft. Not enough leverage to break the plastic, and my fingers had been too far from the ties to reach the connector. Here, hogtied on a bed, I had all the access I needed.

They'd been smart enough to trim the ends off the ties. If they'd left them, I could have bent them back, shoved them under the tab that held the zip tie closed, and stripped them open. It was a little harder to do with my fingernails but not impossible.

I went to work on my ankles first, freeing them easily. I couldn't reach the tab on the connector at my wrists, but now that my feet were free, I didn't need to. Rolling off the bed to stand, I leaned over, pushed my arms out behind me, and brought my bound wrists down hard on the small of my back.

The plastic zip ties cut into my already torn-up wrists but didn't break. I tried again, feeling the plastic strain but hold. It was a lot easier to do this from the front, but I was too impatient to take the time to work my wrists to the front of my body.

I leaned over again, bent my knees and pushed my arms back, hard, as far as I could. I brought them down in a sharp strike against the small of my back. With an audible crack, the plastic zip ties popped open, and my hands were free.

This was where things got tricky. I was alone in the enemy stronghold without a weapon, surrounded by armed men who wouldn't hesitate to shoot me.

I had two choices. I could escape the house undetected, get to Cooper, and go home. Or, I could get a weapon, find Tsepov, and hold him until the FBI was able to breach the house and take him in.

Guess which one I was going for.

I had to.

I wasn't my father.

Maxwell had gone into the family business for the money and the glory.

I like money. Who doesn't? And glory, well, glory is nice when it's deserved.

I wasn't here for money or glory.

At the heart of it, I like helping people. Doing the right thing. It means something to me. I joined the Army because I wanted to serve my country. I joined the Rangers because

I wanted to learn how much I had to give. The answer was a hell of a lot.

I could no more walk out of this house and leave Tsepov behind than I could have left Summer in the hands of that monster. This wasn't about my family anymore. This was about the women who hadn't escaped him and his uncle before him. The children.

Fuck, I didn't like to think about what he was doing with the kids. I knew, I just didn't want to think about it. The guns and drugs were bad enough, but I might have let that slide. Not forever. Long enough to let us regroup and figure out where my father was.

The trafficking put things on a whole other level. None of us could walk away from that.

I had to get a weapon and find Tsepov. I had to signal Cooper. All simple things in theory, none easy to execute in reality. Tsepov's muscle wasn't overly bright, but they were strong, and fast, and armed. Very well armed.

At Rycroft, I'd noticed that aside from the semiautomatic rifles they'd held—overkill in a fucking living room—they'd all had a second handgun visible, and I would bet at least one more hidden away.

I leaned against the door to the room breathing steadily, clearing my mind until I could find my focus. The next few minutes would determine whether I lived or died.

Unless I was incredibly lucky, there was no way through the next step of the plan without loss of life. None of these guys would let me disarm them. They'd fight to the death to protect their boss. If I wanted to walk out alive and help bring down Tsepov, I'd have to be willing to take this all the way.

I was. I didn't like killing. I didn't get off on having power over human life. If I thought I could shoot to maim,

I'd do it, but that only works in the movies. In real life, if you pull your weapon, you'd better be prepared to use it. Leaving the enemy alive is a great way to get yourself killed. I had no intention of dying. Not today.

Hands steady, breath even, mind clear, I crossed the room and opened the window opposite the door. I paused, waiting for an alarm to sound. Nothing. Even the rich cheap out on their alarms, rarely putting sensors on second-floor windows. Their mistake.

Leaving the window open, I crossed the room and eased open the door. The hall was empty. Several hours had passed since we'd made the trade. Plenty of time for Cooper and agent Holley to get set up. They'd be waiting for my signal.

They might have seen the window open, but without knowing their position, I couldn't depend on it. I had to get my hands on a phone. Voices drifted up the stairs at the far end of the hall. I stood completely still and listened.

There was no trace of movement on the second floor. No creak of the floorboards, no voices, no shift of a body in a chair. No murmur of television or radio.

I was the only one up here. That was inconvenient.

I could go back to the room and wait for someone to come check on me. Possibly the smartest approach. It would give me time to get in position, and whoever came up wouldn't expect me to be free. It also meant waiting for God knows how long, leaving Cooper and the FBI in limbo. Leaving Summer to worry.

Or, I could draw attention to the room and hope that only one or two of them came up to investigate. That still gave me the upper hand, but it put them on alert, and it could leave me too outnumbered to take control.

I'm good, but going empty-handed against two or more heavily-armed bodyguards is not my kind of odds.

Then there was the action hero option—go down the stairs and disarm the first goon I saw before going straight for Tsepov. Crazy, reckless, and almost guaranteed to get me killed.

Option number two it was.

Chapter Thirty-Eight

EVERS

I stepped back into the room and looked around. A bed, a dresser, and an armchair. I set a hand on either side of the dresser and threw my weight into it, raising it onto two legs and pivoting it away from the wall. It was a heavy son of a bitch. Solid wood, none of that pressboard modern bullshit that was so popular these days. Perfect.

I lowered it gently enough to mask the sound of the furniture moving. Going to the other side, I repeated the pivot, quietly walking the dresser from the wall to the door. Once I had it in position, I leaned into the heavy piece of furniture, raising it on its side and tipping it over a foot in front of the door.

It landed with a crash loud enough to guarantee an investigation. With the dresser almost blocking the door, they'd be able to get into the room, but they'd be forced to enter one at a time. It didn't entirely even the odds, but it would help.

Shouts were followed by feet pounding up the stairs. I couldn't tell if it was two or three, but it was definitely more than one. I crouched behind the dresser, using its bulk as a shield.

It wasn't as well-built as the chair at Rycroft, but it was close. The multiple layers of thick wood were far better protection than the hollow core door and drywall.

Tsepov's goons were a little smarter than I gave them credit for. The pounding feet came to a stop in front of the door, and four precise bullet holes appeared above my head.

Good thing I hadn't been standing there waiting.

Also, good to know they didn't mind killing me. That changed things. I'd been prepared to do what I had to do to get out of the house, but my conscience eased knowing that my adversaries hadn't given a second thought to taking my life.

I stayed where I was, crouched behind the dresser, and waited. The door slammed open, crashing into the dresser and bouncing back. From the outraged yell, I could only assume it had smacked Goon #1 in the face.

He was about to have much bigger problems than a bruised nose. Goon #2 laughed, and the thud of a fist on flesh told me Goon #1 hadn't appreciated being the butt of a joke.

Good. The more annoyed they were with each other, the less they'd focus on me. One of them decided to try again. The muzzle of a gun showed around the edge of the door as a cautious hand pushed it open. Leading with his gun, Goon #1, red nose giving him away, pushed his head through the gap.

The tall dresser made for good cover. From his angle, all Goon #1 could see was the empty bed and open window. His eyes locked on the curtains fluttering in the breeze, he said something in Russian to his companions.

A set of footsteps moved down the hall, probably to check the backyard beneath the open second-story window.

The seemingly-empty room and open window relaxed Goon #1 as he pushed the door against the dresser and squeezed through the tight opening. He should have paid more attention. Should have been more alert.

He didn't see me until his body had cleared the door. He wasn't ready for me to explode from a crouch, shoving the heavy dresser into the door, wedging it shut and leaving him trapped with me.

Goon #1 still had multiple weapons to my zero, but I was betting I could make up the difference. Startled and struggling to catch up, Goon #1 fired wildly, hitting the far wall, the ceiling, the carpet.

He'd missed me, but he wouldn't for much longer. I was too big a target, and he was only feet away. I was on him before he could get his bearings, knocking him to the ground and jamming a knee in his throat. Closing one hand around his wrist, I wrenched the gun from his fingers.

Bones cracked, my knee crushing his larynx, and still he fought, twisting wildly under my weight. I was tall and strong, but this guy had at least 75 pounds on me. I couldn't hold him like this for long.

Pressing the muzzle of the gun to his forehead, I pulled the trigger twice. Beneath me, his body went limp. I didn't have time to think about what I'd done. Later.

I knew from experience Goon #1 would be back. He'd haunt my dreams and my waking nightmares, his soul lingering, whispering in my ear, reminding me that I'd chosen to take his life.

I'd deal with that later. First, I had to finish the mission. Goon #1 wouldn't be the only casualty.

I hoped I wouldn't be on the list along with him.

I searched for the rest of his weapons. I'd been right, a revolver at his ankle and a semi-automatic in a shoulder holster. His ankle holster was secured by Velcro and easily transferred from his leg to mine. His 9mm I set aside while I completed my search.

I wasn't surprised by the guns, but I was impressed by how many knives he'd managed to hide on his person. A butterfly knife. A switchblade. And a fucking hunting knife in a leather sheath. What did he think, he was going to run into a mountain lion in a suburban McMansion?

I took the butterfly knife and the switchblade but left the hunting knife. No cell phone. Two guns, three knives, and no phone? It said a lot about Goon #1's priorities.

Goon #2 pounded on the door, ineffectually twisting the handle as if that would move the dresser out of the way. There were voices in the hall. I couldn't hide forever.

The bullets from the handgun had made it through the door but not the dresser. Their assault rifles would shred the thick wood and me along with it. Listening hard, I decided there were three of them, two directly behind the door and one in the hall to the right of the door.

Still using the dresser as cover, I fired through the wall, a foot to the right of the doorframe. One bullet hit a stud and veered off course. The second hit its target.

Two endless seconds after I fired, a thump sounded in the hall, the floor shaking from the impact. Goon #4 down, two goons left, and I was running out of time.

At this point, the dresser was more hindrance than help. Staying low, I braced my feet and shoved as hard as I could, pushing the dresser away from the door. Reaching up, I turned the handle.

The door swung open a few inches. Goon #2 took the

bait. Leading the same way as Goon #1, the muzzle of his gun pushed through the opening first.

Didn't these guys realize how clearly that telegraphed their position?

Apparently not.

I raised the gun I'd stolen and fired twice. Goon #2 dropped to the floor, blocking the doorway as a shout of outrage echoed down the hall. Only Goon #3 was left in the hall. For now.

We had no idea how many men Tsepov had in the house. Anything I could do to thin the ranks would only increase my chances of escape and make it easier for the FBI to take Tsepov.

I expected Goon #3 to follow his compatriot through the door, but he was either smarter or had a better sense of self-preservation. Footsteps thudded on the carpet as he fled down the hall to the stairs.

I was running out of time, and I was trapped. I needed to signal Cooper. Goon #2's bulk was wedged between the door and the frame. I crouched over him, searching for his phone, keeping my eyes off his face.

My first shot had gone through his cheekbone, splintering teeth and tearing flesh. The second hit his neck. Barely two minutes had passed since he'd fallen, and his shirt was stained red, the carpet beneath his body soggy with blood.

Ignoring the mess, I checked his pockets, finally hitting pay-dirt on the inside of his suit coat. Wiping the blood from his thumb, I used it to unlock the screen and sent Cooper a quick text.

In bedroom on second floor. Three down.

Tsepov's location unknown. I'm armed. Going hunting.

As I'd hoped, Cooper responded almost immediately.

In position.

On our way.

Stay safe.

Stay safe.

If Cooper thought I was going to sit in this room and wait for them to come to the rescue, he was nuts.

I wasn't looking to be the hero. I was more than happy for the FBI to come charging in, weapons drawn, and arrest the bad guy.

I was a sitting duck up here, and they had assault rifles. Waiting for rescue was a death sentence. Compared to Tsepov's arsenal, two guns and a few knives weren't much.

Leaning over Goon #2, I looked past Goon #4's body, splayed outside the door, to see an empty hallway. It wouldn't be empty for long. Time to go exploring.

Heading for the stairs, I was working out a strategy to deal with the staircase and the unknown layout of the first level when instinct drew my eyes up.

I almost didn't see it in time. A six-inch black cylinder flew down the hall, flipping end over end, headed right for me. My body moved before my brain fully processed the danger.

I dove through the nearest door, throwing myself away from the hall as the flash-bang grenade exploded. Even in another room, the searing light left me temporarily blinded, my ears ringing.

I'd trained with stun grenades before. Back then I could have shaken off the effects a little faster. As it was, I wobbled when I rose to my feet, black dots wavering in my vision.

There would be goons with guns on the way. I wished I had a flash-bang of my own to toss down the stairs and clear my entry. A flash-bang, an assault rifle, anything better than the nine-millimeter in my hand.

If I'd been in the hall when that grenade had hit...

I glanced through the open door to see Goon #4's body on fire. Flames ate at his clothes, rising to lick at the walls.

A flash bang is no party if you're in the same room. If it hits you? The light and the sound are the least of your problems. Not that Goon #4 had problems anymore.

I was out of choices and there was no point in strategy. I couldn't play the odds and hide up here until Cooper and the FBI made their way into the house. Not with Goon #4's body turning the second floor into a bonfire.

Even if I managed to put out the flames, I was vulnerable as long as they knew exactly where I was.

Easing past the burning body, I decided I'd take my chances downstairs.

Chapter Thirty-Nine

EVERS

My back to the wall at the top of the stairs, I peered around the corner. The stair case in Tsepov's McMansion was white marble, curving around the two-story entry as it descended to the white marble foyer.

Pretentious and way oversized for the house, the staircase would have fit better in Rycroft Castle than a suburban house. It did give me a wide-open view of the front door, the stairs, the foyer, and the wide hall to the rest of the house. All empty.

Empty was wrong. After that flash-bang, there should have been someone on the stairs. They must have thrown it and taken off. But why? I didn't wonder for long.

Goon #5 came tearing around the corner, already barreling up the stairs before he spotted me. He looked as surprised to see me as I was that he was alone. His eyes flashed wide as his gun came up.

Not fast enough.

He was down, his head cracking on the marble steps,

and I was vaulting over his body before he had a chance to register what was happening. I hoped agent Holley was prepared to explain all these bodies. I wasn't waiting around for Tsepov to kill me.

I crossed the foyer as fast as I could, not liking the exposure of the open space. Once in the wide hall that led to the rest of the house, I found an empty great room straight ahead, its tall windows looking out to the woods beyond the backyard.

I thought I spotted movement in the trees and hoped it wasn't wishful thinking. On my left was a narrow hall that looked like it led to a kitchen and breakfast room. Tsepov was not the kind of guy who hung around his kitchen.

Another hall led to my left, lined with oil paintings and dark-stained wainscoting. Bingo. I ducked into a doorway as two goons rushed past, weapons out, heading for the back door.

The movement in the trees hadn't been wishful thinking. Those two weren't going after me. Good. The more distracted they were the better my chances of finding Tsepov.

I moved down the hall in the direction the two goons had come from, hoping they'd been getting orders from the boss. The first door I came to was a bathroom, the second a sitting room. Both empty. The door at the end of the hall was ajar.

Flattening my back against the hall, I listened. Voices in the distance. A door opening. The room in front of me was quiet, but I didn't think it was empty. From the sliver I could see through the half-open door, it was an office or a library. Exactly what I was looking for.

I nudged the door open with my toe. A quick glance showed me a single man behind a wide mahogany desk. I was through the door, gun raised before Andrei Tsepov could move.

"Don't even think about it," I said. "I'll put a bullet in you before you can shoot."

Tsepov glanced at the gun on his desk but made no move to pick it up. My finger tightened on the trigger as he shoved his hands in his pockets with an air of nonchalance as if he wasn't the least bit worried about my gun aimed at his head.

I eased into the room, putting my back to the wall so I could see the open door and the windows, keeping my gun trained on Tsepov.

"You left quite a body count out there," he commented, seeming unconcerned with the loss of so many loyal henchmen.

I ignored the internal flinch at the reminder of what I'd done. Later. I could atone for all of it later. I had to finish this first.

"You never should have touched Summer."

It was true. If they'd never touched Summer, they wouldn't have had to trade her for me. If they hadn't taken me, I wouldn't have had to shoot my way out.

"That was an error in judgment, I'll admit," Tsepov conceded with an arrogant nod of his head. "I won't make another."

"I wouldn't bet on that," I said. "You're done."

Tsepov laughed, and the cocky, smug sound of it had my finger vibrating on the trigger of my gun.

A feral instinct in me knew he needed to be put down like a rabid dog.

He deserved it. For his crimes against so many unknown victims. For the women and children he'd sold. For putting his hands on Summer. For fucking touching her. Scaring her. For the role he'd played in my father's bad choices. For every life he'd destroyed, I wanted to pull the fucking trigger.

I didn't.

"The FBI is taking you in," I said, infuriated when he raised his shoulder in a shrug and shook his head.

"They can take me in, but they won't hold me."

I gritted my teeth, adjusted my stance, and kept the gun trained on his forehead.

Your job is to keep him here until Holley and his men arrive, I reminded myself. *That's it. Do your job and stay cool.*

Tsepov must have wanted me to pull that trigger because he couldn't shut the fuck up.

"This is a waste of your time," he said. "I know who has the account numbers. I have men on the way. Once we have the numbers, we'll get rid of the woman, your brother, and then we'll come for the rest of you. You, Cooper, Axel. Your father, his whore, and the girl last."

The venom in his voice burned like acid. My father stealing his money had damaged his pride so much it was worth destroying everyone I loved in revenge. Tsepov didn't care about collateral damage.

I could guess who *the woman* was considering Knox's current assignment. I could only hope that he and Lily Spencer were safe.

What the fuck did he mean by *Maxwell, his whore, and the girl?* It didn't make sense.

"Don't call my mother a whore," I said, trying to shake loose more information.

Tsepov didn't fall for my ploy. "Your mother isn't part of this. She was convenient, that's all."

"Then what the fuck are you talking about? What do you mean by *his whore and the girl?*"

Tsepov's mocking smile stretched across his mouth, baring his teeth, as a voice on a speaker filled the house.

This is the FBI. Surrender your weapons. Face the wall and put your hands up.

Knowing I was out of time, Tsepov shook his head. "You don't know how far heroes can fall, but you will." He laughed, raising his hands in the air and turning to face the wall. With one last smug look over his shoulder, he repeated, "You will."

The door to the office swung open, and agent Holley was there, gun raised, accompanied by three other agents, one of whom flashed a shiny set of handcuffs. Holley read Tsepov his rights, cuffed him, and sent him out with the other agents. I would have felt better if Tsepov had been even a little unnerved by his arrest.

Holley took in my bloody shirt, the flecks of red speckling my hands. "Heard there was a mess upstairs. You're coming back with me."

I started to tell him we'd do it later, but he cut me off. "We'll tell your family you're okay. You don't want your girl to see you like that. She's scared shitless as it is. And I'm not letting you out of my sight until you're debriefed."

I flicked the safety on the weapon and put it on the desk, adrenaline finally starting to fade, leaving my hands shaking. I was ready to sit. To sleep. To walk out of this house and forget everything that had happened here.

Cooper came through the door. His eyes were bright with relief, though all he said was, "Did you have to set the guy on fire?"

"That wasn't me. They threw up a flash-bang, and it landed right on their guy."

Under his breath, Cooper muttered, "Fucking amateurs."

Things moved quickly after that. Quickly and glacially slow.

Lucas headed back to Rycroft to collect Charlie and let Summer know I was fine. I tried to call myself, but agent Holley wasn't having it. No phone calls, no side trips. We were going straight to the FBI building, on communications blackout until they were done with me. Holley wanted this by the book, with no special exceptions Tsepov's lawyers could pick at later.

I rode with agent Holley into the office, and aside from a quick duck under a shower and a change into the clean clothes Cooper brought, I spent the next few hours going over my time in Tsepov's lair in excruciatingly boring detail.

I hadn't enjoyed my visit the first time. Reliving it wasn't an improvement. Finally, Holley released me with a warning to be careful. Just because they had Tsepov and the men who'd been at the house didn't mean he was neutralized.

On the ride home, Cooper said, "You did what you had to do, Ev. Don't let it eat at you."

"I know."

I knew I'd done what I had to do.

I also knew it *would* eat at me. If that was the price I had to pay for getting out alive, so be it.

I'd never been so glad to see Rycroft Castle emerge from the trees. Summer was waiting on the stairs. As I jumped from the passenger seat of Cooper's SUV, she flew down, taking the steps two at a time before skidding to a halt in front of me.

Reaching up, she cupped my face in her palm, searching for any sign of injury.

"I'm okay," I reassured her, "didn't get a scratch."

At that, she threw herself into my arms, wrapping hers around me and squeezing so tight she drove a gust of breath from my lungs. I rested my cheek on the top of her head, drawing in the lemon and flowers scent of her. Home. I was home.

I was thinking I could hold her in my arms forever when she reared back and punched me in the chest.

"What the hell were you thinking? They could have hurt you. They could have killed you."

Her hands waved in the air as she yelled, and I had the feeling she was winding up for another punch. I caught her arms, tugging her close.

"I'd do it again in a heartbeat. I will never let anything happen to you."

Summer's eyes were wide and blue and swimming with tears.

"I never got to tell you. Everything happened so fast, and I never got to tell you."

"Tell me what?" I asked, watching one tear and then another trail down her cheeks.

"I love you. I never got to tell you that I love you."

"I know," I said, smiling down at her.

Summer glared through her tears, outrage all over her face. Rearing back, she swung her fist at my head.

That's my girl.

I caught her hand before she could slam it into my chin.

"You know?" she shrieked. "I finally tell you I love you, and all you have to say is *you know?*"

"I know you love me. Of course, I know. You saved my life, Summer. Your Dad—"

The fight drained out of her. Shoulders drooping, eyes on the ground, she said, "I couldn't let him shoot you."

I pulled her into my arms again, resting my cheek on the top of her head. "I'm sorry. So sorry. But I'm glad you love me enough to pick me."

"Every time," she whispered. "I'll always pick you."

"Is your dad—?" I didn't want to ask.

Summer let out a gust of air. "He's stable. For now. They said no visitors for a few hours. He's recovering from surgery."

"Is everyone else okay?"

"Fine. Tired from whatever Dad slipped in the wine." She pulled back, looking up at me, her eyes landing on mine briefly before skidding away. "I'm so sorry."

Tears spilled over her cheeks again, and my gut clenched in panic. Why was she crying? I was home, we were safe, her dad was alive. Tsepov was in jail. We hadn't heard from Knox, but I knew my brother. He'd turn up. There wasn't any reason to cry.

"What? Why? You don't have anything to be sorry about."

"You knew my dad was a problem, and I didn't believe you. I brought him into Rycroft, and he almost got all of us killed. It was my fault."

"That's bullshit," I said. Summer wasn't taking on her father's guilt. "Your father, my father, Tsepov—they're responsible. They did this. Not you, Summer. Never you."

"I should have known," she said, wiping at her eyes.

"He's your dad, and you wanted to see the good in him. No one gets that more than me."

"I'm sorry," she said again.

"I'm not." Summer looked at me in surprise. "I'm not," I insisted. "You're loyal. You look for the best in the people you love. That's who you are, Summer. I love you. All of you."

"Even when I almost get you shot?"

"Even then. I've loved you since the beginning. I think I've loved you since the day we met. I found you at that conference, told you that you were coming with me and you just stared me down and said *I don't think so* in that snotty tone."

"I was not snotty," she protested, laughing through the last of her tears. "You were a total stranger."

"You came with me anyway," I teased.

"You were persuasive."

"I was a goner. By the time I got you back to Atlanta, I was hooked. You scared the fucking hell out of me."

"I must have," she said, "because you ran away like a little boy."

I cupped her face in my palms, studying every inch of it, absorbing her eyes, her spiky lashes wet with tears, her full, pink lower lip. Every part of her was a treasure.

"I did," I admitted. "I ran like a scared boy. It took me way too long to realize that I'd never have what I wanted most if I couldn't stand up and be a man. I wasn't afraid of you, Summer, I was afraid of me. Of not being good enough. Of fucking everything up. Of hurting you. Then you threw me out, and I knew there was only one thing I was really afraid of. Losing you."

"You stayed away," she said. "I thought you'd come back, but you never—"

"I was working on a plan to win you back."

Summer looked over her shoulder at Rycroft Castle, rising above us, it's turrets and white limestone walls belonging in a different century. "Kind of an elaborate plan. You could have just sent flowers."

"Like that was going to work. You would have shoved them in the disposal and sent me back the stems."

Summer's lips quirked in a grin. "Probably. Still, this was overkill."

"This was just good luck." I thought about our fathers and everything they'd done. "Maybe not good luck. A silver lining?"

"Whatever it was, I'm glad it brought you back to me."

"I was always coming back for you, Summer. I love you."

"I love you, too." Going up on her toes, she kissed me, sliding her fingers into the hair at the nape of my neck, teasing her lips across mine.

When she pulled away, she said, "Are you done with the FBI? Can we go inside so I can take off that suit and make sure you're not injured?"

"I told you, I'm fine."

Summer raised an eyebrow and unbuttoned the top button of my shirt.

"I know, but I want to make absolutely sure. I'm going to need to examine every inch of you."

"Oh, well, in that case, you never know, I might have an injury or two. You'd better check me out. Thoroughly."

Summer stepped back and took my hand, leading me up the stairs into Rycroft Castle. Winking at me over her shoulder, she said, "Oh, I plan to examine you very thoroughly. For a long, long time."

Epilogue

SUMMER

I didn't end up examining Evers. I meant to. I led him upstairs to my room and went to work on the buttons of his shirt, my fingers slow and awkward.

Every time I'd touched Evers I hadn't had to think. I saw him, and my body went on automatic pilot, driven by desire. By need.

I wanted Evers. Always.

The second his fingers unfastened the top button of my cardigan I went stiff.

I didn't mean to. I didn't want to. I didn't even know what was happening until he dropped his hands to his sides, a wave of worry washing across his face.

Lightly, he rested his hands on my shoulders. "You're shaking."

The shame should have flooded my cheeks with heat, but I was cold. Cold and embarrassed and afraid.

I risked a look at Evers. His jaw was tight, the muscle flickering as he clenched his teeth, but his words were gentle. "Cooper said he didn't touch you. He didn't hurt you."

I swallowed hard. My voice grated on my ears. "He didn't hurt me. Not really. But he—"

I still couldn't say it.

I didn't need to. Evers closed his eyes. In a low, guttural voice he said, "He touched you."

I gave a jerky nod and risked a tiny step closer. Evers' hands on my shoulders dropped to my back, urging me into his arms. My heart ached with love for him.

I knew the idea that anyone had touched me must be driving him insane. That it had been Andrei Tsepov only made it worse. Yet he locked it down, only that flickering muscle in his jaw giving away his emotions.

His hands on my back were light, giving me room to step away if that was what I needed.

It wasn't. The idea of being touched by anyone else turned my stomach. Anyone except Evers. I buried myself against him, pressing the side of my face to his chest, the cold draining away as his arms closed around me.

"I'm okay," I whispered. "It was nothing."

Evers' lips grazed my temple. "You're okay, Summer, but it wasn't nothing. I know you want to push it away. Pretend it didn't happen. Don't do that."

"I don't want to think about it," I admitted. "It's over and I never want to think about it again."

Evers let out a sigh, his arms tightening around me. We stood like that for a while. Long enough for me to finally start to feel warm. For me to realize how exhausted I was.

"Can we lay down?" I asked.

Evers didn't answer. He didn't touch his clothes or mine. He led me to the bed and guided me on top, fully clothed, pulling the coverlet over us. I rested my head on his chest and listened to his heartbeat.

I thought he was asleep until he said, "I killed four men today."

I didn't know what to say to that. I squeezed my arm around his chest and whispered, "I'm sorry."

"Not your fault. I didn't have a choice. In each case, it was him or me. I picked me."

"I'm glad you did," I said.

"Me too. You said what happened with Tsepov wasn't a big deal. That it's over. It is. Everything that happened is over. But I know from experience that it's never really over. You have to let yourself understand that because it's going to come back. When you least want it to, it's going to come back."

"I just want it all to go away," I said into his shirt.

"I know you do. So do I. That's not the way it works. Most of our jobs are pretty tame, but the cases that aren't..." He blew out a breath. "Shit happens. We have a few different psychologists we work with. There's one who the women say is good, especially when it comes to assault—"

"It wasn't—he didn't—"

"I think you should talk to her. At least once, okay? Just once."

"Okay," I breathed.

I didn't want to talk to anyone. Talking meant reliving, and I never wanted to go back. While Tsepov had me, I kept telling myself that all I had to do was stay alive. I'd done that. I was alive. Now it was over.

If it would make Evers feel better, I'd talk to his psychologist. Once.

I thought about those four men. How they would weigh on him. "What about you?"

He shifted to kiss the top of my head. "Standard proce-dure. Not after every job, but if there's loss of life? Always."

"Really?" Everyone I'd met on the Sinclair team, men and women, looked tough as nails. They reminded me of soldiers. Commandos. Strong and unyielding.

"Really," Evers confirmed. "Like I said, shit happens. Too much stuff we think we're prepared for. We think we can handle. We can't afford to have it come back on us later. Can't afford to freeze at the wrong moment. We have to deal with it. Process it. Figure out how to live with it before we move on."

Another kiss to the top of my head. "Ignoring the bad stuff doesn't make you stronger. It just leaves you with weak spots you can't see until it's too late. I know you don't want to talk about it. I don't want you to have to talk about it. But trust me when I tell you, you'll feel better after."

"I don't want to tell you—"

His arm tightened around me again. "Unless you need to, I don't want to hear it. I think it's probably better if I don't. We'll get past this. I promise."

Evers was right. About a lot of things. After two more failed attempts to have sex—attempts initiated by me in a desperate effort to convince myself that I'd left Tsepov behind—I set an appointment with the psychologist Evers recommended.

It wasn't a magic fix. She was nice, and I liked her. It was still excruciating going through everything I remem-bered of my time with Tsepov. The bag over my head. Those hands.

Excruciating.

I'm not going to say I walked out of her office feeling back to normal, but there was relief in telling the story. Relief in her lack of judgment, in her easy acceptance of the bad moments I'd had since then. The way I'd wake in the night flinching from Evers. The shame that my head had confused him with someone else in the dark.

I surprised myself by making a second appointment. I needed time, but a little more talking wouldn't hurt.

It helped that things were quiet once Tsepov went to jail. He stayed there for a whole five days before his attorney argued for bail and handed over a fat check that set Tsepov free. Andrei Tsepov strolled out of jail and disappeared.

I didn't have time to think about what that meant. My father made it through surgery but flatlined twice the next day. Eventually, he slipped into a coma. He never woke up. My mom and I sat with him, listening to the machines beep as he quietly faded away into silence.

I was struggling to handle it, my emotions a jumble of contradictions. I couldn't forget that my father was the reason I'd ended up with Tsepov. My father could have killed everyone at Rycroft.

Alive, Smokey was a danger to me. To my mom. To everyone I loved. We were safer with him dead, and I grieved as if he'd been Father of the Year. I grieved for the lost chances. For everything we'd never have.

My mom stuck around for a week, invited to stay at Rycroft by Cynthia. The chance to stay in a castle with two real-life movie stars wasn't enough to offset the loss of her ex-husband, but it helped.

Cynthia, I suspected, was happy for my mom to distract me so she could focus all of her attention on Clint. The two of them mooned around Rycroft like newlyweds. I can't count how many times I came around the corner to find them locked in an embrace.

Cynthia is my favorite client, but there were things I didn't need to see.

After Smokey's funeral, Evers took me aside and handed me a ring. My grandfather's ring.

"This is yours now. Someday, if you want, you can pass it on."

I closed my fingers around the ring and held on to a piece of my father. My history. The past I'd never known.

I brought the ring and my mom to a family party at Winters House. We'd been wrong, the extremely wealthy did do barbecues. The Winters' chef was a master. I don't think I'd ever had better ribs in my life.

My mom fit right in with the Winters, not the least bit awed by their notoriety. I thought I was going to faint when she started lecturing Aiden on one of his subsidiaries' environmental record.

To my shock, he took her seriously, giving her his email and telling her to submit a formal report. He didn't promise to make any changes, but he did promise to review it himself. My mom beamed. She left for home happy that I had Evers at my side and family around.

Cynthia went back to L.A. a few weeks early, Clint in tow, and Evers and I moved out of Rycroft Castle. To say my condo was a letdown after Rycroft is an understatement. I'd always liked it before, but after Rycroft, it felt like living in a closet.

Evers, with his trademark combination of sneaky and sweet, slowly started moving me into his house. He never formally asked me to move in, just said, "You should bring that to my place," about my much better coffee maker, or, "Half of my closet is empty. There's plenty of room for your stuff."

He'd said his house needed work, but it looked fine to

me. The kitchen could use some updating, and the wall-paper and carpet were dated, but his pool was spectacular.

We talked about making improvements but didn't do anything, even though it would have been as simple as calling Charlie and Lucas.

Instead, we waited, stuck in a holding pattern.

The account numbers were still missing, along with Maxwell Sinclair. Cooper and Evers were doing everything they could from Atlanta.

Axel was growing impatient with the delay, not enjoying living with their mother for the first time since high school. Even Emma was ready for her to go back to Florida.

And Knox... Knox was making progress, but not fast enough. Lily Spencer was more than just a widow with security problems. Instead of answers, Lily only brought more problems. Dangerous problems. Evers wanted his brother home. Now. But Knox's priorities had changed.

Tsepov's threat loomed over our all of our heads.

I wanted the situation with Maxwell and Tsepov resolved for the Sinclairs' sake, but I wasn't in a rush for life to move on. So much change so fast, and a part of me was still reeling.

In the space of weeks, I'd gone from swearing I'd never speak to Evers again to practically living with him. I was just fine with things staying the same for a little while.

Evers was not.

We'd gotten into the habit of swimming after dinner. In the heat of summer, it was a great way to decompress after a long day. Me, alone with Evers, mostly naked. I couldn't think of many things better.

One night, a few weeks after Cynthia went back to

L.A., I jumped in, ready to wash away a day of phone calls and social media posts. Most days I loved my job. That was not one of those days.

Evers dove in after me, scooping me up and pinning me against the side. He kissed my neck, one finger toying with the strap of my raspberry bikini.

"What's this?" he asked, deftly untying the bow behind my neck.

"Umm, it's my bathing suit?"

Evers peeled the top down, flicked open the bow at the back, and tossed the bikini top on the flagstone at the side of the pool where it landed with a wet plop.

"Didn't I tell you the new rule?"

I shook my head, distracted by the pluck of his fingers at the bows on my hips holding my bikini bottom together.

"I've instituted a no-bathing-suits rule," he said, freeing my bottoms and tossing them to join my top at the side of the pool.

I thought he'd been wearing trunks when he came out of the house, but as I skimmed my hands down his sides, I realized somewhere along the way they'd disappeared.

"That's going to be awkward when people come over to swim," I commented, reaching to palm his cock, curling my fingers around his hard length.

"The rule is suspended when we have company," he conceded, "but only then. Otherwise, this pool is skinny-dipping only."

I opened my mouth to make a smart-ass comment, but Evers' lips stroked the sensitive skin under my ear and words fell away. His fingers worked between my legs, chasing away whatever I'd been about to say.

Walking backwards, Evers made his way to the stairs in

the corner, drawing me with him. He sat and pulled me to straddle his lap, filling me with his cock in one smooth stroke.

We'd found a lot of ways to have sex in the pool. A lot. This was my favorite.

Buoyant in the water, I rocked on top of him, his hands and mouth everywhere. Tasting, stroking as my clit ground into the base of his cock with every roll of my hips, over and over until I tumbled into orgasm.

Twice.

There's a reason the stairs are my favorite spot in the pool.

The second time I came, my nails digging into Evers' shoulders, he followed me, his hands tight on my ass, his length filling me with each hard thrust, his groan of release music in my ears.

After, when I would have moved away, he tightened his arms around me until I draped myself over him, my wet hair trailing down his shoulder.

His damp lips nuzzled my ear. "Marry me."

"What?" I couldn't have heard him right.

"Marry me," he repeated, leaning back as I sat up to stare at him.

"Did you just ask me to marry you while we're having sex?"

"Not while. After." He braced his weight on one arm, his other hand on my hip, anchoring me in place. I pushed my hair out of my face, mouth gaping, at a loss for words.

"Are you serious?"

"Completely serious." He raised a finger to trace my cheekbone, his eyes level on mine, showing not a hint of levity.

He wasn't joking.

"Do you have a ring?" I asked.

"Not on me."

"Not on you? Does that mean you *have* a ring?" If he had a ring, he'd been planning this. If he had a ring, he hadn't asked by accident.

Evers sat up, wrapping his arms around me, and brushed his mouth across mine.

"I've had the ring for weeks. I was going to wait. Wait until things calmed down. Wait until all the shit with my dad is resolved. But I don't want to wait. I don't want to put our lives off because of other people. I love you. I want you to be my wife. I want to stop this back and forth with your condo. I want this to be our house. I want you to be mine."

"I am yours," I said, reeling.

I'd assumed we'd get here eventually. He'd already told me he planned to propose. Someday. I never expected someday to come this fast.

"We can have a long engagement," he said, a hint of concern in his eyes. "Weddings take a while to plan anyway. But I don't want to wait to put my ring on your finger."

Still trying to figure him out, I said, "What if I want to get married now? What if I want to go to Vegas and do it tomorrow?"

"Do you?" He shifted on the steps as if to stand, startling me into a laugh. My hands closed over his shoulders to hang on.

"No," I gasped, "I don't want to get married in Vegas."

Evers settled back onto the step. "But you do want to get married? To me?"

I thought about teasing him over his clearly unplanned proposal. Then I thought about him buying the ring weeks ago, hanging onto it, probably debating the best time and place to ask. I thought about the words spilling out now, when we were connected, as close as two people could be. I wasn't going to tease.

"Yes," I said. "Yes, I want to marry you. I want to be your wife."

His mouth closed over mine, and when he pulled away he murmured, "Thank God. I was starting to think you were going to say no."

"When have I ever said no to you?" I asked.

"Except for the time you threw me out and didn't speak to me for two months?"

"Well, you deserved that. And aside from that, when have I ever said no to you?"

"Never. I still needed to hear you say yes."

I kissed his jaw, loving the scrape of stubble against my lips, the beat of his pulse under his skin. "Of course, it's yes."

Evers stood, laughing as I shrieked in surprise, tightening my legs around his waist, twining my arms around his neck. Ignoring our wet bathing suits at the side of the pool, he walked us into the house, up the stairs to the bedroom.

Evers dropped me in the middle of the bed, my limbs splayed out, my wet hair everywhere. I started to sit up.

"Stay there," he ordered. "Just for a minute."

Crossing the room to his dresser, he opened the top drawer and pulled out a small, royal blue velvet box. He padded across the room, the planes of his body gleaming in the dim light. I could look at Evers naked all day. Opening the box, he pulled out a ring and slid it on my finger.

"If you don't like it—"

The solitaire sparkled, simple and beautiful.

"I love it."

Evers stretched out beside me, threading his fingers through mine, his eyes locked on the ring on my finger.

"Ever since I bought it I've been imagining seeing it on your hand just like this." He drew our hands to his mouth, kissing my finger beside the ring. "I never knew how much I wanted this until I lost you. Then it was all I wanted. You, beside me, forever."

"I knew," I said. "I just never thought you'd want it, too."

"With you?" Evers asked, "Forever with you sounds like heaven.

Yet again, Evers was right. Forever with him was heaven.

Sneak Peek

UNDONE

CHAPTER ONE: LILY

My eyes flew open in the dark of night. I'd been dreaming of the lake, of moonlight playing on the water, of swimming at night. Of unseen hands pulling me under, water filling my lungs.

Most of my life I'd slept like a log. In the year since Trey died, I'd gotten used to this. To waking in the night, only the shadows on my walls for company.

I rolled over, fluffing the pillow under my head, trying to find a comfortable position. Sometimes I could fall back to sleep. Sometimes I lay awake until dawn.

The dream weighed me down, the dark water in moonlight. I wasn't sure if I wanted to close my eyes again or give up and read until morning.

Sleep. I needed a full night of sleep, and it was possible the nightmare wouldn't come back. I could hope.

My eyes were sliding shut when I heard it.

A thump. A shuffle. Something being dragged, or someone walking in sock covered feet.

I sat up, throwing off the covers, then stopped at the

edge of the bed, my feet on the carpet, leaning forward, straining for a hint of sound.

Had I heard something? It wouldn't be the first time a noise woke me. The house was isolated, on the edge of the lake and surrounded by woods. Between the wildlife and the wind, nighttime sounds weren't unusual.

This was different.

Since Trey had died everything was different.

I listened, breath held, and heard nothing but the faint echo of crickets outside.

I took a deep, slow breath and reminded myself that the doors were locked. The alarm was on. The house was secure.

The last time I'd thought I heard a noise, had been absolutely sure someone was in the house, I'd called the police and ended up feeling like an idiot. Deputy Morris was nice about it.

Castle Falls is a small town. Deputy Morris, Dave, had been fishing buddies with Trey. He was a friend. Sort of. Friend enough that he didn't tell me outright he thought I was making it up, but I'd known Dave for years. I could read between the lines.

If I called him right now he'd jump in his cruiser and head over. He'd search the house from top to bottom, and when he found nothing, he'd give me a sympathetic, worried look and ask if I needed help.

I needed all kinds of help, but not from Dave Morris.

There was nothing there. It was the nightmare, that's all. Stress. Too many nights of interrupted sleep playing tricks on my mind.

I'd almost convinced myself I was imagining things. I turned, ready to slide my feet back under the covers, when it came again. A soft, shuffling thump. Not quite someone walking. Something being dragged?

I didn't know, but I'd have to find out.

I stood slowly, my palms clammy, heart racing. My robe lay at the foot of the bed where I'd tossed it hours earlier. I pulled it on, tying the belt firmly. My hair flopped in my face from where I'd gathered it loosely on top of my head for sleep. I twisted it into a messy knot, crushing the curls, just wanting it out of my eyes.

The house was quiet, but this time I'd heard something. *I had.* I wasn't making it up. I wasn't imagining things. I'd heard a noise from inside the house.

Picking up my phone, I stared at the screen. *Just call Dave*, a little voice whispered.

I unlocked the screen and pulled up Dave's number, then stopped. Dave's face filled my mind, the expression as he stared down at me the last time I'd called in the middle of the night. His patience would have been sweet if it hadn't been tainted by condescension.

He'd suggested I take Adam and move home. Get some help from my family. He laid a hand on my shoulder, intending comfort, and said that it was okay if I wasn't prepared to live on my own. It was okay to need help without Trey. Then the suggestion, voiced so gently, that perhaps I was just lonely.

Like I'd call Dave in the middle of the night because I wanted some company.

Did he think I was that pathetic? I guess he did.

I wasn't pathetic.

I was scared.

Phone in hand, I turned on my bedroom light. I'd known I was alone in the room, and still, I was relieved to see the familiar white walls, my watercolors, and my messy bed.

In the hall I turned on the light, flicking switches on my way to Adam's room. Trey had insisted our son sleep as far from us as possible. I hadn't minded back then. My little guy was a bear to get to sleep, but once he was down he was out. Trey joked that Adam slept like me. Like I used to. Before. Now I hated the distance between our rooms, but Adam didn't want to move.

I left Adam's light off, easing into his room, padding silently to his bedside. He lay face down on the mattress, the quilt shoved to his feet, his cartoon pajamas twisted around his torso.

He slept like a rock, but he moved constantly. Every now and then I'd let him fall asleep in my bed, but I always moved him to his own. I'd woken too many nights from a kick to my kidneys or a small toe in my ear. He slept hard, but he was never still for long.

Tousled blonde hair streaked white from the summer sun spread across his navy pillowcase. I ran my fingers through the silky length so like Trey's. So unlike my own dark curls. He'd need a haircut soon.

I straightened and went to the door, closing it behind me. If I'd been alone I might have ignored the sound. Might have tried harder to convince myself I was hearing things. But I had Adam, and Adam's safety was more important than anything.

At the top of the stairs, I stopped, the darkness at the bottom a cavern hiding whatever had made that sneaky, shuffling sound. I waited, ears straining. Nothing moved in the shadows below. Nothing that I could see.

I flipped the light switch at the top of the stairs, illuminating the empty hall below. The empty hall and the alarm panel on the wall at the base of the stairs. The alarm panel with its blinking green lights. Green, not red.

Green.

My heart kicked in my chest, my breath strangling in my throat.

I'd set the alarm. There was no question. I'd set the alarm. I never forgot.

I'd grown up in the suburbs, not the country. I'd never liked the isolation of the house Trey had built for us. Even when he was alive, I set the alarm every night. I never forgot.

Those green lights glowed up at me, making me wonder. Making me doubt. I never forgot, but had I? Could I have? I descended the stairs slowly, racking my brain.

We'd had dinner early. Chicken fingers with honey mustard for Adam, along with two hated carrots. Leftover lasagne for me. After, a bath for Adam. Pajamas for both of us. Then, curled up on the couch with his favorite stuffed monkey between us, we'd watched half a movie. Curious George. Again. Adam was crazy for Curious George, and we'd watched the movie every night for the past two weeks. Then bedtime for Adam. A story and a back rub later, Adam had fallen asleep.

I'd gone downstairs, set the alarm, and made a cup of tea before bringing a book and the tea up to bed.

I'd set the alarm while I was waiting for the water to boil. Then I'd walked through the first floor, turning off the lights, the alarm panel glowing red. Armed.

How was it green? My mind reeled at the thought. Only Trey and I had the code, and Trey was dead. The alarm had never malfunctioned. If it had, the police would have come.

Someone must have disarmed it. But who? And how? Even if someone had the code, the siren would have gone off when the door opened. The only way to disarm the panel silently was from inside the house.

That thought sent ice through my heart. No. I'd walked the house. No one had been inside. No one. It was impossible.

Not impossible. It's a big house. So many places to hide.

I pushed the voice away. I was not going to get hysterical. There had to be a simple explanation. Maybe the power had gone out while I was sleeping.

Backup battery.

Sleepwalking? Could I have sleepwalked to the panel and turned it off myself?

At the bottom of the stairs, I stopped, turning away from the green glow of the alarm panel. The front door was closed and locked, the windows on either side dark.

Taking a breath for courage, I strode forward and flicked every switch on the panel by the door. Bright light flooded the steps outside and the path from the driveway. Beyond the path, the lake gleamed black in the moonlight, just like my dream. The lights from the dock glowed, warm and welcoming.

No one was there. No one on the lake. No one on the dock. No one on the path.

I peered into the darkness. Most of the first floor was a big open space surrounded by towering plate glass windows. Trey had designed the house with the help of a renown modernist architect. I'd hated it from the start.

This part of Maine is filled with classic New England architecture. Colonials. Saltboxes. Cape Cods. Georgians, Federals, and even a few Victorians. Painted siding. Brick. Shutters and front porches.

This place, with its flat windows and sharp corners, fashioned of metal and concrete, looked like it had been dropped from another world. Or California. Here in Maine that was the same thing.

Modern and aggressive, it jutted out on the peninsula, intruding into the lake, breaking up the shoreline. The house Trey built demanded attention, asserting itself when it should have blended with the trees and the water.

I hated giving my address to anyone who didn't already know it. *Oh, that house*, they'd say. *Why'd you go build a thing like that?*

If I had a dollar for every time I'd heard that I could afford to burn the thing down and move away.

I could have afforded to move away even without those dollars. I stayed put. This was home. It was familiar. Adam's memories of his father were here. I couldn't bring myself to drag him away.

For the first time, I was grateful for the open design. One flick of a switch and I could see everything. Almost everything.

The kitchen, empty. The dining area, the sitting area, empty. The doors to the decks, all closed and locked.

I crossed the empty room and flipped more switches. The deck lights flashed on. Empty.

There was no one here. I was imagining things.

My nerves were shot like Dave said.

I turned on the balls of my feet, phone still clutched in my hand, ready to write the whole thing off as a delusion. An overreaction.

Just two more rooms to check, and I could assure myself that I might be crazy, but at least Adam and I were alone.

I'd barely turned when a sharp crack filled the hall. Something metal clattered. Rolled.

The mudroom. It had to be. The only things down that

hall were the powder room, the mudroom, and beyond that, the garage.

And the back door.

When Trey died I'd sold his guns. I didn't like them in the house with a little boy. Adam, at four, was already climbing like the monkey he loved so much, and there was nowhere I could hide the guns that he wouldn't find.

Trey had never wanted a gun safe, saying what was the point of having weapons if you have to work that hard to get to them? I wasn't a great shot. I hadn't enjoyed target practice like he did, but I would've given anything just then for the weight of his Glock 9mm in my hand. For anything other than my phone.

I looked over my shoulder at the kitchen. I didn't have a gun, but I had an exceptional collection of knives. I love to cook, and my knives are my indulgence. Japanese, hand-made of layered steel, they were as much works of art as tools. And each one was wickedly sharp.

Moving on the balls of my feet, I ran to the kitchen and slid open the knife drawer, pulling free my longest, sharpest blade. The handle fit my palm as if it had been made for me. I could debone a chicken like nobody's business, but I'd never thought about using the knife on a person. I didn't know if I could.

Adam slept upstairs. If Adam was at stake I could do anything. I would do anything. But I didn't want to.

I'd raced to the kitchen. My progress toward the mudroom was a lot slower. I clutched my phone in my hand, thinking it might be worth Dave's patronizing reassurance to avoid facing whatever made that noise in the mudroom. Except...

Except the last time he put his hand on my shoulder, his eyes gentle and worried, and said that maybe the strain of taking care of Adam by myself was too much. Maybe I needed a break. He hadn't said he was going to call social services. He hadn't said he planned to tell them Adam's mother was crazy and delusional. He hadn't had to.

I wasn't calling Dave unless I was sure I had no other choice.

The light in the hall should have been reassuring. It wasn't.

The powder room was empty. Warm, heavy air wafted down the hall, out of place in the sterile, air conditioned house. My fingers tightened on the handle of the knife as I reached through the door of the mudroom and pushed up the light switch with the side of my wrist.

The fluorescent bulbs in the ceiling seared my eyeballs. I blinked hard, the scene in front of me slowly coming into focus. The back door gaped open, the woods beyond the house black. Impenetrable. I couldn't see anything moving, but it was so dark beneath the trees someone could be lurking right outside the door, and I wouldn't know until he was on top of me.

The tall, metal umbrella stand by the back door was on its side, umbrellas spilling out across the tile. The crash I heard. Someone leaving?

I wanted to believe it was someone leaving.

The alternative, that someone was inside the house, was too frightening to contemplate.

My brain was stuck in a loop.

Pick up the umbrella stand.

Close the door.

Pick up the umbrella stand.

Close the door.

I did.

The flick of the lock, the bolt sliding into place, should have made me feel safe. It didn't.

The alarm was off. The door was open. Someone had been in my house.

I could have imagined the sound, the shuffle, and the thump, but I did not imagine the alarm being off. I did not imagine the door hanging open and the umbrella stand knocked over.

I stood there, staring at the locked door, trying to think. I should have taken a picture. I should have called Dave while the umbrella stand was still knocked over and the door was still open. If I called him now, with no proof, he wouldn't believe me.

But if someone had been here I didn't want to leave the door open. I wanted it locked. I didn't know what to do. I gripped the knife and shifted my weight from one foot to the other, trapped by indecision.

Why would someone break into my house?

A thief could have made off with a fortune in artwork from the first floor alone. I hadn't noticed anything missing as I passed through the house.

At a loss for what else to do, I left the mudroom and went back through the first floor. Nothing was missing. Nothing I could see. Why would someone break in if not to steal?

I thought of Adam asleep in his bed, so small. So vulnerable. I had to protect him. I had an alarm and the best locks money could buy. Still, we weren't safe.

We should have been safe.

I'd locked the mudroom door, but I didn't know.

Had I locked someone out? Or locked them in?

I stood in the middle of the kitchen scanning the quiet, brightly-lit house.

What do I do? What the hell was I supposed to do?

And then I remembered. Not long before he died, Trey started talking about a new security system. I'd brushed him off, hadn't really paid attention. The system we had was overkill for a small town in Maine, even considering the artwork Trey had collected.

He'd been restless and anxious those last few months. Promising me everything was fine, then talking about buying more guns and getting a better alarm. He'd been short-tempered and easily irritated. Annoyed when I asked questions, so I'd stopped.

He'd said once that if anything happened, if I needed help and he wasn't there, I should call someone. He had a card. I couldn't remember the name, but there had been a lion's head and a circle. Black on white.

Still clutching the knife in one hand and my phone in the other, I walked past the front door and down the other hall to Trey's office. I rarely went in there. Not before he died and not after. This was his space, his room.

His desk was just as neat as he'd left it. Everything lined up. Everything in its place. No business cards.

I should have paid attention. I should have listened, but he'd been so erratic back then. I got used to tuning him out when he went off on a paranoid rant about guns or a new alarm. About people coming after him. If he'd been afraid for Adam I would have taken him seriously, but it was always about him. Never us.

The top drawer slid open silently, the contents as neatly arranged as the surface of the desk. Pens lined up together, paperclips organized by size, and in the corner a neat stack of business cards.

Reluctantly, I peeled my sweaty fingers from the handle of the knife and set it on the desk. The blade gleamed obscenely against the warm mahogany. The first card in the pile was his stockbroker. The second for a local maid service. The third for the Castle Falls newspaper.

Below that, a white card with black printing. A lion's head surrounded by a circular banner that read 'Sinclair Security'. The name underneath was Maxwell Sinclair. Two phone numbers, one toll-free and the other an interchange I didn't recognize.

It was the middle of the night. No one would be in the office. Before I could think better of it, I dialed the toll-free number and waited. The phone rang. Once. Twice. Three times. A click, as if the call were being transferred. It rang again, and a woman's voice informed me that I had reached Sinclair Security after office hours but was welcome to leave a message.

A long beep sounded in my ear and I began to babble. "This is Lily Spencer. I—my husband—my former husband —I'm a widow—uh, told me to call you if there was ever any trouble. I live—we live—I live up in Maine, and we've had some break-ins. Uh, I think. The police haven't found anything, but tonight someone got in. Turned off the alarm. I don't know what to do. I don't know if you can help, but he said if anything ever happened I should call you, so I'm calling. Please, if you could call me back I'd appreciate it. Again, this is Lily Spencer."

I stabbed my finger at the screen of my phone and hung up. My cheeks were hot with embarrassment no one could see. I should have planned what I was going to say. Should have thought about it, but I was rattled.

Not rattled.

I was scared.

I left the card face up on the blotter and picked up the knife. I thought about making a cup of tea. Turning on the television for company. Of walking through the house again.

I did none of it. I went to the stairs and climbed to the second level, checking every room I passed. I stopped in front of Adam's door and turned the knob, breath held, praying with everything inside me that he was as I'd left him. Safely asleep.

He'd rolled over, pushing his pillow to the floor, Curious George under his head. He was still out cold, cheeks flushed with sleep, his back rising and falling in a regular rhythm.

My sweet boy. If he was okay I was okay.

I shut the door, turning the almost useless lock on the handle, and sat on the carpet, leaning against the bed frame, the only sound in the room Adam's even breathing.

Pulling my knees into my chest, I listened for any hint of a disturbance, for any sign that we weren't alone.

Eyes glued to the door, the knife in my right hand and my phone in my left, I waited for daylight and the false promise of safety.

Sneak Peek

THE TEMPTATION TRAP

HAVE YOU READ AXEL & EMMA'S STORY?

CHAPTER ONE: AXEL

Emma Wright was becoming a problem. She was supposed to be a job. An easy job. Get close to her, find evidence that she was selling confidential data to a competitor. Get paid a ton of money. How hard could it be?

She was the head of Human Resources at a shipping company, not Mata Hari. This kind of thing was the bread and butter of Sinclair Security. I figured I'd take the meeting and pass the case to one of my guys.

Then I got a good look at Emma Wright.

Fiery red hair, creamy skin, abundant curves, and clear blue eyes with a wicked glint. She was irresistible. Luscious, soft, and more than a handful in all the right places. The moment I saw her picture, I knew I'd be handling her myself.

Fucking the suspect wasn't usually my MO, but in this case, I was prepared to make an exception. Normally, my approach was to get the evidence, give it to the client, close the case, and cash the check. Not with Emma.

Getting her into bed wasn't the hard part. Neither was pretending to be her lover. But Emma was tricky. She was smart. Funny. Gorgeous. And surprisingly kinky. Deliciously kinky. I'd never admit it, but it's possible I was taking my time on the case just to have an excuse to keep fucking her.

That, and it was harder than I'd expected to find what I was looking for. I kept waiting for her to slip. Everyone did, eventually. But so far, nothing. I hadn't caught her in even the tiniest lie. The client was getting restless, and I was starting to wonder if I was losing my touch.

I knew she was guilty. Most people were when it came down to it. I already knew what would happen in the end. Tears. Pleading. Excuses and justifications. None of that would matter to me.

I'd taken the contract, and I would do my job. In the back of my mind, I was hoping it would last just a little longer. I hadn't yet had my fill of that lush body, and once I found the data Emma was smuggling out of Harper Shipping, she'd go to jail and our affair would be over.

Tonight my plan was to push her off balance, enough so she might make a mistake. Until now, I'd worked it out so that most of our dates were dinner at her house. More intimate and easier to search her place.

When I did take her out somewhere, I chose places that were upscale, expensive, and not my usual style. I didn't need to be recognized as Axel Sinclair when I was pretending to be Adam Stewart. But tonight I'd picked a quiet, low-key Italian place around the corner from Emma's.

I'd expected her to pout or act annoyed that I wasn't spending a few hundred dollars on her dinner. I should have known better.

Emma was relaxed, drinking her wine and digging into her fettuccine Alfredo. Watching the woman eat pasta was a torturous form of foreplay. When the creamy sauce hit her tongue, she sucked a stray noodle into her mouth with pursed lips, her eyes closed in rapture.

I couldn't help but imagine her sucking me off with that same expression on her face.

She couldn't have cared less if she was in an exclusive restaurant surrounded by the best of Vegas society or a place like this one with paper napkins and a chalkboard menu on the wall. Emma enjoyed life however it came at her. I wondered if that would serve her well when she went to prison.

There was a chance she could avoid going to jail. Either way, I had to remind myself it wasn't my problem. My job was to find proof she was stealing and give that proof to her boss. What happened to her after that was between them.

Most of the time the client didn't press charges. That kind of publicity was worse for business than the crime itself. But the owner and CEO of Harper Shipping had made his intentions clear. As soon as he could prove what she'd done, he was calling the police.

Knowing Emma, she'd get off with probation. She was smart enough to hire a good lawyer, and she'd be able to afford decent counsel. She'd managed to hide the money she was getting for the data she'd stolen. If my hackers couldn't find it, neither would the police. Somewhere out there, Emma had a tidy little nest egg, ready to cushion her when she fell.

Watching her wind pasta around her fork as she laughed over a story a friend had told her, I found it hard to reconcile the woman before me with the liar I knew she was.

I'd been in this game long enough to know that anyone could be a criminal, no matter how innocent they appeared on the surface. But Emma just didn't give me the guilty vibe.

If I hadn't seen surveillance video of her rifling through secured files and copying them, then later handing them off to a competitor in a dark parking lot late at night, I would have sworn she wasn't the one they were looking for.

But I had seen it, seen her face clearly. Even had one of my guys check it. Video could be manufactured. This was real.

On top of that, she treated her briefcase like it held the keys to Fort Knox. And she got jumpy whenever I brought up her job. In fact, it was the only time she acted oddly. Not guilty. Not exactly. But not her usual fun loving self.

All of it added together was more than enough to convince me. Emma was guilty, and I would bring her down. A voice in the back of my head told me to find the evidence and close the case before I got in any deeper.

Sitting across from her, my eyes glued to her lips as she sipped her wine, I knew it was already too late. I was in deep with Emma. And part of me, a part I'd thought long dead, hoped that somehow I'd find a way to prove her innocent.

CHAPTER TWO: EMMA

ADAM HAD THAT LOOK ON HIS FACE AGAIN. I'D SEEN IT before, and I didn't know what it meant. He stared at me as if I was a puzzle and he needed to figure me out. It didn't make sense. There's not that much to figure out about me.

I'm a basic girl. I have a job I like, good friends, nothing out of the ordinary. In fact, the only unusual thing in my life was Adam.

We'd been dating for more than three weeks, and I still wasn't sure what he was doing with me. Don't get me wrong, I'm a pretty good catch. I'm intelligent, not hard on the eyes, and my friends say I'm fun to be around.

I have a few too many curves for guys who like skinny chicks, but that's okay with me. For every guy who wants a waif, there are two who like a full set of DD's and a round ass.

I hate starving myself, and while I don't mind going to the gym a couple of times a week I'm not spending my life there. I'd never be on a catwalk, and I didn't care. None of the few guys who'd seen me naked had complained. That said, I've never dated much, mostly by choice. No offense to any good guys out there but most of the guys I'd hooked up with were assholes.

Going out every night and trying to find a good man is a waste of time. I know they say you have to kiss a lot of frogs to find your prince, but seriously, I've had enough frog kissing to last a lifetime.

Maybe I have a low tolerance for bullshit. Or maybe I'm impatient. Either way, I'd rather hang out with my friends, have fun with my hobbies, and live the good life without one more lying, deadbeat guy asking to borrow money before he cheats on me.

I'm not bitter or anything. I don't have some horrible ex in my past. I have a great Dad and two fantastic brothers. And I have some girlfriends with amazing husbands. I know there are good guys out there, I just don't seem to attract them.

I attract the dicks who have mommy issues and can't hold down a job or think that having self-confidence makes me a bitch. No thanks.

Adam was different. So far, not an asshole. But also, way out of my league. Like I said, I'm a pretty good catch. I've dated men with money. Successful men. Good-looking men. Adam was all three.

He was the kind of man you'd expect to see helping a supermodel out of a Ferrari. Not the kind of man you'd expect to meet in a cooking class at the local community college.

There I'd been, slicing carrots at my first night of learning to cook Thai food, when from beside me I heard a low, deep voice say, "What exactly are we supposed to be doing here? I got in late, and I don't have a partner. Tell me you're not taken."

I'd almost passed out when I got my first look at the new arrival. Tall, at least, 6'4". I've always loved tall men. At 5' 10" it was a luxury to look up into a man's eyes.

Short dark hair, eyes so dark brown they were almost black, sharp cheekbones, and full lips. All of that with broad shoulders, lean hips, and no sign of a beer belly. I was ready to swoon.

I immediately forgave my friend Allison for talking me into Thai cooking class and then bailing at the last minute because she got back together with her boyfriend.

"Nope, I'm free," I'd said with a smile. "I signed up with a friend, but she's a no-show."

He let out a relieved breath and said, "Same for me. I thought I was going to have to do this myself." Holding out a hand, he'd said, "I'm Adam Stewart."

That was the beginning of what had become the wildest love affair of my life. That first night we'd eaten the Pad Thai we'd cooked, and Adam had asked me out for a drink.

The class was on Wednesday nights, and I didn't usually go out drinking when I had to work the next day. Especially with all the stress at the office in the last few months. But cooking with him had been a blast. He was fun as well as hot, and I wasn't ready to say good night.

Two glasses of wine and a scorching kiss later I'd left him in the parking lot and driven home wondering what would happen when I saw him in class the following week. If he even showed up.

I didn't want to get my hopes up. After that kiss, I had no doubt he would've preferred to end the night in my bed, but I didn't sleep with guys on the first date. Not even guys as hot as Adam.

Who was I kidding? I'd never been with a guy as hot as Adam. I still wasn't sure why I hadn't taken him up on his not-so-subtle suggestion that I invite him home.

Maybe I was intimidated. Maybe it just seemed too good to be true that someone as attractive and interesting as Adam Stewart wanted me.

I walked into class the following week to find him waiting at our work table. He looked up and saw me, a welcoming smile spread across his face, bringing light to his intense eyes and melting my caution.

We spent two hours making a green chili curry, and when we were done, I swallowed my nerves and asked him if he wanted to have a glass of wine with me. At my place.

We'd barely made it through the door before we fell on

each other, all eager, frantic hands, his mouth hungry and insistent on mine. That first time he overwhelmed me.

He tore the buttons from my blouse, my fingers slipped on the catch of my skirt, and then the rasp of the carpet against my back as we hit the floor. I was lucky he remembered protection. By the time we were naked, I was too far gone, dizzy and blind from the feel of his hard body against mine.

I'd been going through a dry spell for the past few months, and the press of his cock inside me was almost too much. The first orgasm had crashed through me in a tidal wave of sharp, sweet pleasure.

He fucked me in hard, deep thrusts, dragging out my orgasm until he followed me into bliss, his eyes squeezed shut, teeth clenched. We'd lay on the carpet for a few minutes, trying to catch our breath before Adam rolled to his feet, took my hand and led me to my bedroom.

And then things got a little crazy. As I've mentioned, I'm a pretty normal girl. Not a virgin, not a slut. I don't break any mirrors, but I'm not gorgeous.

I'd had sex before, a handful of boyfriends and one long-term relationship. So far, the sex had been fairly normal, just like me. Not much worth gossiping about with my girl-friends, but not bad. Just sex.

Sex with Adam was not normal. Not that first time when it was all desperate urgency and crazed desire. And definitely not normal the second time when he carefully removed what was left of my bra and used it to tie me to the bed.

It had never occurred to me that I'd like being tied up. I've been thinking about it since that first time. A lot. Because I didn't just like it, I loved it. When we had our clothes on Adam treated me like an equal.

I could be loud, and I could be opinionated. That had been a problem with men in the past. My personality attracted them at the beginning, but once we were together, it always seemed that what they really wanted was a quiet woman who agreed with everything they said.

Not Adam. He enjoyed our verbal sparring. He liked my enthusiasm. And while he was pretty much the definition of confident and assertive, he didn't need to control me to feel powerful.

When the clothes came off, everything changed. Adam was in charge, and what he wanted, he got.

In a million years I never would have thought I'd find that attractive. I don't know if I can explain it because I've always hated it when anyone told me what to do. The easiest way to get me to do something is to tell me to do the opposite.

But when Adam gave me that intent focused look and followed it with an order, I complied immediately, my body heating in anticipation. I think it's safe to say the whole relationship had me spun.

The first time he told me to get on my knees and suck his cock, I'd glared at him in outrage. He'd raised one dark eyebrow and stared me down. By the time I had his belt open, the insides of my thighs were slick with moisture, every cell in my body white-hot with need.

Maybe I would've felt differently if he'd dismissed me afterward, if he treated me like a one night stand or a booty call. But after the sex, after the orgasms, he was always there.

He never slept over, but he didn't rush out either. He'd lay in bed with me, his long body curled around mine, his hands stroking my skin, soothing and sweet. Sometimes we'd talk, whispered conversations about nothing and everything. Other times I'd fall asleep with him and wake alone.

Adam Stewart seemed like my dream man. For the most part, he was. But still, there were things that didn't add up. He was very, very good at distracting me with his body, but I hadn't missed the fact that I'd never met any of his friends, never been to his place, and never seen where he worked.

We hadn't been together that long, barely a month, but by now he should have at least invited me to see where he lived. I'd asked, and his excuse about renovations could have been the truth.

I didn't want to doubt him. For one thing, I trusted him. At least as much as I could trust anyone I'd only known a month. Maybe I just didn't want to believe he was hiding something.

I'll admit it; I worried that if I got any deeper and found out something I didn't want to know, I'd have to give up the best sex I've ever had.

Maybe I should have broken up with him, or demanded he prove he didn't have a wife or girlfriend. Another woman might have tried snooping in his cell phone or his wallet. I didn't do any of that.

My life had gotten very complicated in the past few months, and Adam was a blissful distraction. I was afraid if I peeked behind the curtain I would find out that he had been nothing more than an illusion. I was wary enough to continually remind myself not to fall for him.

Laughing over a shared dinner, mind-blowing kinky sex, and snuggling were all well and good, but I was keeping my heart out of it. At least, I was trying to.

Across the table, Adam broke through my reverie when he put down his fork and pushed his plate away.

"Almost finished?" He asked, his eyes focused on my

mouth as he watched me take my last bite of pasta. Adam had a number of looks I couldn't decipher. His intense gaze and heavy eyelids were not one of them. My belly tightened in anticipation.

I had no idea what he was planning for tonight, but I knew whatever it was, I was going to love it.

I put down my fork, finished chewing, and took a sip of wine. "I'm finished," I said. Adam gestured for the check, not bothering to ask if I wanted dessert.

Normally, I always wanted dessert, but with the way Adam was looking at me, I couldn't have cared less. I'd get my after dinner treat; it just wouldn't be in the form of food. The waiter was at the table a moment later, then walking away a minute after that, cash in hand.

Adam and I rose together, our eyes locked on each other. He helped me into my coat, his gaze leaving a searing path across my skin everywhere it touched.

Standing behind me, settling my coat over my shoulders, he reached around to fasten the top button, his knuckles grazing the bare skin of my upper chest. My nipples tightened at his touch, and I shivered when he whispered into my ear, "I like this dress. I'd hate to damage it. What should we do about that?"

"I guess that depends on how you want to fuck me," I murmured back. "Do you want me naked? Or do you want me to bend over and pull it up out of your way?"

Adam's hands dropped as he fastened the middle button of my coat. I felt the loss of his touch as soon as he stepped away. He took my arm and led me toward the door in silence, my question hanging in the air between us.

Also By Ivy Layne

Don't Miss Out on New Releases, Exclusive Giveaways, and More!!

Join Ivy's Readers Group @ ivylayne.com/readers-group

THE UNTANGLED SERIES

Unraveled (October 2018)

Undone (Early 2019)

Uncovered (Spring 2019)

SCANDALS OF THE BAD BOY BILLIONAIRES

The Billionaire's Secret Heart (Novella)

The Billionaire's Secret Love (Novella)

The Billionaire's Pet

The Billionaire's Promise

The Rebel Billionaire

The Billionaire's Secret Kiss (Novella)

The Billionaire's Angel

Engaging the Billionaire

Compromising the Billionaire

The Counterfeit Billionaire

Series Extras: ivylayne.com/extras

THE ALPHA BILLIONAIRE CLUB

The Wedding Rescue

The Courtship Maneuver

The Temptation Trap

ABOUT IVY LAYNE

Ivy Layne has had her nose stuck in a book since she first learned to decipher the English language. Sometime in her early teens, she stumbled across her first Romance, and the die was cast. Though she pretended to pay attention to her creative writing professors, she dreamed of writing steamy romance instead of literary fiction. These days, she's neck deep in alpha heroes and the smart, sexy women who love them.

Married to her very own alpha hero (who rubs her back after a long day of typing, but also leaves his socks on the floor). Ivy lives in the mountains of North Carolina where she and her other half are having a blast raising two energetic little boys. Aside from her family, Ivy's greatest loves are coffee and chocolate, preferably together.

VISIT IVY
Facebook.com/AuthorIvyLayne
Instagram.com/authorivylayne/
www.ivylayne.com
books@ivylayne.com

Made in the USA
Middletown, DE
16 May 2019